# Sweet Violet

# Catherine Palmer

**Thorndike Press • Waterville, Maine**

Published in 2005 by arrangement with
Tyndale House Publishers, Inc.

Thorndike Press® Large Print Christian Historical Fiction.

The tree indicium is a trademark of Thorndike Press.

The text of this Large Print edition is unabridged.
Other aspects of the book may vary from the original edition.

Set in 16 pt. Plantin by Al Chase.

Printed in the United States on permanent paper.

**Library of Congress Cataloging-in-Publication Data**
Palmer, Catherine, 1956–
    Sweet violet / by Catherine Palmer.
      p. cm.
    ISBN 0-7862-7972-9 (lg. print : hc : alk. paper)
    1. Arranged marriage — Fiction.  2. British — India —
Fiction.  3. Missing persons — Fiction.  4. Missionaries
— Fiction.  5. India — Fiction.  6. Large type books.
I. Title.
PS3566.A495S94 2005b
813′.54—dc22                  2005016551

To my father, Harold Thomas Cummins,
who ushered the beautiful people
of West Bengal into my heart.

"If you refuse to take up your cross
and follow me, you are not worthy
of being mine.
If you cling to your life, you will lose
it;
but if you give it up for me, you will
find it."

— Jesus Christ
Matthew 10:38–39

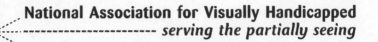

**National Association for Visually Handicapped**
---------------------- *serving the partially seeing*

As the Founder/CEO of NAVH, the only national health agency solely devoted to those who, although not totally blind, have an eye disease which could lead to serious visual impairment, I am pleased to recognize Thorndike Press* as one of the leading publishers in the large print field.

Founded in 1954 in San Francisco to prepare large print textbooks for partially seeing children, NAVH became the pioneer and standard setting agency in the preparation of large type.

Today, those publishers who meet our standards carry the prestigious "Seal of Approval" indicating high quality large print. We are delighted that Thorndike Press is one of the publishers whose titles meet these standards. We are also pleased to recognize the significant contribution Thorndike Press is making in this important and growing field.

Lorraine H. Marchi, L.H.D.
Founder/CEO
NAVH

* Thorndike Press encompasses the following imprints: Thorndike, Wheeler, Walker and Large Print Press.

# Acknowledgments

My deep gratitude goes to the people who make it possible for the words inside me to find their way onto the page and into your hands. To my husband, Tim, thank you for editing my books — some of them over and over as they change and grow. I am so grateful to Linda Highfield Everet, my dear friend, for opening my eyes to the fascinating beauty of orchids. Thank you for teaching me about them and also for putting two little orchids into my life.

Thank you, Kathy Olson, my editor, for shaping and refining each manuscript into a story worthy of publication. Anne Goldsmith and Becky Nesbitt, bless you for acquiring my books and helping me structure them as you see fit. Ron Beers, thank you for your vision and your faith. Karen Solem, I'm so grateful to God for your patience, insight, and hard work as my agent. To everyone at Tyndale — marketing, sales, editorial, warehouse — thank you for being a part of God's ministry team. Bookstore owners, managers, salespeople, may God bless you richly for your service.

And to my Lord Jesus Christ, thank You for redeeming me. My life and my words belong to You. Make of me what You will.

# One

*Calcutta, India*
*1816*

"When I first came to Calcutta from England, I thought I should never grow accustomed to the bazaar." Edmund Sherbourne chuckled as he and his companion, Dr. William Carey, passed a turbaned man seated on a carpet laid out on the dusty street. Surrounded by a throng of gawkers, the man played a simple tune on a reed flute. At the sound of the melody, a cobra emerged from a basket and began to sway from side to side, its hood fanning out and sending the watchers into squeals of terrified delight.

"In the village of Otley near my home, I have never seen such astounding sights or smelled such . . . interesting . . . smells," Edmund went on. Savoring the thought of spicy grilled shish kebabs for their luncheon, the two men made their way down a narrow aisle between a jumble of booths offering for sale everything from sacks of coal to brass pots to mounds of cauliflower, okra, cashews, and seafood. Edmund could not suppress a wry grin as they skirted a pig and five crows rooting in a rubbish heap near some vegetable stalls. "Now, however, I may state with confidence that nothing in India can ever surprise me."

"Nothing, Edmund?" Dr. Carey's bald head gleamed in the bright afternoon sun as he bent to drop a rupee into a tin cup held by a leper whose nose had vanished entirely. "I find I am regularly stupefied by the wonders and tragedies of India."

"True, Calcutta is filled with an amazing variety of things to see. Yet I have come to . . . to . . ." As he spoke, Edmund's attention fell upon a sight so unexpected, so utterly astonishing, that his tongue literally tripped over itself.

A row of sari-clad women lined the fruit sellers' tables as they selected produce for the day's meals. With their backs to Edmund, the ladies' long, glistening, ebony plaits hung to their knees like oiled ropes. All but one. Centered in the midst of the pattern of thick black cords, a single golden braid coiled down the spine of a slender creature in a turquoise sari.

Her hair was golden.

As blonde as a sheaf of winter wheat! Like a shimmering cable that trimmed the most opulent of curtains, this woman's braid formed the perfect adornment to the silken folds of her gown, the gentle slope of her shoulders, the narrow line of her waist, and the perfect curve of her hips.

"You have come to what?" Dr. Carey asked as he paused to examine a religious fresco painted on the wall of an adjoining stone house. "Have you come to view Calcutta as comfortable at last, Edmund? Will you miss it after your return to England? You have lived in India five years. Surely you must feel somewhat at home here now."

Edmund tore his attention from the fascinating vision of the gold braid and forced himself to focus on the painting of various Hindu gods cavorting across the fresco. Like Dr. Carey, he had become accustomed to Calcutta and the region of West Bengal through which he regularly traveled. But was it home?

He thought of the dear town of Otley in Mid-Warfedale, near the center of Yorkshire. Its quaint thatched-roof shops and cobblestone streets could hardly be compared to this steaming city rife with disease, poverty, and paganism. Otley was a quiet place where people called upon one another at teatime, walked side by side to church, and sold lacework and hot cross buns in the market.

Calcutta teemed with thieves and beggars. Street merchants hawked idols made of clay or brass. Cows wandered freely past whitewashed houses so dank their walls seemed to sweat. Burka-clad women and lungi-wearing men padded by in bare feet, while Hindu ladies in their saris . . . ladies in saris . . .

Edmund glanced back over his shoulder at the fruit stalls. Shoppers picked at the pyramids of coconuts, heaps of bananas, and mounds of papayas and mangoes while haggling over prices with the vendors. The row of long black braids appeared unchanged — and yet the gold one was gone.

Who could the woman be? A poor creature afflicted with albinism, perhaps? Edmund had seen such victims — like most others stricken with defects or diseases, they were cast out of their families and abandoned to beg on the streets. But the woman's hair had been gold, not white. And now that Edmund recalled the scene more clearly, he realized her arms had been stacked with brilliant glass bangles above and below her elbows. She was not a beggar. No, indeed. Her sari, in fact —

"You hail from a rather prominent family

in Yorkshire, do you not?" Dr. Carey was asking. "I believe you must be greatly devoted to them."

Deciding the heat had played tricks with his imagination, Edmund let out a breath. Surely the woman had been a mirage, nothing more.

"I confess, home to me will always be Thorne Lodge," he told his friend. "The Sherbourne family has resided upon that great estate for many centuries. I may have mentioned that my brother Randolph recently acceded to the barony at the death of our father."

"Is it this brother whose marriage troubles you so greatly that you are compelled to return to England?"

Edmund nodded. "Randolph has united himself to a most unacceptable young lady from a family that has endeavored to bring utter destruction upon our own. Worse — I am now informed by my brother that he and his wife anticipate the birth of their first child next spring. That the two families should share an heir is abhorrent, for ownership of the estates must certainly come into question. How Randolph was coerced into such an unhappy situation is beyond my ability to comprehend."

"By your recent letter to me," Dr. Carey

said, "you believe this brother may be of unsound mind."

"Indeed so. I fear it greatly." The men turned a corner of the bazaar and entered the area where garment vendors labored — cobblers cutting sandals from water-buffalo hide, sari sellers beading hems, jewelers hammering silver into bangles and rings.

"Our father's demise was most unexpected and untimely," Edmund explained. "He had been an excellent sportsman, and his death by accidental shooting seems most unlikely. Though an inquest was made, no evidence to contradict the conclusion of the coroner could be drawn. Yet, I am hardpressed to doubt that our father fell victim to this detestable family."

"The very family into which your brother married?" The older man's narrow eyebrows drew into a line across his forehead. "This does seem odd. Yet, I wonder if it cannot all be explained in a letter. I understand that you have booked passage on the *Scaleby Castle* already, but may I not persuade you to reconsider resigning your post here in Calcutta? My dear young friend, will you permit me to be frank?"

"Of course, sir. I am eager to know your opinion in all these matters." Edmund had learned of the venerable Dr. Carey's work in

14

India long before he felt God's calling to journey here as a missionary. "You have given me much valuable advice during my years in this country. Indeed, I cannot think how I should have survived without your assistance."

"Then I shall speak my mind. You and I both were sent to India by the Particular Baptist Society for the Propagation of the Gospel Amongst the Heathen. As you may know, several distinguished gentlemen and I formed that society in Kettering in 1792."

"I was but a lad of five at the time."

Carey laughed. "How ancient that makes me, for now we are colleagues!"

"I should very much like to remain so, sir. Your companionship has been —"

There! The flash of gold snapped the words out of Edmund's mouth. Just three stalls down, the woman stood fingering a stack of brightly colored saris. He could see her cheek, as pink as a rose. And her eyes were — blue!

"Our companionship was born of the Holy Spirit," Dr. Carey declared as Edmund's speech once again faltered. "I am certain I should miss your presence here, and our society in England would be greatly bereft. Edmund, our organization was the first ever formed in England, and it now supports a good many missionaries in India, Burma, and elsewhere. If you are unhappy here, may I suggest that you take on a different region? The fields are white unto harvest, and yet the workers are few."

"I fear this reaper is weary and poorly fitted to the task." Disheartened at the turn of the conversation with Dr. Carey, Edmund tried to think of another topic as their path took them nearer the woman. Now he saw that she was conversing with a small Indian, whose darker skin and style of garment identified her as a member of the Untouchable caste. The blonde lady must be English and the other, her servant. Yet both wore saris. Braids. Bangles. Sandals. Alike in every way, they were yet as different as possible. How odd.

"You had hoped to preach here in Calcutta," Dr. Carey was saying. "I do understand your disappointment in that, Edmund. I realize your original calling from God was to build a church and shepherd a body of believers in the city."

Edmund's heart foundered as the woman turned suddenly in the opposite direction and began to walk away. He must know who she was. Why did she dress as an Indian? Was she the wife of one of the East India merchants? a sister of some member of a

16

Royal regiment posted at Fort William?

"I . . . I had indeed hoped to preach in Calcutta," Edmund mumbled as he continued to puzzle over the woman. Increasing his pace to match hers, he felt himself strangely off balance, almost as though stricken by a bout of malaria. Had the heat indeed affected him? Did he hover on the verge of madness, as did too many of his fellow Englishmen in this fevered land? Or was his discourse with Dr. Carey of such intensity that he had become disoriented? He must slow down. Concentrate. Focus.

"I believed God called me to this city," he reminded his mentor, "but I soon learned that the East India Company would not approve of my proselytizing. I have had to travel north into Danish-occupied areas, as you did before me. Though it is now legal for us to preach in the city, I have found it is still discouraged."

"The company is an abominable monopoly," Dr. Carey pronounced vehemently, "just as it has been since its inception in 1600. The act of Parliament three years ago limited its powers, yet we still find it all but impossible to secure a license to preach."

"I do understand that the Indian trade has been much reduced by the act. Indeed,

17

merchants here claim they are gravely threatened."

"Bah! Under the supervision of the Board of Control, the company continues to function as the de facto government of India. It rules this land with an iron fist, controlling everyone and everything within reach of its power. The company serves only itself, suppressing even such a beneficial influence as the preaching of the gospel of Jesus Christ."

Edmund's heart contracted as he listened to this censure of the British East India Company. His entire being had been consumed with the effort of securing a permit to preach in Calcutta, and failing that, to establish small churches in the outlying regions. All to no avail. In five years of hard labor — tramping endless miles of jungle, fording snake-infested rivers, enduring heat that caused him to wonder if he were in hell itself — Edmund had not succeeded in bringing about a single conversion. Still, he could not blame the company for his failure.

"The gospel is beneficial," Edmund stated, "but I have come to believe myself unfit to proclaim it."

"Unfit?" Dr. Carey cried. "Nonsense! Young man, you are as accomplished a speaker as I have heard in all my life. Never have I enjoyed such bold rhetoric, such elegant discourse, or such esteemed oration as that delivered by you upon your acceptance of my invitation to preach in the church at Serampore. My dear sir, I have no doubt of God's calling upon your life. You are willing to venture where no missionary has dared, and at the pulpit you speak with the authority of God Himself!"

Once, Edmund had believed the same of himself. Now he could hardly find the energy to open his Bible. Rather than viewing an outing to the Calcutta bazaar as an opportunity to witness to the pagans who populated its streets, he was thinking about a strange golden-haired woman in a sari. How had he come to this? Where was his direction, his ambition, his fire?

"Dr. Carey, I am downtrodden," Edmund admitted. "All my efforts on behalf of Christ have failed, and I cannot see that they shall succeed no matter how long I might remain in India. Why should a Hindu ever wish to accept the possibility of heaven and hell? Stay as he is, and he can look forward to an eternity of rebirths, eventually resulting in unity with God. And as for the Muslim, he already believes in Paradise and hell."

"As you well know, Edmund, Christianity encompasses far more than belief in an afterlife. Surrender to Jesus Christ produces an abundant life. A peace which passes understanding. A faith in things hoped for and a certainty of things not seen."

"But faith is —"

The woman suddenly stepped out from the shadows of a palm-thatched awning. Clutching a folded length of bright pink silk, she caught her breath and gaped at Edmund.

He stiffened as he jerked off his tall-crowned black hat. "Good afternoon, madam," he said, bowing.

She blinked, and now he saw that her eyes were not blue but an alluring blue gray, like the sky before the monsoon rains. If not for her eyes, her velvety pink cheeks, and the gleam of her golden braid, the young lady would certainly pass for an Indian — and a member of the upper Brahman caste. Shimmering from head to toe in her turquoise sari, she wore so many rings that Edmund could hardly see her fingers. Bracelets encircled her arms. Heavy gold earrings studded with rubies hung from her ears, while a chain of rubies and emeralds set off her fair neck.

*"Nomoshkar,"* she addressed him. *"Shuvo oporanho. Tumi kyamon acho?"*

Edmund's fragile grasp on the Bengali

language selected this moment to loosen completely. Mouth ajar and eyes agoggle, he stared at the woman as though he were a clumsy fish just pulled from the Hooghly River. She smiled and glanced at the smaller woman beside her. The servant shrugged as if to say that the man before them was an utter dolt.

The golden-haired creature chuckled, nudged her companion, and began to walk away.

But Dr. Carey stepped forward. *"Kichu mone korben na,"* the gentleman spoke up, excusing himself for interrupting the meeting between his companion and the lady.

Edmund, to his chagrin, suddenly understood every word, as the native language came rushing back into his head in a flood. His humiliation was utter.

The woman's brilliant smile now turned to Dr. Carey, who saluted her in impeccable Bengali. He asked after her well-being and that of her family. She replied that all were in perfect health, thank you very much, and was it not a lovely day? He assured her that it was indeed the most delightful of days. As no one who knew both parties was available to make introductions, he bade her farewell, took Edmund by the arm, and led him down the nearest alley.

"Fascinating," the missionary said.

"She is . . . she is most unusual." Edmund had located his vocal cords at last. "Quite unexpected."

"You mistake my meaning, young Edmund. It is *you* who fascinate me," Dr. Carey replied. "I believe India has managed to take you by surprise after all."

Edmund cleared his throat. "I confess you are correct. But did you not think the lady most unusual?"

"Lovely, actually. Edmund, admit it — you were instantly smitten by her."

"Nonsense. I was merely taken aback."

Dr. Carey laughed. "I surmise you are in want of a wife, my young friend, for I have never seen a man so captivated by a pretty girl. From the moment she stepped out into the street, you were hopelessly enamored."

"Upon my word, sir, you are mistaken. Her manner of dress and speech stunned me momentarily. Can she be English?"

"Of course she is. She is likely the wife of some merchant, and she has adopted native ways. Such transformations are not uncommon here, though I was surprised at her fluency with the language. Perhaps she is a merchant's daughter and was brought up in India."

"Doubtful, for English children usually are sent back to their homeland for education and left in the charge of boarding schools and relatives. I cannot say I have met an English child above ten years of age in Calcutta."

"True, and so she must be someone's wife or sister," Dr. Carey acknowledged. "At any rate, when you arrive in England, you must ask your brother to attach you to some reputable young lady at once. Make certain she is sturdy, healthy, and a stalwart Christian. And then you may return to India better able to conquer the demons that beset you."

"Sir, I assure you I have no intention of ever marrying. I am wholly committed to Christ and to my labors as a minister — whether in India or in England. I cannot speak more plainly on this matter."

Nearing the shish-kebab vendors, Edmund drank down the steadying aroma of spicy meat. Realization filled him as surely as the fragrant smoke that tickled his nostrils. He had been hungry — that was all. The entire reason for his discomfiture and confusion had been his empty stomach and light head. With a good meal under his belt, all would be well.

"I have testified to you in the past," he told Dr. Carey, "that I was devoted to my own pleasure during my tenure at university. As an accomplished swordsman, I competed often in fencing tournaments, and I won many prizes. This aptitude with the sword, I discovered, brought me great admiration from ladies, and I cultivated their attention toward the end of gratifying myself. Realizing that my visage and form were considered manly, I flattered myself into thinking I was handsome, bold, and witty. And I confess that I pursued the singular objective of becoming the favorite bachelor among my female society in London."

"I am certain the young lady we just encountered thought you admirable," Dr. Carey answered. "Her eyes sparkled at the very sight of your masculine physique."

Edmund could not contain a chuckle. "Indeed, sir. But perhaps her sparkle was meant for you."

"Bosh. I am twice her age and happily settled with my dear wife. But what of marriage for you, Edmund? I believe the companionship would be of benefit."

"Dr. Carey, I am steadfastly set upon my course. The experiences of my past and my subsequent surrender to Christ have altered me completely. I am no longer a carefree youth. My entire attention is taken up with the pursuit of theological enlightenment. I have abandoned the company of women, the diversion of sport, and even the congenial gatherings of family and friends. I find I no longer have any need of such shallow occupations. My greatest joy is reading the Bible. My most beloved occupation is preaching the gospel, and I never allow my discourse to wander far from matters of doctrinal import."

"How deadly dull!" Dr. Carey exclaimed.

Edmund turned to him in surprise. "But surely you are no different, sir. I know you too well to believe otherwise."

"Then you know little of me. I take great pleasure in my wife and my children. I am fascinated with botany, printing presses, the study of language, and any number of activities beyond the theological realm. Indeed, at times I find myself hard-pressed to turn my attention to sermon preparation. Life holds many wondrous things, Edmund. The Bible teaches us that 'every good gift and every perfect gift is from above, and cometh down from the Father of lights, with whom is no variableness, neither shadow of turning.' "

As they joined a queue forming at one of the grills, Edmund reflected on the blue-eyed woman whose golden braid had so allured him. "I cannot allow fleshly pursuits to absorb me," he told Dr. Carey. "The verses preceding that which you quoted me from the book of James state that 'every man is tempted, when he is drawn away of his own lust, and enticed. Then when lust hath conceived, it bringeth forth sin: and sin, when it is finished, bringeth forth death.' I dare not permit a woman — or any other temptation — to enter my life, sir."

Dr. Carey nodded soberly. "You are young ... and good ... and I shall miss your zeal at our mission meetings, my dear friend."

"Thank you, sir." Edmund paid for his shish kebab and joined the elder man in a brief word of prayer. As Dr. Carey tugged off a bite of chicken, Edmund wondered what had become of the golden-haired woman. She had vanished, it seemed, just as the bazaar, Calcutta, and India would one day soon disappear from his life. Perhaps he would miss the surprises of this land more than he imagined.

"Come now, Moumita. You must do as I say, or I shall sack you at once." Violet

26

Rosse crossed her arms and looked daggers at her *ayah,* who stood across the bedroom and glared back. Using the mixture of English and Bengali that the two had always spoken, the younger woman continued. "You are in my employ, and if you refuse to obey me, I shall have you cast out into the street with the other Untouchables. You will have created such a bad *kharma* for yourself that you will thank the gods to have even one grain of rice to eat."

"Oh, you are wicked." Moumita's lips tightened. "Did I raise you to be so evil? *Na,* I taught you every good thing! I loved you and cared for you as though you were my own daughter. And now you threaten me with such a terrible fate?"

Violet swallowed hard at the severity of her *ayah*'s criticism. She could not deny its validity. When Violet was only six, her mother had died of cholera, but the loss was hardly felt. Mrs. Rosse had preferred the wives of merchants in the East India Company to the companionship of her only child — a little girl with golden ringlets and a penchant for making mud pies in the garden.

Moumita Choudhary, a young, childless Hindu widow of the lowest caste, had been hired as an *ayah*. Her only assignment was to look after the child and to keep her as

English as possible — though Moumita had confessed she was not quite certain what that meant. It hardly mattered, for Violet felt sure she could not have had a better mother.

But now was not the time for sentimentality. This very evening in her bedroom overlooking the Hooghly River, Violet had made her decision. She would not turn back.

"If you will not come to Krishnangar with me, Moumita," she said, "I shall go alone."

*"Dushtu meye!"* Moumita stepped forward, hand raised. "Such a naughty daughter!"

Violet stood in stony defiance. "You may not strike me, Moumita. I am a woman now, and I shall chart the course of my own life. I need no one — not even you. I shall go wherever I please and do whatever I wish."

"But you cannot go out into Calcutta at night. Would you risk your very life?"

Violet reflected for a moment on the sprawling city beyond the wall that surrounded the Rosse compound. Three miles long and one mile broad, Calcutta was populated by more than two hundred thousand souls. Though it housed Fort William, a public jail, a general hospital, and other bastions of civilization, the city was a cauldron of every vice known to man.

"Do you suppose I cannot defend myself?" Violet retorted. "I am strong and resourceful, and my wit is the match of any man's. I shall go — no matter what the danger."

"But your destiny has been decided already." Moumita shook her head. "Ah, *meye*. Your father has planned a good future for you. In England, you will marry a rich man. What better life could a woman expect? By rebelling against him, you create a bad fate for yourself. Do you wish to bring about this kind of *kharma?* Certainly not! Then think good thoughts and be grateful to Sahib Rosse. At least in England, if your husband dies, you will not have to make the choice to burn alive on his funeral pyre or be separated from your family and village forever."

"*Na,* Moumita — I do not want a husband. Never." As she spoke the words, a memory flitted through Violet's mind. A tall man bowed before her . . . the English gentleman in the bazaar . . . so handsome . . . regal . . . proper. If ever she had wished for a husband, it might be for someone like him. A man strong enough to protect her, yet humble enough to respect and honor her. A man with green eyes and a manly bearing and soft brown hair.

But of course, anyone Violet would marry must love India and speak perfect Bengali — and with that fellow's silly black hat and fumbling speech, he could never meet her expectations. She dismissed him from her thoughts.

"Moumita, I have no interest in any man, nor do I ever plan to marry. I have important work to do."

"Silly flowers!"

"Whether you approve or not, the study of botany is my occupation, and orchids my specialty. Dr. Wallich has committed himself to teaching me all he knows of the science of hybridization. He has amassed a collection of *Cymbidiums* and *Dendrobiums* that demands careful identification, Moumita, and he needs my assistance. You know very well that I have labored many hours over the catalogue at the Royal Botanic Garden —"

"It is the lot of every woman to marry, *meye,*" Moumita cut in, shaking her forefinger from side to side. "Women are not to study flowers. We are to marry and bear as many children as possible. If the gods are willing, the man your father has chosen will be good to you. At least in England, you will never have to fear drowning in the monsoon floods."

Violet's shoulders sagged. How could she ever explain herself to this simple woman who loved her so dearly? "I cannot go to England," she said. "They have winter there."

"Winter is good. In winter, you cannot become ill from cholera or typhus or malaria."

"But flowers cannot grow in winter. They die — as I shall die if I am forced to leave India."

"You have no choice in this, *meye*. Your father's mind is settled. If you can be obedient to him now, you will bring good *kharma* for yourself — a kind husband, healthy children, and a large house. One day, if you behave properly, perhaps your soul will be reborn into a higher form. Maybe you will even get to live in India again."

As Violet gazed at the intense little woman before her, she struggled against the tears that had threatened all evening. At dinner with several guests present, her father had announced his intention to send her to England to a young ladies' finishing school. Following completion of her course of study, Violet would marry his colleague, a tradesman named Alfred Cunliffe.

The guests, who even now lounged with Malcolm Rosse in the sitting room below, had heard every word. Violet knew her father would never retract anything he had said in public. Her lot was cast — unless she took charge of her own life. Which was exactly what she intended to do.

"Moumita, you cannot predict my future," she said. "All my life, I have tried to be good, just as you instructed me. I have done my best to keep my thoughts pure and never to harm or kill any living thing. I learned everything my tutors taught and more. And I have been kind to everyone. Nearly everyone."

The older woman gave a hoot of derision. "How many times have you run away from me to explore the bazaars? Always, you used to climb over the walls to play with Untouchable children on the banks of the Hooghly. You refused to let me comb your hair. You would not eat your cabbage. You have been a very naughty girl!"

Violet pursed her lips. It was true. She had shouted at the gardener for uprooting and discarding the first orchid she ever planted — a fragile bloom she had buried deep in the heavy, black dirt of the *mali*'s carefully tended beds. She had stolen jasmine blossoms from the neighbor's yard and sweets from a vendor's cart and books from her father's library.

Not only had she behaved badly. Malevolent thoughts had often filled her mind when she reflected on bossy Moumita, or her hookah-puffing father, or the cook who forced her to eat the dry spiced cabbage known as *gobi bhaji,* which she despised. And with great venom she had regarded the gatekeeper who always chased her when she climbed over the whitewashed wall that kept Calcutta's unwashed, diseased, and starving throngs from Malcolm Rosse's opulent house and impeccable gardens.

"Even now," Moumita said, "you are a young lady, and still you are a great disappointment and an annoyance to everyone around you. Every day you go to the Royal Botanic Garden to help that man —"

"Dr. Nathaniel Wallich. We are cataloging species of Asian flora."

"Yes, and the bamboo cages filled with your orchids hang from nearly every tree in the garden outside this house. The *mali* is most unhappy with you. Now you are refusing to obey your father and go to England to get married. If the gods are keeping a tally — and they most certainly are! — your wickedness must surely equal your virtue. *Meye,* I fear you will be reborn as an ant to be stepped on by some low-caste leper in the bazaar!"

"Death would be better than the destiny my father has prepared for me!" Violet cried. "England is a cold and rainy place. It is nothing but moors."

Moumita's eyes narrowed. "What is a moor?"

"Something terrible, I believe, for I have read that there are no orchids in all that place. Moumita, I must flee for my life. Can you not understand?"

"Flee for your life? You will not die in England. Many people live there, and they are healthy. Look at all those fat merchants who sail their East India ships here from that country — do they look ill to you?"

"But those men are not like me. They were born in England. Though I look and speak like an Englishwoman, Moumita, I am not. I am Indian!"

"How can you say such a thing?" The pitch of the *ayah*'s voice rose. "Have I not done my duty to keep you a British girl? Do we not speak English together constantly? Do I not try to curl and pin your hair on top of your head like the women in those books in your father's library? Have I not made you read to me all the stories of the English gods and goddesses? The tale of the red-hooded child who was nearly eaten by a wolf, the story of the woman who pricked her finger with a spindle and slept for one hundred years, the account of the poor Untouchable girl who was given a shoe made of glass. Do you not remember? All seemed hopeless for her, but suddenly a goddess came and transformed a pumpkin into a fine rickshaw!"

"That was not a goddess. It was a fairy godmother."

"And what is that?"

"How should I know, Moumita? I know no more about England than you." Violet picked up the two bags she had packed for her journey. "Of course we read the English stories together. But you also told me the saga of Rama and Sita, and the tale of Ganesha, whose head was chopped off and replaced with that of an elephant, and the story of Hanuman, who is half man and half monkey —"

"But I taught you to be English!"

"I *am* English, Moumita. You did your job well. I am also Indian. I love the Ganges and the Hooghly rivers, the old men with their teeth stained red from chewing betel nut, the temples filled with oil lamps and flowers. I love the smell of spices in the bazaar — cinnamon, cardamom, turmeric, ginger, coriander, curry. I wake each morning to the muezzins calling from the minarets of Calcutta's mosques, bidding worshipers to bow before Allah. How shall I live in a land with no sugarcane? no curry? no mangoes? Moumita, how shall I live without orchids?"

The older woman brushed a finger over Violet's damp cheek and nodded. "You are right, *meye*. I am not able to think of forcing you to live in such a place as England. But where can you escape from your father? Who will help you?"

Violet lowered her voice. "I have heard of an Englishman who lives up the Hooghly in Serampore. His work is to translate texts from English and Latin into Bengali, and he has a strong knowledge of botany. Dr. Wallich told me that he is the one who edited and published Dr. William Roxburgh's *Hortus Bengalensis*, which was the first catalogue of plants growing in the Royal Botanic Garden."

"He works for the East India Company like Dr. Wallich?"

"I do not know his employer, but I understand he is much involved with Dr. Wallich's research. It was they who arranged the plants and shrubs into twenty-three classes: Monandria to Polygamia. In fact, this Englishman is even now preparing the manuscript of Roxburgh's *Flora Indica* for publication on his own printing press."

*"Bas,"* Moumita said, holding up her hand to stop the flow of words. She had little patience for Violet's passionate interest in botany. "Do you think this man at Serampore can help you?"

"I am hopeful he will agree to act as my liaison, transporting to Dr. Wallich the specimens I collect. And after I visit with him and secure his cooperation, I shall travel the road to Krishnangar alone."

Moumita snorted in annoyance. "Then I must go with you on this foolish journey. And when your father catches up to you — which he will — then I shall be cast back into the street from which I came." She sighed. "Better that I should have burned on my husband's funeral pyre than face such a destiny as this."

"Oh, Moumita." Violet dropped her bags, threw her arms around the older woman, and drank in the scent of coconut oil that anointed the long black braid running down her dear *ayah*'s back. Rose water fragranced Moumita's soft brown skin, and her breath smelled of the sweet aniseed she loved to chew.

"I shall never allow anything bad to happen to you," Violet said. "Please believe me. I shall always look after you and see that you are cared for."

"Perhaps in my next life I shall be born a cow for all the trouble you have caused me. Then I can wander the streets of Calcutta with no one to bother me." She shrugged and shook her head. "But if I am reborn as a cow, it is more likely that I shall be owned by a Muslim and get eaten straightaway."

Laughing in spite of herself, Violet shouldered her bags once again and stepped to the door. "Maybe you will be lucky and be reborn a pig. Then the Muslims would never even touch you."

Moumita pulled the loose end of her sari from her shoulder and wrapped it over her head. "*Na,* I shall be rolled into meatballs," she sighed. "Fried and eaten with cauliflower."

"Shh," Violet whispered. Glancing behind to make certain her *ayah* was following, she slipped out into the hallway and crept down the stone staircase. The two women tiptoed to a wooden lattice that screened the front room of the house, and Violet peered through the leaves of the philodendron vine that wound through it.

Near one of the sprawling tufted couches

38

that littered the room stood Malcolm Rosse, smoking his hookah and holding forth on some topic of interest only to himself. No doubt her father was discussing the latest schemes of the East India Company, as he always did when guests came to dinner.

As she took a fortifying breath, Violet spotted a rounded clay pot near the screen. *Cymbidium eburneum.* Standing nearly two feet tall, the green-leafed orchid plant that rose from the pot bore three large white blossoms on a long, arching stem. Each stunningly perfect flower must have measured more than four inches in diameter, and she reached down to touch the petals as though the orchid were a precious child.

"I brought this *Cymbidium* in from our garden this morning," she whispered to Moumita. "Smell it. It is like fruit, I think — mango, perhaps, or apricot."

As her *ayah* obediently bent to sniff, Violet thought of the fate to which her father had sentenced her. This orchid could never grow in Yorkshire. In such a place it would most surely perish.

Taking Moumita's hand, she motioned toward the door. They had a long night's journey ahead.

# Two

While servants set out china dishes covered with silver domes, Edmund regarded the imposing merchant seated across the breakfast table from him. It had been raining since dawn, and a welcome breeze drifted through the arched porticoes of the expansive dining room. The fragrance of jasmine and frangipani blossoms filled the air, giving Edmund a sense of renewed optimism.

Though he did not know why Malcolm Rosse had summoned him, he prayed the subject might be spiritual. The East India Company had made it all but impossible for him to establish a church in Calcutta, but Edmund had determined to shine Christ's love and mercy upon that institution no matter what persecution they heaped upon him. He regularly visited Fort William and counseled with soldiers in the various regiments. He stopped in at the company's hospital to minister to the sick. He made his presence known about the warehouses and offices, chatting with the Indian laborers and their British supervisors.

And early this morning, a servant had knocked upon the door of the house where Edmund stayed while in the city to say that Malcolm Rosse — a respected and wealthy merchant — had need of the missionary's services. Perhaps at last, Edmund prayed, God's people in this foreign land had remembered Him. Filled with hope, he hurried to dress and make his way by rickshaw to the stately home and its surrounding gardens near the Hooghly River.

After greeting Mr. Rosse and entering the spacious dining room, Edmund had offered a prayer of thanksgiving for the meal. Now he leaned forward, eager to learn of the burden on his host's heart.

Though they had never met, Edmund knew Malcolm Rosse by reputation. A cutthroat trader who had enriched himself in India, Rosse lived a life of luxury. He found English culture stifling and had fully adopted Indian ways. Like many of his counterparts in the East India Company, he wore native clothing and kept a "Betsy" — a local mistress who had attached herself to the Englishman in exchange for the benefits he could provide. Guests at Rosse House often joined their host in smoking a hookah and playing at dice and cards. Curry and chutney were staples on his tables. He spoke fluent Bengali, and he had not been home to England in more than twenty years.

Mr. Rosse was no gentleman, Edmund knew. Indeed, if God had led him to India for the single purpose of ministering to Malcolm Rosse, Edmund would consider all the past fruitless years worthwhile.

"How may I be of service, Mr. Rosse?" he asked. "I am willing to do all in my power to assist you."

"Good. Very good." Rosse picked up his knife, cut a plump sausage link in half, and looked at his guest. "Sir, my daughter has run away."

Edmund could not have been more surprised at this information. "You have children?"

"Only one, thank heaven," Rosse said as he chewed the sausage. "A dreadful girl. Violet has been given everything she ever wanted, and more besides. She spends my money willy-nilly, goes off to the Botanic Garden every day to indulge her passion for flowers, and orders the servants to wait upon her hand and foot. Despite all this loving care from me, she is willful, impetuous, brash, disobedient, and ungrateful. She does whatever she likes, and pays little heed to anything I tell her."

"I-I am astonished," Edmund stammered. He hardly knew which was the more amazing: the fact that Mr. Rosse had a child or his appalling description of her.

"Until recently," the man continued, "Violet has been of no use to me at all. But several months ago, I thought to have some profit out of my investment in her, and I began to make arrangements to that end. Last night at dinner, I informed my guests that I intended to pack the girl off to England to marry one of my colleagues in the trade. Everyone thought it a brilliant scheme, of course. Parliament's act reducing the company's power has played havoc with us all, and my profits in particular have suffered."

"I am sorry to hear this, sir. Yet, I must say —"

"Alfred Cunliffe," Rosse went on, "owns several fabric markets and warehouses in York with which I have done business in past years. Connecting myself to such a man seems a most propitious opportunity for me. When I announced the proposed union, Violet said nothing at all, and I thought the matter settled. But this morning at dawn, my servants came to tell me that she and her *ayah* had run away. The *mali* found their footprints in the garden when he was cutting flowers for the breakfast table. Evidently they went over the wall and have disappeared altogether."

Envisioning a poor young English girl running helter-skelter through Calcutta in the middle of the night, Edmund clenched his napkin. "Mr. Rosse, you must alert the authorities at Fort William at once."

"I have done so already, and a search is under way even now. That silly child has been climbing over the wall since she was old enough to walk. I always have her back by nightfall in time for a proper walloping, of course. But now I think she may have gone off for good."

"Mr. Rosse, surely you can understand your daughter's fright," Edmund said carefully. "Child marriages are Hindu in practice and cannot be condoned in any good society."

"My daughter is hardly a child! Indeed, Violet is . . . well, she is —" he looked at the ceiling and counted on his fingers — "she is above twenty, at least."

"Above twenty!" The thought of Mr. Rosse walloping a young lady was more than Edmund could bear. "And she has been kept all these years here in India? Surely you ought to have sent her to England for schooling, sir."

Rosse cleared his throat. "I ought, yes

indeed. But Violet was young when her mother died. She very much reminded me of . . . of my wife . . . and at any rate, I did not think to send her away. If truth be known, I grew accustomed to her presence, and eventually I quite forgot about her."

"You forgot your daughter?"

"She was hardly noticeable in the early years. Such a small thing. Now and again I saw her on the stairs or in the garden, and she often crept under my desk to listen to the letters I would dictate to my Bengali scribe. It was not as though I abandoned her, Mr. Sherbourne. I employed an *ayah* to look after her, and I hired tutors now and again. The tutors hardly stayed more than a month or two, for Violet was far too impertinent. In short, I gave her a good childhood, and I have a fine future planned for her. But first I must find her and pack her off to England."

Edmund tried to think how to respond. He could hardly imagine a father being unaware of his own child. Lord Thorne and his wife had taken prodigious care of their own three sons. Edmund's mother had taught him to read and write. It was by her example that he came to know Jesus Christ — though his conversion had occurred many years after her death. His father had spent many hours teaching his sons to hunt, fish, and ride. All had been taken under his wing and taught to understand ledgers and the workings of the estate, so that upon his passing any of his heirs could take the reins of the baronage. Edmund's childhood had been warm, happy, and filled with parental love.

"Mr. Rosse, I condole with you on the disappearance of your daughter," he said, determined to minister to the merchant despite Rosse's failings as a father. After all, the servant's message that morning had been most urgent, and it was clear that Rosse felt much distress and melancholy at the disappearance of his daughter. "I am so concerned as to be greatly troubled on your behalf. Certainly, I believe God is watching over Miss Rosse, and He must guide those in search of her to her rescue."

"Thank you, my good man," Rosse said. "But you have no idea how resourceful and clever the girl is. By heaven, I should have sent the wretch away years ago. Trouble, she is. Nothing but trouble."

Edmund understood the man had summoned him in order to seek spiritual counsel, yet a true minister could hardly pass up the opportunity to bring enlightenment on the role a father ought to play in his offspring's life. Especially a father so determined to disparage his child.

It was commonplace in India, and in England as well, for a man to arrange a mutually beneficial marriage between his daughter and a well-suited gentleman. But there the similarities ended. In India, fathers married off very young girls, who often lived as veritable slaves until their husband's death. Then they faced the prospect of becoming *suttee* — being burned alive on their husband's funeral pyre, in theory to assure him and all his relatives a happy afterlife.

In England, a young woman was usually permitted at least some opinion on the matter of her future husband. Certainly a respectable father would never make any agreement with a gentleman who was less than well connected, of scrupulous reputation, and very amiable toward the young lady.

Mr. Rosse, in Edmund's opinion, was following the Indian model more closely than he ought.

"Sir, I believe it may be beneficial for us to examine the situation from your daughter's point of view," he said. "Your agreement with this Alfred Cunliffe of York is well intentioned, but I fear it may be misguided. While such a marriage must certainly expedite your trade here in India, it sentences your daughter to a future that may not be beneficial to her. Have you first-hand knowledge of the intended husband — his character, his reputation, his situation in life?"

"He is wealthy. That much I do know."

"Financial resources are essential, of course, but consider the fragile state of your daughter's present condition. She needs much more in a husband than wealth. She will require a man of patience and forbearance, a man of great moral countenance, a man who cares deeply for her. Miss Rosse has lived all her life in India and knows nothing of England. I would suggest you permit her first to acclimate herself to life in that country and thence to form for herself an opinion of the gentleman in question."

At this proposal, Rosse's chest swelled. "Young man, what affair is it of yours the man I choose for my daughter? I did not solicit nor do I welcome your opinion. You and I are neither colleagues nor friends. It is hardly your place to speak about anything to me, let alone my daughter's future."

"I beg your pardon, sir. I assumed you sought counsel from me as a minister."

"Nonsense! What counsel can you offer me? You know nothing of who I am —

nothing of my business dealings, nothing of my motives, and certainly nothing of my daughter. In fact, I know far more about you than you do of me." He leaned forward, jabbing a finger at Edmund. "I am told that you wander about the fort and the company offices as though your presence there is somehow desired. No one wants your proselytizing, Mr. Sherbourne. Do you understand that?"

Edmund bristled. "Sir, my presence in India has a purpose far different from your own. I am called of God, and I have been obedient to His command."

"Employed by God, are you?" Rosse said with a laugh. "How presumptuous."

"If you find my ministry so reprehensible, sir, why did you summon me this morning? Do you wish for my prayers while at the same time reviling the Lord I serve?"

"Wish for your prayers? Upon my word, I never —"

"Sahib! Sahib Rosse!" A woman's voice echoed through the dining room.

Edmund glanced up to see a young Indian in a bright purple, silk sari run to the man's chair and fall to her knees at his feet.

"Good heavens, Betsy, what is it?" he barked. "Has Violet been recovered? Speak up at once."

49

"Sahib, the rickshaw wallah has returned from the Botanic Garden where you sent him. He brings this letter from Dr. Wallich."

Rosse snatched the note the woman held in her outstretched hand. " 'Dear Mr. Rosse,' " he read aloud, " 'I have not seen your daughter yet this morning, but I am expecting her at noon to assist me in cataloguing the —' " He balled the note and hurled it at the wall. "Orchids! By Jove, I shall skin the girl alive!"

"Sahib, I beg you, please do not sack the night watchman because of the disappearance of your daughter." The Indian woman's trembling lips formed the words as her hands folded in supplication. "He has a wife and ten children. The youngest boy suffers from polio, and six of the children are daughters who will require dowries —"

"Hang the watchman! If he had done his job, Violet would be here this morning!"

"Please, sahib," she wailed, clutching his feet. "I beg you also not to sack the *mali,* for his wife died of smallpox only last year, and he has five children —"

"Enough about the servants, Betsy! I want my daughter."

"Sahib," Betsy whispered, her head bowed. "It is possible the daughter and her *ayah* went away from Calcutta last night by boat. The fish wallah who came to the kitchen to sell shrimp spoke of hearing a strange story early this morning at the river. He told the cooks that several fishermen had talked to an Englishwoman who was speaking very fine Bengali. She was seeking a *nouka* wallah in the night."

"But of course that was Violet! Where was she taken?"

"Sahib, we do not know. The fish wallah said the *nouka* journeyed up the river away from the city."

"Send someone down to the river to find out where the *nouka* wallah took my daughter," Rosse commanded. "And see that she is brought back to me at once."

"Yes, sahib, but this already has been done, and no one knows where she was taken."

"Of course someone knows. They simply have not been paid well enough to give out the information."

"Yes, sahib, but the *nouka* wallah has rowed away without giving this information. He must have been paid very well by your daughter." Betsy bowed her head again. "Sahib, we who live only to serve you believe that the girl has gone to the village of her *ayah,* that wicked Moumita, who should be sacked immediately for this bad deed."

"Moumita does not hail from Calcutta?"

"No, sahib, she is from a small village of the Untouchable caste. It is near a river."

"A river? Every village is near a river! How dare she do this to me!"

Edmund assessed whether to speak up and risk another upbraiding from Mr. Rosse. By now, he had come to believe the man was so unpleasant as to deserve every misfortune that came his way. His daughter, however, had done nothing but attempt to flee her father's harsh tongue and uncaring demeanor.

"Why should your daughter not flee Calcutta, sir?" Edmund asked. "What future would she have if she remained here? You mean to send her away to a country she has never seen to marry a man she does not know."

"She is my daughter, Sherbourne, and I may do exactly as I please with her!"

"Indeed, and suffer the consequences. Your failure to show concern for your daughter's feelings compels her to risk going it alone. That an English lady might travel in this heathen land with an outcast Indian woman as her only companion reveals Miss Rosse's utter desperation. That she would believe she could find refuge from her own father in a poor village —"

"You make her sound like a victim! I have never treated my daughter badly."

Edmund swallowed down his anger. Whatever the truth about Violet Rosse, the person most clearly in need of a spiritual minister at this moment was her father. "Sir, I have been hasty in casting judgment upon you," Edmund admitted. "You speak aright when you say that I do not know your daughter well. In fact, I have the barest understanding of the life you have provided her. Please accept my apology and my offer to do anything I can to be of service during this time of need."

Rosse regarded Edmund for a moment, his eyes narrowing. "Anything, eh? Well, yes, then I shall take you up on the offer. You can be of service to me, Sherbourne. That is why I summoned you here this morning. I want you to find my daughter and bring her home."

Edmund stiffened. "Find your daughter? Sir, are you jesting? I am a missionary, and I have —"

"You have nothing to detain you here in Calcutta — no converts, no church, no congregation, nothing. I charge you now, as a minister of God, with the responsibility of finding my daughter."

"But that is . . . why me?"

"You know the countryside better than anyone in Calcutta. I am told you have visited nearly every village in this region in all your fruitless wanderings. You know the rivers, the roads, the towns. As you are not an employee of the company or a member of a Royal regiment, you are able to get about among the people without arousing ill will."

As the situation became clear at last, Edmund's ire rose. "Mr. Rosse, I am under the direction of my missionary society. I cannot possibly go off into the —"

"Yes, yes, the heathen lands. Of course you can. You do it all the time." Rosse produced a wallet and took out a thick stack of rupees. "Take this money, buy passage on a *nouka,* and do whatever it takes to find my daughter. She cannot be too far ahead of you. And see that you bring her back to me unsullied, my good man."

"Upon my word!" Edmund exploded as Rosse put the money on the table and turned to leave the dining room. "You besmirch my character even as you insult me with this ridiculous assignment." He squared his shoulders. "You cannot purchase my services, sir. I refuse to accept your money, nor shall I go in search of your wayward daughter. You are to blame for her heedlessness, and I shall not be given charge of finding her on your behalf. I repeat, Mr. Rosse, you cannot buy me!"

At those words, the older man halted. Turning around, he regarded his guest with a pale blue gaze. "I am accustomed to buying whatever I please," he said. "Are you certain I cannot buy you, Mr. Sherbourne?"

"Absolutely not, sir. I am above such pettiness."

"What say you to the offer of an East India Company permit to preach your sermons inside Calcutta?"

"A permit to preach in the city?"

"Yes, to the British soldiers, and to the Portuguese, and to those rich Armenians — all of whom have been off-limits to you until now. And, of course, you would have permission to make sermons for the Hindus and Muslims in Calcutta, as well." He paused. "And to sweeten the pot, I shall offer you a church of your very own. Inside the city."

Edmund swallowed. "Sir, as you know, the true church is the body of Christ, and I believe —"

"A church is a blasted building, and without one, you have nothing!" Rosse scowled at his guest, but he took a calmer tone when he continued. "Some time ago, I purchased an abandoned Hindu temple, thinking to employ it as a cloth warehouse — for it sits very near the river. The temple is no longer of any use to the priests of Kali, because the water has encroached to within three hundred feet of the building, which means no high-caste Brahman is allowed to receive a gift or take his food there. If you find my daughter and return her to me, Sherbourne, you shall have that temple for your church."

Edmund stared at the merchant in disbelief. A temple to the Hindu goddess, Kali, might become a church? A place where people could worship the one true and living God?

A female figure with blue black skin, Kali was revered throughout Bengal. In the idols and paintings Edmund had seen, she was depicted as having four arms. In one hand she held a sword, in another the head of a demon she had slain, and with the other two she encouraged her followers. Her tongue protruded from her mouth, her eyes were red, and her body was smeared with blood. To the Hindus, Kali represented the universal mother — both terrible and magnificent. To Edmund, she stood for everything that he had come to India to battle in the holy name of Jesus Christ.

"Mr. Rosse," he said evenly, "do I understand you to say that if I return your
daughter to you, I shall be given an East
India Company permit to preach in the city
of Calcutta, as well as an abandoned temple
of Kali to use for a church building?"

"Have I not just said as much?" Rosse's
mouth spread into a slow smile. "I see your
self-righteousness is not without limits,
Sherbourne. No minister in his right mind
would refuse such an offer."

Edmund crossed his arms, fighting the
urge that now assailed him. For five years he
had labored without ceasing on behalf of the
gospel ministry to which God had commissioned him. Five long years. And nothing!
Not one Hindu or Muslim had heeded his
call to repent and be saved. Aware of
Edmund's struggle, Dr. Carey had visited
him often to provide encouragement. The
venerable missionary had preached in India
for seven years without result, he had reminded the younger man as they strolled recently through Calcutta's bazaar. Yet when
heaven's blessings began to pour out, they
came in a deluge. Edmund's mentor had
urged him to be patient, to pray, and to wait
for God's timing.

Was it possible that the time was now?
Could God work through a man like

Malcolm Rosse, who had no morals, no scruples, not even the slightest inclination toward the things of God? The merchant was actually offering a preaching permit and a building in payment for Edmund's assistance. Incredible.

But were these the pieces of silver for which Judas had betrayed his Lord? Or were they the alabaster bottle of perfume with which the woman had washed the feet of her Master?

Impossible dilemma! How could Edmund confess to his missionary society in London that he had struck a deal with an unbeliever to gain the right to preach in Calcutta? How could he report that he had founded a church upon the rescue of a runaway girl?

Yet how could he turn away from such an opportunity?

He faced his tempter.

"I have planned to return to England and never see India again, Mr. Rosse. I believe my work here has been to plant seeds that some other missionary can tend until the day of harvest."

"Bah!" Rosse exclaimed. "Why slink back like a dog with his tail between his legs? You long to stay on and succeed in your mission. You have yet a spark of ambition, young man. I can see it in your eyes. Come, now, make the reasonable choice!"

"Are you an agent of Satan, then?"

"Perhaps I am an angel sent down from heaven. How will you ever know unless you accept my offer?"

Edmund needed time to pray over this. He should speak to Dr. Carey. He ought to go down to the river and have a look at the proffered temple. Perhaps there was no such building. And did Rosse really possess the power to secure a preaching permit? Too many uncertainties . . . too much haste . . .

"Never mind then," Rosse said. "I shall go to Fort William and find some willing young soldier who would —"

"I am that willing soldier, sir," Edmund spoke up. "I am a soldier of the Cross. Whether your offer be of Satan or of God remains to be seen. Yet I accept it out of concern for your daughter's health and safety."

"So pious! You accept it out of greed."

"I want to please God."

"You want to be able to tally your converts and ship them off to heaven, just as I tally the bolts of fabric that I ship away to England. We are cut of the same cloth, Edmund Sherbourne. You are no nobler than I."

"I serve God, not man."

"Do you? How nice." He thumped a finger on the pile of rupees. "This will see you off, then. You must post messages to me each day, reporting your progress. And when you find Violet, you must bring her back to me posthaste."

"What if I am unable to find the young lady?"

"You will find her. Violet is obstinate and unruly, but she, too, has her price. She will want to come back, you see. Though she will deny it, she longs for family and home. This house, the servants, her orchids — these are Violet's family and her home. Use them to lure her here."

"So that you can send her away to England?"

"Exactly." Waving a hand, Rosse turned and stepped away. "Betsy, have a fresh breakfast brought to me in the garden. I shall be sitting under the guava tree. And do tell the *mali* and the night watchman I wish to speak to them both. They have been most derelict in their duties."

# Three

"Thus far, Moumita, we have seen two open-billed storks, a night heron, a cormorant, eight egrets, and countless doves." Violet lifted the skirt of her sari as she stepped over a mud puddle in the main road of Serampore. As it was just past noon, the oppressively dank heat was growing unbearable, and few pedestrians were about.

"While we travel," she continued, "I must keep all these birds in mind until I have had time to write their names in my journal. Dr. Wallich is always most emphatic about my keeping detailed records of everything I observe — though I cannot think he will find my notes useful unless I discover an entirely new species."

"A new kind of bird, *meye?*"

Moumita carried one of Violet's bags in each hand, and on her head she balanced a bundle of her own clothing and possessions. She trudged along three steps behind her charge, as an *ayah* ought. Moumita had accompanied Violet upriver the entire night without complaint. The small boat and the

61

threat of cobras in the water had not distressed her. The long walk up the bank and into the town had prompted no comment. Even Violet's difficulties with her sari had been met with mute resignation. It seemed that once they had cleared the wall of the Rosse family compound, the Indian woman had accepted her destiny.

"Can you imagine, Moumita, discovering a new kind of bird? We have seen bulbuls, sparrows, kingfishers, woodpeckers, owls, ducks, and cuckoos in large numbers. But these are all familiar species. I am eager to find something different — a sort of bird never before seen."

"But, *meye,* there is no such thing as a bird that has never been seen."

"Certainly there is." Violet spotted their destination, the Serampore home of Dr. William Carey, in the distance and pointed it out to her *ayah.* "There are many things in this world that have never been seen. It is the primary job of the scientist to discover, investigate, and record them."

"All birds have been seen by someone," Moumita stated bluntly. "Perhaps the scientist has not seen this bird of the new species, and so this bird may be strange to him. But to the man who lives near the bird, it is very common."

Violet mulled over this observation for a moment, then concluded once again that her *ayah* possessed more common sense than most well-educated Englishmen.

"You are quite correct," she said. "Yet each new species must be recorded by a scientist — preferably an English scientist, for they seem best at such endeavors. This record keeping is very important."

"Does the species not exist unless it is recorded by the scientist?"

"It exists, yes, but the scientist himself wishes to know all that the world contains. He is curious. He longs to discover things that are new to him, and to examine them."

"May the scientist be a man only? Or may he be a woman?"

"Scientists are men." Violet pondered this as they walked. "I wonder why."

"The English have no sense."

"Some of them do not. But a scientist must be brilliant. He studies in order that he might understand and teach others what he has learned. This is his work."

"This is a useless work," Moumita concluded. "He will be paid nothing to find a bird. He ought to plant rice and cabbage. Then he can feed his family, and the gods will be well pleased with him."

Violet sighed as she walked the last few

steps to the whitewashed house and knocked on the door. Several of her many tutors had educated Violet on the incredible impact of the Renaissance. Yet how could one explain such a sweeping enlightenment in a land where nothing like it had occurred? How was it possible to communicate the importance of learning for learning's sake to a poor Indian woman who had worked all her life just to put food in her mouth?

"The world holds more than planting and harvesting," she told Moumita. "Life can be something greater than trying not to drown in monsoons or starve in famines. There are art and theater and architecture and literature. And there is science."

"Those tutors should have been sacked straightaway," Moumita grumbled behind Violet. "They came to your father's house, and they brought their books and their blue-and-brown balls —"

"Globes."

"Yes, and they told many lies to convince your father that they should be given more rupees. If I had been your teacher —"

*"Nomoshkar,"* a voice said in greeting as the front door opened before them. *"Kemon achen?"*

Instead of a servant, a middle-aged En-glishman stood before them. Slight of stature, he had a kind face — a long nose, warm brown eyes, and a gentle expression on his lips. But she knew this man! Their paths had crossed not long before in the bazaar at Calcutta, and they had spoken briefly. He had accompanied that handsome gentleman who bungled his Bengali. Could this be the scholar about whom Violet had heard such accolades?

"Dr. Carey?" she blurted out. "Are you Dr. William Carey?"

"I am indeed," he confirmed. "And you are an Englishwoman . . . wearing a sari. I believe we have met before — just last week in the Calcutta market."

Violet smiled and lowered the length of green silk with which she had covered her head. "I remember you well, sir," she replied, giving him a curtsy. "Your Bengali is excellent. I am Miss Rosse of Calcutta. Miss Violet Rosse."

"How very nice to see you again." He bowed in return. Dr. Carey appeared every inch the man of gentility, education, and high intelligence that Violet had hoped to find. Bald save the half-moon of hair at the back of his head, he wore a black suit of lightweight cotton, and he clutched a heavy tome.

A mere eighteen miles upriver from Calcutta, and here he stood — the learned man of whom she had heard so much. As simple as that. Why had she not run away long before?

"I believe we are now properly introduced," Dr. Carey said, "and so you must come inside where it is cooler. But I have not met your companion."

"This is Moumita Choudhary," Violet said as they stepped into the large front room with its open windows, jute rugs, and comfortable cotton-upholstered seating. "She is my *ayah*."

"Are you not rather . . . mature . . . to have an *ayah*, Miss Rosse?"

"Certainly I am, sir, but I did need someone to accompany me on my expedition."

"An Englishwoman in a sari . . . with her *ayah* . . . on an expedition. Do sit down, please. I must hear more."

Violet arranged her sari carefully as she seated herself on a long, low couch. On Indian women, the wrapped, pleated, and tucked nine yards of silk or cotton appeared graceful. She herself often wore such a garment to dinner or on a stroll about the city. But in the past hours of travel, she had discovered that with any arduous activity it was not easy to keep from treading on the embroidered hem. Such a mishap resulted in three or four yards of fabric suddenly falling loose and puddling to the ground at one's feet. In that regard, Violet had not enjoyed a happy morning.

"Tell me, Miss Rosse, to what do I owe the honor of your visit?" Dr. Carey said as he took a chair across from her. "I sense that God has brought you to my home at Serampore on an important mission."

"Oh, no, it was not God at all," she replied. "It was my own decision to come to Serampore. I am meant to go to England and marry a gentleman from York, you see, but I have elected to take a different course."

"Aha." Dr. Carey looked as if he did not quite see, yet he nodded in a kindly way. "At a time like this, I believe tea might be just the thing."

"I should be delighted, of course."

Violet glanced at her *ayah* as Dr. Carey spoke to a servant waiting in the shadows near an inside door. Moumita was staring at a large picture on the wall, and she did not appear pleased with it in the least. A simple wooden frame displayed a scene of such horror that Violet could not imagine why Dr. Carey had chosen to hang it — especially in his sitting room. She had seen a similar print once, though not this exact artistic rendition. One of her tutors had brought it along with a packet of other famous European artworks to her schoolroom in the house at Calcutta.

Upon a craggy hill stood three tall wooden structures, each built in the shape of a cross or the letter *T*. Hands stretched from side to side and feet held together by a single spike, three tormented men hung upon these crosses. The poor men had been wrapped in nothing more than sheer white fabric at the waist, and their skin was piteously pale. Blood gushed from their wounds, soaking into the ground and dripping onto the crowd gathered below them. The man on the center cross wore an expression of great woe, as though He bore the weight of the whole world upon His shoulders.

Even though she knew it was merely a work of art meant to stimulate the senses, Violet could not feel comfortable in the presence of this painting.

"That one in the middle belonged to my mother," she whispered to her *ayah*. "When she died, I received a small silver statue of Him. Do you not recall it?"

Moumita nodded, her face solemn. "Yes, I know this ridiculous God of the English people. I have seen the statue in your room."

"It is Jesus," Violet said softly. "That is His name."

At that, Dr. Carey turned to her. "Ah, you have discovered my print of the crucifixion. I keep it there to remind my guests of the difference, you understand — the sacrifice that separates our faith from all others."

Though she had no idea what he meant by such a comment, Violet intended to earn this man's favor if at all possible. "It is very well drawn," she remarked.

"Duccio di Buoninsegna. An Italian master."

Violet nodded. "Art is important to civilization."

"Indeed it is, especially when it draws us closer to our Maker. I was careful in my selection of this painting and deliberate in my decision to display it. I did not wish to confuse my converts with any image that might be deemed by them to be worthy of worship. Idolatry is rampant among the heathen, and the missionary must be diligent in avoiding any appearance of it."

"Absolutely," Violet said.

"Duccio's art represents a scene of great emotion and turmoil. It is almost a drama in itself. I felt I might use it much as the early

Christian elders used stained-glass windows among the illiterate masses. The painting is a teaching tool, you see. One can point out Mary of Clopas, Mary the mother of Jesus, Mary Magdalene, and John the Evangelist. One can clearly distinguish the two thieves and the Roman soldiers. By explaining their roles in the crucifixion, one can begin to lead a Hindu or a Muslim toward a better understanding of Christ Himself."

"What a very good thing this is," Violet said. Clearly Dr. Carey knew a great deal more than she about almost everything. Had she the time, Violet would enjoy nothing more than sitting at his feet and listening to his gentle voice as he taught her.

But she had a greater purpose in coming to Serampore, and the sooner she revealed it to him, the better. At the moment of her decision, the servant brought in the tea and began setting it out on a low table made of carved teak and bamboo. This happily ended the discussion of the morbid painting, and it provided the perfect opportunity for Violet.

"Dr. Carey, I have come about botany," she began, but at that moment a knock sounded on the door.

"That will be Krishna Pal," the missionary told Violet. "He was one of my first

Indian converts. I have been awaiting his arrival, for we are working together on a most essential translation."

Rather than sending a servant as any other Englishman would have done, Dr. Carey excused himself and rose to greet his guest at the door.

To Violet's surprise, the visitor on the front porch was not an Indian at all. Tall and broad shouldered, with a strong chin and layers of soft brown hair, a young Englishman removed his black, tall-crowned hat and embraced the elderly scientist. As he focused on the interior of the house, his deep green eyes settled upon Violet. And she knew him at once. He was the man from the bazaar.

"Edmund!" Dr. Carey exclaimed, taking him by the arm and leading him into the house. "Such a delightful surprise, for I was fully expecting Krishna Pal. Do come inside! Perhaps you will remember the young lady we encountered at the Calcutta bazaar last week. She has paid me an unexpected yet most welcome visit."

Edmund could hardly find his voice as he faced the golden-haired creature who had so transfixed him. He made an abrupt bow. "Good afternoon, madam. How pleased I am to see you again."

"Miss Rosse," Dr. Carey said, "I am delighted to introduce to you my dear friend and colleague, Mr. Edmund Sherbourne. Mr. Sherbourne, may I present Miss Violet Rosse of Calcutta."

"I am happy to see you again also, sir." The young woman stood. "I believe Dr. Carey was as unprepared for your visit as he was for mine."

*This* was Violet Rosse — the headstrong, willful, impetuous daughter of Malcolm Rosse? The disobedient child who had climbed over the wall in the middle of the night to run away from home? This most stunning and magnificent of women — could she truly be the very object of his current search? Edmund forced a smile to his lips. What on earth was she doing at William Carey's house?

"Such handsome weather we are having," she spoke up, as though quoting from a book of etiquette. The weather was horrid. "And you are looking well also, Mr. Sherbourne."

"Thank you, but I am . . . I am a bit surprised myself," he told her. "Dr. Carey, I did not realize you were so well acquainted with Miss Rosse."

"I was not acquainted with her at all until

ten minutes ago when she knocked on my door. But we have got along famously since then."

Dr. Carey offered Edmund a seat far too near the young lady, and he had no choice but to take it. He made a brief attempt to look at her but quickly thought better of it. The whole situation was shocking. Edmund could hardly announce that he had come to seek Dr. Carey's opinion on which direction a stubborn and rebellious young lady might take in running away from home. Nor could he simply toss Miss Rosse over his shoulder like a sack of potatoes and carry her back to her father. Yet he must broach the subject soon, for clearly God had directed his path straight to her.

Miss Rosse, too, appeared uncomfortable at being discovered outside of Calcutta and in the home of a stranger. Lowering her head, she made a great business of stirring several lumps of sugar into her milky tea.

Dr. Carey broke the awkward silence. "My dear Edmund, like Miss Rosse, you come to my door as if on an urgent mission. May I ask the purpose of your errand?"

"Advice," Edmund said, suddenly discerning a way to postpone his unhappy assignment. "Indeed, sir, I seek your counsel. You see, a proposal has been made to me,

73

and I am in need of your opinion on it."

"What sort of proposal?"

"As you know, I go to England in three weeks' time, intending never to return."

"And very sad we are for such a loss to our community of believers. May we have any hope you will change your plans?"

"Originally, I should have denied any possibility of my coming back to India, though my holy calling has not been altered in any way. Now I am offered an astonishing opportunity, and I must decide whether it is of God."

"Miss Rosse —" Dr. Carey turned to address the young lady — "if you will permit, I should very much like to hear of this opportunity that has been presented to my colleague. By his anxious countenance, I believe the subject may have deep significance for our future work here in India. Following that discussion, Edmund and I shall be eager to learn the reason for your own visit to Serampore."

"Of course, sir," she said. At this turn of the conversation Miss Rosse seemed to relax, and she began to whisper to the Indian servant at her side. Edmund recognized the woman as the Untouchable who had been with the young lady in the bazaar.

"I am offered a company permit to preach

the gospel in Calcutta," he announced to Dr. Carey. "And I have been promised a building in which to establish a church."

"Upon my word, this is wonderful news!" the missionary cried, raising his hands in delight. "Truly, a miracle has been wrought, for this has been the subject of prayer for many years. Edmund, please tell me more of this offer, which I pray you intend to accept."

"With all my heart I mean to do God's will. But I felt I must consult with you first, for the offer is not without conditions. Tell me, sir, if God's will may arise from a situation in which He is entirely absent."

"God is never absent," Dr. Carey said. "Even in the blackest of hearts, He stands at the door and knocks. I affirm your desire to consider prayerfully this most unusual opportunity."

"Rest assured, I shall pray about the matter." Edmund glanced at Miss Rosse, whose blue gray eyes were now turned upon him. "As to its source and particulars, sir, I must be discreet for the moment. I am sure you understand the delicate nature of such a situation."

"Certainly. In India, few matters that concern our work can proceed without complication. You shall have my support and prayer as you make your decision."

"Thank you, Dr. Carey. I depend upon it."

"Wonderful, wonderful. Miss Rosse, thank you for your forbearance. If you will now impart to us the reason for your own visit, I am certain that Mr. Sherbourne and I shall be most pleased to hear it."

The young woman eyed her companion. Then she plucked at the folds of her sari. Finally, she let out a breath. "You are a scientist, Dr. Carey," she said. "And I have need of your assistance."

The elderly missionary's eyebrows lifted. "I am interested in science, Miss Rosse. But by no means do I call myself a scientist. Rather I am a man of God, come to India to preach the glorious Word of the risen Christ. Mr. Sherbourne and I are missionaries."

*"Sadhus,"* pronounced the Indian servant in a deep, guttural tone. "Holy men."

"But I thought . . . you assisted in the translation and printing of the Botanic Garden's catalogue, did you not? Dr. Wallich told me —"

"If I may please interrupt, Miss Rosse," Edmund spoke up. "Your mission to Dr. Carey — no matter its substance — must give way to another issue of far greater import. Madam, I bring a message from your father. He wishes you to return home at once."

The lady's mouth parted in surprise. "My father sent you to find me, sir? Why you?"

"In my missionary journeys I have become well acquainted with the terrain of West Bengal. Mr. Rosse believed I might have some success in locating you. As, indeed, I have."

"Thank you for your kind delivery of the message, Mr. Sherbourne," she said, her expression sobering. "I now discharge you from your responsibility."

"Then you will go home?"

"Absolutely not."

"But you must. Your father has arranged your journey to England, and he has seen to the details of your future in that land. He expects your willing participation."

"Unthinkable."

"I beg your pardon, madam?"

"I shall not go to York and marry Alfred Cunliffe. I have made other plans."

"Edmund," Dr. Carey spoke up. "I believe we are out of order in this matter. Dear Miss Rosse, perhaps first you should tell us why you came to see me."

After casting a dark look at Edmund, she leaned forward and began to speak to Dr.

Carey. "Botany is of great interest to me, sir. My particular study has been the collection and identification of the family *Orchidaceae,* the orchid. During the past three years, I have been assisting Dr. Nathaniel Wallich in his effort to enrich and add to the index of flora at the Botanic Garden in Calcutta."

"My goodness, but you must be the young lady about whom my good friend has told me so much!" the missionary exclaimed. "Dr. Wallich informs me that you are a woman of great intelligence and a keen understanding of botanical science. I understand you have all but memorized Roxburgh's *Hortus Bengalensis.*"

"Yes, sir." A brilliant smile lit her face. "But it was you, Dr. Carey, who so expertly edited the catalogue. And you are the man responsible for its publication."

At this chorus of mutual admiration, Edmund folded his arms across his chest. Though ostensibly she had come to Serampore to discuss her interest in botany, he felt certain another objective lay at the heart of her visit. But her true mission must be thwarted. Before she could completely enthrall the good missionary, she must be returned to her father.

"Dr. Wallich believes you are quite as capable as any assistant with whom he has ever worked," Dr. Carey sang on, and his praise elicited a glorious pink blush that spread across Miss Rosse's cheeks like a sunrise in summer. "And you were saying, my dear lady, that you have a particular interest in the hybridization of orchids."

"Sir, my passion for this aspect of science cannot be overstated. Were I permitted, I should devote myself wholly to its study. At my home in Calcutta, I have cultivated at least one specimen of every species thus far known in India. Indeed, it is my primary goal in life to discover orchids that have never been catalogued and to develop new types of orchids through hybridization."

"Birds," the small servant at her side murmured, leaning across the arm of her chair toward her mistress. "It was birds that you wished to discover."

"Birds are another interest of mine," Miss Rosse told Dr. Carey. "I keep a log, you see. During my expedition, I mean to record every genus and every species I encounter. I plan to make a thorough catalogue of each region through which I pass. Flora and fauna — both fascinate me. Through having worked so closely with Dr. Wallich, I am far more intimate with plants."

"Your expedition?" Edmund spoke up.

"May one ask your eventual destination, Miss Rosse?"

"The plan cannot be made public, Mr. Sherbourne. My arrangements are as intricate as the offer made to you." She tipped her head at him. "As you and Dr. Carey have noted, such matters call for discretion."

"But your father insists —"

"As you have learned, sir," she continued, "my father has certain goals that would affect my future. I have come to realize that one must be master of one's own life. Or mistress, as the case may be. Society may dictate that a lady ought to marry and bear children, and the lady herself may wish to do just such a thing one day — provided she be allowed to marry a man she loves. But if that lady is not permitted to make some choices for herself instead of having her father make them all on her behalf, she must simply go out on her own and do as she pleases."

"That is understandable, of course. But overt disobedience to a father's wishes is . . . it is obstinate." Edmund glanced at Dr. Carey. "Am I not correct, sir?"

"How can it be obstinate to do what one feels is right and correct?" Miss Rosse spoke up before Dr. Carey could answer. "Did you not choose to come to India, Mr. Sherbourne? Or did your father send you?"

"My heavenly Father sent me," Edmund replied. "In coming here, I obeyed God's calling."

"God sent you to India? This is a most unusual declaration. As for myself, I know only that I was born here, and I intend to stay in this country forever. My father cannot command me to leave."

"A father has the right to declare — yes, and even at times impose — his wishes upon his children," Edmund argued, recalling his own father's example and instruction. "A man must be especially forceful with his daughters, who are by nature weaker and more in need of guidance and protection. Is this not true, Dr. Carey?"

"I am not weak!" Miss Rosse exploded. "I need neither guidance nor protection — and you are a silly man who knows nothing!"

"I submit this matter at once to Dr. Carey," Edmund retorted. "His wisdom will make clear the faults of your position."

In the stillness that followed, Dr. Carey took a sip of tea and savored it before swallowing. He thought for some time. "Personally," he said, "I do not believe a father should impose a plan on his children."

"There!" the young lady crowed. "What did I tell you?"

"I believe," Dr. Carey continued, his brown eyes settling upon Violet, "that a good father ought to mold each of his progeny into the sort of person he can send out into the world. With active training, careful discipline, and much prayer, he can avoid having to use any coercion whatsoever. And they will become exactly what he intended."

Violet eyed him. "That would be the ideal. But what father can achieve this high standard?"

"To my immense satisfaction," Dr. Carey replied, "all my sons have chosen to serve the Lord on foreign fields — just as I prayed they would. Until two years ago, Felix was a medical missionary in Burma. Like myself, he was a printer of the Oriental languages and a scholar, especially in Sanskrit, Pali, Bengali, and Burman. His medical and linguistic talents so commended him to King George that he was conferred with many honors and sent as ambassador to the governor-general of Burma, at which time he was forced to abandon his missionary labors."

"How nice for him," Violet said. "And for you, sir."

Edmund ascertained with relief that the interview was proceeding according to his purposes. At the same time, the look of dismay on the young lady's face tormented him. Though the very idea of a woman wandering unescorted through the rugged landscape of West Bengal was pure madness, Edmund could not hold her at fault for desiring to escape such an overbearing father. Moreover, he could well see the folly in sending such a misfit away to England. Though her beauty must be greatly admired there, her affinity for wearing saris would be ridiculed and her interest in science scoffed at.

"My second son, William, is equally committed to the conversion of the heathen," Dr. Carey was saying. "He labors under much heaviness, however. Two years ago, the brig on which he and his family were sailing was hit by a squall. The ship upset and instantly sank. Those who could swim escaped with their lives. Those who could not perished. Among the saved were my dear William and most of the Bengalis. His poor wife and their two children were lost."

"Dreadful," Miss Rosse exclaimed.

"If that man was so good," her little *ayah* muttered, "he never would have earned such bad *kharma*. The man brought bad luck onto his own head by doing evil."

"Moumita!" Miss Rosse gasped and gave the impertinent woman a disapproving stare before returning her attention to Dr. Carey. "Sir, this is a tragic account. Such suffering your son must have endured."

"Suffering, my dear Miss Rosse, is permitted by God — at times, even planned. As a loving Father, He allows such agonies for the express purpose of shaping His servants into more useful vessels. William understands this, and thus he continues undaunted in his ministry."

"I cannot understand it in the least," she announced. "I believe affliction and misery are to be avoided at all cost. Only when a man's sins grow too great to bear might he then embrace suffering. Dr. Carey, have you not seen the men who pierce their tongues and cheeks with sharp brass needles, or walk on hot coals in their bare feet, or pull heavy carts with chains on hooks sunk into the flesh of their backs? This is suffering indeed, but such punishment is never welcomed except as penance for misdeeds."

"On the contrary, I believe the true purpose of suffering is to turn our eyes upon God and draw us closer to Him," Dr. Carey stated. "At one time, I was tormented by the behavior of my youngest son, Jabez. My suffering was great indeed, for he seemed all but lost to the cause of Christ. Yet my prayer and supplication touched the heart of God. Jabez became decidedly religious, and he now prefers the work of the Lord to every other. After the charter of 1813 removed the East India Company's excuse for intolerance, our Baptist society began to send missionaries and Bibles to the fifty thousand natives of Amboyna. Jabez was baptized, married, and dispatched there even before he could be ordained. I could not be happier."

"Through prayer this was accomplished?" Miss Rosse pondered a moment, then declared, "You will be happy to know that I pray quite often, Dr. Carey. Jesus receives my special homage. I have a small silver statue of Him that once belonged to my mother."

"Excellent, dear lady. I am pleased to know of your devotion to our Lord and Savior."

"You have molded your sons very well indeed, sir." Her smile faded. "I am sure my own father does not take such joy in his only child."

"I fear this is an accurate assessment," Edmund spoke up. "Dr. Carey, I must tell you that Mr. Rosse claims his daughter has given him much distress over the years. He considers her exceedingly headstrong. Her decision to leave her home and undertake a scientific expedition borders on the fool-hardy."

Miss Rosse looked down at her lap. "My father does not approve of my study of orchids, nor does he condone my assistance to Dr. Wallich at the Botanic Garden. He says I am an intolerable nuisance, and I ought to keep my mouth shut."

"Does he?" Dr. Carey asked. "These are hard words for a father to use."

"Yet, he is correct. As Mr. Sherbourne has told you, I am obstinate, and now you see that I have run away." She lifted her head, her eyes filling with tears. "But I had to leave Calcutta, Dr. Carey, or my father would send me to England, where orchids cannot grow. And I do not wish to marry Alfred Cunliffe, for I do not love the man or even know him. If I am married to Mr. Cunliffe and living in the moorlands of Yorkshire with no orchids and no sunshine and no sugarcane or old men chewing betel nut . . . I shall simply die!"

"Come, come, my dear Miss Rosse," Dr. Carey said, rising and crossing the floor to hand her his handkerchief. "Surely your father cannot have planned such a bleak future for you. Mr. Sherbourne would not have come to take you home if he believed that only doom and misfortune lay in your path. Would he now?"

As the young woman studied him through tear-filled eyes, Edmund grew uncomfortably hot. How unhappy she was — and he had caused her woe! Staring out the open window, he fought the unexpected emotion that roiled inside him. Certainly more misery lay ahead for the poor creature. Edmund could not deny it. If she stayed in India, her father would continue to mistreat her. If she went to England, she must know great loneliness and pain. If she continued her so-called scientific expedition, her life might come to a tragic end.

Yet how could Edmund fail to return her to Calcutta? The future of God's work in that dark city lay in his hands. As Dr. Carey had said, this opportunity had been the prayer and desire of every missionary in India for many, many years.

"If only my darling wife had not gone to call on Mrs. Marshman," the man himself was saying gently. He seated himself on the settee beside Miss Rosse and took her hand as she pressed his handkerchief against her damp cheek. "She would comfort you at once. Life often fails to go as we plan it, my dear. That is why we must keep our eyes on our Lord and Savior, Jesus Christ, for His will for us is always perfect. Allow me to tell you about my dear Charlotte."

"Of course, sir," Violet managed between sniffles.

"Charlotte is my second wife, you must understand. My first, and the mother of all my children, came with me to India. Here at Serampore she suffered dysentery and madness, eventually succumbing to her illnesses. Upon her death, I believed that any hope of a wife's companionship must now be denied me forever. But God knew far more than I could ever imagine."

"Really?" Miss Rosse gazed up at him, hope radiating from her face.

Feeling as though he were about to suffocate, Edmund ran a finger around his stiff collar. Clearly the lady thought Dr. Carey the kindest man she had ever met. And himself the most villainous.

"Charlotte Emilia was the only child of the Chevalier de Rumohr of Denmark," Dr. Carey explained to his guest. "During her youth, she was so sickly and so disabled that she could not even walk up and down stairs. Her father sent her to the south of Europe in hope of recovery, but it was not to be. Still seeking relief, she came to Serampore under protection of the Danish East India Company. Here, Lady Rumohr built a house on the Hooghly bank immediately below mine. After much time in the society of myself and the other missionaries, she was baptized."

"And so she was healed?" Miss Rosse asked.

"Baptism expresses the healing of the soul, my dear, not of the body. Nevertheless, she was healthy enough that on the ninth of May in 1808, she became my wife."

The young lady sighed. "Yes, but you knew her character by then. I have no knowledge of Alfred Cunliffe, nor do I wish to become his wife. And how can I think of residing in England when my heart will always be in India?"

He patted her shoulder. "There, there, dear girl. My Charlotte also despaired of her lot in life. Sickly and weak, she was sent far away from her family and home in Denmark. But, oh, what joys God had prepared for her! Do you know that she has become my greatest asset in the ministry? Charlotte knows all the principal languages of Europe, she is a keen student of the Scriptures, and she has learned Bengali so that she might be a loving caretaker to the native Christian families. The education of Hindu girls is her primary occupation, but she is my counselor, above all."

"I am happy for both of you," Violet said. "But I cannot imagine that such a meaningful life awaits me in England."

"Surely it does, and you shall learn to love the quaint countryside of Yorkshire and its charming people. My Charlotte, though so much afflicted, displays always a pleasing cheerfulness. The constant activity of the mind — a quality which you also possess, my dear — is her saving grace. Each morning at dawn when the weather permits, and each evening as soon as the sun is low, Charlotte goes out in her little rickshaw to enjoy the river breeze on her way to and from the schools and homes of the natives."

"Shall I be able to ride in a rickshaw in York?"

"No, Miss Rosse, but there will be something wonderful for you there. Place yourself into the loving hand of Jesus, for He promises an abundant life to all who do."

"Very well put, sir," Edmund said with utmost gratitude to his wise elder. "Dr. Carey is correct in all his observations, Miss Rosse. I shall now see you safely back to Calcutta. Your passage at sea will provide an opportunity — through the study of Scripture and fervent prayer — to ascertain

God's will for your life. I believe He will help you accept the loss of your home in India. God will teach you to embrace the future He has prepared for you in York."

"How do you know God prepares a future for me in York, Mr. Sherbourne?" the lady asked. "It was my father who made this plan. Are they one and the same?"

"Certainly not, for your father is —" He cleared his throat to keep from voicing his true opinion of the man. "God has great compassion on His servants, and He wishes only the very best for us."

"I am not a servant of any god," Violet declared, standing suddenly. "Nor am I bound to my father's wishes. I obey only myself. I listen to my own conscience and act accordingly."

"But surely you are a Christian —"

"Of course I am a Christian!" She pulled back the folds of her sari and stretched out her long white arm to Edmund. "Am I not English? Was I not born to Malcolm and Evelyn Rosse of York? Have I not been taught by five English tutors who have told me everything I need to know about that life? Yes, I am a Christian, and I am English, and I am white, and I am a woman. But I am not a servant! And I shall bow before no one!"

Grabbing the bag that sat nearest her, Violet strode past her *ayah* and directly between Dr. Carey and Edmund. As they leaped to their feet, she dashed out the front door, raced across the porch, and ran out into the street. Edmund called out after her, but she ignored him as she skirted a building and made for a thicket of bamboo, trailing the loops and tangles of nine yards of green silk sari behind her.

# Four

Three days in the presence of the vile heretic Moumita Choudhary, and Edmund had almost made up his mind to return to Calcutta at the first opportunity. For all he knew, this small woman with crooked teeth, a foul temper, and the look of a murderer might be leading him through the jungle to his death.

Insisting she knew Miss Rosse's intended destination, Moumita had offered to guide Edmund there for an exorbitant fee. Dr. Carey urged him to agree to her terms, and Edmund could think of no reason to refuse. Upon the safe return of his daughter, Malcolm Rosse no doubt would reimburse the cost.

More important, he knew he could not afford to earn a reputation as the man who had allowed a young Englishwoman to escape into the wilds of West Bengal, never to be heard from again. Utterly uncertain of God's will in the matter, Edmund was reduced to simple obedience — which he realized was exactly what his Maker had been wanting from him all along.

The question then became whether Moumita would poison him, or whether he would push her off a cliff first. Edmund had been disposed to treat the little creature kindly at the start of their journey. But he quickly found her dark-eyed glares and guttural profanities so disgusting that he could hardly endure her company. Insisting on walking behind him, as Hindu women were wont to do, she muttered such wicked statements that he began to fear she might draw a knife and stab him in the back.

"Not a *sadhu*," she was murmuring as they climbed a hill away from the Jalangi River. "Not a holy man. Not chanting. Not wearing yellow robes. May Sitlamata, the goddess of smallpox, bring disease upon him. May he be stricken with cholera. He is a devil."

"Mrs. Choudhary, who are you calling a devil?" Edmund asked as he halted and turned to face her. "Are all these curses directed at me?"

Moumita pulled the edge of her sari up to cover her mouth and nose. Her eyes glittered. *"Ha, sahib. Ki chai?"*

Setting his hands at his waist, Edmund stared at her. "Speak in English, please. I am certain you know it, for I heard you talking to Miss Rosse, and I understand nearly everything you have been saying."

"Yes, sir. But my English is not so good. What do you want me to say to you?"

"I should very much like to know why you despise me so. I have paid you a great sum of money, Mrs. Choudhary, and I have treated you with utmost respect. Yet you have spent the past three days muttering at me and wishing me ill. Can you give me any reason for such behavior, or am I to assume that you are wicked by nature?"

The woman's eyes narrowed into slits. "You are the wicked one, sahib."

"I am wicked? Upon what do you base this assumption?"

"You tell people that you are a holy man. You lie."

"I have never said I was holy. Far from it, for I know that I am a sinner saved only by the grace of the Almighty. You are correct in stating that I am not a *sadhu*. I am a missionary, and I do not lie."

"Are not missionaries holy men? Yes, this is what everyone is saying. Why do you not make chants?"

"I have no chants to make. If it would appease your malice, madam, I suppose I could muster up a hymn."

"Yet you do not wear yellow robes."

"Of course not. I am an English gentleman, one who wears civilized clothing."

"You wear foolish clothing that is too hot and tight. We know that the white cotton keeps us cool in the heat."

"I do not choose to adulterate myself by adopting the customs of this heathen nation."

"Cannot a holy man be comfortable?"

Edmund considered her words and rejected them at once. Through five long years clad in black wool suits, tall leather boots, and beaver fur hats, he had upheld his refusal to put on the white robe of the Muslim or the soft cotton lungi of the Hindu. A man could not compromise himself in any way, he believed, for then his testimony might weaken. No matter how hot and uncomfortable he felt — which was mightily, much of the time — Edmund knew he represented more than the ideals of English civilization and the majesty of her king. He must do his best to exemplify the character of his heavenly King as well.

This afternoon, as he stood on a muddy track with a small Hindu woman, he would have given almost anything for a drink of clean, cool water. No such luxury was to be found in this part of West Bengal. The dense brush growing close on both sides of the path created a perfect breeding ground for snakes and insects, and he regretted not purchasing a machete in the last village they had passed.

Thus far, his sullen guide had refused to tell him their destination. In silence — save her mutterings — they had journeyed by boat up the Hooghly River and then along one of its tributaries. But now it appeared they were headed into the deep jungle with all its attendant pestilence. Tigers and elephants roamed such terrain, and Edmund did not fancy an encounter with either species.

"I serve the one true God, our Lord and Savior Jesus Christ, and Him alone," he informed the woman whose bare feet left childlike imprints in the muddy path. "I am not a Hindu. I am a Christian."

Her eyes widened, and she lowered the edge of her sari. "Not a Hindu? You do not worship the gods — Hanuman, Ganesha, Rama, Sita, Kali —"

"I serve only one God, Mrs. Choudhary. His name is Jesus."

"Ah, the silver one," she murmured. Nodding, she waved a hand to urge him forward. "Go on, sahib. Now I understand."

"What exactly do you understand?"

"I see why you do evil things. You have

chosen a weak God. He is useless to you, for look how He died with those nails in His hands and feet. But I can no longer fear your power. With that God, you will never have a victory."

"I shall enjoy the greatest victory of all, Mrs. Choudhary, for my God is not dead. He was killed, but after three days He arose from death to newness of life."

"Dead and then alive again?"

"Yes, for by His crucifixion, He conquered death. Those who worship my God shall die once upon this earth, but after that, they shall live eternally with Him in heaven."

She gave a bark of laughter. "You are not even a Brahman! You have no caste at all, sahib. How can one who is not of the highest caste reach Nirvana? This is only possible after many rebirths, passing from the lowest animals to the greatest and then into the human castes — the Untouchables such as I; the Kshatriyas, who are warriors; the Vaishyas, who are merchants and laborers; and at last the Brahmans, who are the priests. Only then can a person hope to be freed from rebirths and enter heaven."

Though he was tired, his feet had blistered and chafed inside his boots, and the mosquitoes were relentless, Edmund felt a surge of tenderness toward the poor woman. Born an Untouchable, she surely had known only the contempt and disgust of others. No doubt her work as Miss Rosse's *ayah* had been her only source of comfort.

"Dear lady," he said, stepping toward her. "Heaven does not depend upon caste, but upon God's grace. Nor can one ever build up enough good *kharma* to enter that blessed realm. Please believe me when I tell you that I do not speak lies. I have journeyed very far for the purpose of bringing truth to you, Mrs. Choudhary."

"To me?"

"Yes, to you and to anyone else who will listen. There is but one God, and He gave His life to free you from all the effects of caste and *kharma*. By His resurrection, He conquered death, and He offers you eternal life — with Him."

Moumita looked down at the path, her mouth working over some of the seeds she had been chewing. When she lifted her head, she spat into a clump of vine-tangled ferns. "You say these good things, sahib, but you are a bad man! Very bad! You chase after the *meye*, and you wish to take her back to her father in Calcutta. She will go on a boat to a land of no orchids. What kind of fate is that? Yes, she is naughty sometimes. But she does not deserve such unhappiness! If your god is so powerful that he can conquer death, he should rescue her. She prays to that silver god, and he ought to help her."

Though baffled over her references to a silver god, Edmund understood the rest of the *ayah*'s message perfectly. "Mrs. Choudhary, hear me, please. The place in England to which Miss Rosse goes is lovely. There are many flowers, beautiful moorlands —"

"Moorlands!" She threw up her hands in horror. "What is it?"

"A moor is a wide stretch of land with large granite stones. Very lovely in its way. Heather, crowberry, and bracken all grow upon the moorlands. In the damp hollows, one can find bog moss, cotton grass, and the marsh violet."

"Violet? This is the name of the *meye*."

"Her mother must have loved the moorlands. I suspect she wished to honor her daughter in calling her by the name of the loveliest flower that grows there. Yorkshire is an enchanting place, and I am sure Miss Rosse will find much happiness. Perhaps a marriage to this Alfred Cunliffe fellow will not be so bad. He is a merchant like her father. He must have a good house and enough money to care for her. Truly, she will be all right."

He paused, trying to absorb the conflicting emotions that must be raging inside this peasant's heart. Unwanted and unloved, she had been given charge over an English child who had become like a daughter to her. Now, as fiercely as a mother tiger, she meant to protect the girl from harm. To that end, she had helped Miss Rosse escape. Then, faced with abandonment herself, Moumita had shrewdly fixed a bargain that would provide enough money for her own subsistence.

"I know Malcolm Rosse," Edmund told her. "I saw his behavior, and I understand his motives. He thinks of himself more than he cares for his daughter. If I believed Miss Rosse were destined to a miserable life in Yorkshire, I never would have agreed to assist that man. But I do not doubt your *meye* will find joy there. It was once my home, too, and I long to return there."

"You do not like India?"

He had to smile. "I love India. More than I ever thought possible." Seeing the softening of her features, he continued. "Please take me to Miss Rosse. I shall do all in my power to protect her from harm and unhappiness."

A small finger emerged from the folds of Moumita's dirty cotton sari. She shook it at him and hissed, "This is a vow?"

Edmund drew back at the intensity of her words. "A vow? Well, I suppose so. Yes, it is a vow. I shall do everything I can to make Miss Rosse happy."

"*Dhanyabad* — thank you. Go on then. She is not far."

Violet did not know when she had ever tasted anything so good. Squatting on the dirt floor of the small hut, she tore apart a *chapatti* and stuffed it into her mouth. The round flat bread was her favorite of the many types enjoyed by Bengalis.

Upon learning that she knew Moumita Choudhary, this family of Untouchables had cautiously welcomed the strange, golden-haired Englishwoman who had appeared at the door of their bamboo hut the night before. Leatherworkers, they made shoes and other items to sell in the large town upriver. Shunned and despised for the unwholesome labor of handling dead animals and their skins, they were not wealthy. But their wages earned them enough for food and clothing.

"*Ami macher jhol ar bhat khabo,*" Violet said, telling the woman of the house that she would love some of the fish curry and rice that had been offered. Seated with the women and children who had waited until after the men ate their fill, she now fell into the meal with gusto.

It was a merry gathering, the half-naked children gobbling their dinner and the women discussing the sweets they had bought in town that day. Violet relished the companionship. No one gave any thought to the East India Company, or to Yorkshire, or even to the orchids that grew in the canopies of the forest that surrounded their huts.

Violet had begun to decide that the Renaissance was not entirely good. There was something comfortable and quiet about a small house in a small village beside a small stream. People did not really need to know about art or architecture or the opera. They needed only to eat and to sleep. And to love and be loved.

This brought Moumita to mind, and Violet's buoyant spirits instantly sank. For three days she had prayed that her *ayah* would come after her. Several times along the path, she had almost turned back to Serampore — even thinking of returning to Calcutta to face her father's wrath.

But Moumita knew that Violet was on her way to the home village. Moumita knew how to find her *meye*. Surely she would come. Surely Violet would not have to face her uncertain future alone.

"You would like a sweet?" Bani, the wife and mother, smiled across the pot of steaming curry. "We have *jelebees*."

She held out a plate of the orange-colored pastries that had been fried in hot oil and covered in sugar syrup. Violet shook her head. "I cannot eat anything more," she said softly. "I am thinking of my *ayah*. I fear Moumita will not come here after all."

"That girl, she was dead to us many years ago," Bani told her. "Her father gave a large dowry and made a good marriage for her, but the boy died before he was even fifteen. Moumita had never gone into his house, for she was still living at home with her own family."

"Ahh," the children said in unison. The mournful cry told Violet all she needed to know about that sad time in her *ayah*'s past. Because she had been so young and had never lived with her husband, there was no chance for children who might grow up to care for their widowed mother. An Untouchable woman without a husband, shunned by society and never permitted to remarry, faced the worst future of any Hindu.

"Moumita told me she did not choose to become *suttee*," Violet said.

Bani shook her head. "After her husband's death, she left our village, and we never saw her again. We thought perhaps a tiger ate her. Or she was taken as a slave. What choice did she have but to leave us and endure her fate? A young widow. An Untouchable. She should have chosen *suttee* — then she and all her family would be in Nirvana."

"But then I should never have met her," Violet said. "She has been a very good *ayah* to me, and I —"

"*Istri!* Wife!" A man burst through the door and into the hut. "She comes! She is not dead! Moumita Choudhary — it is she!"

Violet scrambled to her feet, but before she could gather the yards of sari that had slipped during dinner, Moumita's dear face appeared in the doorway. With a cry of joy, Violet threw her arms around her *ayah*.

"You are here!" she said, burying her face in the woman's warm brown neck. "Oh, I feared you would abandon me! I thought that maybe a tiger had —"

The figure that now darkened the door halted Violet's words. "*Him?* You brought that man?" She grabbed Moumita's shoulders and pushed her away. "How could you

105

do this? He will take me home! I shall be forced to sail to Yorkshire! Oh, Moumita, this very instant I am giving you the sack. Never again will you —"

"Stop talking, silly child," Moumita snapped. "Go and wash your hands. You have put curry on my sari!"

Violet stepped around her *ayah* and faced the tall man whose frame more than filled the doorway. "Go away, Mr. Sherbourne. Go back to your home. You are not welcome here!"

"Good afternoon, Miss Rosse." He bowed. "I trust you are well."

"Do I look ill?"

Edmund scanned her up and down. One dark eyebrow lifted as he appraised her. "I believe I have seen you looking better."

Blushing despite herself, Violet swung around and marched across the hut to the place where she had stashed her bag. She dug inside it until her fingers closed around a gold chain. "Here," she told Sherbourne, striding back to the door and holding out the necklace. "Emeralds and rubies. The finest gold. This was my mother's. It should be enough to pay you for your efforts and fend off my father. Take it and go. I do not want you."

"Nor do I want you, madam. But your

106

father insists that you return to Calcutta at once, and I have promised to take you to him."

"How could you bring this man to your village?" Violet cried, turning on Moumita again. "Did he pay you?"

Her *ayah* stared at her. *"Ha, meye.* He paid me very well. Why should I not accept his money after you ran away and left me at the house of the old *sadhu?"*

"You are a traitor!"

"You abandoned me!"

Violet clenched her fists. "I shall not go back to Calcutta. And I shall never go to Yorkshire!"

"Violets grow in England," Moumita said in a low voice. "The violet is the loveliest flower upon the moorlands. Your mother gave you this name because she believed the violet to be the most beautiful of all flowers in the world. And where does it grow? Not here in India. Oh, no. It is a moorlands flower."

"Moumita, do not presume to tell me about flowers," Violet retorted. "And say nothing about my mother, for you know nothing about her!"

"I know she worshiped the silver God. It is the same for this holy man. He worships only one God, the weeping one who was nailed through foot and hand to the wooden cross. This Sahib Sherbourne, he is not a bad man. How bad could he be, for he worships the same God as your mother?"

"Oh, Moumita!"

"You should listen to him. He has made a vow to take care of you, *meye*. Return to your father now. Go to England on the boat, and then you will see what a good life awaits you there."

"A good life awaits you, does it not? He paid you richly to find me. Now all you can think of is sending me away to Yorkshire so you can begin to enjoy your freedom!"

Violet could hardly believe this turn of events. Not only had Moumita brought Mr. Sherbourne to the village, but she supported Violet's forced return to Calcutta. Well, they would both fail!

"Do you not remember the plan I told you?" she demanded of her *ayah*. "Have you forgotten so soon? We are to live in the palace of the rajah of Krishnangar — the two of us together!"

At this, Bani and her family began to giggle behind their hands. Violet turned on them. "Why do you laugh? No doubt the rajah employs many Untouchables at his palace. Moumita is my servant, and she will be welcomed there. I am an Englishwoman whose father works for the East India Company. The rajah will treat me well. If he does not, I shall tell my father, who will see that troops are sent in to punish him."

"I should imagine your father is more likely to send troops to carry you home to Calcutta, Miss Rosse," the young missionary spoke up. "It is you who will be punished, and not the rajah of Krishnangar."

"I fear you are sadly mistaken, sir," she returned, "for the rajah is a man of science and learning. He has traveled widely and is considered well educated. I believe he will be pleased to meet me. I shall offer to pay him for living quarters and food — though I cannot believe he will accept my money. Moumita has agreed to stay with me there as my assistant. I mean to use the palace as the base from which I shall make my scientific expeditions."

To her surprise, Violet noted that while she spoke, Mr. Sherbourne did not roll his eyes as though she were a silly-headed nuisance. No mockery was written on the turn of his lips. No jest appeared ready to spring from his tongue. Instead, his face wore an expression of understanding. Though she longed to revile this one who had pursued her on behalf of her father, she found she could not. Mr. Sherbourne listened to her even more intently than had Dr. Wallich at the garden.

As she concluded the explanation of her plan, he nodded. "An interesting plan, Miss Rosse. I suppose you went first to Serampore to ask Dr. Carey if he might transport to the Botanic Garden the results of your investigations. We knew you had a logical purpose to your visit there, but we could not make it out. Dr. Carey believed you must have come to speak to him about his work in translating the catalogue of flora. He understands your particular interest in orchids, Miss Rosse, for he finds them fascinating also."

Violet's shoulders relaxed for the first time since Moumita had stepped into the hut. "Dr. Carey is a good man. I knew he must be. I had hoped to ask him to accept the specimens and records I wish to send him. And yes, I believed he might be so good as to transport everything to Dr. Wallich for further examination and study."

"Why not send your collections to the superintendent himself?"

"Dr. Wallich is employed by the company, and no doubt my father would press him into revealing my location. I felt Dr. Carey might make a trustworthy intermediary."

"Indeed, he is the very best of men." Mr. Sherbourne took off his hat and raked a hand through his damp brown hair.

Momentarily mezmerized, Violet watched as each strand sifted through his fingers and fell back into place. Such thick hair. The color of teakwood. And how very soft it looked.

"Miss Rosse, despite what you believe of me," he was saying, "I very much understand and respect your quest. I am driven by a passion also. My zeal is so great that I have journeyed much farther than you and have taken an equal number of risks to my health and safety. Though I find myself defeated at every turn, the fire still burns brightly inside my heart. I cannot quench it, and neither will Satan."

Outlined in the late-afternoon sunlight, Mr. Sherbourne suddenly appeared to Violet as a giant of a man. His heart was large and filled with compassion. His intellect was sharp. His broad shoulders, well-muscled legs, and erect posture gave his words substance and merit. Indeed, were he not her foe, she might consider herself smitten. As it was, she must turn away, remembering his purpose in speaking to her.

"You are to be commended for your efforts at success in India," she told him. "I was born here, and I am well suited to this country. But many who venture here find it intolerable. They fall ill from malaria or typhus or cholera. They go mad slowly — or make everyone around them so. Many flee India at the first opportunity. But you have stayed and labored for your faith, Mr. Sherbourne. That is admirable indeed."

A gentle smile tilted his mouth. "I see we have some understanding of each other, Miss Rosse. Perhaps we might discuss our differences and reach a pleasant resolution. Shall we sit together? Tea would be welcome, if your hostess can part with some."

The thought of spending quiet moments in conversation with the man intrigued Violet. But then she glanced at Bani, who had been staring wide-eyed at the two white people who chattered back and forth in an unknown tongue. The bamboo walls of the hut were thin and tattered, the thatched roof ridden with insects, the floor bare dirt. Though its inhabitants had enough to eat, they could spare little extra.

"Let us not burden this family, Mr. Sherbourne," Violet said. "Their lot is heavy enough. Come, we shall walk along the river. The town of Krishnangar is not far, and perhaps we shall see the rajah's palace."

Bani would not allow her guests to leave

without first drinking a cup of mango juice. Thus refreshed from their journey, Mr. Sherbourne and Moumita stepped outside the hut. Violet expressed her deepest gratitude to the whole family, picked up her bag, and made her farewell.

Though she knew she might need to return for the night, she hoped Mr. Sherbourne would accompany her to the town. If he — an English gentleman of the finest ilk — spoke to the rajah on her behalf, Violet could not imagine that her plan would fail. Perhaps Mr. Sherbourne would stay on at the palace for a time. He might call upon her as a gentleman ought. They would discuss science and God, and other subjects of interest. Perhaps they would dine together or attend a celebration. Or a dance.

Now that she knew such a kind and handsome man existed, Violet did not like to think of his departure. But he planned to go to England, and the safety and comfort of the palace would ensure her a full, rich life. Eventually, she would write to her father and inform him of her happy situation. Her years would be spent in travel around the countryside and in the pursuit of scientific acquisition.

Dr. Wallich would be delighted to receive her specimens, and even Dr. Carey must take great interest in everything she would send. She had neither the training nor the education to call herself a scientist, yet she might make some little difference in that world. A new species. A special collection. A path as yet uncharted. The possibilities held endless fascination for her. How could she be anything but content?

Determined to make the most of these next hours, Violet slipped her hand around Mr. Sherbourne's arm and lifted the hem of her sari. She once had harbored the small dream of a home and family — children gathered around a table, a comfortable house with wide verandahs, and orchids hanging from every tree, and, of course, a loving husband.

But this would not be her fate — especially if she journeyed to England and married Mr. Alfred Cunliffe. No matter the will of the gods, Violet would accomplish her own goals. Her life belonged to her and to no one else. She held the power to make all her dreams come true.

"Shall we walk, Miss Rosse?" Mr. Sherbourne asked. He smiled at her, his green eyes soft and warm. "I believe the Lord in His mercy has provided us the perfect afternoon for a stroll along the riverbank."

# Five

"Dear Miss Rosse," Edmund said as they followed a path toward the river. "Please permit me to tell you of Yorkshire, for I believe most sincerely that you will come to love it as I do."

"Do you love it, sir?" the lady asked. Her arm looped through his, Miss Rosse strolled beside Edmund as though they were walking along an English garden corridor. A discreet distance behind them, Moumita Choudhary filled the role of elderly chaperone treading silently along and pretending not to listen to their conversation.

But the Hindu was neither elderly nor English, Edmund reminded himself, and her motives served only herself. Nor was this the pleasant pastoral Yorkshire countryside, for tigers hunted in the brush, cobras slithered among the vines, and crocodiles eyed them from among the reeds that lined the riverbank. And Violet Rosse — in her silk sari, curry-stained fingertips, and sandaled feet — was anything but a proper young English miss.

"I wonder that you profess such passion for your native country," she said. "My love for India compels me to stay here. But you seem to have left Yorkshire without a second thought."

"I had many a second thought, madam, I assure you," Edmund replied. "My family is of noble lineage, our situation is comfortable, and Thorne Lodge is my dearly loved home."

As he spoke, Edmund conjured the immense manor house built of gray stone by the first Baron Thorne centuries before. Once, he had been willing to forgo that place in light of his holy calling to the mission field of India. But now the image of home beckoned him with its promise of security and comfort. The thought of embracing his two brothers, of sleeping beneath down-filled bedding, of eating three wholesome meals a day, and of riding a fine horse along the hedgerows filled him with an unexpected longing. *England.* Edmund eagerly anticipated the moment when — a few months from now — the misty shores of that dear isle would come into sight.

Had he been driven to India by some misguided need to atone for the sins of his past? Edmund often wondered. Or had God truly

116

called him to carry the gospel to the heathen masses? Was he fleeing India now because of his seeming failure as a missionary — running home like a shamed dog with its tail between its legs, as Malcolm Rosse had charged? Did England truly beckon because Edmund needed to satisfy himself as to the safety of his family? Or did he wish to escape India's hardships in favor of the cloistered existence he had known in Yorkshire?

The answers to these questions did not come readily, and Mr. Rosse's accusations and mockery haunted his waking hours. Should he return to England and make a new life for himself there? Or should he journey home, stay for a short tenure, and then return to India, as William Carey had urged? Though Edmund had prayed for vision, God had not given him clear direction.

Of only one thing was he completely certain. He must convince Violet Rosse to return to Calcutta. He must assure her of England's beauty and bounty. And he must do all in his power to make her understand that God would provide a good life for her there.

"Yorkshire is a much cherished countryside," he told her. "My own childhood there could not have been more pleasant. Thorne

Lodge is grandly built, and it boasts of eighteen fireplaces. These keep it warm in winter and provide ample opportunity for cozy gatherings with quiet conversation and genteel pastimes. The tall windows offer as fair a prospect as any in the whole of England — rolling moorlands, heathered fells, glassy lakes, and rich sheep pastures. The village of Otley, with its thatched cottages and cobblestone streets, is home to a mill, several fine churches, and an assembly hall where occurred some of the most delightful events of my youth. The people of the region work hard and love deeply. They are generous and thrifty and kind. I daresay, Miss Rosse, that you cannot find a better place anywhere in the world."

"Yet, if you dare me to find a better place, Mr. Sherbourne," Violet said as they walked along the riverbank, "I shall happily provide you with the city of Calcutta."

At the name, he gave her a sharp glance. "Calcutta? You cannot mean it. I have never seen such poverty, such wretchedness, or such ignorance in all my life."

"Nor have you seen such beauty. Calcutta is a treasury of wealth beyond measure. It is a jewel box filled with the richest of gems. The Hooghly at sunset might be a river of molten gold. The bronzed bodies of the children gleam as they play at the water's edge. Their mothers squat flat-footed in the dust to chop ruby red onions and emerald green chilies and coconuts the hue of milky white pearls. Orchids and vines and a thousand flowers of every color brighten each patch of uncut forest — like glimmering stones on a green velvet cloth."

As she spoke, Miss Rosse's melodious voice turned Edmund's imagination toward a city seen through her eyes. Had he overlooked its beauty in the press of humanity, squalid conditions, and oppressive heat?

"Have you not seen the domes of the mosques?" she asked him. "Jade and salmon pink, they leap out above the roofs of the other buildings like great soap bubbles! And what of the Hindu temples filled with incense and garlands of marigolds?"

Edmund shook his head. "I am sorry to disappoint you, dear lady, but I cannot view mosques and temples as anything but heathen shrines."

"But think of the bazaars!" she continued undaunted. "Pyramids of green beans, papayas, and peppers. Baskets filled with gooseberries, tomatoes, onions, mangoes, and gingerroot. Bundles of coriander and mint lie beside burlap sacks filled with rice, lentils, and ground cinnamon. Small yellow bananas still clustered on the stalk dangle from street stalls. And what of the colored glass bangles and the saris and sandals piled in great heaps? Mr. Sherbourne, surely you have never seen such a sensory feast in your wet, foggy Yorkshire."

He had to laugh. "You paint a lovely picture of a damp, odorous, and crowded city, Miss Rosse. And yet I confess, I have failed to appreciate the charms of Calcutta as I should. When we return, I promise to allow it another opportunity to enchant me as it does you."

"You speak of our return as though it were a foregone conclusion, sir. It most certainly is not. Indeed, I fully intend to stay here at Krishnangar." She gestured toward the mud-brick huts that formed the center of the small city a short distance down the Jalangi River. A wooden bridge crossed the crystalline water to a road leading up a hillside to a magnificent palace, no doubt the home of the rajah.

"Miss Rosse, I do appreciate your desire to stay in India," Edmund told her, concerned that they had come so far toward the object of her quest. "Though I cannot speak as well as you do of Calcutta, my small village house has been a place of solace these five years. Clearly you love this country. It is your home, after all."

"You understand that?" Her eyes deepened as he nodded. "Then you are the only one. To every family in the company, India is foreign soil. England is home and always will be. But I was born here. When other children were sent away from their parents to board at English schools, I stayed here. My father ignored me. He hired tutors now and then, but he paid me little heed. Mr. Sherbourne, my roots are sunk deep into the muddy delta of the Ganges and her tributaries. I am as much an Indian as Moumita."

Edmund sighed, hearing pain and love mingled in her words. "You were brought up in India, Miss Rosse, but you are not Indian. Your parentage is English, your blood is English, your appearance is . . ."

He glanced at her and tried to remain unmoved by the gleam of her golden hair and the soft, full curve of her lips. Had this woman any idea of the natural grace and beauty she wore more easily than her mud-hemmed sari? Her hair curled away from her forehead and down her temple, flowing behind the pink shell of her ear into a long braid that fell down her back. The kiss of the sun on her cheeks and the sparkle of violet blue in her eyes made Edmund's heart thud

121

dangerously each time he looked at her. Yet she thought herself Indian? No, certainly not. No, indeed.

He drank down a deep breath. "Despite your sari and bangles, Miss Rosse, you are as English as the wild violets that grow along the hedgerow in Yorkshire. And you cannot escape it."

"Then you do not understand me after all."

"I do, much better than you suppose. I know your feelings for India are strong. I see, too, that your interest in orchids and other flora compels you to stay in this country. But please, dear lady, can such a future be reasonable?"

"What has reason to do with anything?" she replied, throwing up her slender hands. "I follow my heart, Mr. Sherbourne, as do you. My heart tells me to stay in Krishnangar, to live out my days in India, to pour my intellect and the hours of my days into the study of botany. Reason offers me no better prospect than life with a man I do not know in a country I have never seen. So why should reason weigh more heavily?"

"I cannot answer that, for although you say I follow my heart, you are mistaken. I follow neither heart nor head, Miss Rosse, for I am led only by my God. I tread the straight and narrow path upon which He leads me, and I do not permit myself to stray from it."

They walked in silence for a moment before she spoke again. "Moumita tells me you worship the English God, Jesus."

He glanced at her in surprise. What a curious way to describe the Lord. "But Jesus is not English, of course. He was a Jew, born in the town of Bethlehem and brought up in Nazareth. Surely, as a Christian yourself, you know this?"

She shrugged. "I am familiar with most matters of religion, Mr. Sherbourne. Yet I confess that I have become hopelessly disobedient. Upon making my decision to leave Calcutta, I surrendered all thought of happiness in the life after this, and I committed myself to making the most of the one I have been given already. I simply do not know what Jesus wants of me, as you do, nor do I intend to try to please Him. It is quite impossible to be good enough to satisfy a deity. My resolve, therefore, is to please myself and no one else."

"You are honest, at least," Edmund said, "though I cannot admire your intent. I fear you will find, Miss Rosse, that serving oneself leads only to misery and despair. Obedience to the Lord and service to one's fellow man — though seemingly burdensome — are the only hope of true joy. Jesus said, 'Take My yoke upon you, and learn of Me; for I am meek and lowly in heart: and ye shall find rest unto your souls. For My yoke is easy, and My burden is light.' "

"Jesus said that about Himself, did He? Meek and lowly? I cannot imagine what sort of God would want that description. The Hindu gods are powerful and demanding. I believe I should rather bow to a mighty god than to one who is meek, Mr. Sherbourne. Let me assure you, sir, that although I am a lady, I am neither meek nor lowly. In fact, I am quite strong-minded and ever ready to suffer the consequences of my decisions."

"Upon my word," Edmund said, "this is the oddest of confessions I ever heard fall from a Christian's lips. Miss Rosse, surely you jest. You most certainly know that Jesus' might was displayed upon the cross when He gave Himself in sacrifice for our sin. It was His power that gave Him victory over death."

"Yes, but what use is all this ancient history to me when I am alive now and facing this terrible fate? Alfred Cunliffe awaits me, and I assure you that I do not mean to satisfy him. It is true that I am not the very best of creatures, but I do not deserve such a destiny. I shall not suffer it, Mr. Sherbourne. And nothing you or my father can say or do will change that."

Such bemusement and confusion befell Edmund as they arrived on the outskirts of Krishnangar that he could hardly think what to say. What an unusual perspective Miss Rosse offered. None of the other young women of his acquaintance had ever made sport of the truths of Christianity. He was not sure whether to be amused or concerned. But what should he find to concern him? Surely Miss Rosse was only teasing.

"Moumita — where are you going? *Tumi kothai jaccho?*" Miss Rosse beckoned, her silver bangles jingling. "*Asha!* Come here at once. Honestly, you are so slow!"

The Indian woman stepped up her pace along the dusty street. "Do you go now to the palace of the rajah, *meye?*" she asked when she was standing before Miss Rosse.

"Yes, I am going, for this is my destiny."

"I believe you make a mistake in this," Moumita said. "While you and the sahib were walking toward the river, Bani came out of her hut and spoke to me. She told me she is afraid that the rajah will not permit you to live at his palace. This rajah is not the same one who ruled at Krishnangar when I was younger. That rajah who loved learning is now old and ill, lying on his bed day after day and very near to death. He has surrendered power to his son, Jatindra. Bani says the new rajah is young and strong, and he does not like the British who presume to rule his land and people. She believes this Jatindra will not want a daughter of the East India Company staying at his palace."

Edmund watched in concern as Miss Rosse's face paled, and she brushed a hand over her forehead. He, too, had faced a hopeless future once — a time when it seemed that turning to the left or to the right offered nothing but misery. He had known the face of despair that he saw in her wide blue eyes.

"Miss Rosse," he said gently, "please allow me to offer you comfort. Come away with me before it is too late. I promise you that I shall see you safely back to Calcutta. My ship sails soon, and I am happy to prepare your way in England. Indeed, my home is not far from York. If you wish, I shall travel directly to that city and visit Mr. Cunliffe after we land. If he is a gentleman of integrity and honor, then I shall assist in introducing you after your own arrival. But if I find him to be a villain, then . . ." He paused, trying to think what on earth he could do to reassure this forlorn, lost creature who wanted neither him nor his assistance. "If Mr. Cunliffe is as wicked as you fear, Miss Rosse, I shall protect you from him."

"And how will you do that — you and your meek and lowly God?" The eyes flashed at him like great blue sapphires. "I do not need your protection, Mr. Rosse. I shall speak to this new rajah and present my case. If he is intelligent, he will understand that my presence in his palace can benefit him. If he refuses to admit me, then I shall leave Krishnangar and find another place to live. Perhaps I can stay with Bani and her family."

"With Bani?" Moumita clapped her hands against her cheeks. "*Chokhkhaki!* Blind fool! How can that poor family take in another mouth to feed? Did you not see how hard they and the other Untouchables in the village work making shoes to sell here in Krishnangar? What will you do each day, *meye?* Will you scrape the skin from the dead water buffalo? Will you cut the hide and sew it into sandals? Perhaps you will sit on the street corner and call out to the customers to buy your wares. Is that it? You, who have no caste, believe you will be welcomed by a family of the lowest caste? Bani was kind to you because she remembered me and the tragedy of my life. But you? You are no one here. You are nothing but a young girl, one of the despised English occupiers. *Na, meye,* you should go back to Calcutta with the sahib."

"No, Moumita!" Miss Rosse cried. "I have my jewels — the emerald-and-ruby necklace. I have rings and bangles. I can even sell my mother's silver statue if I must. If Bani will not have me, I shall go up into the mountains. I shall build myself a house in . . . in Darjeeling!"

"Come, Miss Rosse," Edmund said, reaching toward her, "you cannot live alone in the Himalayan Mountains. It is too cold there. Certainly you would not be able to build a house warm and secure enough to see you through a Himalayan winter. And who in that poor land would have the wealth to purchase your jewels? I beg you to put away this notion of following your heart. You must see reason, and come with me to England."

"He has made a vow, *meye,*" Moumita said. "This sahib promises to take care of you."

"Him?" Her blue eyes flashed Edmund a look of disdain. "Why should I trust him? No, Moumita. I rely on no one but myself!" Turning, she stormed away from them, the hem of her sari stirring up wisps of dust in the street. Edmund studied the *ayah,* whose anger turned down her mouth and sharpened the lines in her forehead.

"Let her go," Moumita said. "Your words cannot change the mind of that girl. Nothing can change her."

"On the contrary, Mrs. Choudhary. The power of God can change anyone. I trust Him in all things, including the future of Miss Rosse."

"You are foolish to trust a god, sahib. The gods play with us, but they do not love us. They use us, but they do not care for us. We can beg them for help, and perhaps they will grant our wishes. But no one should ever put trust in a god. A person makes his own *kharma.* You have lived your past lives well enough to be reborn an Englishman with wealth and education. But you are too ignorant to hope that your *kharma* might bring you back as a Hindu — even someone of the lowest caste."

"As I told you before, Mrs. Choudhary, I serve the one true God. My God acknowledges but one rebirth — the one that occurs when a person accepts God's Son, Jesus, as Lord and Savior. Those who worship and serve Him are taken to heaven after death. Only faith — not good deeds — can earn this gift of eternal life."

The woman lifted her eyebrows. "We can try to earn it. We must try."

"Yes, and you will fail because you are a human. No human — not even a Brahman — can be good enough to enter paradise."

"But what of the *suttee?*" Her face took on an expression of guilt and fear, as though Edmund's words themselves might reach out and strike her. "Surely a woman who burns herself upon her husband's funeral pyre can gain heaven for herself and all her family. This is what we are taught."

"What satisfaction does the death of one poor widow bring to the almighty God? Do you suppose this somehow pleases Him? In your heart, Mrs. Choudhary, you know such a sacrifice is useless, for you chose to run from it yourself. God does not want our death. He wants our love. Our faith. Our fellowship and communion with Him. *Kharma* means nothing to my God. Instead, we must accept salvation as freely given to us by Him. And yes, He does love us. He loves us very much indeed."

The woman drew a line in the dust with her bare toe. "Though I believe you are ignorant, sahib, I can excuse it because you are English and have had too little education in the ways of the gods. And even though you are foolish — wearing your hot coat and black hat and speaking very poor Bengali — I have learned to like you. I see how your eyes grow soft when you look at the girl. I know that you care for her. You are kind with your words and with your actions, and I believe you mean well. You will not permit my *meye*'s father to cause her pain."

"Thank you, Mrs. Choudhary, for your faith in me. I should hope to prevent pain to anyone, especially Miss Rosse."

"Very well." She crossed her arms. "Because of this, I shall tell you to stay here in Krishnangar for two days. There is an inn for travelers just down this street near the river. Wait for me there. I shall go up to the rajah's palace to see how the *meye* is received. If all is well, you may go back to Calcutta and inform Sahib Rosse that his daughter was bitten by a cobra. Tell him she died an agonizing death in her *ayah*'s arms, her body was burned, and her ashes were taken away to be thrown into the holy Ganges River. But if all is not well, then I shall bring the girl down to you, and you may bind her with ropes and force her to return to Calcutta."

Edmund did not know whether to laugh out loud or groan in frustration. "First,

Mrs. Choudhary, Mr. Rosse's daughter has not been bitten by a cobra, and I should never presume to tell her father such a preposterous story. Second, I cannot afford to wait here in Krishnangar for even one more day. I have been away from my work too long already. It will take me some time to travel back to my home and settle my affairs. I have still to pack my belongings and make decisions regarding my house and my ministry. Then I must journey to Calcutta to board the *Scaleby Castle*. If I delay any longer here, I may miss the departure altogether. In England, my brother will anticipate the arrival of the ship only to learn when it docks that I am not upon it. Such an event is unthinkable."

"You would abandon us here? But you made a vow to take care of the *meye*."

Edmund clenched his jaw, fighting the urge to surrender in spite of all he knew was sensible. "I have taken care of her as long as I was able — and I have seen to your future as well. You have the money I paid you to bring me here, Mrs. Choudhary. Miss Rosse has her jewels. You are both intelligent and resourceful. I am sure all will be well."

*"Chucho!"* she spat.

Though Edmund knew that he spoke

Bengali rather poorly, he understood that Moumita was calling him a mean and cruel man. He looked away from her snapping black eyes and focused instead on the small figure now crossing the bridge over the Jalangi River. Miss Rosse hurried along, her sari gathered in her fists and her face tilted toward the palace ahead.

What could one do with such a willful and self-possessed young creature? How could her mind be changed except by God? And why, when Edmund closed his eyes even now, did her blue gaze beckon him?

By the time she arrived at the entrance to the rajah's palace, Violet's heart was beating so loudly she feared she might startle the saber-armed guards in their tall red turbans. It was not the exertion of the short climb up the hill that had left her breathless, for she was accustomed to walking much farther each day in Calcutta. Nor did fear of the ruler's response cause her such violent palpitations. It was the mighty battle raging within herself that had brought on these tremors and throbbings.

Was this truly where she belonged? There must be some place in this world where she would fit in and be able to find hope for her future. As she hurried across the bridge,

Violet suddenly wondered whether Mr. Edmund Sherbourne would run after her and catch her up in his arms. Perhaps he would call out her name, passionately profess himself enchanted by her, and then fold her into his embrace.

Secure and protected, she would agree to become his wife and bear him many children as they lived out their happy years in a house beside the Hooghly River. He would continue telling everyone about his dearly loved God. She would grow orchids and hybridize them for Mr. Wallich at the Botanic Garden. Moumita would tend the children. And all would be well forever and ever.

But that was silly, was it not? She barely knew the man and shared none of his passion for preaching about Jesus. Even as she peered nonchalantly over her shoulder, Violet could see Mr. Sherbourne bidding Moumita farewell. He intended to walk away, and he *ought* to walk away. He was handsome and kind and strong — but he had nothing to offer Violet. He wanted only his dream of a church in Calcutta and the memory of his beloved Yorkshire.

And she did not want him. Certainly not.

Silly man in his black wool coat and stifling hat. Edmund Sherbourne knew nothing of India. What little Bengali he spoke came directly from a book and sounded ludicrous to anyone who truly understood the language. He seemed to despise Calcutta. He found temples and mosques appalling. In fact, he understood only the English ways he had brought with him to try to shove into poor Hindus' mouths. He was like the merchants of the East India Company, here to enrich themselves while caring nothing for the country itself.

As she climbed the marble steps that led to the row of arches along the palace verandah, Violet peeked behind her again. And there he went — strolling off as if he had not a care. She was worth no more to him than a single coriander seed. Or an inch of dry sugarcane. He did not admire her sari or think well of the way she had braided her long hair. Perhaps he believed blonde tresses to be hideous, as did Moumita and the other Indians who teased her by calling her a Hanuman langur — a golden-haired monkey.

Violet clenched her fists and squeezed her eyes shut. Let him go. She had her own plans. Her own future. Edmund Sherbourne had said he understood her, but he did not. His eyes were soft, but his heart lacked sympathy. His smile was kind, but his aims were selfish. No doubt her father had paid him well. Paid him . . .

With a gasp, Violet swung around. The church in Calcutta! Of all the merchants she knew, only Malcolm Rosse had the wealth to offer such a gift. And a permit to preach! Of course, that had been his doing, too. Mr. Sherbourne had not followed Violet out of obedience to her father's wishes. Nor did he care about her future. He wanted permission to preach. A building in which to worship his god.

Her eyes narrowed as she watched him walk down the street. No wonder he had been so persistent in following her. But she had not succumbed to his charms. No, indeed! She had not fallen prey to his broad shoulders and handsome face. Certainly not! And now he must skulk back to Calcutta empty-handed. He would sail away on the ship, leaving behind his hopes and dreams, and he would live out his life in that misty moorland he loved so well.

Good.

Let him find some featherbrained English girl to fawn and simper over his thatch of thick brown hair and his green eyes. Violet had better things to do than marry and bear children and sit by a fire knitting stockings. She had botany — the orchids, hybridization, her expeditions. She had India. And now she had Moumita, her dear *ayah* who had climbed the hill and was ascending the steps to meet her.

"He has gone, *meye*," Moumita said, lifting her small brown face. "That man is ignorant, but he is good. His understanding of the ways of the gods is weak, but he is kind. I believe he is strong and brave and rich also. He would have been a good guardian for you. Now you must face this young rajah who does not like the Englishmen who live in India. I believe your fate is very bad."

Violet moistened her lips as she focused on the rows of red banners floating above the seven stone arches of the palace verandah. Soaring pillars festooned with gold-leafed carvings supported the second floor and its rows of balconies. Fluttering in the breeze that drifted up from the Jalangi River, rich purple curtains hung in open windows. Inside each archway stood a Hindu guard wearing a *dhoti* of billowy white fabric that covered his knees and swept up between his bare legs to form a sort of pantaloon. Each had on a red coat and a crimson turban adorned with gold ornaments. Tall, menacing figures, the guards were armed with curved sabers and long lances. Like statues carved of banyan wood, they studied the pair of women advancing toward them across the outer porch.

The moment Violet made to step between two of the guards, they stretched out their arms and crossed their lances to prevent her passage. Moumita cried out, fell to her knees, and covered her head.

But Violet lifted her chin and addressed the taller guard. "I am Miss Violet Rosse from Calcutta," she said. "I am here to see the rajah of Krishnangar."

# Six

Aware of the filthy hem of her poorly wrapped sari, the yellow tinge of curry stains on her fingers, and the bright gleam of golden sunlight on her blonde hair, Violet stood trembling before the rajah. Yes, trembling. She knew it, despised it, and yet there was nothing she could do to make herself stop shaking. The moment the fifteen-foot-tall studded brass doors had swung open to admit her into his throne room, her knees had turned to melted butter, and her whole body had begun to quiver as though she were suffering a bad bout of malaria.

On an elevated platform layered with thick wool rugs sat an enormous gilt chair embedded with gems of every hue. The back of the throne rose upward in carved peacock feathers enameled in shades of turquoise, white, and black, and their eyes seemed to fix Violet with a malevolent glare. Behind the throne, more chairs were decorated in similar style, but none held so regal and commanding a figure as Jatindra, the rajah of Krishnangar.

His rich purple satin coat and red silk shoes were adorned with gold trimming and embroideries. His turban of white silk had been ornamented with gold, pearls, and gemstones. The scimitar at his waist hung in a golden scabbard inlaid with ivory and emeralds. Diamonds and rubies glittered on his neck, and his hand sparkled as he waved it at her.

"Miss Violet Rosse," the rajah addressed her in perfect English. As he spoke, his mustachioed mouth turned down at the corners, as though he were smelling something unpleasant. "Why have you journeyed from Calcutta to my palace?"

Violet made a wobbly curtsy and saved herself from a fall only by grabbing the arm of the guard who stood at her side. He jerked to attention, his saber instantly drawn. With a gasp, she backed up and clenched her hands at her waist.

"No, please," she sputtered to the guard, whose eyes narrowed as she fought to maintain her dignity. "I have come to see the rajah. I mean no harm. None whatsoever."

"Let the Englishwoman answer my question," the ruler called down from his throne. He turned to the men who sat behind him. "We shall learn what she wants before I decide what to do with her."

Speaking Bengali, he ordered a servant to bring forth a silver tray containing attar of roses and to sprinkle some fragrant essence on the malodorous and ugly woman who stood shivering before him. Before Violet could regain the little aplomb with which she had arrived, the servant hurried forward. Scurrying around her, he used a whisk to shower her head and shoulders with perfumed oils. Then he pushed a rolled palm leaf full of spices into her hand and scrambled back to his place behind the rajah.

Feeling every bit as small and unwanted as a louse upon a leper's head, Violet made an effort to smile. "Yes, well . . . thank you very much, Your Highness," she said. The rose-scented oil began to slide down her cheeks and drip from her chin as she continued. "As I was saying, sir, I come to you in peace."

Raven brows slashing across his dark face, the rajah leaned forward, stared at her, and made no answer. Violet considered attempting another curtsy or even full-length prostration on the floor, but she gave it up. The sunlight from the open windows overhead sent dark spots dancing before her eyes, and she dared not move again. The guard beside her had not sheathed his saber, and she sensed his eagerness to lop off her head and shove it onto a fence post as a warning to any other presumptuous English girls who might come calling. She summoned her strength and addressed the ruler again. "I understand that your dear father, the previous rajah of Krishnangar, is a man of great understanding —" She caught her breath at the scowl that darkened the man's face. "As are *you,* of course," she added hurriedly. "And I am certain that you have as strong an interest in science as he does. Being father and son, you must be very alike. Or . . . perhaps not."

Still trembling, Violet waited for a response. When the rajah made none, she continued. "I have a great interest in orchids, sir. They are a sort of flower, and as you may know, many unique varieties grow here in India. I have been studying orchids at the Botanic Garden in Calcutta."

"That garden belongs to the East India Company," the rajah growled.

"Indeed it does, but that fact means nothing to me. I do not care about the company at all, nor am I loyal to England in any way. I was born in India, sir. This is my home country."

His frown deepened. "You are not an

Indian. Your hair is yellow like a Hanuman monkey's!"

This sent all the turbaned men behind the rajah into gales of laughter. Trying to keep her chin up, Violet blinked through the oil that was fogging her vision. She knew she had made a poor impression, and the ruler of Krishnangar did not respect her. But she saw that this was her last opportunity to state her mission. If he refused her request, she would have no choice but to leave the palace in defeat. Should she return to Calcutta, she would be forced to sail away to England. Edmund Sherbourne had been correct in his understanding of her predicament. What hope of survival did she have as a white woman alone in India?

She took a step and fell to her knees, throwing her arms forward and touching her forehead to the floor. Speaking in fluent Bengali, she addressed the rajah.

"Oh, great lord, blessed by the gods," she began, "I come humbly before you. I am nothing compared to your greatness and power. I am lower than the dust beneath your beautiful feet. Oh, master of the mighty and magnificent land of Krishnangar, I throw myself upon your mercy, for you are my only hope of happiness. Permit me the gift of one small room in your great palace. I wish to live here and never again return to the home of my English father in Calcutta. My presence will not trouble you, for I require only a little food, and I bring my own servant who will tend me day and night. From your palace, I shall make journeys throughout India to collect orchids for study by the scientist at the Botanic Garden, Dr. Nathaniel Wallich, whose loyalty to knowledge and learning is much greater than to the East India Company. This is my request, oh great Rajah Jatindra, and if you grant it, I shall be the most content woman in all of India. I shall be honored by your munificence, and I shall grace your palace all my days."

Having poured out her request in a great rush of words, Violet felt more spent than she had in her entire life. Tears flooded her eyes as the rajah spoke in a low voice to the men who sat behind him. Waiting for his response, Violet spread her fingers across the carpet and pressed her forehead into its soft tufts of wool. How she wished she could pray at this moment and beg the gods for mercy. If only they would be kind to her. Though she had been disobedient to leave her father, surely the gods would not punish her for it. Surely they understood that her motives were good — that she wanted to benefit the world through scientific under-standing.

Violet thought of the gods her *ayah* had given her, each one wrapped in a soft cloth and lying at the bottom of her bag. Ganesha, the elephant-headed god whom Moumita adored, was crafted of gold. Hanuman, half monkey and half man, had been made of brass. Kali and Devi were clay figurines. And then there was the small cross on which hung the little silver Jesus.

Why had her mother loved Him? And why would He not help her? If she had that statue in her hand now, Violet thought, she would rub some rose oil on it and light incense before it and pray with all her might that He might hear her. But what use was any god at all when one first had to unwrap him and set him up on an altar? She needed a god now — here on the palace floor!

"I have considered your request and have consulted with my advisors," the rajah spoke up at last. "It is preposterous, and you are foolish. I utterly despise everything English."

Violet closed her eyes and let out her breath. This was it, then. The end of hope.

"Only one thing about you intrigues me, Miss Rosse of Calcutta," the rajah continued. "You speak Bengali as well as I."

Hope flickered to life again inside her heart.

"Science means nothing to me," he spat. "And the East India Company will have only my hatred as long as I live. But you have walked into my palace as though the gods had brought you. An English lady who speaks Bengali. Tell me, can you write in my language?"

"Yes, oh great rajah," Violet said into the carpet beneath her face. "I write the Bengali script very well indeed. As a child, I used to sit beside the scribe who came into my father's library to take down messages and letters. I wanted to be near my father, sir, but he rarely took notice of me. Instead it was the scribe, Ashok Kumar, who became my friend. Babu Kumar taught me how to write in Bengali."

"Very well, then. I have a plan for you, Englishwoman. It should please us all greatly."

Violet lifted her head. "May I live here at the palace, sir?"

"Yes, of course," he said, but his smile held no warmth. "For a time."

He motioned to his advisors, who leapt to their feet and bowed before him as he spoke his pronouncement. "Before my father dies, I shall give him this young Englishwoman as

146

a wife. It will be a good match — two power-less creatures bonded together. Prepare a wedding, and see that it is quickly done. We should hold the ceremony tomorrow, if at all possible. After my father breathes his last, we shall have a widow to place upon the burning pyre."

Violet choked out a cry of horror. "You would have me become *suttee?* But I . . . I am English! My father would . . . he will . . ."

"He will read from your own hand how you willingly wed my father and gave your life for the salvation of the family of the rajah of Krishnangar. You will write this letter in English and also in Bengali, that no one may mistake its meaning."

He stood and smoothed the creases in his purple coat. "You can have no objection, English girl. You left your father and came to me willingly. You placed your life in my hands. If I choose to end it, how can you object?"

"But I —"

"No, indeed, your death will be welcome. Many will rejoice, as should you. For you, *suttee* provides a direct path into Nirvana — a place of holiness you would never have attained without this opportunity. For me, it will mean saving the life of my mother, who would have been placed upon the pyre as a rajah's wife always is. And of course, I have the additional benefit of my own entrance into Nirvana upon my death. And for all those who despise the Englishmen of the East India Company as I do . . . well, Miss Violet Rosse of Calcutta, it will be as though I have slapped them in the face."

Edmund paused on the path and took off his hat. Tugging a handkerchief from the pocket of his black frock coat, he blotted his brow. Never mind about Miss Rosse, he told himself — as he had a hundred times since watching her walk across that bridge toward the rajah's palace. Never mind the lost permit to preach in Calcutta. Never mind the loss of the church building. Never mind all the things that might try to claim his heart.

He would go home to Yorkshire, sit beside the fire with Randolph, and discuss sheep. They would chat about the current price of wool. They would sip their tea. Perhaps they would go riding or grouse shooting. They might fence — a favorite sport for all three Sherbourne brothers. They might fish in one of the streams that ran through the Thorne estate. They might walk into Otley and call on the minister or purchase something in one of the shops.

Perhaps they would sit about and do nothing at all, as gentlemen of leisure were wont to do.

One day India would fade from Edmund's consciousness as though it had never existed. He would forget the masses of hungry, illiterate, disease-ridden people. He would forget the temples with their bloody idols and marigold garlands. He would forget the mosques with their rows of men kneeling in prayer.

And he would most certainly forget Miss Violet Rosse.

Staring down at his finely wrought, tall-crowned, beaver hat, Edmund considered the impractically small brim that was useless for protecting his face from tropical rays. He recalled the small Hindu Untouchable woman who had so reviled him for his choice of clothing and his poor Bengali. He had thought her ignorant and blind. But perhaps she was correct in her assessment. Why had he thought it so important to wear this hat?

It was a symbol of civilization, he had told himself. He was an ambassador of enlightenment and aesthetic training. He brought to this heathen land all that was right and proper in the world. Manners, culture, etiquette, and, of course, Jesus Christ.

Hurling his hat into the tangle of vines beside the path, Edmund sank down on a fallen log and covered his face with his hands. What good had any of it done? No Indian man in his right mind would wear a black hat in these sweltering temperatures. The people wore clothing that suited their climate, not his. He stripped off his black wool coat and dropped it onto the crumbling log. The Bible did not speak of beaver hats and frock coats. Jesus cared nothing for such trappings! Indeed, Jesus had cautioned His followers to have no concern at all about clothing, for their heavenly Father would provide for them just as He provided for the birds of the air and the flowers of the field.

Disgusted by his own blindness, Edmund thought of the wasted hours he had spent trying to teach his Hindu servants about the importance of cutlery. Forks, knives, spoons. Fish forks, butter knives, soup spoons. Bah! The servants had stolen the silver utensils and probably melted them down to make idols!

*What an utter fool I have been,* Edmund thought as he ripped off his damp neckerchief. Tightly woven of fine, thin wool, it was worn to prevent a chill while hiking up a misty English fell. In this sweltering country, it did nothing but increase his perspiration and thereby his misery. He dropped it onto the path.

His boots had been crafted for riding horses on the moorlands, not slogging through the muddy rice paddies of West Bengal! Yet he had spent much time explaining the intricacies of polishing leather to the curious crowd who had gathered at his house. No doubt they had ridiculed him behind his back for giving such attention to the hide of a dead cow. To the Hindu, the cow was a holy creature — but Edmund had strolled about the countryside in his fine leather boots for five years.

He was as great an idiot as Violet Rosse and her *ayah* had declared him to be. His ability to speak Bengali had suffered from his misguided belief that his servants would be grateful to learn the civilized lilt of the King's English. Instead of pouring India into himself, as Dr. Carey had so wisely suggested when he first arrived, Edmund had tried to pour England into India.

England was not God.

God was God!

More despondent than he had ever felt in his life, Edmund sat upon the log and watched a row of ants scurrying back and forth between his ridiculous leather boots. As he mused, the sins of his past crept into his thoughts and began to dance before his eyes. His youthful licentious and profligate ways — the women he had used for his own pleasure, the hours spent in drunken revelry, the carousel of hedonism upon which he had ridden around and around. How many years? Three? Or was it four? The memories blurred into a sea of heedless decadence.

How much further might he have fallen had God not rescued him? With humiliation darkening his heart, Edmund recalled the night he had been too inebriated to find himself a carriage back to the university at Cambridge. Sitting outside a tavern in the pouring rain, he had felt a touch upon his arm. A man in a dark coat bent over him, lifted him to his feet, led him inside a warmly lit room where others had gathered.

Seated at the back of the congregation while rainwater puddled beneath his chair, Edmund had listened to a heated discussion of several verses in the tenth chapter of the biblical book of Romans: "Whosoever shall call upon the name of the Lord shall be saved. How then shall they call on Him in whom they have not believed? And how shall they believe in Him of whom they have not heard? And how shall they hear without a preacher? And how shall they preach except they be sent?"

Edmund now knew those verses by heart. But at the time they were foreign to him and utterly meaningless. The leader of the discussion, a man named Andrew Fuller, was a member of the group known as the Particular Baptist Society for the Propagation of the Gospel Amongst the Heathen. It was Fuller who had brought Edmund out of the rain and Fuller who had taken the besotted young university student to his own home after the meeting.

The next day and for many days after that, Andrew Fuller had gently shown Edmund that he was among the lost — far from God, full of sin, and completely without hope of eternal life. That very week, Edmund had called upon the name of the Lord and been saved. Not only saved from the clutches of his own wickedness but transformed into an entirely new man.

Completing his education at the university, he had devoted himself entirely to the study of Scripture. And the more he read, the more he knew that St. Paul had written those verses not only to the Romans but to Edmund Sherbourne. Those who had not heard must hear. And he must be the one to tell them.

How clear his calling had seemed once,

Edmund reflected now as he watched the ants creating a new supply trail around the sole of his boot. Filled with determination, strength, and the joy of the Holy Spirit, he had sailed to India to win the heathen hordes to Christ. Five years later, he was sitting here on a rotting log in the midst of the jungle, half hoping that a tiger would leap out of the nearest banyan tree and put him out of his misery.

Wrongheaded and still too full of himself, Edmund had utterly failed his Lord. Dr. Carey had tried to encourage him by saying that planting seed was just as important as harvesting grain. The small missionary with fire still burning in his eyes had recounted his own seven years of labor without a convert. And on their last encounter, he had pleaded with Edmund to return to India and continue to preach the gospel in obedience to his holy calling.

Could he remain obedient in the face of such defeat? Edmund squeezed his eyes shut, struggling against the tide of emotion that surged inside him. Dare he come back to India and try again? Did God even want him anymore?

The hard face of Moumita Choudhary slipped into Edmund's thoughts. How the little Hindu woman had ridiculed him and spat out her bilious mockery of his ineptitude. Yet even then, God had given him the courage to speak the truth of Jesus Christ. Could Edmund share the healing power of salvation even one more time? Could he face the rejection of the Word yet again? Even now, in the midst of overwhelming despair, could he find some small grain of courage with which to sustain himself?

He lifted up a prayer — brief, silent, simple, and heartfelt. And then he stood. Though he had heard no voices from heaven, seen no brilliant lights, and had no certainty of victory, he did know one thing: He could go on. And he would.

Violet knelt beside the low bed upon which she had placed the row of her small clay, brass, gold, and silver statues. "Great gods of wisdom and power," she murmured, "please spare my life. Take away this terrible *kharma* I have brought upon myself. Help me. Oh, help me, please."

Weeping, she could say nothing more — and why bother? All was hopeless. After addressing the rajah, Violet had been dragged off, shoved into this room, and locked away as though she were a rabid dog. Moumita, who had been awaiting her *meye*'s return from the reception hall, had vanished. No food had been brought during the night Violet had spent in the room, and only twice was she given a small cup of mango juice to drink.

Each time the guard outside her door opened it, Violet pleaded with him for mercy. She begged to see Moumita. She offered the man all her jewels in exchange for escape. She threatened to bring down the fury of every British soldier in India. But each time, the guard shut the door in her face and locked it.

From the small bag that contained her jewels and clothes, Violet had taken out the little figurines. As Moumita had taught her to do, she prayed to them for many long hours. She had no incense to light before them. No bowls of steaming curry to offer. No rose water with which to bathe their metal and clay forms. Instead, she had stared at the familiar faces until the sun went down and left her in darkness.

Lying alone upon the hard bed, Violet had thought of her many wrongdoings. This terrible fate was the punishment for running away from Moumita so many times in the bazaar. For climbing over the compound wall and causing the watchman such trouble. For slapping the *mali* when he inadvertently harmed her orchids. For stealing sugarcane and lying to her tutors and swimming with the Indian children in the Hooghly River.

Most of all, this horrendous destiny resulted from her willful disobedience to her father. She never should have run away. She ought to have boarded the boat and sailed to England and married Alfred Cunliffe. She should have been a good daughter instead of a stubborn, selfish, impatient, and ugly beast of a girl.

Now she would become *suttee*. As the sun rose and Violet could hear the bustle in the courtyard below, she stared at the unmoving, cold little gods on her bed. For the thousandth time, she recalled the long-ago afternoon she had viewed the burning of a widow upon her husband's funeral pyre. Drawn by the clangor of drums, gongs, and conch-shell horns, she had escaped her napping *ayah,* clambered over the compound wall, and raced toward the nearby temple.

At barely ten years of age, she was small enough to slip unnoticed among the crowd assembled on the riverbank. There she saw a dead man lying atop a three-foot-high pile of firewood. His young widow and her mother stood beside the pyre, and near them sat a small basket of sweetmeats. All around Violet, the crowd murmured in admiration of the great act of holiness taking place before them.

Violet had watched as the widow's mother led her daughter six times around the pile of wood, scattering the sweetmeats among the people, who eagerly picked them up and ate them. Then the young woman left her mother's side, calmly mounted the pile of wood, and began to dance upon it with her hands raised.

After lying down beside her husband's body, the widow put her arms around him. Violet clearly remembered how the girl's mother then heaped dry cocoa leaves over her still form. Ghee, the melted preserved butter so favored by Hindu cooks, was poured over the top of the whole pyre. Two long bamboo poles were then laid across it and tied down with thick ropes so that the widow could not move.

Before Violet realized what was happening, the widow's mother took a burning torch and thrust it into the pyre. It burst into crackling flames, and all the people called out in a great shout of joy, *"Hurree-bol, Hurree-bol!"*

Rooted to the ground, Violet had covered her mouth with her hands and stared. Transfixed with shock and horror, she watched the fire shoot toward the clouds overhead and the black smoke waft away in the breeze. If the burning woman had groaned or even screamed, no one could have heard her over the commotion of voices. Nor could the widow have struggled to escape because the bamboo poles held her down. In moments, it seemed, the entire pyre burned to ashes, the crowd dispersed, and Violet was left standing alone beside the riverbank.

"The widow is happy now, *meye,*" Moumita had explained to the child that night, when the image of the burning pyre kept her from sleeping. "I chose not to become *suttee,* and now I have a lifetime of pain. Many lifetimes. That woman chose a moment of pain, but now she has an eternity of joy."

*Joy?* Even now, all these years later, Violet's stomach churned as she left her bedside and stepped to the barred window of her room. Why was such horror and sacrifice necessary to reach heaven? And what assurance had she that the gods would even accept into their heaven an English girl with monkey hair?

Peering through the slatted shutters, she saw the preparations being made for her wedding to the old, sick rajah. She had seen dozens of these ceremonies, and she knew this one would be little different — though no doubt greatly shortened. When it ended, she would be just another of the old man's many wives. Soon he must die of whatever was ailing him, and she would be tied down beside his corpse and burnt into ashes. And that would be the end of Violet Sarah Rosse, who had been silly and ignorant and disobedient, and who deserved everything she got.

The chamber door swung open and an elderly woman entered, bearing in her arms a red-and-white sari heavily embroidered with gold thread. Four guards stood by as two younger women carried large pots filled with fragrant water into the room. The door slammed shut, and the women quickly began unwinding Violet's soiled sari and combing out the braid she had put into her hair.

"Please," she whispered in Bengali as they bathed her with the rose-strewn water. "I have made a terrible mistake. I am an English girl, and I cannot marry the old rajah, for this is entirely impossible according to my family's custom. Please help me, I beg you. You must find my *ayah*. Her name is Moumita Choudhary, and she stays in the village of the Untouchables near Krishnangar. She can explain everything. She will tell you that I came here only to look for orchids. Rajah Jatindra has captured me. He is holding me against my will. The English rulers will not tolerate —"

"Be quiet!" the old woman cried suddenly, giving Violet a jerk that nearly knocked her to the floor. "We do not hear your words!"

"But you must hear me!" Violet rushed on. "You must listen — I beg you! This is a terrible mistake. I am not Indian, so I cannot marry the old rajah. I am not even Hindu!"

"Look on your bed," the woman ordered. "You have placed the gods there. Ganesha and Hanuman and Kali. They brought you to Krishnangar to become the fourth wife of the Rajah Biharilal."

"But that is only because his son, the Rajah Jatindra, wishes to save his mother from *suttee!*"

"Of course." The woman drew back and smiled. "Why should my son not save me from this fate?"

"*You* are the wife of the Rajah Biharilal? You are the rani?"

"I am the first and most highly favored of the ranis. These are his other wives." She gestured to the two women who had accompanied her. "I would have become *suttee* by tradition. It was my destiny from the day I married the rajah, and I accepted it. But now I am saved, for the gods brought you to take my place upon the funeral pyre."

"No, that is a lie!" Violet tore away from their soapy hands and grabbed the small silver cross. "Those are your gods, but they cannot control me. Look at this one! You do not recognize him, do you? That is because this one is the Christian God. He is the God of English people."

"Then ask Him to save you if He can." The rani knocked the figurine out of Violet's hand, and it fell to the floor. "See? The English God is weak, as are the English people. He will be defeated and driven from our country — and so will you all."

Grabbing Violet's arms, the women pulled her back to the bathwater and continued scrubbing. After combing out the tangles in her wet hair, they twisted it into a tight knot. Then they drew a long red skirt over her head, tied it at her waist with ribbon, and fitted her into a red bodice. As the sound of clanging metal filtered up into the chamber, the women began tucking the edge of the red silk sari into the waist of the skirt.

"I cannot become *suttee*." Violet wept, knowing even as she did that it was useless to beg for help from the very women whose

162

lives her own death would spare. "If you release me, I shall go home to Calcutta and never disturb the rajah again. I am very young, and I do not wish to die!"

"You have been brought to us by the gods. This marriage is your fate. To become *suttee* is your *kharma*." The senior rani jabbed a large hibiscus flower into Violet's hair and took her by the arm. "Yes, cry, English girl. The more you weep, the better the wedding will go, for it is our tradition that the bride must appear unhappy. No one will take pity on you. My son, the rajah, has decreed this celebration."

"But please! Please can you not see that —"

"Put this over your hair," another of the ranis said, lifting a length of the sari and draping it around Violet's head. "No one should see this ugly monkey hair."

"It is good that the old man has gone blind!" the third whispered with a giggle. "He would die before the ceremony if he saw this monster!"

Their hands tightly gripping her arms, the women led Violet to the door and out onto the steps that led to the courtyard, where her future husband awaited.

# Seven

Violet sat on a golden throne, her head bowed and her eyes downcast. Above her, a four-poled canopy of fringed red silk provided scant shade and a bit of shelter for the small fire that had been built beneath it. Around this central pavilion, those who had gathered for the wedding shouted, sang, and ate the sweetmeats that had been heaped on silver trays for the festivities.

A happy day, Violet thought. A rajah wedded, a widow saved, an eternity in heaven for generations of a family. Rejoicing for everyone except the unwilling bride beneath the canopy.

With sickening finality, Violet understood at last that this was a nightmare from which she would never awaken. There was no hope of escape. Though the townspeople of Krishnangar had been admitted through the gates and into the palace, high stone walls surrounded the heavily guarded courtyard. Edmund Sherbourne had gone away to Calcutta. Moumita had been banished from the palace. No one could possibly get word to the English regiments at Fort William in time to prevent the ceremony. And thus, Violet knew she must accept her fate.

She realized, too, that Moumita had erred in her teachings. There were no gods. None of the figures Violet and her *ayah* venerated with such faithfulness had taken a single step to help. Though she had known they were made of nothing more than metal and clay, she now admitted to herself for the first time that the little gods had no power whatsoever.

Violet was alone. Abandoned. About to die.

The fragrance of jasmine, hibiscus, orchids, frangipani, and countless other blossoms decorating the canopy swirled around her. Before the crackling fire sat small clay pots filled with fresh coconut, rice, ghee, and vermilion powder. A priest in orange robes squatted near the fire and chanted prayers to Ganesha and to the nine planets of the solar system. The sound of clanging metal reverberated in the distance — no doubt it was the dancing girl.

In the Hindu custom that Violet had seen enacted so many times, a young woman danced before the arriving bridegroom's procession. Tradition decreed that in order to keep him awake, she must shake over his head a metal pot filled with coins and a betel nut. Violet managed to lift her eyes as the retinue came into view.

Garlanded with necklaces of marigolds so that his face was barely visible, the rajah was borne toward her on a palanquin carried by eight armed men. As he drew nearer, Violet sucked in a breath of surprise at his fearsome appearance. Was this a man? a beast? or some strange demon sent by the gods to punish her for disbelief? Even the raucous crowd fell silent as the rajah was paraded before them.

When the palanquin arrived at the canopy, Violet gazed through a veil of numbed disbelief. Gradually she recognized that the black, mottled mass she had viewed from a distance was not the rajah himself but a large tumor on his face. Blinded by the cancer and struggling to breathe, the rajah appeared to be in a drugged stupor as his guards carried him into the shade and placed his chair beside Violet's golden throne. Clearly in pain, he twitched and groaned as though urging death to take him.

Mesmerized by the man about whom she had heard so many tales at her *ayah*'s knee, Violet realized that she could neither fear nor hate him. This was not the rajah who had condemned her to death. This poor man was the kindly ruler of Moumita's childhood — the rajah who had loved science and art and who had been fair and just in dealing with his minions.

Pity filling her heart, Violet swallowed to hold back the flow of tears that had been threatening ever since she was dragged to her own chair beneath the canopy. Gazing at the diseased man, she thought of the crippled beggars she had seen on the streets of Calcutta. The countless lepers roaming the riverside in the hope of alms. The malformed children who crowded at the fringes of the temples and pleaded for the food brought in offering to the gods. This pitiful rajah was no different from any of the wasted and disfigured creatures Violet had seen all her life. She had never reviled any of them, and now she longed to reach beyond her own fear and pain to touch the man with a word of comfort or hope. But as she leaned toward him, the priest began to address the horde gathered around the canopy.

"Welcome one and all," he droned, breaking momentarily from his chanting. "We celebrate now the marriage of Rajah Biharilal to the woman sent by the gods to become his wife."

From past experience, Violet knew this

was the moment known as *hastamelap,* when the bride's parents were to join their daughter's right hand to that of the bridegroom. But as the priest returned to his recitation of sacred verses, no one stepped forward to perform the ritual. At first she believed their hesitation must arise from dislike of her. Who would wish to play the role of parent to the monkey-haired English girl? Yet it took only a moment for Violet to realize that she was not the source of the silence and discomfort.

Everyone in the crowd was afraid to touch the diseased rajah. By custom, his illness made him unclean. His impending death would leave him to the Untouchables, whose job it was to prepare corpses for the funeral pyre. Violet eyed the poor man's family — the pompous Rajah Jatindra, his array of wives and consorts, his mother, the other wives of his father, the children. Aunts and uncles, cousins, nieces and nephews. Even the advisors, who had stood so stalwartly behind their rajah only yesterday, now sat paralyzed. None dared make a move.

For a moment, Violet thought this might be her opportunity for freedom. She could stand and declare the ceremony nullified — for how could a marriage be valid unless all parts of it had been properly performed? But she knew such a gesture would only delay the inevitable. Rejected by a people whose ranks she had wished to join, she made up her mind to accept her fate with dignity.

As the priest chanted, Violet reached out and took the rajah's hand in her own. The crowd gasped and drew back from the canopy. Keeping her eyes on the old man, she stood and lifted a marigold garland from her neck and slipped it over his. Then she took one of his garlands and put it on herself.

"Do you see?" she said, throwing the edge of her sari back from her hair and facing the crowd. She called out to them in Bengali. "I have no fear of the Rajah Biharilal. I have no fear of you. Nor have I any fear of your lord, the Rajah Jatindra."

Ill at ease, the onlookers backed farther away, stumbling into each other and murmuring loudly at this white woman who spoke their own tongue with such ease and familiarity.

"My name is Violet Sarah Rosse, and I am the daughter of English parents," Violet cried over the hubbub. "But I was born in Calcutta, and all my life I have believed I was an Indian like you. I speak in Bengali as you do, wear a sari, and pray to Ganesha, Kali, and Hanuman. If I am Indian, then I am a worthy wife for the man who once led you. This man — Rajah Biharilal — was your lord and master, a kind ruler who treated you well and made peace in Krishnangar. But his son Jatindra says I am not Indian. He says I am English. He says I am a Christian. Yet, see how he weds me to his father?"

"Stop this woman!" Jatindra shouted at his guards. "She speaks nonsense!"

As several sentinels left their posts and began to push through the crowd toward the canopy, the priest spoke up. "It is the time for *ganthibandhan*. We must place the white cord around the shoulders of the bride and groom and tie them together."

"Yes, tie the cord around us," Violet said, lifting the old rajah's hand into the air. "Bind us as one — the Indian lord and the Englishwoman!"

Ripples of displeasure ran through the onlookers as they shoved and elbowed their way closer to hear what Violet was saying. Taking courage from their curiosity, she faced the men who had been sitting behind Jatindra when he pronounced her sentence.

"You advisors heard what your rajah said about me. But were you not loyal to

170

Jatindra's father before him? Do you not still love the Rajah Biharilal? Or are you too frightened of his illness to defend him? Will you stand by and permit him to marry an English Christian woman who can have no hope of taking him to Nirvana on the funeral pyre? Jatindra says I shall become *suttee*. But surely you must know my death will count for nothing!"

Shouting erupted at one end of the courtyard. Four guards at last broke through the crowd and rushed the canopy. Someone screamed — the rajah's mother — and Jatindra drew his scimitar from its jeweled scabbard. Violet caught her breath, certain it must be her last.

"Quiet, foolish woman!" the younger rajah shouted at Violet. "What do you know about my advisors? You know nothing of our beliefs!"

"Hear the words I speak!" Violet faced him down and squared her shoulders, determined that if she must die, she would die bravely. "Declare me Indian and fit to become your father's wife! Or if I am English — if I am truly Violet Sarah Rosse — then release me to my own people!"

"You were sent to us by the gods!"

"Jesus Christ is the Lord of every Christian!" a distant voice cried out in English.

171

"In the name of Jesus Christ, I command you to release this woman!"

Violet swung around to find that Edmund Sherbourne was striding toward her through the restless sea of wedding guests. He had gone away to Calcutta, and yet he was here now! How could this be?

Again, Violet felt the dizzying sensation that she was inside a dream — a multihued, shifting place where people disappeared and then suddenly reappeared at random. And how strangely the missionary moved, almost as though he were floating. Though led by two guards and followed by three more, he approached the canopy unhindered as the throng around him fell away.

But no, was this really Mr. Sherbourne? Striding forward in knee-high black boots, but without his black frock coat and tall-crowned hat, he hardly looked himself. With white shirtsleeves rolled to his elbows, he was no longer the severe holy man . . . he was simply a man.

His green eyes met hers.

"Miss Rosse, I have come to take you back to your father in Calcutta," he stated, and then he turned to the Rajah Jatindra. "Sir, this woman is a subject of the king of England and a Christian. With this ritual, you make a mockery of her country and her

172

God. I demand that you release her to me at once."

"Who is this man?" Jatindra cried. "Guards — seize him!"

The guards beneath the canopy moved forward, but Violet now saw that Mr. Sherbourne was armed with a saber. Gleaming in the sunlight, its bright silver blade dripped with blood as he raised it. "Stand back," he called. "I mean no harm, but I shall be satisfied in my quest. Miss Rosse, please step out from the canopy, and come to my side at once."

Though his eyes were fastened on the guards who surrounded him, Mr. Sherbourne clearly spoke to Violet. She glanced at the old man beside her and then moved to obey. But Jatindra caught her arm. "Stop! The wedding will proceed!" Pushing her toward the golden throne, he shouted at his men. "Guards, take this man. Remove him from my sight!"

"My lord!" A tall, hook-nosed guard stepped out from among the others, fell to his knees before the rajah, and pressed his forehead to the ground. "As commander of the palace regiment, I humble myself before you. Please hear me when I tell you that this man is a great warrior of the English people! He says that his Christian God has power over death, and my lord, this is true, for we cannot kill him. It is impossible for our sabers even to touch him. Already, he has wounded three royal guards, though he chose not to kill them. He has taken many weapons. His skill is beyond ours. Not even ten of us can subdue him!"

"Then order twenty to take him!" Jatindra roared.

"My lord, the men fear him and his God. I cannot force them to attack him. They refuse to obey me. At the gate he . . . he defeated us. His God is with him. He cannot be stopped."

"Do you defy me?"

"Yes, they defy you," Violet said, jerking her arm out of the rajah's grasp. "How can anyone respect a man who treats his own father in such a cruel manner? Look at the Rajah Biharilal, who once ruled Krishnangar with might and justice! You have brought a sick man into the heat of the sun on such a day? You have carried him here to parade his disease and shame him before his own people? You have tried to wed a devout Brahman to a Christian woman who cannot possibly take him to Nirvana — an act that must certainly bring you and the good citizens of Krishnangar great trouble from the East India Company in Calcutta? What sort of a ruler are you?"

"Miss Rosse!" Sherbourne shouted as the surging crowd threatened to topple the canopy. "I beg you — come to me at once!"

Violet assessed the distance between them. Dare she run? The rajah's scimitar glistened. She could see the priest rocking back and forth, chanting prayers to the planets. The women in the royal party clung together as the men attempted to move them toward the safety of the portico. The Rajah Jatindra stepped toward her. "I command you to wed my father and become *suttee!*" he snarled. "The gods have decreed it!"

"*You* are the one who should burn," she cried, leaping to the fire and kicking the glowing coals at him. Pots of spices tipped over and spilled their contents. Ghee spattered across Jatindra's tunic and burst into flame.

As he screamed, Violet threw herself toward Mr. Sherbourne. He caught her with one arm and hurried her into the flood of people now escaping the growing mayhem inside the courtyard. Saber drawn, he led her beneath the portico, across the verandah, and down the steps toward the bridge.

As they fled, Violet stumbled out of her

sari, its billowing yards of silk unwinding behind her like a red flag. They crossed the bridge, turned south toward the jungle, and found the path down the hillside. Running hand in hand, they splashed across streams, leapt fallen logs, slid across patches of bog, and pushed through vines that clutched at their legs.

At last, when Violet felt certain she must collapse in a heap, they burst out of the jungle and into the village of the Untouchables. Arriving at Bani's hut, they threw open the door, rushed inside, and tumbled into the arms of darkness.

Curled on the floor, Violet clutched her heaving stomach. The dream that could never end had ended. With his bloodied saber, Edmund Sherbourne had shattered the nightmare. She reached out, found his hand, and pressed it to her lips.

"Yes, three," Edmund said. He swung the saber before him, cutting a swath of tangled vines from the path that led down the hillside toward the river that would return them to Calcutta. "I am not proud of that fact, Miss Rosse, and I beg you to refrain from speaking of it again."

"But *three* guards!" Miss Rosse, whose bare feet padded along behind him, had done little else but weep since her rescue. Only when she paused from that activity did she take up her second and favorite pastime — that of chattering on and on until Edmund had to grit his teeth to keep from shouting at her to cease at once.

"How could you possibly have wounded three guards without assistance?" she questioned him for the hundredth time. "They were the rajah's guards and very well trained, and you are a holy man — a missionary. A *sadhu* is taught chanting and begging, yet you must have fought them as a warrior, for I saw the blood on that very saber!"

"Miss Rosse, first of all, I am not a *sadhu,* and secondly —"

"But what else can you be, for have you not told me that you devote your whole life to the study and worship of God?"

"I am a minister, which is very different from a Hindu *sadhu*. I am a Christian missionary."

"Christians train their missionaries in swordsmanship? It must be so, for the captain of the guard said your God made you invincible against his men. Fighting is not an occupation associated with holiness in my mind — although I sincerely hope I have conveyed to you how very much I appreciate —"

"Yes, Miss Rosse, you have conveyed your appreciation," he said. "Repeatedly."

"But how did you know to come and rescue me? What led you to return and capture me so boldly after you had already made up your mind to go to Calcutta? Did someone offer to pay you? Or were you fearful of my father's wrath?"

Edmund shook his head. Why was all this so difficult for the young lady to comprehend? No matter how many times he told her that he had acted merely out of Christian compassion, she could not accept it. Determined to attach either reward or punishment as motivation for his deed, she discussed it so much that he began to wonder at her sanity.

Glancing over his shoulder, he assessed the slender blonde woman who so fiercely had defended herself before the rajah of Krishnangar. Her tale was far more twisted and confusing than his, yet she found nothing odd in the notion that she had very nearly been forced to marry a dying man and burn on his funeral pyre in order to take him and his family to heaven. Clad in only a red blouse and an ankle-length petticoat as she hurried down the path, Miss Rosse seemed much more baffled by Edmund's experience at the palace than by her own.

"To assure myself of your safety and well-being," he explained to her once again, "I returned to the palace to speak to the rajah. I had decided that I could not go back to Calcutta unless I brought a message of hope to your father."

"It was because of your vow," Moumita Choudhary spoke up from the rear of the company. "You made a vow to care for the *meye,* and you knew you could not break it."

Edmund again glanced behind him. The small Indian woman had hardly spoken to him since he had found her standing at the foot of the bridge on the morning of Miss Rosse's forced wedding. As he soon learned, she had given all her money to a man who promised to bribe the guards and kidnap Miss Rosse from the palace. Of course the man had gone off and never returned, leaving the penniless Moumita alone and without hope.

When Edmund appeared, she told him of the new rajah's intention to force her *meye* to marry and then become *suttee.* She begged him to save Miss Rosse. Hardly able to believe such a far-fetched account, he decided to continue with his plan to speak to the rajah and assess Miss Rosse's situation. Meanwhile, he had instructed Mrs.

Choudhary to go home to her village and await him there. She had done so, and now all she could talk about was his so-called vow.

"I fulfilled my vow by accompanying Miss Rosse to Krishnangar," he told her. "Furthermore, Mrs. Choudhary, I beg you to stop insisting that I am bound by a statement you have taken entirely out of context."

"But you promised that you would care for the *meye*," Moumita argued. "You said, 'I shall do all in my power to protect her from harm and unhappiness.' How can you tell me you fulfilled the vow? This vow has no ending, sahib. You can never be released from it."

"But that is absolutely ridiculous!" he protested. "I am bound by no vow other than that of obedience to my Lord and Savior, Jesus Christ. Furthermore, I did not rescue Miss Rosse because of a vow. Nor, Miss Rosse, did I go to your aid because someone had paid me. And I most certainly did not go out of fear of reprisals from your father. Is the notion of chivalry and Christian kindness quite foreign to both of you?"

The silence behind him stopped Edmund on the path. Turning, he set his hands at his waist and surveyed the two strange creatures with whom he had been saddled. Moumita, small and dark, stood beside fair, blonde Miss Rosse, who was a head taller. So completely opposite in appearance — yet they might have been twins as they stared at him with utter innocence and confusion in their eyes.

In the quiet heat of the jungle, Edmund shook his head. The vast gulf that lay between himself and Miss Rosse had little to do with her willful obstinacy and impetuousness. It had everything to do with the tiny woman at her side. Miss Violet Rosse was *not* English. Despite her blue eyes, pink skin, and flaxen tresses, she was an Indian.

"But how did you disable *three* guards, Mr. Sherbourne?" Violet asked into the awkward space between them. "I never saw a weapon upon your person during the whole of our journey together, sir."

Edmund's urge to snap back a retort fled before the realization that she knew nothing. Nothing of English ways, English customs and manners, English thought or opinion. To her, he was as complete a mystery as she was to him.

"First, Miss Rosse, you must understand that my late father was a baron," he told her gently. "A baron is among the lowest-ranking classes in the British peerage."

"Like an Untouchable?"

"No, indeed. In England, no human being is untouchable. Yet, I confess there is a sort of caste system. We call this way of ordering ourselves classes. We have an upper class, a middle class, and a lower class. Peers are like Brahmans — very high caste, if you will. Barons are included among the upper-class peerage, but they are not as highly ranked as others, such as viscounts, earls, and dukes."

"I see," Violet said. "And of which class is my father?"

"He is a merchant."

"Is this ranking among those who belong to the peerage?"

"Certainly not."

As he spoke the words with such disdain, Edmund suddenly felt like a complete idiot. From the moment he arrived in India, he had deplored the Hindu caste system with all its prejudice and injustice. Yet, suddenly, he was confronted with his own country's hierarchy — a remnant of feudal times, but as fully alive as India's.

"I fear a merchant is rather lower than a peer," he said more gently, wishing it were not so. "But never mind, for merchants are often far richer."

Violet smiled, pink lips parting beautifully over her straight white teeth. "And is your family rich or poor, Mr. Sherbourne?"

"The Thornes are quite wealthy, in fact, and family members have all the training, education, and luxuries normally associated with our rank. Among the studies my two brothers and I pursued was swordsmanship. Fencing, it is sometimes called. Being inclined toward athletics, I became a rather accomplished swordsman. I took a great many prizes at school, actually, and my fencing master declared me the best pupil he had ever trained."

He paused for a moment, recalling those days of glory when comrades had slapped him on the back and ladies had clustered around him in admiration. How shallow it all seemed now.

"On the day that I became a Christian," he told Miss Rosse, "I put away such earthly things. Fencing had been a way to exalt myself, and I no longer felt the need to do that. I longed only to honor and uphold my Master, an aim I strive for to this moment. Certainly I would never boast about rescuing you from the rajah. This is why, dear lady, I should prefer not to speak of the events at the rajah's palace. Please do not mention them to me or to anyone ever again."

She stared at him as though he had been speaking Chinese. "You fought your way through the palace guards and saved my life — and you wish me never to speak of it again?"

"That is correct."

"Impossible! I shall tell everyone I meet what you have done for me. I shall speak of my hopeless fate, and I shall tell how you entered the courtyard with your bloodied sword drawn —"

"No, indeed!" he cut in. "You are not to talk of it at all. My reputation is to be built on nothing more than the reflection of my Savior!"

"But you are *my* savior!"

"I most certainly am not. I am nothing but an English gentleman blessed to have a talent for fencing."

"Ooh, you are too odd!" she declared, stamping her foot.

"I find that a most interesting comment from a woman who goes about in bare feet and a red petticoat."

"How should I not? I have lost my sari."

"A proper English lady does not wear saris."

She swallowed, her blue eyes suddenly misting. "But I am not a proper English lady. Nor am I an Indian." Pursing her lips, she looked away before speaking again. "I do not know who I am."

As though an arrow had been shot through his heart, Edmund reached for a tree trunk to support himself. How absolutely lost she looked. How forlorn and empty! At that moment, it was all he could do to refrain from taking her in his arms and holding her tightly until every tear washed from her eyes and every sorrow fled her breast.

He stepped toward her, his arm outstretched. "Miss Rosse —"

"Nor do you know who you are!" she cried out. "You have come to India to teach the people about God, but you speak Bengali no better than a baby! You live here, but you dress as though prepared for a winter's day upon some damp and chilly moorland where no orchids grow. You have labored for five years, yet you have convinced no one that your God exists."

"I know He exists!"

"I begin to think that you do not, for you are fleeing India for England as though He had deserted you here and you can only find Him if you go back home! What kind of faith is that? What sort of God is He anyway?"

So saying, she shouldered past him, lifted

the hem of her red petticoat, and padded down the path. Edmund looked at Moumita. She shrugged.

"That girl is rude," she said. "It is the fault of her father and mother who gave her birth. I raised her very well, but her blood is bad. Everywhere she goes, she brings bad *kharma* upon herself."

"I must say, I have a difficult time disagreeing with you on that point, Mrs. Choudhary."

"You are a holy man and a warrior, and you would make her a good husband. I could try to arrange a marriage between you, but after the wedding, you would regret it at once. Besides, why should a man as great as you wed such an ugly woman? Yes, she is the *meye,* and I love her as my own daughter. But oh . . . the monkey hair."

With a sigh, she, too, stepped around him and trudged on down the path.

Edmund studied them for a moment. Violet Rosse had the most beautiful hair he had ever seen. As she disappeared behind the great green leaves of a philodendron, it occurred to Edmund that if he touched that hair, his heart might be lost to her forever. And that would never do.

# Eight

"It is a bad idea," Edmund declared. "Your daughter absolutely cannot be forced to go to England, Mr. Rosse."

"How dare you be so presumptuous!" Malcolm Rosse glared down his nose at the missionary across the sitting room. Violet had seen her father angry many times, but never had he been this enraged. His plump cheeks shone a bright pink, and the wattle beneath his chin trembled as he spoke. "You hardly know the girl, and yet you pronounce her unfit for English society. Upon my word, Mr. Sherbourne, you do try my patience."

"Forgive me, sir, I beg you. It is not my aim to annoy you but only to protect Miss Rosse."

"Protect her from what?"

"From England. And England from her!"

The young man stood and rubbed the back of his neck as he paced the floor. His saber was gone, Violet noted, and so were his tall-crowned hat, black coat, and white neckerchief. With his white collar unbuttoned and his sleeves rolled to the elbow, Mr. Sherbourne had entirely lost his pious air in the three days since they left the palace at Krishnangar. His light brown hair began to reveal a trace of curl, his arms went bronze from the sun, and the green in his eyes took on a strange fire.

But just when Violet began to believe Edmund Sherbourne the most fascinating and tantalizing man of her acquaintance, he decided to hate her. From the moment they had hurried away from the village of the Untouchables, he had been testy and short with her. The more she tried to talk to him, the less he responded. The more she stared at him, the more he looked away. And when by chance their eyes met, he went as rigid as a statue, clenched his jaw shut, and turned in quite the opposite direction.

After returning Violet to her home in Calcutta, he had gone away with hardly a word of farewell. But the following morning, he came back to the house to inform her father that she could not go to England. Of all the marvelous things Edmund had done for Violet, this might be the greatest. Yet he had hardly glanced her way when she entered the sitting room. He greeted her with the briefest of bows. And the things he now was saying about her made her feel as small and helpless as a child.

"She cannot possibly succeed in England," he told her father. "Her mannerisms are Indian, her thoughts are Indian, her entire being is Indian. She will find herself a complete alien among her society in Yorkshire, and her desolation will be utter. You must not send her, Mr. Rosse. I simply cannot allow it."

"Allow it? What right have you to say what I may and may not do with my daughter? If I wanted to marry her off to that diseased rajah, I could!"

"Father!" Violet gasped. "You would have me become *suttee?*"

"When will you learn to be quiet, daughter? You are just like your mother — chattering on and on . . ." He paused, bit his lower lip, and breathed heavily for a moment. "You will do very well in England, Violet. Your mother hailed from Yorkshire, and she was happy there. I brought her to India and . . . and she was never the same. First, there was you — a great trial from the time of your mother's confinement, through your birth, and all the way until her death. I am sorry to say it, my dear girl, but you have been nothing but trouble your whole life."

"I see." Violet glanced at Edmund, who was staring intently out the window at a bougainvillea bush. She had known she was difficult, but never had anyone put it quite so bluntly.

"The heat of India made your mother suffer so," Mr. Rosse continued, as if completely unaware that his daughter was wishing to sink into the carpet and become a tuft of wool. "She spent all her time with friends — the wives of the company merchants. They took laudanum, you know. It was the thing to do. Opium. They had no time for children or husbands or housekeeping. Just the laudanum and their sleepy laughter. No, Violet, you had better go away to England before India ensnares you as it did her."

"India has captured your daughter already," Edmund spoke up, turning from the window. "She is as Indian as any poor sari seller in the bazaar or any rani in the finest palace in the land. Sir, may I speak frankly?"

"You have hardly restrained yourself to this point."

"Mr. Rosse, nearly everything your daughter knows of life has been taught by her Hindu *ayah*." He pointed at Violet. "You can hardly consider her English. She is, in fact, an Indian."

"An Indian?" he barked out as he leapt from the settee and started across the room

190

toward the younger man. "An Indian?"

"Yes, indeed!" Edmund shouted back, holding his ground. "How can you possibly think of sending her to England? She will be ridiculed. She will be reviled. At best, she must become an object of pity to all her society!"

"My daughter is English, Mr. Sherbourne, not Indian. And if you dare suggest anything else, I shall be forced to throw you out on your ear!"

"Order me to leave if you will," Edmund retorted. "I can do nothing less than defend your daughter from the dismal future to which you mean to subject her. Sir, she goes about shoeless, eats with her fingers, and is more comfortable squatting on the floor than sitting in a chair. She despises gowns and longs to wear saris —"

"Yes, I long for saris, Mr. Sherbourne, but I could learn to be comfortable in English gowns." Violet decided she had had quite enough of this recitation of her failings and weaknesses. "You saw yourself how my sari was always slipping out of my petticoat and trailing off down the path."

"It was?" her father blurted out, gaping at her and then at Edmund. "He did?"

"Indeed he did, and he knows very well that I could learn to wear a proper gown if I wanted to. I can do anything if I make up my mind to it!"

"You made up your mind to live in the rajah's palace at Krishnangar, and you very nearly ended on a funeral pyre," Edmund retorted. For the first time that morning, he faced her, his green eyes as hard and shimmering as emeralds. "If you go to England, Miss Rosse, you will have to learn to eat with the proper utensils, stitch fire screens, paint landscapes, play whist, and dance a minuet! You must wear a bonnet and gloves, play the pianoforte, speak French, and go to church every Sunday."

"I can do that," she declared.

"You may not chew aniseeds and spit them on the floor, wear bangles to your elbows, or tie bells on your ankles! You must learn to curtsy properly and give up sucking your teeth at the end of a meal. You must put your hair in a bun and curls, and you must surrender your long plait. There will be no wearing of kohl around your eyes or red stain on your lips. You will sit beside a fire and become as pale and quiet and obedient and devout — and entirely as boring as possible! Do you wish to do these things, Miss Rosse?"

She shook her head. "Well, I —"

"I thought not! There, Mr. Rosse, you

192

have your answer. She does not wish to do it, and therefore, she must certainly fail. If you send her to England, she is doomed. I beg you to keep her here in India where she may continue to study botany and go on speaking Bengali like a native and be happy!"

So saying, he slammed his fist down on a table, which sent a collection of brass bells jingling so wildly that one leapt off, fell to the floor, and rolled under a settee. Violet quite wished she could do the same. According to both her father and Edmund Sherbourne, she was the most troublesome of human beings ever to exist.

*Never mind,* she thought. She had survived her father, the rajah, and even her own wrongheaded blunders. She *would* go on.

"Mr. Sherbourne," she said, "you are correct in your understanding of my preferences. I should be more comfortable in India, and I should like very much to stay here. You are wrong, however, in your predictions of doom. I am capable of success in England, for I am not altogether without social refinements."

"Indeed you are not," Mr. Sherbourne agreed. "Mr. Rosse, your daughter has many welcome attributes. I find her charmingly forthright, comfortable with conversation, and of course, very beautiful. Despite being abandoned by both her parents into the care of an uneducated Hindu widow, she has managed to turn out well enough. Here in Calcutta she will thrive, especially if she is permitted to assist Dr. Wallich and continue pursuing her interest in orchid hybridization. Indeed, I believe that one day she may make a valuable contribution to botany, and I feel that she ought to be allowed to follow her heart in that direction. I consider myself a friend to your daughter, sir, and because of that, I contend most firmly that she *must* stay in India."

Violet felt that she had been fastened to the settee with a hundred nails. This amazing man who had overcome three of the rajah's palace guards and rescued her from death thought her beautiful? Beautiful? He called himself her friend? Found her charmingly forthright? And beautiful? *Very* beautiful?

"Well done, Violet," her father was saying as she sat unable to move, staring at Edmund Sherbourne and trying to make herself breathe. "That you are so admired by this respectable gentleman proves my point all the more. You will do well in England. The *Scaleby Castle* sits anchored in the harbor, and you will board it with your chaperone, Mr. Sherbourne, within the week. And now, my good man, I do thank you for your assistance in retrieving my daughter —"

"Sir, surely you are not serious," Edmund interjected. "You expect *me* to chaperone your daughter? Unthinkable! And after all I have told you, there can be no doubt that she is unsuited to life in England."

"Unsuited, perhaps, but as Violet herself said, capable of altering herself to fit her circumstances."

"But why? Why must you be so set upon this course that is likely to end in disaster?"

"Because I need the money." Mr. Rosse smiled and gave a small shrug. "The company's monopoly on trade with India is ended, as you well know. Our hold over Calcutta and the shipping lanes has waned in past years, and with it my own profits. Alfred Cunliffe, to whom my daughter is promised in marriage, offers an unending market for my cloth goods. He will take everything I can supply. With his money, I shall establish myself here once again, and both of us must profit greatly."

"You would sell your daughter to a total stranger?" Edmund asked in a low voice. "How desperate are you, sir?"

"I prefer to call myself determined. I built

my trade, and I shall continue it."

"To what end? You have no sons to carry on your name. What is your purpose, Mr. Rosse?"

"My own happiness, of course." He swept a hand around his house. "My servants, the luxuries of life, comforts, playthings — these are the dreams of any man, are they not? If I can assure my own contentedness until the end of my days, why should I not? And when I am dead, my dear daughter and her husband will inherit what remains for themselves and their progeny. Perhaps they will see fit to name one of them after me. What more can a man expect or hope for?"

"He can hope for a great deal more. Morality. Good deeds. Salvation for himself and his fellow man."

"Yes, yes, yes. You would say that."

"I should think you would expect and hope for a happy life for your daughter, Mr. Rosse. Have you so little regard for her? Do you not long for the sweet companionship of family — for the warmth of a daughter's loving arms about your neck, her gentle conversation at mealtimes, and her laughter in your corridors? Have you such little care for this young lady that you would sacrifice her chance at happiness in order to promote your own indulgences?"

196

"But I do not disregard my daughter at all! If I believed Alfred Cunliffe to be low or ill bred or in any way poorly suited to this match, I should not wish to form a partnership with him. Nor, of course, should I think of attaching Violet to him. But his reputation is excellent. I am told he is a young widower with no children, a fine house, and a most successful enterprise. Violet will arrive in Yorkshire, attend the finishing school, and wed Mr. Cunliffe apace. Your objections have no foundation whatsoever, Mr. Sherbourne, and as our discussion is at an end, I should very much like my servant to see you to the door."

"I shall see him to the door," Violet said, standing.

"I may see myself to the door, thank you." Edmund gave her a bow. "Good day, madam. Mr. Rosse, before I go, I must assure you that I shall expect some written acknowledgment that the specifications of our previous agreement are intact."

"Ah, the church and the preaching permit. Yes, of course. You shall have them, Mr. Sherbourne, provided you accompany Violet to England."

"That was not a part of our original contract, sir, as you well know. I prefer not to serve as your daughter's escort on her

197

voyage. It is unseemly for me, an unmarried man, to act as a chaperone for your daughter."

"For heaven's sake! You are a minister and very pious. I have no qualms. Why should you?"

A faint flush stained Edmund's cheeks as he stared unblinkingly at Violet's father. "Because it . . . because I . . . your daughter is hardly ten years my junior. Were our shipmates to observe us together on board, they might make inaccurate assumptions. With a church and a preaching permit awaiting me in India, I mean to return here as soon as I am resolved that my family is in a stable and happy condition. I cannot allow the slightest whisper of a possible indiscretion to reach the ears of my mission society. Upon my return to India, I shall require their constant support, and therefore, I cannot escort your daughter, Mr. Rosse. I shall not."

"And upon whom am I to rely? At the first port of call, Violet will leave the ship and run off. Before I can breathe a sigh of relief that she is at sea, she will be back in Calcutta."

"I shall take Moumita," Violet said. "She watches me very well, and she will like to see Yorkshire."

"You must be joking," her father scoffed. "I shall not pay passage for a wee Hindu who would take one breath of England's winter air and drop dead of pneumonia. Certainly not!"

"I shall not go alone," Violet countered. "Moumita has been both a mother and a sister to me, and I cannot imagine my life without her. Besides, what will happen to her when I am gone? You know very well she is a widow, and she was cheated of all the money Mr. Sherbourne paid her to take him to Krishnangar. Abandoned and penniless, she must surely be forced into indecent labor before dying of some nefarious disease. Who would burn her body and cast her ashes into the Ganges? Better she should perish of pneumonia in England, for at least I could be at her side. Father, if you do not agree to let me take Moumita, I shall indeed leap overboard and swim straight to Ceylon."

"And cause them as much trouble as you have done me!" Mr. Rosse studied his daughter. "By St. Peter's gates, you do sound very much like your mother these days, Violet. Until the laudanum, she had a fiery spirit I thought could never be quenched. You look like her, as well. Your eyes . . . they remind me of your mother's when we were young and she was so much in love." He paused. "You are not in love, are you?"

"Father! Of course not!"

"With that botanist . . . that fellow at the Botanic Garden?"

"Dr. Wallich? Certainly not. He is thirty years old and long married to his dear wife. How dare you suggest such a thing!"

"Well, now . . ." He touched his daughter's chin and then glanced at Edmund. Eyes narrowing, he addressed the young man. "Have you formed a secret attachment to my daughter, sir? I see the way you look at her —"

"I am a missionary, Mr. Rosse," Edmund shot back. "I am wholly devoted to my ministry. I assure you I have no romantic interest in your daughter."

"You certainly defend her with some gallantry."

"If she were better protected by her father, she would not warrant my defense."

Mr. Rosse and Edmund stared as though each would like nothing more than to strike the other. Violet thought of calling for tea — if only to fortify herself. But as it was, her father spoke up at that moment.

"I shall accompany Violet to England myself," he announced. "I have not been home these twenty years, and I believe I ought to meet this Cunliffe fellow for myself. I shall see that my daughter is educated at the finishing school and wedded forthwith. Furthermore, we shall indeed take the little Hindu *ayah* with us, for what proper Englishwoman does not have a lady's maid?"

Edmund's face revealed nothing as he nodded crisply. "I see, sir. You have made your decision, and now I bid you farewell."

As he turned and strode out of the sitting room, Violet picked up her skirts and hurried after him. "Mr. Sherbourne," she called. "I must speak to you for a moment, sir. Do you really believe I shall be a complete failure in England?"

He slowed his step. "It will be difficult. An orchid cannot survive on the moorlands."

"An orchid?" Moving to his side, she looked into his face. "Do you think I am like an orchid, sir?"

"Very much so." He stopped near the door and gazed at her. "You are Indian and tropical. You are more fragile than you suppose. I fear you will not travel well, and I certainly believe you are unsuited for the climate and society you will find in Yorkshire."

"And do you find me beautiful?" she asked. "Like an orchid? You said that just now to my father. I heard you. You said I was beautiful."

Unspeaking, he searched her eyes. His own went deep and dark, and his lips moved slightly. He breathed in once, and then he let it out in a rush.

"Well, yes . . . I suppose," he mumbled. "I think . . . of course, anyone would . . . well, certainly."

"Truly?" She touched his arm, and then drew it away again, aware suddenly of his bare skin. "But my hair. Is it not rather like . . . like a sort of . . . perhaps like an animal's?"

"An animal's? Your hair?" He frowned. "I have never seen anything quite like it, and certainly not on any animal. Your hair, Miss Rosse, is exquisite. Magnificent. The gold color is utterly —" He reached out and laid his fingertips on her temple. Slowly, he stroked her hair, tracing around her ear, and sliding back toward her braid. And then suddenly, nostrils flaring, he stiffened and jerked back his hand. "Good heavens, I —"

"Mr. Sherbourne?"

"I must go at once." He grabbed the door handle and wrenched it open. "Many things to do. Packing and settling my accounts . . ."

As Edmund fairly ran across the verandah without even a final bow, Violet reached up and pressed her fingers to the place his hand had so recently caressed. *"Exquisite,"* he had said. *"Magnificent."*

Yes, he certainly was.

Built ten years earlier in Bombay, the three-masted *Scaleby Castle* was the finest ship upon which Edmund had ever sailed. Weighing over a thousand tons and well armed, she ran a full one hundred and fifty-seven feet in length and had made many successful voyages on behalf of her merchant owners in London. Captain John Loch, a Scotsman, took a personal interest in his ship's passengers, and he settled Edmund into a fine cabin with a single bunk and a gimbaled lantern by which the young minister might read and study Scripture.

To this occupation Edmund devoted himself both day and night. He had decided, in fact, to spend the three-month journey from India around the southern cape of Africa and up to England in reading the entire Bible, seeking to permanently fix the Scripture in his head. Also, he thought it a perfect way to avoid contact with the other passengers.

Especially one of them.

Having fled the Rosse house in Calcutta, Edmund had taken a boat up the Hooghly to his own small abode. There he packed and repacked his trunks, all the while reminding himself not to think of the young lady. He could not remember the violet blue of her eyes. The pearly whiteness of her teeth. The sweet curve of her pink lips. The shining golden halo of her hair —

Dash it all! Why had he ever touched her hair? Her voice slid through him like sugarcane syrup: "Do you find me beautiful?" she had asked him. Well, of course he found her beautiful! What man in his right mind would not find her mesmerizing, alluring, enchanting —

"Oh, bosh," Edmund said aloud in the silence of his cabin. How many times this evening had he read the same passage in Exodus? God was instructing Moses as to the exact dimensions of the ark and the tabernacle, the details of the priests' garments, and the construction of altars and incense burners.

Surely this was important, for God did keep giving Moses the same information again and again. And Moses kept writing it down. And Edmund kept reading it. And reading it. And thinking the whole time of nothing but Miss Violet Rosse and her comely shape and her bare feet and her stacks of golden bangles.

What was an ephod anyway? Edmund focused on the passage concerning the priestly garments. According to God's will, Moses' brother, Aaron, and Aaron's sons were to be adorned as regally as the rajah of Krishnangar. How fierce that man had appeared despite his flashing jewels and soft skin, Edmund recalled. Scimitar drawn, he had been ready to slice Miss Rosse's head from her body had Edmund not intervened.

He was glad he had fought his way into the palace courtyard and rescued the young lady — with bold assistance from Violet herself. But he was not at all happy to have drawn the blood of three guards. Why were they not better swordsmen? Ritualistic in their movements, they had been easy to outwit and disarm.

Nor had Edmund been the least bit pleased to spend three days returning Miss Rosse to her father. How she did chatter! And Mrs. Choudhary chattered back at her in their strange mix of Bengali and English until Edmund thought he was in a cage of parakeets. They reviewed every moment leading up to the escape from the palace, endlessly discussed the young rajah and his family, fretted about the elderly rajah and his deadly tumor, and made plans to send gifts to Bani and her family in the village of the Untouchables.

Exhausting those topics — and Edmund along with them — they went on to debate such fascinating issues as embroidery on the hems of saris, the fashion for pointed toes on slippers, the merit of glass bangles as opposed to silver ones, and the proper way to greet a Muslim. It was too much! By the time they arrived in Calcutta, Edmund had been ready to tear out his hair. Yet when the constant babble ended and he found himself alone in his own house, he missed it far more than he could have imagined.

Now, three weeks into the voyage, he thought he might tear out his hair from the silence. He ate in his cabin, slept in his cabin, spent all his daylight hours in his cabin, and only ventured out in the dark of night when he would not be recognized. And would recognize no one.

It was necessary, he reminded himself as he attempted once again to ponder the significance of ephods to Moses and his brother. Clearly, God had provided this journey aboard the *Scaleby Castle* to train His servant. Edmund must learn diligence. He must focus on the task at hand. He must think about the Ark of the Covenant and what it meant to the Hebrew people. And he must turn his thoughts completely from a young woman who might even now be leaning on the ship's rail and looking out to sea . . . her eyes the color of the Indian Ocean, her cheeks kissed by the sun, and her laughter caught up in the salty breeze. . . .

"Are you quite certain, Captain Loch?" Violet leaned forward at the dinner table, her fork poised over a serving of freshly grilled tuna. "I have seen nothing at all of Mr. Sherbourne, and we have been at sea for more than a month."

"I know he is aboard, Miss Rosse," the captain replied, "for I escorted him to his cabin myself. The cook's boy takes his meals down three times a day and always brings back an empty tray. I am told Mr. Sherbourne is much occupied in the study of Scripture."

"But perhaps he is actually seasick," Violet offered. She glanced around the table for affirmation. The other passengers were a deadly dull lot — Mr. Rosse, two portly East India Company merchants and their gossipy wives, a physician who was nearly deaf, and a Brahman family on the way to Ceylon to visit relatives. They stared at

Violet as though she had dribbled soup down her chin — all except the Brahmans, who sat at another table and felt themselves far too superior to commune with the class-less Englishmen.

"A man could not study Scripture for a full month without ever tasting the salt air, could he?" Violet went on. "I should think he must die of boredom."

"Mr. Sherbourne ventures on deck at night, I believe," Captain Loch told her. "I have spoken at length with him several times when the moon was out, and I understand he has been teaching some of the crew to play chess."

"Chess at night? That is very curious."

"Oh, what of it, Violet?" Mr. Rosse spoke up. "I cannot think why you continue to inquire about the man day after day. More than once, the captain has assured you that Mr. Sherbourne is aboard the ship. Let the poor fellow study his Bible if he likes."

"I continue to ask about Mr. Sherbourne because I am concerned for his well-being. As you may recall, Father, he is my friend."

"He is a minister who wants nothing to do with a featherheaded female. Clearly he had more than enough of you during the Krishnangar debacle. Let him be."

Violet clenched her jaw. Her father

thought her ignorant and dull, and he evidenced no understanding whatsoever of her lively character. At least Mr. Sherbourne had been willing to share his opinions and make an effort at congenial conversation. The more she thought of the man — which was quite often indeed — the more Violet decided she would like to see him. How could someone who described himself as athletic enjoy staying in a ship's cabin day and night? Violet herself felt she was going mad.

Life aboard ship had turned out to be far more tedious than she had anticipated. She and Moumita found little to do all day but sit on chairs they carried up to the deck. They watched the ocean, listened to the snapping of the sails overhead, and mourned India. Sometimes Violet spoke to one of the sailors, all of whom seemed eager to chat with her. Mr. Rosse had expressly forbidden his daughter any contact with the seamen, however, and Moumita rebuked her *meye* each time Violet dared reply to their questions or comments. Moumita lived in terror of being tossed overboard — which Mr. Rosse had threatened to do more than once — and she followed Violet about like a rickshaw behind a wallah.

Truth to tell, she was bored. They had

visited only one port, and the bazaars at Madras were a disappointment. Fish, fish, and more fish. Swordfish and tuna and shark and eel. The odor was horrid. And what did they eat on the ship day after day? Fish.

"Dr. Nathaniel Wallich of the Royal Botanic Garden in Calcutta has developed a highly successful method of transporting orchids and other flora from India to England," she observed. "He packs them in brown sugar."

Violet sat back and waited for a response to this intriguing bit of information. Instead, everyone at the table went on eating their grilled tuna. In the total silence that followed, she picked at the fish and thought about Dr. Wallich, who was probably watering orchids at this very moment. And then she thought about her cabin, which had not a single orchid or plant of any kind, because her father had forbidden her to take them to England. The prospect of more long hours in her empty cabin led her to look for an alternative. Moumita, who ate with the other passengers' servants, never went on deck after the evening meal. How strange that Mr. Sherbourne left his cabin only for the nightly chess games.

Violet had learned to play chess from

Babu Kumar, the man who took down her father's letters and taught her to write in Bengali. Perhaps Mr. Sherbourne would welcome her at the game table if she appeared there some night. In fact, chess might be just the very diversion she sought this evening.

"Excuse me," Violet said, pushing back from the table. "I believe I have had quite enough fish today. Good evening, Captain Loch, Father, ladies, gentlemen."

"Bolt your door," Mr. Rosse called after her. As she stepped out onto the deck, Violet heard him mutter to the other guests, "As much to keep her inside the cabin as to keep anyone else out."

To tinkling laughter, Violet lifted her face to the breeze and drank down a deep breath of sea air.

# Nine

Standing at the ship's rail, Edmund scanned the moonlit sea. In the far distance, a dark mass lined the horizon. Africa. Truly the Dark Continent, it beckoned with mysteries as yet undiscovered by any European. Where did the great Nile River begin? How far did the desert sands stretch? And how many souls had perished without holding in their hearts the good news of Christ's salvation?

Edmund linked his fingers as he leaned upon the rail. Bowing his head, he prayed that the Lord might yet use him. He was weak, ignorant, a failure in so many ways. Yet God had used many flawed men to accomplish His will. Moses was a murderer. David committed adultery. Peter betrayed the Messiah.

Edmund had spent five years of his life preaching on street corners, teaching the Bible to any who would come and sit on his verandah, trekking through jungles and climbing mountains to reach those who had never heard the gospel, and doing all he could to heal the sick and minister to the needy at his doorstep. In all that time, not one man, woman, or child had prayed a prayer of repentance and surrendered to the sovereign power of Jesus Christ.

Doubt assailed Edmund day and night. Would he ever make a difference in anyone's life as Andrew Fuller had altered his? The memory of that man's hand on Edmund's shoulder as he sat in a drunken stupor would remain with him forever. If only he could touch the heart of some lost soul, some heathen who wandered in darkness with no knowledge of the love and compassion —

"There you are, Mr. Sherbourne!" The voice shot straight down his spine, through the backs of his legs, and into the deck as though he had been struck by a bolt of lightning. "Captain Loch says you have been on promenade at night, and I must tell you I think it quite discourteous of you to avoid the companionship of your fellow passengers."

Gripping the metal rail, Edmund turned to find her standing in the moonlight, a silver beacon in a white gown, blue pelisse, and flowing hair. Forcing air into his lungs, he bowed.

"Good evening, Miss Rosse. You are looking well."

"You are very pale, sir." She offered an awkward curtsy, and he was reminded of the difficult adjustment that awaited her. If she could not perform a womanly dip better than that, she was doomed to censure by all good society.

"I have not been out in the sun," he explained. "My days are occupied with much study."

"You ought to put your books away and come on deck in the mornings. You looked better after you lost your hat at Krishnangar. A bit of color does you very well."

He froze as she stepped up beside him and leaned on the railing, her arm not two inches from his own. Swallowing down his discomfort, he said, "I am studying Deut . . . Deuterom . . . Deuteronomy."

With a laugh, she shook her head. "What sort of book can it be with such a preposterous title?"

"It is the fifth book in the Old Testament, of course. It was written by Moses as a collection of exhortations and instructions to the Hebrew people."

"And why are you making a study of this obscure tome?"

"Deuteronomy is hardly obscure, Miss Rosse. The book has been studied, discussed, dissected, and analyzed for thousands of years."

"If it is so well-known, sir, then why do you study it still?"

"Because it . . . because I . . . upon my word, Miss Rosse, why are you not at dinner with the other passengers?"

"They are eating grilled tuna again, and so I came out to find you. Captain Loch says you are teaching the sailors to play chess at night. I shall have you know I am quite good at chess."

"Are you? How can you know chess but not the Bible?"

"Babu Ashok Kumar used to play with me while we waited for my father. He had a little board he had painted himself, and small figurines he had carved of dark and light stone. Babu Kumar was my father's secretary — much occupied in translating letters into Bengali so they could be read by the managers of the Rosse warehouses and factories. I learned to write in Bengali from Babu Kumar, and he taught me to play chess as well." She tapped her lip for a moment. "We did not read the Bible, Babu Kumar and I. He is a Hindu. I did read it when I had Mrs. Van Camp for a tutor. I was eleven, and she taught me on Tuesdays and Thursdays for a whole year before succumbing to smallpox."

"Good heavens."

"Oh, never fear. Mrs. Van Camp did not die of smallpox, but she was terribly disfigured by it and refused to come out of the house ever after. Her husband packed her off to England, and then he promptly perished of malaria. They were an unlucky family. Moumita could never understand how such tragedies beset the Van Camps, for they were very kind and never beat their servants."

Edmund listened with a familiar sense of disorientation. Once again, he realized how differently Miss Rosse viewed the world. "Excuse me, dear lady," he said, "but what had the Van Camps' kindness to do with their physical maladies?"

"Nothing at all. You see, they were good people and should have had excellent luck. Instead, the worst sorts of things befell them. Did I tell you their house flooded in the monsoon rains? It is a wonder to me that neither of them was bitten by a cobra, for you know very well how snakes often go inside houses when it floods."

Edmund shook his head as if to clear his mind. "Are you saying that good behavior ought to bring good luck?"

She turned to him, her mouth parted in

surprise. "Of course. Why do you suppose I am on my way to England?"

"Well . . . you are going there to marry Alfred Cunliffe."

"Yes, because I have been wicked. Wicked people earn bad *kharma,* while kind people earn good *kharma*. Did they teach you nothing in your missionary school beyond swordsmanship?"

"I did not learn swordsmanship in seminary, Miss Rosse, and furthermore —"

"I cannot believe you dispatched three guards at the palace at Krishnangar," she said. "I am sorry to interrupt you, sir, but it baffles me to this very hour. If I had not heard the testimony with my own ears, I should have doubted it entirely. How can a man so skilled and athletic bear to spend all his days inside a cabin studying a book that has been studied for thousands of years already? I cannot make you out at all, Mr. Sherbourne. Either you are the most interesting and dashing man of my acquaintance, or you are deadly dull."

With a laugh, Edmund rocked back on his heels as he held the ship's rail for support. "And you, Miss Rosse, are either the most beautiful and fascinating woman of my acquaintance, or you are quite mad."

"Beautiful and fascinating," she said, her

voice suddenly sober. "I am not beautiful. It is not kind of you to mock me, sir, and I should very much appreciate your not doing so again. On the other hand, I believe I am definitely fascinating, for I have much to discuss if anyone will listen. I know a great deal about botany, especially orchids, and I can give you the scientific particulars on any number of plants." She thought for a moment. "That is the primary area in which I am fascinating. Botany."

Edmund regarded Violet Rosse solemnly, realizing that she had absolutely no idea how stunning she would appear to the male population into which she was about to be introduced. In fact, even if she were slow to cultivate the social graces, she still might find herself quite popular due to her exquisite beauty. How quickly England would absorb and alter her. How soon she would lose her startling innocence and childlike chatter. He regretted the thought of it.

"You must find sea travel rather tedious," he said.

"How did you know?" Blue eyes wide, she stared at him. "I am ready to scream!"

"There is very little of botanic interest to be found on a ship. A bit of lichen, perhaps. And the usual mold."

Her spontaneous giggle tickled the edges

of his heart. "Oh, Mr. Sherbourne, you are too right! I have seen nothing green for more than a month. Madras gave me no reprieve whatsoever."

"A great many fish. That is all I saw to the town."

"Every sort of fish. Such a smelly bazaar — not a sari or a bangle in sight. And Father would not permit me to set one foot into the jungle for fear I should run away."

"Which was very wise of him, under the circumstances."

"Hmm, yes. But I believe he may rest assured now, for I am unlikely to flee into the middle of Africa." She studied the long dark outline of the approaching shore. "Does botany interest you, Mr. Sherbourne?"

"I like shrubberies, flowers, vines. Yes, very much indeed. But I know little of their scientific description, as you do. My field of study, as you know, is theology."

"Theology — in Latin: *theologia,* the study of God. You and poor Mrs. Van Camp would have had a lovely time together. She liked nothing better than to read the Bible. We read it very often. We did our grammar lessons out of Romans, for of course St. Paul had a masterful way with the King's English."

"I beg your pardon! St. Paul did not speak English."

"Mrs. Van Camp said he did. To the Romans he wrote: 'And not only so, but we glory in tribulations also: knowing that tribulation worketh patience; and patience, experience; and experience, hope: and hope maketh not ashamed; because the love of God is shed abroad in our hearts by the Holy Ghost which is given unto us.' Fifth chapter of Romans, verses three through five. There you are, Mr. Sherbourne. Do you see how theological I can be?"

"You certainly are." Edmund was intrigued to hear her quoting the New Testament. "Miss Rosse, I must say I am relieved to hear that you do, after all, know something of the saving work of Jesus Christ. I confess I was beginning to wonder if you knew much about Him at all."

"Do not be absurd, Mr. Sherbourne. Christians worship Jesus, as you so wisely reminded the rajah of Krishnangar. I had Jesus in silver. The statue was quite small and shiny, and I lost it inside the palace. The eldest rani knocked it from my hand. I thought it terribly cruel of her, for I had gotten Jesus from my mother, who believed in Him most sincerely."

"You got Jesus from your mother?"

"Yes, after she died. But there again, my own wickedness came into play. You see, I had decided at Krishnangar that I did not believe in Him — or in any of the gods, for that matter. That might be why I nearly had to marry the tumorous rajah, for one cannot doubt the gods without severe repercussions. When I told Moumita I had left all the gods at Krishnangar, she was horrified and hurried off to the bazaar to buy more. Now we have Ganesha, Kali, and Hanuman, all in gold, as well as a large supply of incense. But we no longer have Jesus, and I cannot think where we shall get another unless you can purchase Him in England."

Edmund could hardly think how to begin untangling the massive knot of semantics. "Upon my word, madam, you do express yourself most unusually! I presume you speak of a crucifix, which your mother no doubt wore on a chain around her neck. And yes, I believe you may be able to procure another one when we reach England."

"Mine was a silver one on a cross. You could carry him in the palm of your hand, and he was so delicately crafted that —"

*"Meye!"* Moumita Choudhary's voice cut off her words. "Why are you not in your cabin?"

"I am with Mr. Sherbourne," the young

woman called over her shoulder. "We are discussing matters of great doctrinal import."

Miss Rosse tossed her head, and a tendril of golden hair came loose from the roll pinned at her nape. The long tress drifted in the breeze and came to rest on Edmund's chest, an event that momentarily paralyzed him. Though the little Hindu woman approached, he discovered he could do nothing but gaze at his white shirt and the silken threads that now embroidered it in gold.

Oblivious to his discomfort, Mrs. Choudhary began to scold her charge in rapid-fire Bengali. Her pointed finger flew as she gestured toward the dining room, then to the cabins below deck, out to the ocean, and repeatedly at Edmund himself. No sooner did she take a breath than Miss Rosse responded with equal ardor in a torrent of Bengali that rushed past Edmund's ears like so much water. In moments, the two were shouting at each other, both gesticulating with arms, fingers, and chins. And all the while, Edmund stared down at the length of golden hair that had settled like a seal emblazoned upon his shirt.

"Do you hear what she says?" Miss Rosse turned upon Edmund all at once. With a fling of her hand, she caught the loose hair, tugged it away from the row of buttons on Edmund's shirt, and flipped it behind her shoulder. "This silly *ayah* believes you have dangerous intentions toward me! Have you no response to her accusations, Mr. Sherbourne?"

He gaped, his mind completely blank. "None."

"But you championed me so boldly before the rajah! You are a brave man, and you ought to defend yourself now. How can you say nothing to her?"

"I did not . . ." Swallowing, he forced his focus from Miss Rosse's hair to her eyes. "You are both speaking too rapidly for me."

The young woman set her hands on her hips and gave her head such a shake of fury that the entire knot of hair at her nape came loose and was captured by the wind like a brilliant golden flag. "Allow me to translate then. She very plainly stated that you are a man, and therefore, you cannot be trusted to behave properly! She insists that I am to go directly from the dining room to my cabin each night, and that to be seen conversing with you in public will bring the worst sort of luck. She says that on the journey down to Calcutta from Krishnangar you looked at me very often, even though I

223

assured her that you never did look at me no matter how hard I tried to capture your attention. Can you even listen to such infamous accusations? Must you not defend yourself against these falsehoods?"

Edmund glanced back and forth between the two women. "Madam," he said to the younger, "I fear my Bengali is hardly adequate to the task."

"Oh, hang your Bengali! Anyone who has lived in West Bengal at all ought to speak it well enough to defend himself."

"But I did not have as good a teacher as yours, Miss Rosse," he said, attempting a smile at Mrs. Choudhary, who was glaring at him with her small dark eyes. "Although I did not understand all of what your *ayah* was saying, I feel quite certain she means you well. In fact, I agree it is best for you not to walk about on the deck at night."

"You do it. Why should I not?"

"You are a lady."

"I can keep my balance as well as any man."

"Dear Miss Rosse, you can hardly even curtsy! One wave followed by a deep trough and you are likely to go straight overboard."

"Oh!" She pursed her lips. "And I suppose you can curtsy very well indeed."

"A gentleman never curtsies."

Her eyes narrowed. "I wager that I curtsy better than you speak Bengali."

"That is probably quite true."

"Well, then, you ought to learn it." She grabbed her loose hair, divided it into three equal strands, and in full view of him, she began to braid. "Very well, Mr. Sherbourne. I can see that Moumita and I must take it upon ourselves to teach you to speak proper Bengali, for you cannot return to Calcutta in such an ignorant state. We shall do lessons in the daytime, here on deck where everyone may see that you have no improper intentions toward me."

Edmund considered the opportunity with far more trepidation than she could imagine. Certainly the thought of lessons in the befuddling language from two women who knew both English and Bengali tempted him greatly. But dare he spend hours in the presence of Miss Rosse?

Even now, she absently tugged a ribbon from her sleeve and began to tie it around the end of her long braid. This loosed the scrap of fabric that had been puffed over her arm and sent it flipping about in the breeze, which left Edmund nothing to do but stare in blank wonder at the supple curve of her bare shoulder.

What on earth was wrong with him? Had

he been so long denied the companionship of females that he was rendered an utter fool by the first of them to come along? Or was Miss Rosse truly as bemusing and enchanting as she seemed?

"What do you think of my plan, Moumita?" she was asking her *ayah*. "We shall teach Bengali to Mr. Sherbourne every morning at teatime, and then in the afternoon, we shall make a review of his efforts and evaluate his progress."

"I think you ought to go to your cabin and stop being naughty!" Mrs. Choudhary snapped. "Your father will throw me into the sea if he learns of your misbehavior."

"Shall we see you tomorrow morning, sir?" she asked Edmund, turning her back on the *ayah*. "Tea is served on deck at ten."

He gripped the railing. "Miss Rosse, I begin to concur with your father. You are a tribulation."

She beamed. "And I concur with St. Paul. 'We glory in tribulations,' Mr. Sherbourne, 'knowing that tribulation worketh patience; and patience, experience; and experience, hope: and hope maketh not ashamed; because the love of God is shed abroad in our hearts by the Holy Ghost which is given unto us.' "

With a laugh, she flung her braid behind

226

her, took her *ayah*'s hand, and skipped away.

Violet could not think when she had ever been so disappointed. Though she had taken great pains to plan a marvelous Bengali lesson for Mr. Sherbourne, it was not to be. The following morning shortly after breakfast, the *Scaleby Castle* sailed into harbor at Mombasa, a city on the eastern coast of Africa. Mr. Rosse ordered his daughter and her *ayah* to accompany him and several other passengers on a sight-seeing mission into the old town.

The family of Brahmans had drifted away weeks before on a smaller boat headed for Ceylon, and now all that remained to show any interest in the outing were the deaf doctor and two of the East India Company merchants' wives. Though Violet searched carefully among the sailors and passengers scurrying about the deck as the anchor dropped, she caught not even a glimpse of Mr. Sherbourne. With much disappointment at having to give up on her Bengali lesson — and Mr. Sherbourne's expressive green eyes along with it — she boarded a bobbing little outrigger without him.

The journey to shore saw her sandwiched between Mrs. Congleton and Moumita on a damp plank of wood. The former shrieked as each wave lifted the narrow boat out of the water and then sent it rushing downward in a stomach-clenching plunge. Violet would have laughed out loud at the sheer pleasure of the bright morning were she not immobilized by the hold her little *ayah* had around her middle. Eyes closed and head bowed, Moumita murmured prayers to every Hindu god Violet had ever heard of and many more besides.

As the outrigger skimmed toward shore, a line of coconut palms came into view behind a stretch of sand as white as salt. Beneath the turquoise water, schools of bright fish darted to and fro in flashes of green, turquoise, and yellow. Starfish tipped with crimson lay along the sandy ocean bed, while shells and corals of every hue clustered like flower beds planted by a master gardener.

When the boat scraped up onto the sand, Mrs. Congleton let out a screech that halted even the traders who had been much engaged in shouting prices back and forth to each other. Violet looked up in time to see a group of sailors crossing the beach not a hundred paces away — and among them was the object of her recent musings.

"Mr. Sherbourne!" she shouted. "Oh,

Mr. Sherbourne, it is I — Violet Rosse!"

"Quiet, daughter!" her father scolded. "What do you mean by crying out in such a manner? Give a thought to your reputation."

"But there is Mr. Sherbourne, and see how he walks away without us."

"He is not to be among our party. Captain Loch informed me at breakfast that Sherbourne is afire to visit a church built two hundred years ago by the Portuguese. Can you imagine anything more deadly dull, Mrs. Congleton?"

The woman, who had by now hoisted her skirts to an entirely unbecoming height above her ankles, gave Mr. Rosse a flutter of eyelash. "Why, no, sir. I should think such a church must be polluted by every sort of heathen riffraff by now. We go into town, do we not?"

Up to his thighs in water, Mr. Rosse held out his hand to Mrs. Congleton. Violet barely stifled a cry of shock as the woman promptly sank into his arms and begged him to carry her ashore. To Violet's further surprise, her father did not drop Mrs. Congleton straight into the sea as he ought to have done. Instead, he sloshed his way toward the land, set her on her feet on the beach, and held out his arm to escort her to

229

the shade of the palm trees.

"Do you see that?" Violet asked Moumita. "Look at my father and Mrs. Congleton!"

"He wishes to take her into his bed," Moumita observed bluntly as she and Violet clambered out of the boat and staggered onto the warm sand without the slightest assistance from anyone.

"But he cannot do that! Mrs. Congleton belongs to Mr. Congleton. They are married!"

"Do you think marriage stops men from trying to get whatever they want? Oh, *meye,* you are foolish."

Violet scowled as she hurried to catch up to the rest of the party. After her mother died, her father had brought several Betsys into the home. Violet was not so foolish as to suppose he kept these women from his bed. But she had always believed marriage was meant to be something truly special. A promise that ought not be broken. An agreement between two people who intended to keep only to each other and not go hopping in and out of other people's beds.

Despite the brilliant morning sunshine, the day had taken a rather unpleasant turn. Violet did not like the thought of Mrs. Congleton dallying with her father. Mr.

Congleton had unwisely stayed on the ship. To make things worse, Moumita kept grumbling that the weight of the seawater in her sari was pulling it from her petticoat. The deaf doctor was shouting at the other person in the party, a Mrs. Ambridge, who shouted back at him, neither making sense to the other. And Mr. Sherbourne had quite vanished between two thatched huts that perched among the palms.

Perhaps this was why the young missionary had never married, Violet mused as she followed the others along a path toward the old city. He seemed a gentleman of high scruples who would not stand for his wife going off in a boat and then leaping into another man's arms at the first opportunity. And Mr. Sherbourne would be unlikely to welcome any woman leaping into his own arms. He certainly did his best to avoid Violet. Contrary to Moumita's claim, he had not looked at her often during their journey from Krishnangar. Mr. Sherbourne had insisted that Violet remain in India rather than accompany the minister on the ship. He refused to escort her when Mr. Rosse told him that she would be going. And then he hid in his cabin as though he were dreadfully ashamed of something.

Perhaps he was, Violet thought. Perhaps

Mr. Sherbourne once had been a pirate like those her father had told her about — men who roved the open seas looting other ships of their gold and slitting the throats of mutinous sailors. Or perhaps he was a vile murderer who feared he might be driven to kill again at the slightest provocation. Maybe he was a thief who had barely escaped the hangman's noose and —

"Do hurry along, Violet!" Mr. Rosse stood at the corner of a large stone building and beckoned. "Mrs. Congleton wishes to look inside the shops. You must not keep her waiting."

"Oh, certainly not," Violet muttered under her breath.

Having determined to be mean-spirited toward Mrs. Congleton and to ignore her father completely, she was taken quite by surprise when she rounded the building and stepped onto a street that swept her straight back to Calcutta. Like fat little men, open sacks of spices sat about on the steps of small shops. Curry, cloves, cardamom — the scents swirled about Violet's head in a delicious blend. She beheld strings of garlic, mounds of red chilies, piles of mangoes, and squawking chickens tied together by their feet as she lifted her skirt and hurried along the cobbled road.

"I feel as if I am back in India!" she exclaimed.

Her father nodded. "You might as well be. Did you not see those lateen-rigged boats moored in the harbor? They are *dhows,* and they sail back and forth on the trade winds. The monsoons blow to the southwest between June and October bringing *dhows* here from India and Oman. And from December to April, the winds blow in the opposite direction to take them back again."

"Such a clever plan," Violet murmured, pondering how wise the gods had been to design the world in such a way. Thinking of religion put her in mind of Mr. Sherbourne again. The English God — though Mr. Sherbourne had insisted He was not actually English at all — must be extremely powerful to have persuaded a well-born gentleman to abandon his friends and family, his athletic pursuits, and even the possibility of marriage and children, in favor of toiling in a foreign land. Violet had been unwilling to leave India, and she could not imagine any deity persuasive enough to convince her to spend her whole life in his service — going where he willed, doing what he asked, obeying his every wish. But perhaps Jesus was such a god, for Mr. Sherbourne and Dr. Carey and many others had done just that.

If the truth were known, Violet could not say she understood much about Jesus Christ. Moumita knew nothing at all of Him and, therefore, had imparted no wisdom, teachings, or tales of Him to her charge. Through prints of famous artworks, books of religious poetry, and even a few lessons from the Bible, Violet's various tutors had brought Jesus to their pupil's attention. But other than poor Mrs. Van Camp, who had hardly benefited by her love for Him at all, her tutors had given only superficial attention to this God. And poor Mrs. Van Camp's many misfortunes had made Violet extremely leery of Jesus.

What sort of God would rain down such disasters upon His loyal followers? The more Violet had studied the paintings of Jesus hanging on the cross and the more she gazed upon His sad face, the less she admired Him. Jesus was nothing like Ganesha — he of the cheerful elephant head and perky trunk. The crucified man certainly caused nothing like the fear that bloody Kali, with her black skin and skull necklace, induced in her followers. And God was never seen frolicking with voluptuous, half-naked female gods, as Krishna did.

No, indeed. If her mother had not been so fond of Jesus, Violet might have put Him in a drawer and never thought of Him again. As it was, she had always set the silver statue up among the others and lit incense before it, and washed it, and brought it mangoes and rice, and otherwise honored it with the others.

"This city was built by Arab and Portuguese traders," Mr. Rosse was telling Mrs. Congleton as they promenaded arm in arm ahead of the others. Violet realized with a sickening thud in her stomach that her father was trying to impress the woman with his knowledge of the region. Moumita had been correct. He gave every appearance of wanting to seduce Mrs. Congleton.

"Slavery built many of the cities along the east coast of Africa," he announced grandly. "Kilwa is the largest slaving port between Zanzibar and Mozambique. Do you know, my dear, that the French have more than fifty thousand slaves on the island of Mauritius?"

"Good heavens," Mrs. Congleton said with a giggle, as though this were delightful news.

Fuming, Violet paused before a shoemaker's stall. The sandals she saw must have been made by Muslims, she realized, for they were crafted of cowhide and quite supple. She considered purchasing a pair adorned with tiny turquoise beads and small round mirrors, but the thought of walking across dank and soggy moorlands in such footwear deterred her. What sort of shoes did one wear in Yorkshire?

"Sayyid Sa'id al-Busa'idi holds the Omani throne at Muscat," Mr. Rosse proclaimed loudly. "He is only twenty-three years old, but he poses a constant threat to Mombasa. The governor here, a Mazrui by the name of Abdullah, has appealed to the British at Bombay to protect the city's independence."

"Are we assisting?" Mrs. Congleton asked as Violet caught up with them.

"We are, but most unhappily. The Mazrui keep more than one hundred and fifty thousand slaves on Zanzibar, an island not far down the coast, and Abdullah hopes the British will assist him in preserving his despicable trade. As you know, our good King George and his Parliament are violently opposed to slavery. Yet we help Abdullah, because we far prefer negotiating with the Mazrui over the Omanis."

"Dreadful!" At this, Mrs. Congleton leaned her head on Mr. Rosse's shoulder, as if he might protect her from the savagery of the feuding Arabs.

"We fully expect Sayyid Sa'id to send his Omani troops to attack Mombasa or Pate or one of the other cities in the region at any time."

As Violet stopped to inspect a stack of brightly colored saris, she saw her father lean down and whisper something in Mrs. Congleton's ear. At the next moment, Violet glanced down a narrow alley to discover Mr. Sherbourne standing beside the carved wooden door of the old church. And in the moment after that, she left the saris, her father and Mrs. Congleton, the deaf doctor and his shouting companion, and even Moumita, who had paused at a stall a few yards behind and was buying some seed to chew.

Violet picked up her skirt, stepped over a puddle on the cobblestone path, and crossed to the church. "Good morning, Mr. Sherbourne," she said, making him the best curtsy of her career.

He turned in surprise. "Miss Rosse? I thought you meant to tour the city with your father."

She gave a little shrug. "My father is quite occupied with Mrs. Congleton at the moment," she told him. "Under the circumstances, I thought it most prudent to take my leave of them. At least for the afternoon."

The smile that lit up his green eyes at the sight of her told Violet she had done exactly the right thing.

# Ten

"It is indeed a church," Edmund said as he escorted Violet out of the humid air of Mombasa town and into the cool sanctuary. "A very old one. The Portuguese built it almost two hundred years ago."

"Much as they did the fort we sailed past on the way into the harbor?" she asked. Seating herself on one of the smooth wooden pews, Violet folded her hands and gazed up at the paintings that adorned the walls. "My father told me that Portuguese invaders crafted Fort Jesus out of coral blocks. They must have been very fond of Him."

"Fond of whom?" Against his better judgment, Edmund sat down beside her.

"Jesus. They named their fort after Him, and they built Him this church." She turned and studied Edmund for a moment. "You prefer Him, too; do you not? You sailed to India to tell people about Jesus. I must say I find that an odd thing to have done."

"As I recall, you and I previously acknowledged that we think each other rather odd. I have never met anyone quite like you, Miss Rosse."

"Really? But I am common. In fact, the more I consider the matter, the more I think perhaps I am not so fascinating as I should have hoped. After all, I am accomplished only in botany and Bengali."

"Few of us are accomplished in anything — yet you may boast two areas of proficiency."

"But knowing the flora of India and speaking Bengali will hardly serve me in Yorkshire. I fear it must be as you said, Mr. Sherbourne, and I shall not fit into society there at all. Moumita and I have for several years been attempting to pin my hair in rolls, but we have not discovered the proper method. I cannot make trivial conversation at the tea table. I know nothing of dancing or embroideries. And, as you said, I am quite hopeless at curtsying."

"You made a very good one just now outside the church."

"Did I?"

She appeared so pleased at this news that Edmund had to swallow down his urge to tell her how wonderfully uncommon she really was. Her speech fascinated him. Her approach to life intrigued him. And her beauty . . . Miss Rosse was beyond compare.

"Why did you think it important to bring Jesus to India?" she asked him, her blue eyes shining. "The people there have plenty of gods already. Do you truly believe you can convince them that Jesus is better than the gods they already know? And the Portuguese carried Him all the way to Africa. Tell me, Mr. Sherbourne, are people taking Him everywhere?"

Her childlike question softened Edmund's heart toward her even more. "As much as they are able, Miss Rosse. Telling others about Jesus is a Christian commandment. I confess I have been unsuccessful in winning souls to Christ, but that does not excuse me from trying. Jesus' very last words to His disciples were an order to go and make followers in all nations, baptizing them into the name of the Father and of the Son and of the Holy Spirit, and then to teach these new disciples to obey all His commands. A true Christian must be obedient to this final mandate."

"Oh, dear," she said softly. "I cannot think that I have told anyone at all about Him."

"Perhaps you do not know what to say."

"That is quite true." She sighed. "Well, I suppose I shall learn it all at the finishing school."

"They do not teach Christianity at finishing schools, Miss Rosse. There you will learn manners and etiquette. But you will not learn what is truly important."

"But if I am to be properly English, Mr. Sherbourne, I must be Christian in every way — although I confess that I do find it hard to imagine myself sailing about the globe to tell others of Jesus. One must be very pleased indeed with one's god to take such extreme measures. The only thing I like that much is orchids."

She leaned toward him and spoke in a low voice. "I shall make you another confession, Mr. Sherbourne, but you must not let Moumita know of it. Nor must you take offense."

Uncomfortable with her closeness, Edmund struggled against the urge to leap up from the bench and flee the church. The last time he had been so near a woman, his behavior had reflected the carnal life he then lived. He thanked God for the ten thousandth time for changing him, and he prayed for strength in the present moment.

With the scent of Violet's hair in his nostrils and the press of her shoulder against his, Edmund felt a rush of sudden desire hammer in his chest and make him ache to take this beguiling creature into his arms.

But she was promised to another man. And Edmund was promised to God. Nothing could compromise that. Nothing.

His resolve steeled, he nodded, encouraging her to confess this secret truth that burdened her.

"I do not think very highly of any god," she admitted. "Not one of them. Even Jesus."

Edmund tried to think how to respond, but his brain had turned to porridge. Before he could form one sensible word, Violet rose and stepped toward a series of religious scenes that had been carved into the coral wall. Slumping over for a moment, he breathed the quickest and most earnest prayer of his life. It consisted of only one word — *Help!* — but it could not have been more heartfelt.

He had no resistance to Violet Rosse, and every fiber of his being now demanded action. As on the morning he had rescued her from the rajah of Krishnangar, Edmund knew the surge of tension in his muscles and the incredible heat that poured through his chest. He must have her. He must take her as his own. Everything within him commanded it.

And yet he must surrender. To purity. To truth. To goodness. To honor. Christ must

243

rule within him, and flesh must fall under subjugation to the Holy Spirit.

"Oh, these poor gentlemen!" Violet exclaimed, clearly unaware of the torture her presence was inflicting on this poor gentleman. "This sign says that Father Prior and the chaplain of Fort Jesus were killed for refusing to convert to Islam."

Edmund forced himself to his feet and walked toward the plaque she was reading. Aware of God's comforting counsel, he took a deep breath. "Religion has been at the heart of many wars, Miss Rosse," he began. "Believers attempt to convert others — sometimes by force — and conflicts arise. We Christians are hardly exempt from the sin of trying to force our faith onto those we have conquered. But the true believer understands that surrender to Jesus must come as a result of genuine faith. That sort of faith will survive any assault."

"I do not have faith like that," Violet said. Turning, she gazed up at him. "Do you think me very wicked, Mr. Sherbourne?"

He smiled. "I think you entirely innocent, Miss Rosse. You know too little of the harsh realities of life to have been tainted toward any wickedness."

"On the contrary, I know a great deal about harsh reality. I have grown up among lepers and cripples and orphans. I have seen corpses of people drowned in floods, and I once observed a widow burning alive inside a *suttee* fire. I have watched children die of starvation, and my own mother perished of a pestilent disease. My whole life has been cobras and tigers and cholera and monsoon floods. Not to mention my father's succession of Betsys. Indeed, I am so far from innocence as to be quite blackened by the stain of the world."

"Oh, how far from the truth this is, Miss Rosse. The realities of which you speak are brought by life itself, by the corruption sin brought to this fallen world. But what do you know of mankind's foul heart? Have you seen how alcohol can ruin a man and destroy his family? Do you know the pain that divorce can bring? Have you watched war divide one nation or bring terror upon another? What do you know of real evil — of murder, treachery, prostitution, thievery, betrayal? No, you have been sheltered inside the compound walls with your *ayah* and your gold bangles and your tutors. Not even your forays into the bazaar have tainted you, Miss Rosse."

"If I am so wonderful, I should be enjoying God's greatest gifts," she countered. "But I have been willful and disobedient all

245

my life. That is why I now reap the painful consequences of my wickedness. I am forced onto a ship that sails away from my beloved homeland. I am torn from my only true love . . . the orchids of India. I am swept away to a man I do not know . . . a merchant . . . a man very much like my father who may . . . who may one day find himself a Mrs. Congleton . . ."

To Edmund's utter dismay, he realized that Violet was weeping. She covered her face with her hands and broke into sobs. "I am sorry, but I do not wish to go to England," she cried softly. "I shall not like it there, and I shall never again see an orchid, and Mr. Cunliffe may be . . . ugly . . . and devious . . . and . . . and . . ."

"There, now," Edmund said, laying a hand on her shoulder. "It will not be so bad. I shall introduce you to my brothers, and I am confident they will know of some very nice ladies who —"

"Oh, Mr. Sherbourne!" With a sob, she wrapped her arms around him and laid her head on his shoulder. "I shall never again go to the Botanic Garden or roam the bazaar or walk along the banks of the Hooghly."

"No, but you will see the hedgerows of Yorkshire." Touched by her distress, Edmund folded her into his embrace and held her close. "Dear Miss Rosse, I assure you the streams are very pretty, and the sheep are . . . oh, bosh, I have nearly forgotten how it looks myself."

"It is all moorlands!" she wailed.

He could not deny it. Yorkshire *was* nearly all moorlands, and he honestly could not make himself remember a single thing to recommend them. The moors were cold and windy and foggy and nothing at all like the lush, tropical jungles of India that he had grudgingly tolerated for five long years. York's quaint little shops along cobbled streets seemed drab compared to Calcutta's teeming bazaars with their rich mingling of sounds and smells, which he once had found so offensive. And what was a sheep next to a tiger? No, there was nothing that could even approach . . .

"Oh, violets!" he exclaimed suddenly.

"What?" She lifted her head, her cheeks streaked with tears. "Did you call my name?"

"I was speaking of flowers, Miss Rosse." As gently as he could, Edmund set her away from him. "Violets are worth every pain you will face in leaving India. Small and delicate, they are as lovely as any orchid. Their fragrance is enchanting. Their color is . . . well, it is very like your eyes. Please, dear lady, have hope. God has not abandoned you, nor is He punishing you for your failings. God is with you. He has a marvelous plan for your life if only you are willing to submit to His guidance."

"God has a plan for me?" she asked, wiping her cheek with the back of her hand. "How can you possibly know such a thing?"

"Again and again, the Bible repeats this promise. In Jeremiah, God says, 'For I know the thoughts that I think toward you . . . thoughts of peace and not of evil. . . . Then shall ye call upon Me, and ye shall go and pray unto Me, and I will hearken unto you. And ye shall seek Me, and find Me, when ye shall search for Me with all your heart.' In Matthew, Jesus assures His followers, 'Lo, I am with you alway, even unto the end of the world.' "

Edmund tugged a handkerchief from his pocket and gave it to her. "Here, Miss Rosse. A lady always carries a handkerchief."

"I am not a lady!" she said, breaking into sobs again and weeping into the square of white fabric. "I am not anything I ought to be!"

Without thinking, Edmund took her into his arms again and drew her near. Never in his life had he felt such tenderness toward

248

any creature. If he had the power, he would do anything to comfort her. A part of his mind plotted to whisk her back to India, somehow do away with her father and Alfred Cunliffe, install her in a house filled to the ceiling with orchids, and make her as happy as she had the right to be.

What was the point of that kind of thinking? He had no right even to hold her as he was doing now. She did not belong to him, and he had not been designated by God to defend her from misery. He had his own heavenly commission, and she was to spend her life with another man. Yet, the ache in his heart could not be denied.

"Sweet Violet," he murmured, his lips pressed to her warm, golden hair. "How I long to keep the vow I made to your *ayah*. Could I ease your every pain, I should do it without hesitation. But you must be strong — as I know you are. You must —"

"Mr. Sherbourne, is that you?" The voice echoed against the whitewashed coral walls. "I say, my good man, it is very dark in here. Are you there? Have you seen my daughter?"

Just as Edmund turned, Violet sank to the floor. From the corner of his eye, he could see her duck under the bench and out of her father's line of vision.

"Good morning, Mr. Rosse." Edmund stepped forward quickly to greet the man. His heart hammered so loudly he felt certain it must be heard all the way up to the high wood beams that supported the church's roof. "This is a surprise indeed. I thought you must be touring the city with your party."

"We had hardly begun when my daughter vanished." Mr. Rosse uttered an oath so vile Edmund wondered that the beamed ceiling did not suddenly collapse upon their heads. "I ought to beat her soundly. She will have gone straight into the jungle, of course. We shall miss the departure of the *Scaleby Castle*, and I must be forced to stay in Mombasa until I can find her and book passage on another ship."

"I cannot imagine she would wish to cause you such consternation, Mr. Rosse," Edmund said as he watched a dark shape edging from the shadows of one bench to another down the length of the church. "Your daughter is a woman of great moral character, I believe. Perhaps she was merely diverted by some unexpected attraction."

"You think that, do you? Well, you have much to learn about her, Mr. Sherbourne." As Edmund saw the dark figure slip through a side door and out into the street, Mr.

Rosse frowned. "If Violet is aboard our ship this evening, I shall shake your hand for a wiser man than I suspected."

"I look forward to the event, sir." Edmund let out a deep breath of relief. "I have great faith in Miss Rosse. Clearly, she is distraught at the prospect of a future in a country foreign to her. She dreads marriage to a man she does not know. Yet I am confident she means to complete the task you have set before her."

"And how do you have such faith?"

Edmund smiled. "I am a man of faith, after all, sir."

"Bah!"

"Mr. Rosse, your daughter has given every evidence of her submission to your will. After the frightful events at Krishnangar, she knew she had no choice but to do as you asked. She boarded the ship, and I am certain she means to complete the journey. In fact," he said, arriving at a conclusion he realized God had placed before him, "Miss Rosse told me herself that she intends to be aboard the *Scaleby Castle* tomorrow morning."

"She told you that?"

"In a manner of speaking. She has offered to give me Bengali lessons. She and Mrs. Choudhary had planned to begin this morning had not the ship docked at Mombasa Harbor."

"Mrs. Choudhary? Who is that?"

"Her *ayah,* of course. You cannot suppose I should be seen alone with your daughter, sir. Indeed, I must do all in my power to protect her reputation as well as my own."

"Well," Mr. Rosse said. He cleared his throat. "Aha. Bengali lessons."

"Your daughter seemed quite enthusiastic at the opportunity to assist me."

"Mr. Rosse? Are you there?" The female voice at the door caused both men to turn. Mrs. Congleton stepped into the church and waved a glove. "We have found her! We have found your daughter! Miss Rosse was looking at saris, if you can imagine."

At that, into the church crowded the entire touring party from the *Scaleby Castle* — the deaf doctor, the two merchants' wives, and the little *ayah.* Moumita dragged Violet through the door and pushed her toward Mr. Rosse.

"Violet Sarah Rosse!" he exclaimed. "Where have you been?"

"I am sorry, Father," the young woman said. She looked down at the floor. "I was momentarily distracted."

Mr. Rosse took off his hat and slapped it

on his thigh. "I thought you had run away again! By heaven, I should leave you here! Perhaps the natives would cook you and eat you for dinner. Serve you right. Cheeky girl!"

Brushing past her, he took Mrs. Congleton's arm and led the rest of the party back out into the morning. Violet eyed Edmund for a moment as a slow grin crept across her face.

"Good day, Mr. Sherbourne," she said.

He swallowed as she turned and hurried after the others. "Good day . . . dear, beautiful lady," he murmured.

*"Tumi kothae thako?"* Violet asked.

Seated beside her at a tea table on the deck of the *Scaleby Castle*, Edmund translated the question into English. "Where do you live?"

Violet nodded in satisfaction. "Very good, sir."

As he answered, *"Ami e grame thaki* — I live in this village," she had to congratulate herself on her success.

In the past month, they had left Mombasa, made port briefly in Zanzibar, rounded the southern cape of Africa, and sailed up the west coast of that continent, making a brisk pace toward their destination. In the meantime, Mr. Sherbourne had learned his alphabet, his greetings, his numbers, and was making a brisk pace toward proficiency in Bengali. Every morning, promptly at ten, they joined Moumita for tea on deck. Every afternoon, promptly at four, they returned to their tea table to practice once again. Edmund turned brown from the sun, became a regular in the dining room, and despite past evidence to the contrary, proved himself quite adept at learning Bengali. Violet turned pink from the sun, learned to tolerate tuna, and despite past evidence to the contrary, proved herself patient, cooperative, and helpful.

Edmund had insisted from the beginning that they talk of nothing but Bengali, and Violet had to agree. Although their stolen moments together that morning in the Portuguese church haunted her, she sensed that Edmund viewed her as nothing more interesting than his language teacher. He focused all his attention on the pages of conversational lessons that she had laboriously inked for him. Working with intense effort, he practiced forming the curious curls and horizontal lines of Bengali letters. And when not otherwise occupied, he stared out to sea.

When his gaze did accidentally fall upon

Violet, he went almost utterly mute, and she had no doubt it arose from his distaste of her. In fact, he must feel himself somehow tainted by her, much as a Brahman would upon inadvertently brushing the arm of an Untouchable. Violet knew this because if their hands accidentally met over the sugar bowl, he immediately whisked a small black Bible from his coat pocket and began to read it as if to purify himself.

Though she did not like to dwell on this truth, Violet came to believe that Edmund considered her more than a little repulsive. He had spoken with disdain of her Indian habits — going barefoot, wearing bangles, sucking her teeth after a meal. And he believed her chances of transformation to be slim indeed.

So did Violet. She abhorred the thought of taking up needle and thread. After all, sari embroidery was done by poor women of one of the lowest castes, and Violet could not imagine that English ladies actually enjoyed such a laborious task as a hobby. She dreaded the very idea of dancing at balls, for as Edmund had noted, she could hardly curtsy. Her feet went wherever they liked, it seemed, and they were more sure on a stony jungle path than on a slick marble floor. Except with Moumita, Violet did not enjoy making idle conversation, moreover, for she preferred to have some purpose in everything she said — whether it be a discussion of Bengali verb forms or the identification of botanical names of flower species.

But worse than her bad Indian habits and her failed English prospects was her poor appearance. No matter how hard Violet and Moumita tried to put her hair up in coils and poufs, it all came tumbling down at the first strong gust of ocean breeze. When once by chance a strand of her blonde monkey hair happened to fall upon Edmund's arm, he stared at it as though it had sullied him.

No matter how much Violet liked Edmund — and she did, very much indeed — he was determined to keep their acquaintance merely as friendship. He allowed nothing more intimate than the time of day or an observation on the weather to cross his lips. He bowed each time they met, addressed her as "Miss Rosse" without fail, and smiled very much more at Moumita than he did at her. In fact, Violet began to wonder if he had taken a fancy to the *ayah,* who was, after all, not more than five years his senior.

*"Apni amar ekhane ca?"* Edmund asked, breaking into Violet's thoughts.

She looked up at him and their eyes met.

"I am having tea, quite obviously."

"No, it was part of the lesson, Miss Rosse. I am to ask if you want to have tea. You see?"

He showed her the page she had written out the night before. Violet looked at it and then back at him. She glanced at Moumita, who, as always, was dozing off during the afternoon lesson. Leaning forward across the table so as not to disturb her, Violet addressed Edmund. "I am very tired of these lessons, Mr. Sherbourne, and I believe it is time to cease them altogether. *Apni khub bhalo bangla baulen* — you speak Bengali very well. There. Enough."

"*Dhanyabad. Ami bangla likhte o porte o shikhechhi.* Thank you. I have also learned to read and write Bengali."

"Stop it!" She grabbed the page out of his hands. "Now you are not even using the lesson I wrote."

"No, because you have taught me enough Bengali to speak on my own. In fact, Miss Rosse, you have given me such confidence that I believe I might one day have a real conversation with someone."

"Will you talk about the weather?" she asked. "Or would you prefer to discuss the time?"

He glanced at Moumita, whose eyes had

slid open and whose mouth now curved into a grin. "Mrs. Choudhary," Edmund asked the small woman, *"tumi keno hashcho?"*

"You ask why she is laughing?" Violet spoke for her *ayah*. "I shall tell you the answer. She laughs because many times I have told her how annoyed I am that you discuss nothing of interest beyond the weather and the time. Mr. Sherbourne, if the other English gentlemen in Yorkshire are anything like you, I shall most certainly go mad of boredom."

"Of course I discuss nothing of interest, Miss Rosse," he protested. "This is not an occasion for conversation. We are studying Bengali."

"Yes, and when we pause from our lessons for even a moment, we talk only of the time or the weather."

He turned his focus to the sea. "Well, it *has* been looking a good deal like rain of late."

"Upon my word, sir, you are the most infuriating man!" She tossed the day's lessons down on the table. "Yes, it usually rains in the morning, and sometimes in the afternoon, and — dear heaven — occasionally even at night! And when it is not raining, to everyone's astonishment, it is sunny! We have clouds and sun and rain and ocean.

That is all, Mr. Sherbourne, and it is deadly dull."

He shifted in his chair. As she had anticipated, the very next moment he took out his pocket watch and glanced down at it. "Five o'clock," he said. "It is rather early to end the lesson, but I suppose —"

"Talk to me, Mr. Sherbourne!" Violet hissed. "Tell me something of interest. What was your life like before you sailed to India? Did you have tutors? Did you learn how to dance?" She caught her breath. "Perhaps you ought to teach me to dance! Yes, we must make a trade. Bengali lessons in exchange for dancing lessons."

"No, I —" he ran a finger around the back of his collar — "I am not overly fond of dancing, Miss Rosse. I believe, in fact, that it can lead to licentious behavior. I am convinced it does, actually. In Yorkshire, you ought to avoid going to balls if possible. There will be men who —"

"Who what?" She leaned toward him, genuinely interested. "What sort of men will I find at balls?"

"Bad ones," he said. Before she could respond, he took out his small black Bible and opened it. "Of late, I have been reading in the book of Proverbs, and I —"

"Hang Proverbs!" Violet cried, snatching

the Bible from his hands and leaping to her feet. As her chair tipped over onto the deck, she raced to the rail and flung the little book as far as she could into the ocean. The sound of its splash barely registered over the snapping sails, groaning masts, and rushing wind.

"There, Mr. Sherbourne!" she cried, swinging around and clutching the rail behind her. "That is what I think of your silly Bible!"

To her dismay, she observed Edmund's face darken and his eyes narrow. Like an angry bull, he rose from his chair and charged across the deck toward her. "You threw God's holy Word into the sea!" he bellowed into Violet's face. "You desecrated my Bible!"

She lifted her chin. "Yes, I did, and what of it?"

"That . . . that . . ." He looked over her shoulder. "It is gone! I scarcely believe what I just saw!"

"I say good riddance."

"How could you do that?" Teeth clenched, he glared at her. "It was mine! Mr. Fuller gave it to me!"

"Well, you are better off without it. It made you very boring and not the least bit —"

"I do not care if I am boring! I am not meant to be interesting!"

"Yes, you are," she hurled back at him. "You have been interesting before. You were thrilling at Krishnangar. I thought I had never met such a bold and marvelous man. And when you returned to my house in Calcutta to assert my right to stay in India, you amazed and delighted me. You . . . you said I was beautiful! I heard you say it. And in the church at Mombasa —"

"Do not talk of that!" he warned, his forefinger extended in her face. "You very nearly disgraced me before all the party. If we had been seen, I might have lost my support from the missionary society."

"You told me you were rich! What sort of support can you possibly need from a missionary society?"

"I need their prayers, something which you — a heathen of the worst sort — clearly do not understand!"

"You call me a heathen?" She set her hands on her hips. "How dare you say such a thing!"

"Yes, you are a heathen!" he shouted at her. "I cannot believe I have not seen it before this. You threw my Bible into the Atlantic Ocean! You callously discarded the Word of the Lord! You have no respect for

Christianity. Indeed, you are entirely ignorant of the whole Christian faith! You are as
blind and misguided and lost as . . . as . . . as
Mrs. Choudhary!"

Violet glanced at Moumita, who was
looking on with her hands clapped to her
cheeks and her dark eyes wide with fear.

"My *ayah* is a Hindu," Violet said, enun-
ciating each word. "I am not!"

"No? Then who is Jesus Christ?"

"He is a pathetic God who got Himself
nailed to a cross and who forces people to
sail the seas telling others about Him even
though He turns them into boring, stupid,
lifeless slugs!"

Fearing she must burst into tears at any
moment, Violet picked up her skirts and
started for the steep wooden staircase that
led down to her cabin. She could hear
Moumita scurrying to follow, but before
Violet took the first step, Edmund's hand
clamped over her arm.

"Miss Rosse," he said as he whirled her
around to face him. "I am *not* a slug."

She stared at him — all green eyes and
flaring nostrils and heated face. Fierce and
manly. He was a warrior now and not some
pale scholar hiding in his cabin. The
muscle in his arm flexed as he drew her
closer.

"Do you hear me, Miss Rosse?" he demanded.

"I hear you," she answered. "You are not a slug. Not at this moment. But unless you are very careful, you shall become one. Then there will be nothing left for me to do but pour salt on you and watch you melt in order to keep you from eating the life out of the orchids."

Without thinking, she stood on tiptoe and kissed his lips. "I am an orchid," she said softly, "and you must not eat away my life."

He dropped her arm at once. Taking a step back, he wiped the back of his hand across his mouth. "Please, Miss Rosse," he said, his voice husky, "do not *ever* do that again."

Looking away, she nodded, aware of how revolting it must be to endure such an intimacy from a monkey-haired heathen like herself. "I am sorry, sir," she said. "It was wrong of me."

"Yes, it was," he said in a low voice. "Very wrong indeed. You are entirely obstreperous, Miss Rosse. You threw my Bible into the sea. You are promised to Mr. Cunliffe. And you are altogether and totally wrong . . . wrong for me."

"Yes, Mr. Sherbourne. I promise I shall never do it again. Any of it."

His green eyes deepened. "No?"

"Never."

He swallowed as he nodded. "Good. That is very good. And right. And moral. And proper."

She turned to go, but he caught her again. "And boring," he added, taking her in his arms and pressing his lips to hers. "Miss Rosse, forgive me," he whispered, kissing her again. His hands slid up her back, and his fingers threaded through her hair. "I ought not . . . I must not . . ."

As he kissed her once more, Violet felt someone jerk her by the hair, snapping her head back and nearly causing her to fall. *"Bas!"* Moumita cried out, barging between the two of them. "Enough. Come, *meye.*"

The small woman shoved Violet onto the steep staircase. As Violet reached the deck below, her head dizzy with joy and her heart singing, she heard Moumita scolding Edmund overhead. In a flood of Bengali, the *ayah* cursed him and his entire family for fifteen generations, wished them every scrap of bad *kharma* in the universe, and vowed to pray to the gods that all Sherbournes would be reincarnated as dung beetles.

*"Ekhon ektu ektu brishti porche!"* Edmund shouted back at her. *"Pacta*

264

bejece!" "It is drizzling now," he had said. "It is five o'clock."

Violet laughed aloud. *Yes, Edmund Sherbourne, resort to the weather and time when you can think of nothing else to say. But I know you better now, and you are most certainly not a slug.*

# Eleven

The *Scaleby Castle* dropped anchor at the city of Cape Coast in the Bight of Benin off the coast of West Africa. Mortified and repentant at his reproachful behavior toward her, Edmund had done all in his power to avoid the young lady in the days following his kiss. No, his *three* kisses. Thrice he had pressed his mouth against hers. Thrice he had drunk of her sweetness. Thrice he had permitted himself the luxury of hedonistic passion.

What a fool.

After that reckless moment, he could not get Violet out of his head. When he had learned that she intended to tour Cape Coast with her father's party again, he determined he must stay aboard the ship in order to avoid her. But he had weakened, and like a sot in search of his next drink, he boarded a small boat and combed the port city in search of her. Unable to contain himself, he had purchased a length of fine blue cotton embroidered with tiny white flowers, a comb carved of ebony, and a bracelet of hammered gold. When such gifts seemed insufficient to reward her magnificent beauty, his eye fell upon the perfect and most wonderful treasure of all. High in a tree grew an orchid — a fragile thing with glossy green leaves and fragrant yellow flowers. Edmund had climbed the tree, carefully lifted away the orchid, and bought a small clay pot in which to set it.

He might have gone on in such a way, heedless to all his training and beliefs, had he not rounded a street corner and come upon a slave market. The sight of such profound misery, such sinful abuse by those who whipped and heckled their fellow man, such unconscionable wickedness and unadulterated suffering brought him to his senses at once. He had not been called away from England to pursue a blue-eyed enchantress; he had been commissioned by his Lord to preach the gospel to people such as these who now cowered before him on the auction block!

Standing with his packets under one arm and the orchid in his hand, Edmund suddenly saw himself as God must see him. What on earth had he been doing? What had possessed him to succumb to such a temptress — a woman with neither faith in the one true God nor understanding of Edmund's very purpose in life.

Violet Rosse had thrown his Bible into the sea! She had verbally demeaned Christ's sacrifice. She cared nothing for Christianity, nor did she make any apology for her views. No, indeed, she had blatantly confessed that she did not think highly of God.

Were he not careful, Edmund knew he must soon admit himself to be in love with her. Impossible! Not only had her father attached her to Mr. Cunliffe, but she was an unbeliever. Rather than kissing her and tracking her through a city in Africa, he ought to be teaching her about Christ. Rather than viewing her as the potential fulfillment of his own fleshly desire, he should see her as a lost soul in need of a Savior.

How stupid he had been! What an addlepated fool! How could he have spent so much time in her company and been blinded to the truth? So many things now made sense — Violet's comments about her "silver Jesus," her frequent comparisons of Jesus to the Hindu gods she knew so well, and especially her reluctance to trust Christ for her future. Despite her English birth and her white skin, Violet was no more Christian than her Hindu *ayah.*

Edmund had seen himself as a missionary

sent to bring the Light of Life to such wretches as these poor slaves who stood without hope and without faith on the auction block. He believed God had sent him to teach Hindus and Muslims about Christ Jesus and His ultimate sacrifice. He thought he was to witness to people of a different color, tongue, and custom.

And right before him had stood a young lady who was among the most needy of all. Violet Rosse knew nothing of Christ. She had been taught by her *ayah* to worship idols. And she had concluded that God was not worth her time or respect.

And what had Edmund done to change her poor opinion of God? Nothing. Nothing but hide from her until she had lured him into her presence with the offer of Bengali lessons. Nothing but gaze at her with love-sick eyes and then kiss her only moments after she had hurled God's holy Word into the ocean.

Utterly disgusted with himself, Edmund returned to the *Scaleby Castle* and hurried to his cabin, where he fell to his knees in repentance. As he prayed, he felt a complete certainty that Violet must become his new mission. She and her *ayah,* like all people, needed to hear the beautiful message of Christ's love.

But Violet did not appear at the dinner table that night, and her father mentioned that she had returned from the tour of the city feeling unwell. The next day, Mrs. Choudhary came to the tea table at ten o'clock as usual, but she informed Edmund that Miss Rosse would no longer teach him Bengali. She was ill.

Could it be a ruse? Day after day, Edmund sat at the table watching the green shores of Africa slip away and wondering if his brash behavior had so unsettled Violet that she believed she must avoid him. Or had Mrs. Choudhary confined her to the cabin out of fear that another such despicable scene might occur? Or had her father learned of the indiscretion and ordered her to keep out of sight? Worse, might the man in his rage have harmed his daughter?

Certain he was the cause of Violet's disappearance, Edmund berated himself. Ought he to write her a letter of apology? Ought he to approach her father and offer to make atonement for his behavior? Or ought he simply to accept that he would never meet the young lady again, while counting himself blessed to have escaped the turmoil she caused in him?

"Sahib?" The tap on his shoulder brought Edmund out of his unhappy thoughts. He turned to find the small *ayah* standing nearby, hands knotted before her. "Sahib, you are a holy man. You must come and make prayers now. You must chant. And if you have brought holy water from the Ganges, you must put it on the *meye,* for she is dying."

"Dying?" Edmund leapt to his feet. "You cannot mean it. Is Miss Rosse truly ill?"

"Yes, sahib." The woman's face crumpled. "She cannot live another day."

"But an entire week has passed since we left the port. Upon my word, why was I not told of this before now? Is there not a ship's surgeon aboard? Has Captain Loch been informed of the situation?"

"Come, sahib," Mrs. Choudhary urged, taking his arm. "You come now and pray for her. It is too late for doctors."

Hardly able to accept what he was hearing as truth, Edmund ran to the staircase and took the steps down two at a time. He knew Violet's cabin was at the far end of the corridor, for they sometimes encountered each other on their way to a meal or a Bengali lesson.

"Miss Rosse?" He knocked softly on her door, and it fell open. "Dear Miss Rosse!"

The odor of illness hit him as though he had run into a brick wall. A dark pall hung about the cabin, an oak-paneled room crowded with trunks and lit by only a single gimbaled lantern. With no window to admit fresh air or sunshine, the chamber had become a cramped and darkened coffin. The small shape lying on the wooden bunk did not move, yet Edmund heard muffled moans of agony. Dropping to one knee at bedside, he took the thin hand that lay atop a damp sheet.

"Miss Rosse, it is I, Edmund Sherbourne," he addressed her gently. "I come as a minister of God, and I shall do all in my power to assist you."

Her eyelids slid open and she gazed at him. "Mr. Sherbourne? Thank the gods, you have come. Somehow I have swallowed a tiger. Please, sir, I beg you . . . can you drive it away with your saber?"

Alarmed at her delirium, Edmund brushed a strand of hair from Violet's flushed cheek. "Miss Rosse, have you been seen by a doctor? Does your father know of your condition?"

Attempting futilely to moisten her dry lips, she squeezed his hand. "How are you, Mr. Sherbourne? You are looking very well."

"Thank you, Miss Rosse, but I must tell you I am most concerned as to your well-being." He turned to the *ayah*. "Mrs. Choudhary, I adjure you to fetch Mr. Rosse at once! He must be informed of his daughter's illness. And the captain has to be told, as well. The ship should weigh anchor at the nearest port, and we must find Miss Rosse a doctor."

"Yes, sahib!" With a wail of despair, the *ayah* vanished.

"You need water," Edmund assessed. "You must be bathed and placed in a dry bed. Dear lady, do you suffer fever?"

"You are very brown," she murmured. "I fear you are not wearing your hat, Mr. Sherbourne."

"Miss Rosse, may I be so bold as to place my hand on your forehead to ascertain —"

"I should prefer to go to the bazaar, sir. I very much fancy a banana."

"A banana? Yes, of course. You shall have one at once." He set his hand on her brow. The blazing heat told him she was consumed with fever. "I must see that cold water is brought at once. Have you eaten anything at all in this past week, Miss Rosse?"

"I should like a banana," she repeated. "A yellow one. Small and sweet. Not the long green ones, Mr. Sherbourne. They are bitter."

"Indeed, we shall find you a banana immediately." As he got to his feet, he heard the thunder of boots down the corridor. Momentarily, Mr. Rosse, Captain Loch, Mrs. Congleton, and Mrs. Choudhary all crowded into the room.

"Pfaugh!" Mr. Rosse cried, jerking his handkerchief from his pocket. "This odor is enough to kill anyone! What have you done to my daughter, you wicked little Hindu?"

"Oh, sahib!" Moumita fell prostrate onto the floor and clutched the man's foot. "Please do not throw me into the ocean, sahib! I have tried to care for her, but she does not improve!"

"Fool!" He shoved the small woman with his boot, sending her scrambling to a corner of the room.

"I say, sir," Edmund cried, stepping forward. "How dare you abuse Mrs. Choudhary in such a manner! Upon my word, I shall see you reported for such a deed. Captain Loch, may we heave to port at once? Miss Rosse must see a doctor. An English one, if at all possible."

The captain squared his broad shoulders. "Mr. Sherbourne, we are fast at sea and pushed along by a good wind. We have passed Dakar already, I fear. We shall not pass another port with a doctor of any nationality until we reach Casablanca."

"How long, Captain?"

"Another week at least."

Mr. Rosse burst out with a profane oath and made for the little *ayah,* who was cowering behind a wooden trunk. "This is your fault!" he bellowed. "You told me nothing but that my daughter was unwell. Had I known she was so gravely ill, I should have tended her at once! I shall have you beaten and thrown into the sea that the sharks may —"

"Mr. Rosse, this is hardly helpful," Edmund cut in. "With your permission, Captain Loch, I shall carry the young lady to another cabin while this one is thoroughly cleaned and the bedding is changed. We must have cool water to bathe her if we mean to reduce her fever, sir, and I beg you to search your ship's apothecary box for any medicines that may be of use."

"Of course, my good man. But I have no free cabin. Can you take her to the deck? Perhaps the fresh air will do her good."

"Fresh air is known to cause all manner of vile illnesses," Mrs. Congleton spoke up. "Chills and colds and agues. I believe the poor thing ought to be bled. It is her only hope. Captain Loch, surely you have been trained to cut the vein and drain out ill humors."

"I can do that, aye, and I shall be glad to offer my services."

"Have you any leeches, sir?"

Frustrated by the ongoing discussion, Edmund bent down and scooped Violet off the bed. "I shall take her to my own cabin until hers is made ready, sir. Captain Loch, if you will see to the provision of fresh water, I shall be much obliged. And she wants a banana."

"Aye, sir. Very good, sir," the captain said with a bow. "I shall bring the medicine box to your cabin and, of course, the surgical implements required for bleeding."

"Thank you, Captain. Mr. Rosse, if you would be so good as to restrain yourself from any further mistreatment of Mrs. Choudhary, you will find her to be very much use to us." Turning to the small woman, he spoke in Bengali. "Please clean the room and throw out the refuse. Provide clean sheets for the *meye*'s bunk. Fetch her a new pillow. And when you have done that, come to my cabin, where you may begin to care for her again."

A pair of dark eyes appeared over the top of the trunk. "That evil sahib will throw me into the sea," she murmured in a tremulous

276

voice. "I shall be eaten by a big fish with sharp teeth."

"*Na,* Memsahib Choudhary," Edmund said gently. "I shall look after you. I give you my vow."

Unwilling to delay a moment longer, Edmund carried Violet out of the cabin and down the corridor. She weighed nothing, and he drew her closer against him to assure her of her safety. Her loose golden hair swept the floor, and her arm dangled from her shoulder, but her blue eyes searched his face.

"You kissed me once," she said.

Edmund's heart faltered. "Please do not speak of that, Miss Rosse. It was a grave error on my part."

"I liked it."

He shook his head as he kneed open the door to his cabin. Though he now had no Bible, he retained all of his scriptural concordances, commentaries, and theology texts. These lay strewn across his bunk, where he had been studying them that morning. Before he could think how to proceed, Moumita's arms appeared in his vision as she whisked the books to a side table and drew back the sheet.

"She will die," the woman whispered in Bengali. "It is my fault. I have killed her."

"What on earth can you mean by such a statement, Mrs. Choudhary?" Edmund asked, wondering if he had misunderstood her. He settled Violet on the bed and drew the sheet up to her chin. "How have you killed her?"

"I did not tell the sahib to come to her room because I was afraid of him. I did not tell you to come because I was angry with you. Now she will die, and I will never see my *meye* again!"

With that, Moumita burst into keening wails of such intense volume that Edmund instinctively covered his ears. Regaining his presence of mind, he clapped his hand over her open mouth and shook her by the shoulder. "For heaven's sake, Mrs. Choudhary," he ordered in English, "do not carry on so. Miss Rosse is not gone yet. Go back to her room at once, and clean it."

"I shall be reincarnated as a caterpillar!"

"Dash it all, madam," he cried. "You shall not become a caterpillar or any other such creature. If I had done my duty to God, you might eagerly anticipate walking streets of gold. As it is, you . . . well, just get on with you!"

As Moumita left the room, a young shipmate no more than fourteen years of age hurried into the cabin with a pail of water

278

that sloshed from side to side with his every step. " 'Tis rainwater, sir," he announced. "Very soft and sweet. I drink it meself from time to time."

"Good work, lad." Edmund took the bucket and dipped a clean cup into it. "See that you bring me another pailful with which to wash her."

"She is very pretty. All the sailors fancy her."

"All the sailors should keep their fancies under better rein. Now, be gone with you, lad!" Growing increasingly annoyed, Edmund slid an arm under Violet's shoulders and lifted her head. Her eyes met his. All dark fringed lashes and great blue depths, they seemed to cry out to him for help.

"I have clean, fresh water for you, Miss Rosse," he said. "Please take a sip."

As he slowly trickled the liquid between her dry lips, she swallowed. No sooner had she done so than she curled over and began to retch. So depleted that nothing was expelled, she groaned in anguish.

"There, there." Edmund drew her close as shudders racked her body. "I am here, my dearest. I shall not leave you."

"Oh, Edmund . . ." She clutched his sleeve, her fingers thin and white on the fabric. "Hold me, please, for I am going to die."

"Nonsense." He could hardly bring himself to speak another word. "You must banish such thoughts. Captain Loch brings medicines even now. Your father means to do all in his power for you. And I . . . well, I shall pray for you. I ought to have done it at once."

"Where is Jesus?" she murmured. "I wish to look at Him while you pray."

Edmund cradled her as the spasms subsided. "Jesus is here with us, in this very place. He has promised that wherever two or more are gathered in His name, He is there among them."

"But I cannot see Him. Go and fetch yours, please, Mr. Sherbourne. I lost my Jesus at Krishnangar. The silver one."

Silent for a moment, Edmund tried to think what to say. "Dear Miss Rosse, Jesus is not a silver statue. He is not any sort of idol or man-made object. Rather, Jesus is the living God who has sent His Holy Spirit to dwell in us. This Spirit of God cannot be seen, but if we serve Him, we will feel His presence every day. He has promised that if we seek Him, we shall find Him. Shall we go before Him now?"

"Oh, yes. Please, sir."

Edmund held her against his chest and bowed his head. "Dear Father, we beseech You now on behalf of Violet Rosse. You have called Yourself by the name Jehovah Rapha — God Who Heals. I beg You now —" he swallowed, fighting the emotion that threatened to undo him — "I beg You, most Holy God, to heal Miss Rosse of this violent illness that has beset her. Lay Your hand upon her body and restore her to perfect health. Lay Your Holy Spirit upon her impoverished soul that she may know You. Make Your presence felt by her, that she may surrender to Your saving power. I pray all of this, in the precious name of my Lord and Savior, Jesus Christ."

"Very good, Mr. Sherbourne," Violet's father said as he stepped into the room, followed by the captain, Mrs. Congleton, and the shipmate carrying a second pail of rainwater. "Nothing like a prayer to solemnize the occasion. Might do us some good, as well, eh? Come then, Captain Loch. Show us what you have in the medicine box. I believe Mrs. Congleton was correct, and my daughter warrants a good bleeding."

Things were not as they should be. All her trunks had been carried away. A stack of books in leather bindings lay upon the table where her sandalwood jewelry box was meant to stand. The bed on which she lay was not in its proper corner. And high on a shelf, all alone and forlorn, sat an orchid.

An orchid!

"I am in India again," she said with gratitude, but her voice sounded as though it belonged to another person entirely. She listened to its echo in the small, wood-paneled room and wondered if she had indeed spoken. Perhaps the words had come from elsewhere, though she knew she had said them herself.

Studying the orchid, she saw that its blooms were yellow — three long, drooping canes laden with golden blossoms. Seven leathery green leaves sprouted from the base of a small clay pot inlaid with strange red and blue beads. She had never seen such an orchid in her whole life.

"Am I in Calcutta?" she asked in someone else's voice.

"*Meye?*" Moumita's face suddenly took the place of the orchid. Two black eyes and haphazard teeth adorned the woman's familiar thin nose, mouth, and glossy black hair.

Violet blinked. "*Ayah,* please tell the *mali* to come and talk to me at once. I must know where he found that orchid."

Moumita let out a shriek as though she had seen a demon. The door banged behind her as she fled the room.

Violet sighed. Why had the gods not given her an ordinary mother?

She enjoyed remembering her first mother — a flaxen-haired, wispy creature who always wore purple gowns and lay in her chair fanning herself while drinking something pale and pink in a tall glass. That mother had clutched her small silver Jesus and wept and told Violet to go out into the garden to play.

The second mother had been this small, dark-eyed imp who ordered Violet about, hugged her tightly, braided her hair, taught her to pray, and was given to loud arguing and the occasional wild screech. Moumita Choudhary had been a good mother, all in all, but Violet did consider herself quite prepared now to be on her own.

She looked at the orchid again just to make certain it was still there. How could an orchid grow in a dark corner of a room at the top of a shelf without sunshine or rainwater? Where was the *mali?* A gardener would know such things, and despite Violet's ongoing tribulations with her father's knock-kneed *mali*, she did respect his knowledge of plants.

The skinny old man had labored inside the Rosse compound for as long as Violet could remember. When she had brought home her first orchid and mistakenly planted it in the rich black soil of the rose bed, the *mali* had taken great offense and had torn it out and thrown it into the fire. That is when Violet had slapped him. Later, however, he helped to build her orchid collection — hanging the plants in baskets from the trees and tending them as one might a favorite child.

"Moumita, where is the *mali?*" she called. That silly *ayah* had no doubt gone off and forgotten her mission. She was probably in the kitchen even now sampling the curry and dipping her fingers into the lentil soup. Wondering why she could not hear the usual bustle of the servants in the corridors, Violet pushed herself up from her pillow. At once, a sharp pain shot through her head and the room tilted on its side.

With a frightened cry, she grabbed for the edge of the bed as she tumbled to the floor. As she landed on the hard wood, her head hit the corner of the table. Stars spread out across the ceiling, and the walls swam in and out as though they were made of water.

"Moumita!" she wailed. *"Ma!"*

*"Meye!"* The *ayah*'s face appeared inside

the melting, oozing room, then Mr. Sherbourne's green eyes emerged from somewhere near the door, and her father's mouth tiptoed in and out of the scene all the while shouting, "Pick her up! Pick her up, you idiot!"

Strong arms wrapped around Violet, Mr. Sherbourne's chest pressed against her cheek, and his voice slid down into her head. "There, now, dear lady."

She turned her face and buried her nose against his neck. He smelled of sunshine and cotton and clean shaving soap, and as she drank in deep breaths of him, the world stopped spinning. Holding on to his arm, she fought the tides of panic and waited for the stomach pains she knew must come.

But they did not come, and now she remembered that she was not in India, and the *mali* could not toddle in from the garden, and there was no orchid in the corner. They were all sailing to the moorlands on the *Scaleby Castle*, and she must go to finishing school and marry Alfred Cunliffe and never again smell Edmund's clean neck.

"You ought not to have left her alone!" Mr. Rosse admonished Moumita. "Look, she has fallen out of bed, and who knows what else might have happened to her if we had not come in when we did! Had I given it half a thought, I should have abandoned you to the streets of Calcutta where you belong!"

"Really, Mr. Rosse," Edmund said. Like a cat's purr, the rumble of his deep voice settled into the pit of Violet's stomach. "Can you leave off this chastisement for once and see to your daughter's health?"

Violet snuggled in closer to him, hoping he would go on talking. Everything he said felt like magic, a sweet dream that sifted down through her and calmed her every fear. She could go on this way forever, she realized. Nothing else mattered. Not Moumita or Calcutta. Not her father. Certainly not Mr. Cunliffe. Not even orchids.

In Edmund's arms, she was safe and warm and at peace. All her life, she had been taught that if she was good enough, she might deserve the right to be born again into a better life. If she were lucky, she might be reborn a Hindu. If she earned exceptionally wonderful *kharma,* she might even return to life as a Brahman. The ultimate goal was Nirvana — a blissful state in which all cares and worries were banished.

And here she was! All her wicked sins notwithstanding, Violet had somehow been blessed by the gods and placed into the Nirvana of Edmund Sherbourne's embrace.

"Put her down!" her father's voice intruded into her sweet dream. "That is my daughter, Mr. Sherbourne, and I do not like the manner in which you are holding her."

"I merely lifted her from the floor where she had fallen." Edmund drew her closer, as if to protect her from her father's wrath. "Sir, this poor woman has suffered every manner of difficulty. She was nearly burned on a *suttee* fire. She has been forced to leave the only home she ever knew. She was put on a ship and deprived of every joy in her life. And now she has fallen so ill as to assure us all of her imminent death. Yet you find things to criticize in those who seek to help her?"

"Yes, I do! You are entirely too familiar. Put her onto the bed again at once." Mr. Rosse cleared his throat. "Mr. Sherbourne, may I remind you that the *suttee* incident was entirely Violet's own fault? May I beg you to acknowledge me the privilege of every English gentleman — that of making his daughter a decent marriage? And may I request that you not lay blame for her illness upon me or any other?"

"You may, sir. But you may not make any assumptions regarding my familiarity toward your daughter. I assure you that although I have the highest regard for her, I view her as merely another lamb in the fold of the Almighty."

"Then put her down, by George! And stop . . . stop cradling her! *Ayah,* see that her ankles are covered."

Instantly, Violet knew the sorrowful absence of Edmund's broad chest and warm neck. Deposited back onto the cold, hard bunk, she groaned and curled into a ball as if she might preserve something of him deep inside herself. She felt very weak. Like an orchid blossom at the end of its bloom. At any moment, she might come loose and float away on the breeze, a mere shadow of what she once had been.

"You are too much occupied with my daughter, Mr. Sherbourne," her father was shouting. "How many hours of every day have you spent at her side? Ten? Fifteen?"

"Upon my word, she is most unwell, and I am a minister! I should be derelict indeed were I to abandon anyone at such a time. Sir, inside this room, we have been always in the company of Mrs. Choudhary. The majority of my time has been spent in prayer. That and reading."

"And talking Bengali," Moumita put in.

Violet smiled at that. Now that she thought of it, she recalled their voices in the room . . . Moumita and Edmund . . . the soft ebb and flow of Bengali as they discussed houses and shopping and the proper way to make a cup of tea.

"Yes, I have practiced my language skills," Edmund admitted. "I have found Mrs. Choudhary's assistance to be most useful."

"And feeding," Moumita told Mr. Rosse. "The holy sahib is feeding your daughter. It is always a banana. He makes her drink water, also. And we change the sheets and pillows every day. Sometimes he sings —"

"Thank you, Mrs. Choudhary," Edmund cut in. "I believe Mr. Rosse understands the scope of our care for his daughter. I merely minister to her needs, sir. Were you ill, I should do the same."

"You would sing to me? I think not!" Violet's father harrumphed. "At any rate, she is awake now, and better. Captain Loch tells me the *Scaleby Castle* is expected to make port next week in London, and I mean to take her directly to York where she will not be bothered by oversolicitous ministers!"

"You cannot mean that, sir. You would transport Miss Rosse to York by land? Why not take a bark to Hull and thence inland? I believe your daughter should have as much rest as possible. In fact, if you so choose, I should welcome all three of you to stop at

Thorne Lodge for as long as you wish."

"All three of us?"

"You intend to take Mrs. Choudhary, do you not?"

"Ah. Well, yes, of course." He paused, as though to remind himself that Moumita was actually a person. "Have you room enough at your estate?"

"Mr. Rosse, the house is very large, I assure you. One wing of it could contain all the contents of your compound at Calcutta with plenty of room for you, your daughter, and all your servants."

"My goodness."

"And I have no doubt of my brother's warm welcome. He will be very happy to meet all of you."

"But this new wife of his? I understand there to be some question as to her character."

Violet was growing sleepy again as her father and Edmund chatted back and forth. She felt grateful to be free of the pain that had twisted through her insides and tied everything into terrible knots. Though she was thirsty and her arms felt as fragile as butterfly wings, she sensed that all was well. Her father was talking of transporting her to Edmund's house. And Edmund himself stood just to the side of her bed, his tall form nearly blocking the light of the lamp and his hand just inches from her face. She studied his fingers, the way they curved just so. Strong nails. Perfect knuckles. Coarse gold hair covering his bronzed arm.

Yes, this was all very good indeed.

"If your sister-in-law's family is as disreputable as you suggest, Mr. Sherbourne, I cannot countenance taking my daughter into her presence at all."

"Nor should I ever suggest that you do so," Edmund replied. "Yet I am certain one of two things has occurred. Either my intelligence about their marriage was somehow in error, or the lady has undergone a great transformation. My brother Randolph is in every respect a gentleman of high standing and great moral virtue. In no way would he undertake a marriage that might threaten his own reputation or that of our family name."

"Very well, then," Violet's father said. "We shall accept your offer and remain at Thorne Lodge until my daughter is recovered enough to be transported to York. I thank you, Mr. Sherbourne. So long as your motives are pure and your intent is amiable, I can see no reason to subject Violet to undue stress."

"I assure you, Mr. Rosse, my concern for

your daughter is of godly impetus. I have no feeling for her whatsoever beyond that of a minister for an ailing soul."

"You do not . . . fancy Violet?" Mr. Rosse asked. "As a woman, I mean?"

"Certainly not. My loyalty is to God. I have committed myself to Him alone. Indeed, it is my aim to see that Miss Rosse is made well enough that I might return to India with every assurance of her health and well-being."

"Ah . . . excellent. Then, perhaps you might be so good as to perform her wedding ceremony to Mr. Cunliffe."

At that, Violet opened her eyes and looked up at Edmund. He was staring at her father. Nearby, his hand closed into a fist that whitened his knuckles and sent ripples through the muscles of his forearm.

"Perform her wedding?" he asked. "Perhaps . . . perhaps I might."

"Good. Very good." Violet's father stepped to the door. "Carry on with your ministry, then, Mr. Sherbourne. Good afternoon to you." Without another glance at Violet, he left the room, shutting the door behind him.

Moumita let out a sigh and sank down onto a stool near the bed. Edmund stood staring after Mr. Rosse, his back to Violet and his fist still clenched.

She tried to feel as happy as she had a moment before, but the joy had quite left her heart. Edmund did not fancy her, he had said. Certainly not. He did not see her as a woman. No, his love was only for God.

Edmund meant to help her get well enough to marry Alfred Cunliffe. That was all. Well enough so that he could go back to India.

Well enough to leave her.

Unable to move, unable to protest or argue or stamp her foot or any of the things she had always done to express her strong opinions and emotions, Violet lay on the bed and gazed at the plane of white sheet that stretched out before her eyes. This was all. She had nothing, then. Nothing but this white sheet and the damp moorlands and Mr. Cunliffe.

"Here is an orchid." Edmund's voice was gentle as he knelt by her bedside. In both hands, he cupped a small clay pot from which an orchid grew.

So she had not imagined it. But now, closer, she could see how greatly the poor thing had suffered. The golden flowers clung to the cane by threads, hanging their heads in sorrow.

"I found this orchid at Cape Coast, Miss

Rosse," he said. "I climbed a tree and brought it down for you. I thought . . . I hoped that perhaps it would please you."

Violet looked at the orchid and then at Edmund's green eyes. "It wants light and water," she whispered. "It is very lovely, sir, but I fear it cannot last."

She lifted her hand to a blossom. As she touched it, the flower separated from the cane and drifted to the floor. "You see?" she said. "It is dying for want of love."

# Twelve

Edmund thought he had never seen anything more beautiful. Outside the coach, an expanse of glittering snow stretched as far as the eye could see.

Like the thick, almond-flavored marzipan icing he had loved as a boy, the snow covered every dale and fell, every granite outcrop, the bare branches of every tree, and the thatched roofs of cottages in the villages that clustered along the roadway. Overhead, the sky climbed endlessly from the horizon like fine Italian marble — a magnificent display of white clouds etched with jagged lines of gray, blue, even black. Shaggy sheep, thick with winter wool, pressed together, barely distinguishable save their simple black faces and slow movement as they ambled along the hedgerows.

And in the midst of all this glory sat the pièce de résistance, a tropical flower in a glowing array of golden hair, sapphire cloak, indigo bonnet, pink cheeks, and violet blue eyes. As she stared out the open window of the coach, Violet Rosse's delicate profile sent a stab of pain through Edmund's heart. How beautiful she was. How utterly perfect.

Yet she was meant for another man, another life, another love.

Though the thought of losing Violet tore through Edmund as nothing ever had, he could thank God for one thing. She was alive. Despite her undiagnosed agonies aboard the ship, Violet had survived. And he knew without doubt that she would continue to survive here in Yorkshire. She would draw sustenance from the dear memories of her Indian childhood, from her beloved *ayah,* and yes, from her new husband and family.

Edmund had to accept this. Violet would go on without him, as he must go on without her.

He had disputed God concerning this matter, but in no way could he hear anything but the truth. God had called Edmund to India. In His servant's darkest hour, God had shone down a light — the promise of a permit to preach and a building in which to worship as a church. As soon as he had satisfied himself that his brother was well, the unexpected marriage was acceptable, and the family name and estate were in good hands, Edmund must return to India.

Violet would marry the man her father had chosen for her. A businessman and landowner, Alfred Cunliffe must be well settled in his life. If not for the death of his childless wife, he might have been content with his lot. Feeling the loss, he had agreed on a satisfactory marriage to his associate's daughter. No doubt one look at Violet Rosse would confirm the wisdom of Cunliffe's arrangement with Rosse. She would make a fine wife, an entrancing jewel in Yorkshire society, and a good mother to the children she would bear him.

In time, Violet would find happiness, too. Of that, Edmund had every confidence. She had confessed her desire for a home and a family, and now she would have them. What more could she want?

"I have never seen anything so gloomy or desolate in all my life," Violet said into the silence of the coach. "Snow is horrid."

Seated alongside Violet, Moumita lifted her head from the layers of woolen scarves around her neck, peered out the window, and nodded. *"Kadarjata,"* she stated. Edmund recognized the Bengali word immediately as a great insult, for the little woman had used it often aboard the *Scaleby Castle* to describe the vast ocean and all the sea monsters it contained.

"You believe the snow to be ugly, Mrs. Choudhary?" he asked in surprise. "Detestable? An abomination?"

*"Ha,* sahib. *Kadarjata."* She nodded again and sank back down into her scarves.

Violet's great blue eyes turned on Edmund. "Surely you cannot disagree, Mr. Sherbourne."

"I can disagree completely. I was thinking just now that I have never seen anything more lovely."

"But I have looked everywhere and can find not one growing thing. Every tree in this forsaken land is dead. Every blade of grass is dry and yellow. Every leaf on every bush is brown, withered, and ready to drop to the ground. Most of the leaves have done so already. It is a barren wilderness with no life at all."

"But surely you know the trees and plants are not dead. They are merely resting. In spring, when the sun shines and the days grow long and warm, the limbs will begin to bud. Bright green leaves will unfurl and flowers will bloom in all their glory once again."

She turned to the window again. "In India, if a tree looks like that one just there by the roadside, it is dead."

"Believe me, Miss Rosse, what you see is not dead."

She gave a small harrumph. "Perhaps you are correct, but I find nothing in it to give me pleasure. An artist would hardly have need of paints to capture the scene. It is every shade of gray from white to black, and no color anywhere. As for the snow itself, it might be pretty enough, but everyone has been walking about in it."

Edmund laughed. "Of course they have! The roads must be traveled and the streets traversed."

"But their footsteps have turned it all to mud and dirt. Look how the snow has been gashed by all the carriages and coaches along this road. It is utterly besmirched."

"And cold," Moumita offered from her cave of scarves. "The snow out there is very cold."

"Well, yes," Edmund agreed. "That is the nature of snow."

As he looked out the window again, he tried to see the scene through the eyes of these two women who had never encountered such a phenomenon of nature. To Edmund, snow was both familiar and delightful. It filled him with memories of Christmas trees, sledding down hills, throwing snowballs at his brothers, Randolph and William, and spending countless hours watching snowflakes fall as he sat beside the fire with his dear family.

In his childhood, Edmund had considered the occasional snowfall great fun — a blissful change from endless winter days of frost and fog and soggy rain. As a man, he found it a beautiful reminder of his heavenly Father's creative majesty. Only God could have thought to transform water droplets into white crystals — no two alike — that fell like feathers from the sky.

But Violet and her *ayah* had no such pleasant memories or happy encounters with winter weather. To them, snow was as foreign as the monsoon rains had been to Edmund when he first arrived in India. Until he came to realize that when the flooded rivers finally receded, they left behind the fertile silt that provided moist black soil for crops, Edmund had greatly disliked the season. He hated the weeks of constant rain and heat; the swarming clouds of mosquitoes; the threat of cobras; the mold and mildew that grew on clothing, walls, and food; and the flooded streets that made it impossible to travel except by boat. Several seasons passed before he came to accept the beauty and beneficence of the monsoons.

Now Edmund willed himself to view winter in a new way as well. Through the eyes of an alien unaccustomed to snow, it was strange and uncomfortable and perhaps unsettling.

"Does the snow frighten you?" he asked Violet in a low voice. Her father had been dozing all morning, and even now, Mr. Rosse's head bumped against Edmund's shoulder. Though his inquiring was not of an intimate nature, he did not want to embarrass the young lady.

But rather than shame, tears filled her eyes. "Of course I am frightened," she said, her nose turning pink as she tried not to cry. "Yorkshire is as horrid a place as I had imagined. Indeed, it is worse. You tell me that the trees will have leaves again, Mr. Sherbourne, but how can I know that what you say is true?"

"You must have faith, Miss Rosse. In fact, our conversation illustrates the very essence of faith. In his letter to the Hebrews, St. Paul tells us that faith is the assurance of those things for which we hope. Faith is the certainty of that which we cannot see. But like the disciples who knew the Christ, witnessed His resurrected body, and bore testament to His divinity, I have seen the spring, Miss Rosse. I assure you that it will come again. You must trust me."

"It seems I have a great many things to

accept on faith," she said with a sigh. "I am to believe I shall find happiness here. I am to assure myself that Mr. Cunliffe will like me, which I feel quite certain he will not. I am to trust that I shall like him, which is even less certain." She fell silent for a moment. "I do not like very many people, you know. Especially stupid ones who have nothing to say. Here in Yorkshire, I shall be the stupid one with nothing to say."

"Impossible," Edmund said. "I always find you interesting and charming. As I recall, Miss Rosse, you have a great deal to say on any number of subjects."

"India subjects. I have nothing to say on Yorkshire subjects."

"You may be surprised to learn that you have much in common with the people of this country. I am certain my brother will introduce you to many lively young ladies of his society."

"I do not wish to talk to lively young ladies. I wish to go to the Botanic Garden and assist Dr. Wallich in his examination and identification of orchids."

Edmund let out a breath. "That you may no longer do."

"Nor may I go to the bazaar and look at saris. Nor eat sugarcane. Nor buy bangles."

"No, but you may walk down to Otley and

look in all the shopwindows and purchase great numbers of bonnets which you may decorate with ribbons and feathers and jewels. That occupation has always been of great interest to the ladies of my acquaintance."

"I do not like bonnets." She gave a hostile glare at the indigo velvet creation that framed her face. "The brim of a bonnet is too wide. It wraps around my forehead and all the way down to my cheeks, and I cannot see what is above me or beside me but only what is directly ahead. The bow threatens to choke me. And as for the blue flower someone has stitched on the side — well, I can assure you, Mr. Sherbourne, there is no species in all the world that resembles it. Were it not for the chill wind blowing through this open window, I should take off my bonnet at once. But I cannot, for if I did, my ears must surely freeze and break off and fall into my lap."

Edmund tried to stifle a grin. He could see that Violet's tears had vanished and she was now in a petulant mood, an alteration that pleased him no end. Since falling ill, she had been all but transformed from her delightfully opinionated and willful self into a quiet, obedient, malleable waif. Despite himself, he preferred the petulant princess to the submissive invalid.

"If your ears fall off, you will be quite deaf," he said. "And then I may say anything I wish, and you will not hear a word of it."

Glancing at him, she gave the first hint of a smile he had seen since they debarked in Hull on the previous afternoon. "What might you wish to say to me, Mr. Sherbourne?" she asked.

Though he was mightily tempted toward some indiscreet flirtation, the sight of Moumita's dark eyes peering at him from her tunnel of scarves stopped him at once. He studied the scene outside for a moment, recognizing familiar landmarks that told him the coach was nearing Otley at last.

"I should say that I shall be very sad to bid you and your *ayah* farewell. I have enjoyed your company more than I ever thought possible, and I shall miss you both."

"Which of us will you miss the most?" Violet asked.

He thought for a moment. The two dark eyes across the coach glittered. *Careful, Edmund,* he reminded himself.

"I shall miss you equally. You have taught me Bengali and entertained me and shown me things about myself that I did not know."

"What sorts of things?"

"I had not realized why I was such an unsuccessful missionary until you so thoughtfully pointed out all my failings to me. I had been walking about in boots made of cowhide, desecrating the creature that Hindus hold most sacred. Despite the discomfort of my Yorkshire clothing and the uselessness of my British manners in India, I had been clinging to them because I mistakenly believed that to be a Christian meant also to be English in custom and deportment."

She giggled. "That was very silly of you indeed."

"Thank you, Miss Rosse." He nodded at her, and to his delight, she blushed beautifully. "And finally, I have come to understand that the two women I know best and care for with the greatest affection have no saving knowledge of Jesus Christ. Despite my missionary zeal and my best intentions, I have utterly failed to lead you and Mrs. Choudhary into the kingdom of God."

"I think you may have done a better job than you realize," she said. "Moumita told me yesterday that she believes Jesus is the greatest of all the gods."

A jolt of surprise nearly lifted Edmund off his seat. He glanced at the little Indian woman, whose eyes had never left his face.

Her two brows lifted, and she spoke from the folds of her woolen fortress. "I like Jesus," she announced. "That God has made the holy sahib into a good man."

"There, you see?" Violet stated. "Moumita and I both like you very much, Mr. Sherbourne, and therefore we are inclined to like Jesus, as well. Of all the men we know, you are the best." She studied her father as he snored on Edmund's shoulder.

"You are brave," she went on, lowering her voice. "You rescued me from the rajah of Krishnangar. You are kind, for when I was ill, you sat beside me day and night to make certain I had food and water. Moumita told me this. She said you are also very wise. You knew how to mash the bananas for me, and pour water into my mouth, and make my blood stop flowing after Captain Loch had cut my arm. Also, she said that you read many pages in your holy books without looking up or talking aloud. You are able to read all the way through one candle without stopping until it sputters and goes out."

"I suppose that is true," Edmund acknowledged.

"Moumita and I admire these things about you. We believe that you are kind and brave and wise because you are a true Christian. You are not a Christian like my father and the other men and women of the East India Company. They are only Christian by birth and not by belief. But you are a Christian who truly worships Jesus. That is why you are different, Mr. Sherbourne, and that is why Moumita and I have decided to favor Jesus above the other gods."

Edmund listened to this recitation of his attributes with a mixture of wonder and despair. Somehow — despite his bumbling inadequacies and human frailties — he had testified to the life-changing power of Jesus Christ. By trying his best to live as a Christian, he had shown the two women the Light.

His life had illustrated his faith, and yet his words had failed him. How little these women still knew.

"I am glad you have seen my love for Christ," he said, aware that both Violet and Moumita were listening intently. "Yet, what you see in me is only a shadow of His character. Jesus is far wiser than I. In fact, He is omniscient, for He knows all that was and is and ever shall be. He is kinder than I, for His mercy endures forever. And most certainly, Jesus is braver than I. Although He is God — the one and only true God — He chose to give up His own life. Jesus

Christ sacrificed Himself on the cross for me. For *my* sin."

At this, Violet gave a loud gasp and clapped her hand over her mouth. "Oh, I knew it! I knew you were too good to be true! What did you do, Edmund? Did you kill someone? Was it your wife?"

"What . . . what?" Mr. Rosse lifted his head and gave a loud snort. "Who killed someone?"

"Mr. Sherbourne!"

"Upon my word, I never killed anyone!" Edmund squared his shoulders. "Miss Rosse, we are all sinners. You, I, and everyone in this coach. Like sheep, we have gone astray, each of us turning to our own way. But God laid upon Jesus Christ our iniquity. He bore our sin, and by His stripes, we are healed."

"I am not a sinner," Violet averred. "I never killed anyone or stole anything — nothing more than a piece of sugarcane. Perhaps I did slap the *mali* once, but I was very small."

"You slapped the *mali?*" her father growled. "Whatever did you do that for?"

"He tore my orchid out of the ground."

"Your orchid? Are you still ranting about flowers, girl? Why would you slap the *mali* for such a trifle as that? By heaven, you are the one who ought to be slapped — clambering over the compound wall day and night, scampering off to Krishnangar and nearly getting yourself burned alive, vanishing right in the middle of Mombasa, where you might have been captured and sold as a slave! Serve you right, it would. Sell you off to some planter in the Americas. Teach you to go stealing sugarcane from the bazaar and slapping the *mali* for no good reason."

"Mr. Rosse, the pertinent point is that we are *all* sinners," Edmund said before Violet could respond. "You keep Betsy at your beck and call. Your daughter is disobedient and willful. Mrs. Choudhary worships idols. And I . . . I am a sinner also."

"Fancy you to go lording it over me because of Betsy!" Mr. Rosse said loudly. "I shall have you know, she is a very nice young woman and a great comfort to me."

"Idols?" Moumita sputtered from the depths of her scarves. "What does he mean by that, *meye?*"

"I am not always disobedient," Violet protested. "And while you are naming our sins, Mr. Sherbourne, you had better name your own."

Edmund gritted his teeth. Well, he had botched this one. Aflame with the zeal of

Christ's passion, he had managed to indict and offend everyone in the coach. And now he must own up to his own misdeeds. Moumita's face had emerged from her woolen tunnel, and her thin lips tightened in silent accusation. Mr. Rosse glared at Edmund as though the missionary were a scrap of rubbish he had inadvertently stepped on. And Violet's blue eyes glittered with a mixture of dread and curiosity.

"What is your sin, Mr. Sherbourne?" she asked.

He drew down a deep breath. Offered up a prayer of supplication. Attempted to still his heart. "At one time, I was a drunkard," he said at last. "And a libertine."

"What is a libertine?" Moumita asked Violet under her breath.

"A very bad man," Violet whispered back. "With ladies."

Moumita's dark eyes flew open. Violet turned to the open window.

Mr. Rosse let out a bark of laughter. "You? The missionary?" he cried. "By george, this is delicious news."

"Thorne Lodge!" The coachman's voice rang out into the winter afternoon. "All passengers, make ready."

Edmund steadied himself as the coach came to a stop and sat rocking on its bolsters. The footman opened the door, let down the folding steps, and reached inside for Violet's hand.

She gazed at Edmund for a moment, her eyes accusing. Then she picked up her skirt, set her palm into the footman's hand, and slipped out of the coach. As she moved to one side, the front door of Thorne Lodge fell open.

"Edmund? Is it you at last?" Randolph Sherbourne emerged onto the long stone staircase that led from the house down to the snow-covered drive. His face broke into a broad smile. "Welcome!" he cried as his brother stepped out of the coach. "Dear Edmund, welcome home!"

Although Violet had made up her mind to dislike everyone and everything in Yorkshire, she was instantly defeated by the onrush of a lovely young woman who hurried to greet the party just entering the marble-floored foyer of Thorne Lodge. With glossy brown curls, a radiant smile, and a kind voice, the lady embraced Violet as though she were a long-lost friend.

"Welcome, welcome!" she cried, her hands on Violet's shoulders and her deep brown eyes shining with compassion. "You must be Miss Rosse, of whom Mr.

Sherbourne wrote to us in such great detail. Oh, my dear girl, you are surely exhausted from your long journey. You must take off your cloak and bonnet and then come into the parlor to rest. You will want tea, of course, and I have ordered a hearty dinner."

With a laugh, the woman shook her head. "But I forget my manners in all this excitement! I must first introduce myself. I am Olivia Sherbourne, Lady Thorne, and near the door stands my dear husband, Lord Thorne. Randolph, darling, please give your brother a moment to breathe. You must meet his charming guest."

A tall gentleman with chestnut curls and blue eyes broke away from Edmund to give Violet a smart bow. "Miss Rosse!" he said, taking her hand and kissing it gallantly. "Welcome to Thorne. We are delighted to meet you at last. My brother wrote to us from India saying that he might escort you, and we had confirmation of this in a message he sent posthaste after your arrival in Hull. How pleased we are that you are able to stop with us until your recovery is complete."

Violet had wanted to hate him, this Yorkshire man who cared nothing for India and had never been anywhere interesting but had lived his whole life upon his own foggy

312

moorland. Instead, she admired him at once. He had eyes of sapphire and a face very much like Edmund's, yet different in appealing ways. He spoke like Edmund. He bowed exactly like Edmund.

But Violet seriously doubted that this gentleman had ever been a drunkard and a libertine.

She glared at the missionary who was standing near the door and directing the footmen into the house with the trunks. Edmund Sherbourne was no better than her father with all his Betsys. Worse, in fact. Malcolm Rosse drank his wine and port and sherry just like all the men of the East India Company. But he was not a drunkard. Not a drunkard *and* a libertine. One was bad enough. But both? Both?

"Miss Rosse?" Edmund's brother stared at her. He spoke again, more precisely and loudly this time, as though she were deaf. "We are happy to have you here. Welcome to Thorne Lodge."

"Yes, thank you." Violet tried to smile. She did like this man and his brown-eyed wife. But Edmund . . . again her gaze slid across the room. He had said Jesus Christ died on that horrid cross as a human sacrifice. A sacrifice for him. For Edmund!

Violet had seen plenty of sacrifices in her

lifetime. Goats slaughtered in the temple, blood running everywhere, bits of hair stuck to the stone floor. Bowls of rice and bread and curry set out on the altar steps. Pots of fragrant incense burning day and night. Flower garlands and money strewn across the altar where one god or another sat looking out with brass or silver or golden eyes.

These were the sacrifices Violet knew — but they were not *human* sacrifices. Edmund Sherbourne claimed that Jesus was like a bride who had chosen to become *suttee*. He had allowed Himself to be nailed to that cross in order for Edmund's sins to be forgiven. This was too much to comprehend.

Had Edmund really been so bad?

Had Jesus really been so good?

"I did not realize she spoke so little English." Lady Thorne turned to her husband and asked in a low voice, "Did your brother tell you she was unfamiliar with our language? What are we to do? How shall we talk to her?"

They both stared at Violet. She stared back, wondering if they, too, had secret sins so terrible that Jesus had been compelled to die for them as well. Perhaps they were murderers, Lord and Lady Thorne. Edmund had told her he was unhappy with his brother's choice of a wife. That was one reason he had made the journey from India to England. This woman with her sweet smile and soft hands must be a secret sinner. And the man who had married her? What sort of villain was he?

"Ah, I see you have met already," Edmund said, joining them at last. "I regret to tell you that Miss Rosse has suffered a great deal aboard ship. She is very weak, and I am certain a time of rest will do her much good. Thank you, brother, for welcoming her and her party. And . . . Lady Thorne. How interesting . . . how pleasant, of course, to . . . to know you."

She smiled, warmth radiating from her brown eyes. "This need not be awkward for us, Mr. Sherbourne. I am well aware that our families have been at war these many generations. But allow me to assure you how completely all enmity has been erased between us. I love your brother as dearly as I love my own. And more! Our meeting was no accident — although we believed quite differently at the time. Had God not brought Randolph and me together, Thorne and Chatham should be fighting still. But our Lord is good, and His mercy is great."

"Edmund, I know you must have been surprised to hear of our unexpected marriage," Lord Thorne said, slipping an arm around his wife's shoulders. "But permit me to join my dearest Olivia in telling you that all is well. Our two families, once bitterest foes, are wedded in a bond of love and peace. The hedgerow that once separated our lands is now a symbol of our unity. Our flocks are joined. Our shepherds work side by side. The town is no longer divided in its loyalties. In fact, we employ a great many of Otley's most stalwart citizens. My wife and I have built a woolen mill near the bottom of the stream, and we now control all the production and sale of our fabric."

"Do you, indeed?" Mr. Rosse moved into the group. Only just now entering the house, he had been directing the unloading of trunks and boxes from the coach. "Please permit me to introduce myself. I am Malcolm Rosse of the East India Company. I trade primarily in fabric myself — cotton, in fact. Did I understand you to say you own a woolen mill, sir?"

"Aye, Mr. Rosse." Edmund's brother bowed again. "I am Randolph Sherbourne, Lord Thorne. May I present my wife, Olivia, Lady Thorne?"

"Lady Thorne, good afternoon." Mr.

Rosse took off his hat and made a fine bow in return.

Violet felt slightly sicker than she had in the past few days. Here they all were — bowing and introducing themselves and talking of peace and love and unity. Yet right in their midst stood Edmund Sherbourne, a libertine and drunkard of such infamy that Jesus had been compelled to sacrifice His own life on the man's behalf.

No doubt Edmund would assure Violet that she — in her willful disobedience — was equally guilty. He had said Mr. Rosse was a sinner with his Betsys, and Moumita with her idols. What was an idol anyway? And how could all sins be equally bad and deserving of such a great sacrifice? Everyone knew that small sins reaped slightly bad *kharma*, whereas terrible wickedness earned the evildoer rebirth as a pig or a worm or an Untouchable.

"How are we to speak to your daughter, sir?" Lady Thorne was asking Mr. Rosse. "It appears she may be more familiar with the Indian language than with our own."

"There is no such thing as an Indian language," Violet answered for her father. "Each regional group within the country speaks its own tongue — Hindi, Bengali, Tamil, Telagu, Urdu, Gujarati —"

"Well, yes, Violet, we all know that; thank you very much." Mr. Rosse gave an embarrassed chuckle. "Pardon my daughter, madam. Her mother died when Violet was a child, and she was not brought up well."

*"Shaytan,"* Moumita muttered from someplace nearby, calling her employer a devil.

"My daughter has been poorly educated; I regret to say," he continued. "Though I have hired various tutors, and she is well read in the classics, I fear Violet is lacking in the etiquette and accomplishments to which all ladies aspire. I have every intention of seeing to her formal education, of course. I am given to understand that a Mrs. Jane Brewster owns a very good finishing school in York. Upon my daughter's complete recovery from this regrettable illness, she will go to live with Mrs. Brewster and the other young ladies who board there. When she is fully fitted to the task, Violet is to marry an associate of mine, Mr. Alfred Cunliffe."

At the mention of this name, Lord Thorne and his wife exchanged surprised glances. "Do you speak of a Mr. Cunliffe of York?" the man asked. "Is he a trader in woolen, linen, and cotton goods — a gentleman who owns a large cloth market near the river?"

"He is indeed. The very same."

Edmund spoke up. "Do you know this Cunliffe fellow, Randolph?"

"I know him well," Lord Thorne responded. "He is among our colleagues in the trade."

Violet swallowed as both Lord and Lady Thorne trained their focus on her. Clearly they had found something about which to be very unhappy. Perhaps they did not wish her to marry Mr. Cunliffe, who might be their rival. Perhaps they did not like Mr. Cunliffe and the way he conducted business matters. Or perhaps it was something else entirely. Perhaps they did not like Violet herself.

She knotted her hands at her waist and glanced at Moumita for support. Still bundled up to her eyes, the little *ayah* was standing against the wall shivering. She would be of no help.

Violet turned to Lady Thorne. "What is wrong?" she asked, touching the wad of pins and ribbons with which she and Moumita had attempted yet another coiffure. "Is it my hair?"

The lady's expression softened. "Oh, my dear Miss Rosse, your hair is quite —" she seemed to see the bun on Violet's head for the first time — "quite the most beautiful golden shade I have ever witnessed. Is her hair not a lovely color, Randolph?"

Her husband smiled. "Very nice."

Violet crossed her arms. Well, they were both liars — as wicked as their besotted, womanizing missionary brother. Such a place, this Yorkshire! How would she ever endure it?

She gave a loud snort of disgust. "I have monkey hair, Lady Thorne, and you very well know it," she said. Without waiting for anyone to respond, she headed for the parlor, where she hoped a fireplace might warm her frozen toes.

# Thirteen

Edmund had not seen Violet for two days, and his concern for her well-being had increased to the point that he felt he must address the situation with his brother. As Randolph and his wife sat in the drawing room taking afternoon tea, Edmund made up his mind to join them even without invitation. Though he could still scarcely believe that his family were now united with their sworn enemy, the Chathams, the alteration in Randolph's humor could not be denied. The man was positively beside himself in love with his wife.

And who would not be? Lady Thorne, the former Olivia Hewes, proved a delight. Her family were all of Chatham lineage, and her younger brother stood to inherit the estate and title, yet nothing about the young woman could be faulted. She was warm, witty, and kind. Clearly, she was intelligent as well. For several years following her father's untimely death, she had managed Chatham on her own and had succeeded at a task many found daunting if not impossible.

Moreover, Lady Thorne clearly adored Randolph, whose first child and heir she now bore. Despite all the pain and heartache that Chathams had caused Thornes throughout the centuries, how could Edmund disdain anyone who loved his brother with such ardent passion? With God's help, Randolph and his wife had managed to bridge a chasm that once seemed far too deep and wide ever to cross. Delighted at this newfound peace, Edmund readily buried his own inclination to carry on the traditional grudge.

"Ah, there you are!" cried the lady herself as he stepped into the drawing room that opened onto the eastern prospect of Thorne estate. "Just now, my husband and I were speaking of your countenance this morning at breakfast. Despite your expressions of gratitude and contentment, you appeared distraught. Are you well, my dear brother?"

Edmund smiled, welcoming the term of endearment. "I am very well, indeed, Lady Thorne."

"Please, I cannot ask you again — you must call me Olivia. And do join us for tea. You are a part of our family, after all, and you must never suppose you need permission to participate in our gatherings." So saying, she reached for the bell rope and gave it a tug to signal a servant. "Our guests from India make themselves scarce. Mr. Rosse has taken himself to London just now with hardly any forewarning."

"Has he?" Edmund was surprised. He seated himself across the tea table from his brother. "To what end?"

"He told me he must speak to the board of the East India Company," Randolph answered. "Apparently, Mr. Rosse has suffered great financial loss due to the British government's decision to open trade and end the monopoly of the company."

"I understand it to be so," Edmund concurred. "The company controlled the trade routes for many years and enriched both its board and its tradesmen. This recent development has lightened the pockets of most of the merchants with whom I have connection in India."

"And Mr. Rosse is among them," Olivia said. "Poor man."

"Although I sympathize with his plight, sister, I must tell you that I am grateful the stranglehold of the company upon India has been loosed. Many of their strictures seemed without reason. Do you know that until recently, preaching the gospel of Jesus Christ was utterly forbidden in the city of Calcutta and in all the region controlled by England?"

"The East India Company prohibited the spread of Christianity?" Randolph asked.

"Absolutely. Even now it is difficult to obtain a license to preach, though Mr. Rosse has promised to secure one for me upon our return."

"Then you do mean to return?" Olivia asked. "We understand your mission, of course, dear Edmund. But you must know how happy we are to have you living here with us at Thorne. You are more than welcome to stay as long as you like. Or . . . Chatham Hall is empty at the moment. My brother, Clive, is away at school in London. You may make your home there, if you prefer privacy."

The offer astonished Edmund. Olivia Hewes — a Chatham — would share her family holding with him? She would invite a Thorne to take up residence in those forbidden halls? Unthinkable. And yet she reached for his hand and took it into her own.

"Do not look so startled," Olivia said softly. "My home is Thorne Lodge now. And as you know, I shall present you with a new niece or nephew in a few months. All this land belongs to our two families, for they are one. You are as welcome at

324

Chatham as you will always be at Thorne."

Beside himself, Edmund lifted her hand and kissed it. "My dearest sister," he said, "never should I have dreamed of such peace. God is very good."

"Indeed, He is." She reached for the teapot as a footman carried a new tray of tea into the room. "And if God must return you to India to preach His Word, then your brother and I shall send you away willingly — though with heavy hearts."

The conversation paused as servants set out the tray laden with strawberry tarts, scones, clotted cream, butter, and a selection of cold meats. Clean cups were passed all around, and Lady Thorne poured out the freshly brewed tea.

As Edmund stirred a lump of sugar and a dollop of warmed milk into his, he elected to broach the subject that had been weighing on his heart. "I have been concerned for the well-being of Miss Rosse," he began. "She does not come down to meals, nor have I seen her in the drawing rooms. Do you know, sister, how she fares?"

Olivia's dark eyes flashed at her husband for an instant. Then she returned her focus to Edmund. "Miss Rosse is well enough, I believe. I visit her several times each day, and I find her growing stronger and more hale since her arrival at Thorne. I have made certain that all manner of healthy meals are taken into her rooms — good meats, fish, poultry, cheeses, and newly baked breads. Because the old conservatory at Longley has been restored by its owner and his wife, we are now able to purchase fresh oranges and vegetables during winter. Of course, my guest has been served these fruits that she may increase her strength."

Edmund nodded. "Thank you, Olivia. Your kindness has not gone unnoticed, I am certain."

Again, she glanced at her husband. He cleared his throat. "We fear Miss Rosse's spirits flag," Randolph said. "My wife informs me that the young lady lies abed or sits beside the window and will hardly speak. Their conversation is limited to no more than two or three sentences. Do you know if Miss Rosse suffers from some . . . poverty of intelligence . . . or perhaps a speech impediment?"

"Hardly!" Edmund said with a laugh. "I have never heard such a flow of chatter as may emerge from that lady's mouth at any time. She and her *ayah* — her nurse — are wont to argue loudly at the most inopportune moments. Together, they speak an odd mixture of Bengali and English, yet Miss

Rosse has no trouble conversing fluently in the King's tongue whenever she likes. As for her intelligence, I assure you I have found the young lady to be among the liveliest wits of my acquaintance. She is particularly knowledgeable in the field of botany, and she has a special interest in orchid hybridization. In Calcutta, she assisted the curator of the Botanic Garden in his classification of Indian flora. I understand from my colleague, Dr. William Carey — himself an expert in the subject — that Miss Rosse has memorized most current books and catalogues of such flora, and she is considered highly educated in that realm."

Lady Thorne let out a breath. "My goodness. I had no idea. But now my fears are increased rather than abated, for I believe her withdrawn behavior indicates that she is feeling very dull indeed. Truly, she must be made to go out, Edmund. She needs the comfort of society. She should be given diversions and entertainments. She must have companions, for she is entirely too dispirited."

"I agree. If I may be so bold as to offer a suggestion, sister . . . perhaps you might invite some of your friends to call here at Thorne. A tea, perhaps. Or a luncheon."

"I have stated such intents to Miss Rosse

already, and she declares she will not come out of her room should I invite King George himself. In fact, she has told me — quite pointedly — that she does not mean to leave that place at all. Ever."

"Well . . . at least in the outspoken determination of her will, she has not changed at all. That sounds very like something she would say." Edmund set down his cup and leaned back in his chair. "I dreaded such an outcome. I must speak openly with you both. Miss Rosse is . . . difficult. She can be obstinate. She did not wish to come to England, and I believe what we witness now is evidence of grief more than of anger. She mourns India and the loss of her life there. She cannot see her way to joy here, and as a result, she stubbornly refuses to leave her room."

"You speak somewhat disparagingly of the young lady," Randolph said, "and yet I sense in your manner a measure of goodwill toward her."

How could Edmund be anything but honest with this elder brother he had always admired and emulated? Though separated by years, the two had been utterly united — along with their brother, William — as companions and playmates throughout their childhood. William currently was away in the north on matters pertaining to the woolen mill, but Edmund knew the moment they met again, they would instantly become confederates just as they always had been.

Edmund met his brother's frank gaze. "I like Miss Rosse," he said. "I like her very much. She is . . . odd."

"Such high praise!" Olivia cried with a chuckle. "Randolph has told me of your former fame with the ladies of London's ton society, and I am certain they could hardly resist such flattery."

"Dear sister, you must know that I prefer to leave my past behind me," Edmund told her solemnly. "The man my brother knew no longer exists. I am a new creature in Christ. I should pray that none of the ladies with whom I once displayed such ungentlemanlike and dissolute behavior can remember me at all."

"Oh, Edmund, can you not see that my wife teases you?" Randolph exclaimed. "You have expressed your admiration for Miss Rosse by calling her odd. That is amusing!"

"It is more flattering than you may realize." He smiled at their puzzled expressions. "I have become rather odd myself, Randolph. One cannot exist in another culture without somehow becoming a strange mixture of the two. While in India, I swore I should give almost anything for a glimpse of these beloved Yorkshire moorlands — the gentle sheep, the bracken growing on the fells, the quaint streets of dear old Otley. I believed myself cursed by every mosquito that slipped through the netting over my bed, every beetle that found its way into my wheat flour, every droplet of perspiration that seeped from my body even as rain fell in sheets all around me.

"Yet, now that I am here — at *home* — I can hardly cease thinking of my small bamboo shack perched high on stilts with the wind rustling the palm leaves of my thatched roof. I miss the heart-pounding alertness with which I went through each day, always on the lookout for a monkey that might swing through the window and snatch my morning toast, or a cobra curled up in my boot, or a tiger crouched over my head as I walked beneath a banyan tree. Life in India pulsates, Randolph. There is no peace, no calm. Nothing like the security of Thorne or the serenity of a walk across the moors. Yet, India beckons me with its vibrancy. Its vitality.

"You see, I am not myself, Olivia. I suddenly find I prefer curry and rice to lamb chops. I miss the fragrance of frangipani blossoms in the night. I long for the sight of the old men who squat as they chew betel nuts and smile at me with their bright red teeth and lips as I walk along the pathway near my house. I am no longer the man I was in any way, Randolph. And I am not quite certain who I am. In short . . . I, too, am odd."

Olivia and Randolph were silent for a moment, and Edmund wondered if he had said too much. How could they ever imagine the world he had known? No atlas or geography book could capture the reality of the streets of Calcutta, the swirl of the Hooghly River, or the teeming jungle that pressed close on every side.

"You are not odd," Olivia said at last. "You are the man God intended you to be. He is shaping you into His servant, molding you for His purposes. And He is doing the same for Miss Rosse."

"But she cannot *stay* odd," Edmund protested. "If she is to survive here, she must learn how to become English. Yorkshire must become her home. She will have to suppress the Indian part of herself."

"Surely not. As far as her past life is concerned, I shall be eager to hear her tales of adventure," Olivia said. "Everyone in our society will wish to learn of her existence in India."

"But Miss Rosse is hardly a lecturer on a speaking circuit, and she will not like to be gawked at as though she were on display in a traveling museum of curiosities."

"No, of course not —"

"You see, sister, even though you treat her well, Miss Rosse will *feel* odd. That is because she *is* odd."

"And you like that about her," Randolph concluded.

Edmund looked away, pondering his brother's insight. "I do," he said at last. "Very much. I understand her. To Miss Rosse, life in India has never felt like an adventure. It has been normal. It is all she has ever known. But England is not normal. It is frightening and fearsome and discomfiting. Unless she is somehow able to embrace this new world, I fear the lady may wither of sadness and mourning for the home she has lost."

"Edmund, I believe you love Miss Rosse," Olivia said gently.

"In my way . . . as a minister . . . I do love her."

"Bosh!" Randolph cried, reaching across the tea table and slapping his brother on the arm. "*As a minister.* What a great load of rubbish! What utter rot!"

Edmund could not help but laugh. "You

mock me, but it is true, brother. I care for her as one of my flock."

"Bah!" Randolph said, leaning back in his chair and chortling. "*Baa-baa!* One of your flock . . . as a minister . . . oh, Edmund, I know you far too well for this tripe! You have not changed so much that I cannot see straight through you. You, my dear brother, have fallen in love with the girl, and you might as well admit it."

"What if I have?" Edmund retorted. "Her father has attached her to Alfred Cunliffe, who is —"

"Who is a scoundrel and a murderer!"

"A murderer?" Edmund's heart faltered. "What is this news?"

"Alfred Cunliffe is rumored to have done away with his wife," Olivia said in a low voice. "The allegations were never substantiated, and therefore, he cannot be formally charged."

"A constable found the poor woman's body in an alleyway in York . . . stabbed," Randolph continued the gruesome tale. "Cunliffe had been discovered in flagrante delicto with another man's wife. Mrs. Cunliffe, whose wealthy family provides the primary source of his capital, had begun proceedings to divorce him."

"But Mr. Rosse told me that Cunliffe is a

successful cloth merchant," Edmund protested. "They have engaged in trade together for some years."

"Cunliffe has built a successful enterprise, true. Yet its foundation rests upon the five thousand pounds a year that his wife brought into the marriage."

"Five thousand a year!"

"Nothing to sniff at. And without it, the trade was unlikely to stand on its own. I assure you that York is a highly competitive marketplace, for Olivia and I sell our wool primarily to merchants in that city."

"This is appalling," Edmund said. "Have you informed Mr. Rosse?"

"At once. The moment we were alone together, I enlightened him on all the details. His first reaction was one of doubt. But he soon came to accept that my allegations may have some basis in truth. Of course, we cannot say for certain that Cunliffe killed his wife."

"Yet he is a skilled swordsman," Olivia said. "He prefers the rapier to the gun, it is believed. And his wife was not merely stabbed . . . she was run through."

"Good heavens!" Edmund exclaimed.

"Dreadful," his brother concurred. "All signs point to his guilt, and yet proof of it cannot be discovered. There were no witnesses to the crime, and no weapon has been found. Meanwhile, Cunliffe goes on collecting five thousand a year as per the mandate of his deceased wife's will."

"What of the . . . the woman with whom Cunliffe was exposed?"

"Banished. It was put about that her cuckolded husband sent her on an extended tour of the Continent. But we are given to understand that she may have entered a nunnery in Italy. Certainly, she will never be seen again."

"This tale of atrocities grows more astonishing by the moment," Edmund exclaimed. "Do you know what Mr. Rosse intends now for his daughter?"

"I cannot say," Randolph replied. "He makes for London to speak to the board of the East India Company. Following that, he returns to York to meet with his barrister. And thence to confront Cunliffe himself."

"Alone? I should think that unwise. The man sounds as if he may prove a danger to any who dispute him."

"In no uncertain terms did I warn Mr. Rosse of this very thing. Edmund, if you believe you ought to make for York to stand up with Rosse, I am happy to accompany you."

His wife let out a small cry. "Oh, Randolph, I beg you, no! Under any other circumstance, I might agree. But to put yourself in danger . . . at such a time . . ."

Both men glanced down at the obvious swelling beneath her white tea gown and then quickly faced each other. "I cannot go," Randolph stated at once. "I beg your pardon, Edmund, but my wife is absolutely correct. In no way shall I abandon Olivia during her confinement, and certainly I dare not put my own life in danger when my heir has not yet been born."

"Of course not. Nor do I believe either of us may do Mr. Rosse any good. I do not know Alfred Cunliffe, I have no certainty of his guilt, and I am confident that Mr. Rosse would consider this business none of my affair."

"Except that you care deeply for his daughter," Olivia said. "May I suggest, dear brother, that you do not go to York. I believe that instead, you should do your ministerial duty by a very sad member of your flock. Take poor Miss Rosse out into the world."

Randolph chuckled as Edmund gave a shrug. "It is not as you suppose, Randolph," he insisted. "Miss Rosse is like a sister to me. In many ways, she is no more than a friend. Indeed, that is absolutely correct. She is simply a friend and a sister."

"Ha! She is an enchantress with golden hair and blue eyes and a pair of pink lips that you dream of kissing."

As Olivia scolded her husband, Edmund quickly tipped down the last of his tea. What if they knew he had sampled the honeyed sweetness of Violet's lips already? Such a transgression was better left unmentioned. Now he must concentrate on seeing to the young lady's welfare, for if by some terrible chance her father still intended her to wed Cunliffe, Edmund must do all in his power to ensure her safety.

"You ought to take her to the conservatory at Longley," Olivia suggested. "I should imagine it is very like India inside, for I understand it is filled with lovely plants and fruit trees. Perhaps they do not have monkeys, tigers, or cobras to keep the both of you company, but Miss Rosse will surely enjoy the warm, damp air and the array of lush greenery."

"Possibly, yet I cannot think how I may draw her out of her rooms to begin with," Edmund said. "I fear she will not find the prospect of visiting an English conservatory temptation enough."

"But surely she must enjoy escaping the cold and the snow. I am told the conservatory is quite warm in winter. I believe it even boasts a palm tree or two. And I am certain that Mrs. Richmond has brought in flowers of every kind — roses, lilies, camellias —"

"Ah, but that is just the thing!" Edmund exclaimed as an idea was born in his mind. "My dear sister, will you escort me to Miss Rosse at once?"

She gave her husband a smile of victory as she set down her teacup. "But of course, Edmund. Follow me."

"I believe he must be a vicious liar," Violet stated as she looked out the window at the melting snow. "Mr. Sherbourne confessed to his drunkenness and debauchery, so why should we suppose him to be wholesome in any way whatsoever?"

Moumita clucked her tongue in disgust. "How many times must I remind you, *meye?* The sahib told us that he did those bad things long ago."

"He could not have done them very long ago. He is hardly old enough to have lived a sordid life and then reformed himself. Do you know . . . I suspect that in India he had a Betsy."

"*Na!* This cannot be true."

"All the Englishmen in Calcutta have Betsys. Why not Mr. Sherbourne? You saw how dastardly he behaved toward me. He kissed me! He took me into his arms and kissed me — three times. And how could he have been so bold and so . . . so wonderful . . . and so perfect at it, if he had not had a great deal of practice?"

"I think he seemed good at kissing because you wished him to kiss you."

"Moumita! No, but he is a villain. I see it all so clearly now. Remember that he wounded those guards at Krishnangar? When he rescued me, his saber was covered in blood, and he did not think a thing of it."

"He did think many thoughts of it, for he was very sad all the way back to Calcutta. He told you he did not wish to talk of those injured men. He felt very bad for harming them." Moumita cast Violet a disparaging look. "*Meye,* you wish to think bad things about the sahib, but he is not bad. All those days of your sickness on the ship, I sat with him and we talked. He is very kind. Also smart. And he was strong to rescue you from your foolishness at Krishnangar. I believe it is all as he said — his God has changed him. Jesus has great power. Power to make a bad man into a good one."

Violet traced her finger down the frost that coated the inside of the window. "I cannot bear to talk any longer of Mr. Sherbourne," she murmured. "I want to go home."

"You are home. This is your home now."

"No, it is not!" Violet cried, whirling around and stamping her foot. "Edmund promised it would be green and warm again here, but see how he lied! Look outside there! Everything is utterly dead, Moumita. Now the snow melts, and all we see is brown grass. Bare tree limbs. Gray sky. It is dead, all of it."

"But we came here only a short time ago. Two days. What is that? Bringing new life to dead things must take longer than that."

"Well, it is too long for me. Oh, Moumita, let us sell what remains of my jewelry and buy passage on a ship back to Calcutta."

"I cannot think about another boat! Please! No more ocean. No more fish."

"Then I shall go by myself. I can leave at night and take a horse."

"You do not know how to ride a horse. You will fall off and break open your head like a chicken egg."

Violet sank down onto the window seat again and covered her face with her hands. Since arriving at Thorne Lodge, she had spent her days and nights trying to think what to do with herself. How could her life ever hold any joy again? Sometimes, all she could do was weep as she recalled the enormity of her losses. No Botanic Garden or orchids or specimen catalogues to challenge her mind. No dances in the temples or trained elephants to entertain her. No bazaars, no Hooghly River, no rickshaws, no curry and *chapattis* — nothing that meant home to her. All was lost.

When she was not crying, she found herself flying into fits of fury. She pounded her pillow and kicked a trunk so hard she feared she might have broken her toe. How could her father have done this to her? How dare he take her away from India. Why did Moumita comply so easily? It was all a great conspiracy to make her utterly miserable!

During those times when she was too drained to cry and too exhausted to rage, Violet plotted her escape. She decided to dress like Moumita, cover her head with a sari, and slip out of the house unnoticed. Or she might climb down the ivied wall and vanish away in the night. She could take a horse from the long row of stables near the end of the drive. Better, she would steal a gun and force a coachman to carry her to the seaside city of Hull.

When she slept, she dreamed of India. And when she awoke, she pretended she was still there. But soon a servant always knocked on the door and stepped into the room bearing a tray of dry little cakes and strange-tasting meats and sour oranges. These English servants wore tight, buttoned boots, black gowns, and small white caps on their heads. Gone was the barefoot *swish-swish* of the sari-clad maids passing by or the pounding of the *mali* as he worked in the garden.

At the sound of a rap on the door even now, Violet fought tears. Here must be her tea once again. Maids would tiptoe in bearing an array of strange foods, none of which appealed to Violet. They would stare at her as though they had never before seen an ugly, monkey-haired girl from India, and then they would drift away like silent ghosts.

"It is Lady Thorne," Moumita announced. "She comes to talk to you again."

Violet lifted her head. She did like the brown-eyed Englishwoman, though not well enough to bother trying to make conversation. Standing, she smoothed down the wrinkled gray gown she had been wearing day and night. She had not allowed her *ayah* to fix her hair or pour her a bath or lay out clean clothes. All Violet wanted to do was sleep. Sleep and drift away to India and never ever wake up again.

"Good afternoon, Miss Rosse," Lady Thorne said. "I hope you are well."

She wore a soft purple gown that draped

over the swell of her unborn baby. A warm wool shawl of deep indigo and green plaid covered her shoulders, and her hair was caught back in a white mobcap.

"Thank you, Lady Thorne," Violet said. "I am very fine."

"This is happy news, for you have a visitor who wishes to make a proposal that will require your good health." Standing to one side, she held out her hand as Edmund Sherbourne strode into the room.

He bowed. "Miss Rosse, I am pleased to learn you are so much recovered."

Yet even as he said the words, Edmund's face registered dismay at the sight of her. Violet reached up to try and push some of her hair into place, but it was a hopeless tangle. Instead, she made a slight curtsy and then shrugged.

"You are looking well enough, Mr. Sherbourne," she observed. "I am sure you must be rejoicing to be home at last on your beloved moorland."

"I am pleased to see my brother and to meet his lovely wife. But I find I miss India far more than I expected. Perhaps you feel the same."

"Yes, sir, I do." Violet swallowed back the lump that rose in her throat. "I am sorry I came to England. I should rather have ended on the pyre in Krishnangar."

The dark green shadows in his eyes deepened as he gazed at her. "If so, then we should be sadly deprived of your company, Miss Rosse. I know I should miss you far more than I miss India. And Lord and Lady Thorne might never know you at all. That would be a great loss indeed."

Violet studied Olivia Sherbourne for a moment, hoping she had not offended her host too much. After all, Lady Thorne had been nothing but kind and solicitous since the arrival of her guests.

"Thorne Lodge is very nice," Violet managed. "But I believe you were mistaken about the spring, Mr. Sherbourne. See how the snow melts and yet nothing is green."

A tender smile crept across his face. "January is not yet complete. We shall not begin to see spring until March, Miss Rosse."

"March!" she gasped and sagged back down onto the window seat. "Oh, it is too, too horrid! I am going to die! How I wish I could die!"

Before she could speak another word, Edmund was kneeling at her feet. "Violet," he said in a low voice as he took her hands from her damp cheeks. "You are not alone. Look, Mrs. Choudhary is with you. I am here. We both miss India, as well. We long

344

for warmth and light and the fragrance of growing things. And here is something else that is dying of the need for sunshine."

She opened her eyes to find him holding out the little African orchid in its sad clay pot. All the leaves had fallen off, and the canes hung limp and sagging as though they, too, wished to weep in mourning.

"Miss Rosse," Edmund said. "I believe you and I can save this orchid."

She shook her head as she ran a finger along a cane. "It is too cold in England for orchids to live. There is no sun here, and the windows are covered in frost — even on the inside."

"Then we must take it to a special place. Very near Thorne Lodge sits a glass house, a conservatory. Inside it, we shall discover for ourselves a very small India, a place where it is hot and fertile and alive. If we set the orchid there, and if we return to tend it, perhaps it will revive. Perhaps it will even grow and thrive. And maybe one day it will blossom."

Violet took the clay pot and studied the poor, bedraggled specimen that had no name. "I doubt this orchid can survive. And I must tell you, Mr. Sherbourne, that I do not believe there is such a wonderful place as you describe. Not in the midst of all this winter."

"Will you come with me, Miss Rosse? Will you trust me?" He lifted her chin with his finger. "Come to the conservatory, dear lady. Come and find life."

Despite herself, Violet knew a small surge of hope. She glanced at Moumita and then at Lady Thorne. Both wore expressions of pleading. Gazing into Edmund's green eyes, she knew she could never refuse this man anything.

"Yes, sir," she whispered. "I shall go with you wherever you will take me."

# Fourteen

Snowflakes stung her cheeks. Wind bit at her nose. Icy cold sucked the blood from her fingers and toes. As though facing a fearsome foe, Violet peered out from under her bonnet brim at the swirling white froth. Though Edmund had told her the snow was harmless, she knew she could not trust it.

Winter had proven its fickle, malevolent, and scheming character that very afternoon. Upon Violet's first step out of the grand house at Thorne, a patch of black ice flipped her feet out from under her and sent them straight up into the air. Down she went with a thud, cushioned only by a heap of damp snow that instantly froze solid the folds on the back of her skirt and stuck the fabric to her legs. Inside the carriage, the more she sat upon her frozen skirt, the wetter it became, until at last she felt as if she were sitting in a puddle.

Not only had this wicked winter chill toppled Violet, but it was determined to gnaw through her skin and nibble away her fingertips. Even now, she could feel nothing beneath her gloves. And where had her toes gone? She tried to wiggle them as Edmund pulled on the reins and the carriage drew to a halt before a soaring house made of nothing more substantial than glass. Though she would have liked to bemoan her missing lower digits, Violet realized that Edmund had decided to hold forth on the beauty of the conservatory.

"Countless panes . . . almost unimaginable labor . . . water pipes . . . tunnels . . . flora collected from all around the world," he was saying as he waved his hand across the scene. She tried to listen through the heavy velvet that covered her ears. Wondering if Moumita had survived the journey, she glanced to her side to find only a heap of colorful wool blankets, scarves, and capes. Perhaps the little Hindu had vanished entirely, escaping this frigid wasteland and wafting away to Nirvana. A pleasant thought indeed.

"When I went to India," Edmund said as he surveyed the glass house through the carriage window, "the conservatory was little more than a heap of rusty, twisted iron framework and a million shards of broken windowpanes. But look at it now! My brother tells me that Mrs. Richmond has overseen the restoration of the building, and such a magnificent piece of architecture it is!"

Violet found herself distracted by the clouds of white steam that emerged from her nostrils and mouth. "It is lovely," she puffed out, as though she had just smoked one of her father's cigars.

"I have never seen its like!" Edmund exclaimed with boundless enthusiasm. "Do you know that my brothers and I used to play here with Colin Richmond when we were all very young lads?" He set the carriage brake and leapt down into the snow. "It was a bit dangerous with all the broken glass, but we thought it brilliant fun. We would hide from each other in the tunnels and clay pipes that brought water down from the grand heights of the Chevin."

Violet realized that he was speaking of the mount — little more than a hill, really — that rose above the town of Otley. Edmund considered the Chevin a stunning and wondrous example of God's handiwork. As the carriage had rolled along the muddy, rutted road to Longley Park, he extolled the glories of this rounded heap of golden stone from which much of the village had been built. He talked of how difficult the Chevin was to cross, how valuable in bringing water to the village, how marvelous a peak from which to view the surrounding countryside.

To Violet, the Chevin looked like nothing more than one of Lady Thorne's dry little cakes with stiff white icing. After all, she had seen the Himalayas — massive, soaring mountains that pierced the clouds and rose straight up into the heavens. And above them all stood Everest, that unconquerable giant. Certainly one would never consider taking a Sunday picnic onto its slopes as these Yorkshire people did their paltry little hump.

No, Violet could not say that she liked one thing about England. She despised the snow. She detested the bleak landscape. And she seriously doubted she would find anything pleasant inside this glass house.

"Come, Miss Rosse," Edmund was saying as he held out his hand. "Mrs. Choudhary carries the orchid, and we must hurry it inside lest it meet with disaster."

The poor orchid had met with disaster already, Violet thought as she placed her hand in Edmund's. Taken down from its comfortable perch in a tree on the western coast of Africa, shoved into a clay pot where it did not belong, deprived of sunlight and water while forced across the ocean to a frozen and hostile landscape — no, the orchid could not be happy in the least.

"Although I never saw this conservatory in its prime," Edmund said as he helped Violet down into the ankle-deep snow, "I have viewed several in London and on the Continent. I believe you will find it astonishing."

"I am astonished indeed, for snow has gone straight down into these boots which Lady Thorne lent to me, and now my feet are wet and even colder than they were before."

"I have lost my toes," Moumita moaned as Edmund lifted her down beside Violet. "They have gone away. I cannot feel them inside my boots at all."

"Nonsense!" Edmund cried. "Come, ladies. You will both thaw momentarily. Let us enter the tropics once again!"

So saying, he pushed open the conservatory door and gestured for Violet to enter. It was not the tropics. But Violet took one breath of the humid air, fragrant with the scent of decomposing vegetation and loamy soil and pushing roots and unfolding leaves, and she burst into tears.

"It is alive!" she cried. Blurting out a flood of Bengali, she grabbed her *ayah* and folded the wet mound of blankets in her arms. "Oh, Moumita, just look and see! It is the jungle! The trees have leaves, and there

351

are flowers! Flowers!"

Throwing off her cloak and stepping out of the too-big boots, she grabbed up her damp skirt and raced barefoot down a path. "A philodendron!" she called out as her eye fell upon an enormous potted plant with huge green leaves. "Edmund, I have found a philodendron! I cannot name the species, but certainly it must be a philodendron. And look — a palm tree! I thought I should never see one again! And here is a lily of some sort. Fruit trees! Oh, an orange tree, and what are these? Lemons? But so small!"

She danced along the path as though her frozen feet could float. "I feel as if I am in Nirvana!" she shouted. "The smell is glorious and the heat is like home! Home! Home!"

At the sight of a row of terra-cotta pots — each filled with small, round green leaves and delicate purple, pink, and white blossoms — she caught her breath. Such tiny wonders! They were small and fragile, yet in their bearing Violet saw some trace of the orchids she knew and loved so dearly.

"What are these?" Violet asked into the empty space around her. "Edmund! Are you there? Please come and tell me the names of these wonderful flowers."

"They are called violets," a woman answered as she emerged from behind a hedge of giant ferns. "And may I ask your name, madam?"

"I am Violet." She looked down at the flowers again. "And these flowers are violets, too."

A small girl appeared at the woman's side. Her wide blue eyes and golden waves of long hair caught up with sapphire ribbons made her an astonishing sight to Violet. In fact, this child was the first person she had ever seen besides her mother with hair so much like her own.

"Why does the lady speak oddly?" the girl asked. "Is she a gypsy?"

"Hush, Clemma." The woman held out her hand, realized her glove was muddy, and peeled it off. "Excuse me . . . Miss Violet. Perhaps I should curtsy instead. I am Mrs. Colin Richmond. And this is Miss Clementine Bowden."

"Oh dear! If you are Mrs. Richmond, then this is your house, and we have come inside without invitation." She searched in vain for Edmund and Moumita. "I am here with my *ayah*. And the missionary. We came to see the tropics. He said it would be like India, and it is not quite West Bengal, but very nearly the same in its smell and lushness. Please, Mrs. Richmond, have you any orchids?"

The woman's gold-flecked brown eyes tilted up at the corners as she smiled. "I fear it is quite impossible to transport such exotic flowers so far from where they grow. I have only read of orchids and studied pictures in books. But as you can see, I have brought into Longley's conservatory every sort of flora I am able to manage. I have collected a great many plants from Spain, Greece, Italy, and even the Holy Land. May I ask how it can be that you know of orchids but you have never seen a violet?"

"Violets do not grow in India. That is my home. Calcutta in West Bengal on the banks of the Hooghly River. I came to England on a ship with my *ayah* and the missionary. My father made me do it. He wishes me to marry." She sighed. "Is the monkey-haired girl your daughter?"

"Monkey-haired?" Miss Clementine giggled. "Ivy, she says I have monkey hair!"

"Miss Clementine is my youngest sister," Mrs. Richmond explained. "Her hair is blonde, as is yours. We think it very lovely."

Now it was Violet's turn to laugh. "Lovely! Your poor sister is an ugly child, Mrs. Richmond. But not to worry. Perhaps her father can provide a good dowry. A man may choose an ugly bride who is rich, even though his heart belongs to a more beautiful woman. I have seen this happen many times."

Both the brown-eyed woman and her blue-eyed little sister were staring at Violet as though she had stepped out of a bad dream. A look of disbelief mingled with horror on their faces. Violet sucked in her lower lip, wondering what she had said wrong.

"But in England," she said, digging her big toe into the gritty sand of the path, "perhaps marriages are arranged another way, although I think not, because my father has —"

"Ah, there you are!" Edmund strode down the path toward the three as Moumita hurried along behind, trailing blankets. "Mrs. Richmond, how lovely to see you again. I am Edmund Sherbourne of Thorne. We knew each other as children. You have married since I left to begin my missionary labors among the heathen. I congratulate you most heartily on your happy estate."

"Thank you, Mr. Sherbourne." She dipped him a graceful curtsy. "Of course I remember you and both of your brothers. I believe we had your family to tea at Brooking House more than once. Welcome home."

"I am delighted to be back in Yorkshire. And I see you have already met Miss Violet Rosse. Miss Rosse and her father are staying at Thorne, having lately arrived with me from India. May I introduce Mrs. Choudhary, the lady's maid to Miss Rosse?"

"Miss Rosse says I have monkey hair," the little girl announced after she and her sister had nodded briefly at Moumita. "She thinks I am ugly."

"You are hardly ugly, Miss Clementine," Edmund assured her. "Indeed, you are enchanting. You must understand that in India, no one has blonde hair. Miss Rosse's hair is the color of a certain monkey, the Hanuman langur. It is often seen scampering about the temples of West Bengal, and she has been told — quite wrongly — that because of this, she is ugly. But you and I know, my dear young lady, that blonde hair is lovely. A woman who has been blessed by God with such glorious locks may count herself among those to be the most envied in all the land."

Miss Clementine grinned. "That is what I thought all along."

"My sister and I have just been repotting violets in preparation for spring," Mrs. Richmond said. "And now as we meet Miss

Rosse, we discover a most intriguing and charming new Violet."

Everyone looked at Violet, who had managed to dig a rather large hole in the path with her big toe. She had never thought herself charming or lovely in any way. Yet Edmund once had called her beautiful. He had held her in his arms. He had kissed her lips. And now, as they stood inside this glass jewel box, she wanted nothing more than to step to his side and lean on his shoulder for support.

Though she had doubted him too many times, Violet knew deep inside herself that Edmund could be trusted. Moumita was correct. If he once had been as dissolute as he claimed, his God had changed him completely. Edmund was no drunken libertine. On the contrary, he had proved himself again and again as kind and gentle and good a man as anyone could ever wish to find.

If Violet needed him to educate her, he would explain everything he knew from violets to blonde hair to the God he worshiped. If she suffered from the winter, he would protect her from it, just as he had saved her from the rajah of Krishnangar and death on a funeral pyre. If she could somehow cross the barrier between them, Violet knew Edmund would gently cradle her heart just as he had nestled her against his chest when she was so ill. This man, above all others, would make everything all right.

Violet edged sideways to place herself nearer to Edmund. "Thank you for your kind words, Mrs. Richmond," she said, feeling as awkward as an egret stuck in a mud bog. "Your violets are very nice indeed. Lovely."

"We have white ones," Miss Clementine announced. "We found them near the stone wall where my sister tends her very special ivy. We dug them up and put them into pots, and now we have more."

"Aha," Violet said, sliding closer to Edmund and reaching for his hand. At her touch, he stiffened and took in a deep breath, but she could not bring herself to draw away. "Miss Clementine," she said softly, "you are propagating an aberration in the species. This is a good thing. I had hoped to experiment in such a way with orchids, but I was brought to England instead."

"I very much admire flowers from many different countries," Mrs. Richmond declared. "I should like to have an orchid one day. My husband grew up in India, as you did, Miss Rosse, and he has told me all about them. We purchased several wonderful books on Asian flora, but of course it is quite impossible to think that I might ever see such an exotic flower unless I return with him to India."

The whole time the woman talked, Violet was squeezing Edmund's hand as if she might draw strength out of him and take it into herself. She knew she was disconcerting him, but she could not help it. He must understand how desperately she needed him.

And he did understand, for no matter how forward Violet's behavior, he did not push her away. Instead, he moved nearer to her, so that their joined hands were hidden in the folds of her skirt. His own much larger hand covered hers as he held it tightly, firmly, comforting her with the steadiness of his presence.

"And I understand there are many different species of violets," Mrs. Richmond was saying. "I have heard of African violets, which have a thicker leaf and a grander flower. But we have not been able to bring such beauties all the way to Yorkshire."

"We have an orchid here," Moumita spoke up. "It is from Africa. The holy sahib brought it down from a tree in the city of Cape Coast."

Both Mrs. Richmond and her sister now

turned to further examine the small, black-haired woman who had stood all this time to the far side of the group. Moumita stepped forward and held up the clay pot with its pathetic limp canes.

"Here is the orchid," she declared. "Memsahib Richmond, you must put it here inside this warm glass house where you live, so that it may grow again."

Mrs. Richmond took the pot. "This is an orchid?"

"It looks dead to me," Miss Clementine announced. "And it is very ugly." At this, she gave Violet a sharp glance. Then she took the orchid and set it down beside the row of pots with their small purple and white violets.

"This girl can make the orchid grow again," Moumita said. Giving Violet a jerk that loosed her from her hold on Edmund, she thrust her toward the clay pot. "She knows how to make anything grow."

"Even inside this conservatory, Mrs. Richmond, the orchid is in the wrong environment," Violet explained. "An orchid does not belong in a clay pot. It wants air about its roots. And rainwater. And perhaps some peat and a little crushed bark. It ought to be put it into a basket and hung on one of those palm trees. In India, orchids often grow on trees or in the crannies of stone ledges — but they are not parasitic. Your palm tree will not be harmed by a basket containing a small orchid."

"I know where to find a basket," Miss Clementine said, seeming to abandon her efforts to stay annoyed at Violet for calling her ugly. "Come with me, Miss Rosse. Bring the orchid. We shall put it into a basket so the roots can breathe."

Feeling more comfortable with the child than with the others, Violet hurried after her. On a far table covered with clay pots, spades, and sacks of black dirt, they found a small basket woven in the shape of a bird's nest. Violet lifted the orchid from the pot and loosened its roots. Then she set it into the basket, and Miss Clementine tucked bits of peat moss and leaf litter around it. As they completed their task, they spotted a strapping young man bearing a large pail of water along the path.

"Oh, it is Michael!" Miss Clementine exclaimed. "His father, Mr. Hedgley, is the chief gardener for the conservatory. I forgot that Ivy and I sent him to fetch water for our violets. Michael! Do come and let us have a bit of that rainwater, please!"

The man gave a nod and altered his course. " 'Tis not rainwater, Miss

Clementine," he told the child. He tipped his head at Violet. "This water flows down from the Chevin in long clay pipes. I think it comes from a spring."

"All water is rainwater at some time," Violet informed him. "The gods send water from the sky onto the land and into the rivers and deep down to the caverns and springs."

"Which gods do that?" Miss Clementine asked.

Violet looked into eyes as blue as her own. "I do not know," she whispered. "I have been told there are many gods, but I think perhaps there is only one."

"What you think is true," Miss Clementine said. "There is only one, but you see, God has three parts to Him. That is why you are confused. Is that not correct, Michael?"

"Quite right," he said. He scratched the back of his head with stubby fingers as he thought for a moment. "Three in one. The Trinity. Never made a lot o' sense to me, but there ye 'ave it."

"God is like an orchid," the little girl explained. "An orchid with leaves and stems and flowers. It is all one orchid, but it has got different parts to it. The Father part is called God. The Son part is called Jesus.

362

And the Spirit part is called the Holy Ghost. But they are all God, and there is only one. It may be quite complicated for gardeners or for people who come from India and think that hair like mine is monkey hair. You must listen carefully in church, Miss Rosse, as must you, Michael. And then you will understand it all as well as I do."

"Thank you," Violet said.

Michael nodded solemnly. "I shall do me best."

"And when may we expect leaves and flowers on this orchid, Miss Rosse?" Clementine asked. "I should very much like to see them. I am a painter, you know. With watercolors I paint flowers and trees and all sorts of things. My father says I am as good a painter as Leonardo da Vinci, which is very good indeed."

"I cannot say if this orchid will live. It may be dead even now."

"It is not dead, even though I thought so too at first. Do you see that wee green bit? Just there?"

She held up the basket and Violet peered down at the orchid. Just as the child had said, a small green lump was pushing out from the side of a cane. A thrill shot down Violet's spine and sent bumps along her arms.

"It *is* alive!" she gasped out. "Come quickly! We must show Edmund and Moumita!"

Taking the child's hand, she abandoned the gardener and ran down the conservatory's paths until they came upon the group who stood at its center near the potted violets.

"Look, Edmund!" Violet thrust the basket at him. "It is alive! It is putting out a new cane, or perhaps a leaf. I believe it may survive. Now that we have found this warm place, I think there is hope!"

He smiled. "Then you must come here every day and tend it."

"Of course," Mrs. Richmond said. "Please, Miss Rosse, I beg you to return to the conservatory. Just now, Mr. Sherbourne has told me of your work at the Royal Botanic Garden in Calcutta, and I should be honored to have your insight as I attempt to grow these difficult specimens."

The hope inside Violet grew into a flickering flame, but she was afraid. "I cannot come," she said. "As soon as I return to health, I am to go to York to attend a finishing school."

"Your father will not be back from his travels for some time, Miss Rosse," Edmund reminded her. "Why not come to the conservatory while he is away? It can only aid your healing. Certainly your knowledge and expertise are very welcome."

"Ivy can teach you anything you might ever want to know about manners," Miss Clementine put in. "There is no need for you ever to go away to York, for we all have very good etiquette here in Yorkshire, and we shall be most pleased to teach it to you."

Mrs. Richmond chuckled. "My sister is quite right. I see no reason for you to board at a school in York. I am perfectly willing to teach you all the accomplishments a young lady needs to be successful in society. Lady Thorne can have no objection either, and I believe she may enjoy the task as well. She was brought up a Chatham and the daughter of a baron. One can hardly ask for better breeding than that."

"Upon my word, this is a happy plan," Edmund said. "Mrs. Richmond, please, will you write to Lady Thorne and ask if she may be willing to assist you in the education of Miss Rosse?"

"I shall write her directly upon my return to the house."

"You do not live here?" Violet asked. "In the conservatory?"

"Heavens, no! Perish the thought. I should never get any sleep at all, for I can always think of one more branch that wants pruning or one more rose that must be repotted." She took Violet's hands and clasped them warmly. "I shall be delighted to assist you — on one condition. Please, will you tell me everything you know about India? My husband talks of it all the time, and I am certain that it cannot be too long before we shall set sail for that country ourselves. He has not seen his father in several years, and I know the pull is strong."

"Very strong," Edmund confirmed. "I find I can hardly wait to return there myself."

Violet's shoulders sagged. "I shall never go home again. But I shall tell you everything about India that you wish to know, Mrs. Richmond. You will learn all about being Indian, and perhaps you can transform me into an Englishwoman."

"A perfect trade. I am delighted."

Violet glanced around in search of Moumita. "If we can find my *ayah,*" she said, "I believe we must return to Thorne now, for I am very tired."

"I saw the lady's maid go off!" Miss Clementine exclaimed. "She went down that path. I believe she has gone to talk to Michael."

"Miss Rosse, do let me urge you to sit

down," Mrs. Richmond said. "Just beyond those palms, you will find a bench. Please, Mr. Sherbourne, take her there while my sister and I search out your lady's maid."

"Thank you, Mrs. Richmond," Edmund said. "I had not considered the toll such an outing might exact on one in such fragile condition as Miss Rosse."

While Mrs. Richmond and her little sister hurried away, Violet accompanied Edmund to the bench near a copse of potted palms. Though the thrill of the conservatory had given her new hope, she now realized how exhausted she had become. Running up and down the paths, meeting Mrs. Richmond, potting the orchid — all had served to sap the last reserves of her energy. She sagged down onto the bench and tugged the ribbons of her bonnet.

"I am too weak," she said. "I must do all in my power to regain my strength."

"If you will come out of your room and walk about at Thorne Lodge, you will certainly regain your land legs. The meals are hearty. Mrs. Richmond and Lady Thorne will visit you to bring their cheer and goodwill. And if you return to the conservatory often, I believe your health will recover soon enough."

Violet's eyes misted as she turned to him.

"Thank you, Edmund," she said softly. "Thank you for bringing me here to this warm place. Thank you for introducing me to your brother's wife and her friend. Thank you for taking the orchid at Cape Coast. Thank you for everything you have done for me!"

Unable to stop herself, Violet threw her arms around him. "I cannot care that you were once a drunkard! And if you had a hundred Betsys in India, I forgive you all of them!"

"Betsys in India!" Edmund exclaimed. "My dear lady, where on earth did you get such an idea?"

"A libertine is a man who is very wicked with ladies."

"Miss Rosse . . . Violet . . ." He sighed as he took her shoulders and set her away from him. "Despite my untoward behavior on the ship, I am no longer a dissolute drunkard, and I certainly never kept a Betsy in India or anywhere else. I behaved improperly with you. I know that, and I have repented. The man who once wore the name Edmund Sherbourne has died. I am born again, and my new life must give evidence of the righteousness of the Holy Spirit that lives inside me."

"The Holy Spirit is one of the three parts

of God," Violet told him. "Miss Clementine explained it."

"She did?"

"Yes, and I do understand. Perhaps you do not know that there are some people in India — *sadhus* mainly — who claim that Hindus worship only one god. According to Moumita, these people say that all the many gods are simply manifestations of a single being. They say that this one god is in all things, and all things are a part of this god. In some way, you are god, and I am god. These people believe that Hanuman and Ganesha and Kali and the others — there are millions of Hindu gods, you know — these lesser gods are aspects of the character of this one being."

"I have heard this said of Hinduism. And what is your opinion on it, Violet?"

"We discussed this, Moumita and I, and we do not think that any Indian from Brahmans all the way down to Untouchables truly believes it. How a person *acts* reveals what he *believes*. In India, everyone who is a Hindu acts as though each of the gods is separate from the others. People like to choose particular gods that can bring fortune or good luck or a happy marriage. Then the person prays to those gods in the hope of getting what he wants."

"I understand that Moumita has taught you to worship the Hindu gods," Edmund said.

"We had a little altar in my room. We put up the gods we had chosen as our favorites, and we bathed and dressed them and brought them sacrifices. We burned incense before them and prayed to them. But you should not be angry about this, Edmund, for I had the little silver Jesus that once belonged to my mother. I put Him on the altar, too."

"You did not put Jesus on your altar, Miss Rosse," Edmund said gently. "What you put there was nothing more than a silver statue. Although we cannot see Jesus, He is alive and real, and no picture or statue can contain any essence of Him. God has forbidden the worship of anything like a statue or a clay figurine. These creations are known as idols, and we are not to revere anything made by the hand of man."

Violet bowed her head. "In my heart, I have always known it. I used to argue with Moumita and tell her that because we had seen the men who poured liquid silver and gold into molds or formed clay to make statues, we knew the gods could not be real. I asked her why we worshiped gods that were not real. She said they were real, because the god is inside the clay or the brass, and I should not ask so many questions."

"It is better to ask questions and learn the truth than to believe a lie. Man cannot create God. God is the creator of man. There is only one God, Violet, and I wish you to know Him as I do."

"You continue to tell me your God is alive, but you also have said He died on a cross."

"Yes, He did." Edmund mused for a moment. "Violet, did you ever see the sacrifices in the temples of Calcutta? Goats that had been slaughtered, or gifts of grain left near the altar, or incense burned around the idols?"

"Of course I saw sacrifices. Moumita and I burned incense for our own gods and brought them food very often. If you do not make sacrifices, the gods will become angry."

Edmund's brow furrowed. "I have come to understand that there is something of truth in every religion, for God has placed inside every man and woman a yearning for Him. God has given each of us a deep-seated certainty of His existence. How could anyone behold the Himalayas or a freshly fallen snow and doubt His hand at work? Hindus, Muslims, even the natives of

Africa, I am told, are aware that the Supreme Being demands sacrifice. But anyone who does not worship Jesus Christ has placed his faith in a wrong understanding of the one true God."

"Are you certain of this, Edmund?"

"Absolutely, for my own life has proven it out. Because of Jesus Christ, I am a new man."

"How can that be?"

"God has changed me completely, and He has done it through sacrifice. In the Bible, God delineates His requirements for sacrifice. These sacrifices are meant to cleanse us and make us acceptable to Him. The book of Leviticus lists each aspect of the sacrifice and how it is to be undertaken. For guilt, for jealousy, for sin, for cleansing, for all things displeasing to God, a sacrifice is required."

Violet listened, trying to absorb what Edmund was telling her. Somehow, she had sensed this throughout her life. Guilt required atonement — and everyone was guilty.

"In the coach when you confessed your wicked past," she said, "you insisted that all of us are sinners. I tried to deny it, Edmund, but you spoke the truth. While I have never been a drunkard or a murderer or any such heinous villain, I have been sinful. My many lies haunted me as a child. Even as I grew older, I continued my bad behavior — running away from home, deceiving Moumita and my father, constant disobedience and willfulness. I made many sacrifices at the altar in my room, and I tried very hard to correct myself so that I might earn good *kharma*. But I find it quite impossible to be good all the time."

"Of course it is impossible. No one is perfect. Only God can claim that quality. Although He requires sacrifice, Violet, our paltry efforts can never be enough to earn us His forgiveness for our wrongdoings. We are simply too human — too prone to go our own way."

"That is very true," she acknowledged. "And because of it, I am doomed. Moumita believes I may be reborn an ant or a worm. She fears she will become a pig."

Edmund smiled. "Violet, do you really believe an animal has a soul? Do you think that God has given a worm the same essence of Himself that He gave to you? Certainly not. Your soul is unique to you, and when you die, it is destined for an afterlife with God. Or without Him. Because God cannot accept us into His glorious presence if we are covered with the stain of our sin, failure, willfulness, and disobedience, He chose to provide a sacrifice He would find pleasing. It is a sacrifice far better than any goat, sweetmeat, or incense."

Into Violet's mind came the painting she had seen on Dr. Carey's wall. Jesus had given Himself in sacrifice. And Clementine Bowden had said Jesus was God.

"God sacrificed Himself," she said softly. As she thought about the horrible, agonizing pain reflected on Christ's face in the painting, her eyes filled with tears. "Oh, Edmund, He gave Himself for me! Why did He do that?"

"Because He loves you, Violet. He wants you to come to Him now and after death. He wants your presence, your worship, your whole life. In essence, He wishes you to sacrifice yourself to Him."

"Like a widow on the pyre of *suttee?*"

"God does not seek from us a literal death. Jesus said that to follow Him, we must take up our own cross. He also said that if we want to save our life, we must lose it. Violet, God wants you to give Him all that you are — your hopes, your dreams, your willfulness, your disobedience — everything about you that is both good and bad. He longs to complete you as a bridegroom would his bride. To take you, to fill

374

you, and to make you completely His. On your own, you will never be right with Him. But if you give yourself to Jesus, His sacrificial death can make you pure in the eyes of God."

"But . . . if Jesus died on that cross, then what is the use? God is dead."

"There is far more to the story than a cross on a hillside. Jesus remained dead for three days, His tomb sealed, and His followers in mourning. But on the third day, He came to life again. On our behalf, He conquered death, and now He reigns in heaven, seated on the right hand of the Father. When Jesus left the earth forty days following His resurrection, He sent the Holy Spirit to live inside all who choose to turn their lives over to Him. That is who I serve, Violet. I am filled with the one true God — the Father, the Son, and the Holy Spirit."

Violet could see Miss Clementine skipping toward them down the path. Her sister was walking quickly to keep up, and behind them came Moumita. She had shed her blankets and scarves and had thrown back her sari from her head. A radiant smile beamed from her face as she hurried along, a red rose clutched in her hands.

"I want to do it, too," Violet said, taking

both of Edmund's hands in her own. "Please, sir, tell me quickly how to sacrifice myself! I wish to be perfect and pure and filled up to the brim with God."

Edmund swallowed. "Are you certain? Because I have not completely explained everything. I am not . . . there is more to be understood . . . and I think —"

"Oh, please hurry, for they are almost here!"

"Pray," he said. "Tell God that you love Him, that you wish to turn from your sin, that you long to become a new person — fully cleansed by His sacrificial blood. And you must —"

"We found her!" Miss Clementine exclaimed. "She was talking to Michael, and he gave her a rose, which was very nice of him, and we all thought so, too, especially Mrs. Choudhary! And she taught us how to say thank you in Bengali, which is *dhanyabad,* and you ought to fold your hands and bow your head a little bit before you take the gift. That is how they do it in India!"

"How lovely, Miss Clementine," Violet said, trying to focus her attention on the child.

But Edmund now took her hands. "You must read the Bible and go to church in order to learn and grow," he said in a low voice. "And you cannot expect to be perfect, for you will sin again, but —"

"And in India, everybody wears long cloths wrapped round and round," the little girl continued, "at least all the women do, the ones who are Hindus. They eat with their hands, and they walk about barefoot, and do you know that I should very much like to go to India when I am grown? I mean to travel all around the world and see everything and paint lots of lovely pictures of orchids and tigers and ladies in long wrapped cloths!"

"But you are covered," Edmund was saying, his mouth near Violet's ear. "Covered always by His sacrifice. Nothing can separate you from the love of God. Do you understand? Do you comprehend what I am telling you?"

Unable to respond, Violet stood to greet Mrs. Richmond and Moumita as they arrived at the bench. Edmund rose beside her, and she could feel his presence — so near and so certain — that a lightness flooded her heart.

All the voices around her floated through Violet's head: "You must come here tomorrow . . . the orchid is alive . . . Lady Thorne will be so pleased . . . red roses in winter . . . how very nice . . . so lovely. . . ."

"And are you better now, Miss Rosse?" This question came from Mrs. Richmond.

Violet looked into her eyes. "I am much better, thank you," she said. "In fact, I believe that after today, I may be an entirely new woman."

Mrs. Richmond laughed in delight as Clemma clapped her hands and spun circles. Even Moumita gave a giggle of joy.

But Violet turned to Edmund and folded her hands. *"Dhanyabad,"* she said, bowing her head. "Thank you."

# Fifteen

"I must see her, Randolph," Edmund said. "Truly, I cannot wait another day."

He and his brother rode side by side between two rows of arching oak trees that framed the great house in the distance. They had spent the afternoon jumping their mounts over the low stone walls and small streams that crisscrossed the Thorne estate. As when they were boys, the two had competed to see who could race his horse the fastest, whose steed might leap the highest hedge, whose could brave a splash across the deepest pond. And as always, Edmund had won. The more athletic of the two, he had no fear of pushing his animal to the utmost, and he relished the brisk moorland air that filled his chest each time he tested his own limits.

But now, as they cooled their horses on the long walk back to the stables, Edmund could not refrain from voicing his concerns. "I have told you that I was forced to separate myself from Miss Rosse in the midst of a most delicate conversation," he said.

"Nearly three weeks have passed since Mrs. Richmond and your wife conspired to take her away from Thorne and ensconce her at Longley Park. I do understand that in putting the young lady nearer to the conservatory they hoped to promote her healing as well as to teach her the feminine graces. All that is well and good, of course, and yet in doing so, they removed her entirely from my presence. Randolph, I must be permitted to conclude my discussion with Miss Rosse. I implore you to arrange a meeting between us."

"Honestly, Edmund, why must you refuse to tell me the subject of this so-called 'delicate conversation'?" Randolph took off his tall black hat and raked his fingers through his hair. "I have concluded that you were speaking with the young lady so urgently in order to propose marriage to her. You must see that I cannot foster the continuation of such a conversation, for Miss Rosse's father left her in my charge while he went off to meet with her intended husband."

"Upon my honor, Randolph, you leap to conclusions with greater skill than you surmounted those walls today."

"Speak plainly, brother. Did you or did you not mean to form an attachment?"

Edmund let out a breath of frustration. "An attachment, yes. But not to me."

"To whom then? You cannot mean to engage her to our brother. William is far too engulfed in the management of the mill to consider marriage. You heard him at dinner last night. He can talk of nothing else. Once, he was all agoggle over the ladies. I thought he must surely engage himself in marriage to two or three of them a year while he was in the Royal Navy at Portsmouth. But the moment my wife and I began construction of the mill, he abandoned all interest in his former pursuits and took up a new one. William is determined to make Thorne wealthy and himself along with it."

"Thorne is a rich estate as it is," Edmund said. "I pity our brother such a shallow aim, yet nothing I could say last night dissuaded him in the least."

"No, and I fear not even Miss Rosse's glorious golden tresses could tempt the man. He is besotted by gold of another ilk."

Edmund stroked his palm across his horse's mane. Though winter tried to hold on, the most recent snow was gone and the sun had warmed the earth. The horses' hooves trod upon solid ground, and their breath sent little vapor into the evening shadows.

"Randolph, I have no interest in attaching Miss Rosse to my brother," Edmund said. "That is not my aim at all."

"Then to whom do you mean to attach her?"

"To God."

Randolph turned to stare. "You were attempting to convert her? But is she not a Christian already?"

"Hardly. Mrs. Choudhary is all the mother Miss Rosse has ever known, and the young lady was brought up in the practice of Hinduism."

"Do you mean . . . she worships idols?"

"That is exactly what I mean. I am ashamed to tell you that even though I suspected this for some time, I could not bring myself to accept it. As is common in England, I foolishly equated her having pale skin with her also having a saving knowledge of Jesus Christ. She was English, and therefore, she must be Christian. It took me far too long to comprehend that Miss Rosse knew no more about our Lord than did her little Hindu nanny. I had hardly begun to believe this truth about her when she fell ill aboard the ship. Since then, I have made it my object to teach the lady about Christ, but time and again I have failed. That day in the conservatory, we had a few moments to speak alone. Randolph, I felt as though she was hungry for God. She asked me many questions, and at last, she begged me to help her give her life to Him. But just at that moment we were interrupted, and immediately thereafter, she was taken away to Longley."

The brothers rode in silence for a time, and Edmund tried to still his anxious thoughts. All too soon, Violet's father must return to Thorne. They had received a message from him earlier in the week to say that he had arrived in York, spoken to his barrister, and now was attempting to locate Mr. Alfred Cunliffe. Edmund had little doubt that when Malcolm Rosse arrived at Thorne, he would take his daughter away with him. Either he would have discovered nothing ill about Cunliffe and would wish to wed her to the man forthwith. Or he would mean to settle her elsewhere, perhaps with a brother he had mentioned living near London.

"Edmund, permit me to speak openly with you," Randolph said at last. "I can hardly mince words with one who was my constant companion throughout our childhood."

"Of course, brother."

"I ask you one question, then, Edmund.

Is it Miss Rosse's soul you wish to save . . . or is it her heart?"

"I know your meaning. You and your wife have not been wrong in your assumption that my affection for Miss Rosse is more than that of a minister for his congregant. I do care for her."

"You love her."

Edmund gazed across the vast prospect of his family's property. "I love this land, Randolph. I love you and your wife. I love my brother William. And in a way that overwhelms me more than I ever imagined, I love Violet Rosse. I adore her. She brings me joy and life and challenge. She makes me laugh. Her beauty stirs me, and her intellect astonishes me. Everything about her delights me. But I cannot wish to save her heart for myself. I must go back to India, and her father will keep her here in England. My life is not my own. I have given it to God, and He will send me away from her. I must accept this, Randolph."

"You are a better man than I. I cannot imagine leaving my dear Olivia. Not for all the world."

"It is for the world that I do leave Violet. For the salvation of the world. That is my commission. It is my calling. I can do no less."

"And thus, before you go, you wish to make certain that her soul belongs to God."

"I am desperate for that certainty. Indeed, I cannot think of returning to India without it."

"Then you will be pleased to learn that I have not been entirely deaf to your constant pleas these past three weeks. I encouraged Olivia to return Miss Rosse to our company, and this morning she informed me that she has invited the young lady and the Richmonds to dinner this very evening."

"Thank God!"

"But Edmund, the purpose of the dinner is not the continuance of your conversation. My wife and Mrs. Richmond intend to display their protégé. They believe Miss Rosse is now an accomplished young lady, and she will prove herself by demonstrating her alteration."

As they turned their horses toward the stables, Edmund knew a moment's sadness. "I do hope they have not altered her entirely. I did very much enjoy Miss Rosse as she was."

"Perhaps you did, but she never could have entered our society with such manners. Do you know . . . Olivia told me that when presented with a dish of rice, Miss Rosse began to eat it with her hands!"

"Only one hand. The right."

"Upon my word!"

"Randolph, in India, rice is always eaten with one's fingers."

"But that is savage! And my wife said that one afternoon, she discovered Miss Rosse seated cross-legged on the floor while painting a design on her palm with ink!"

"A very common mark of beauty. It is customarily done with henna. And you must understand that one rarely sits on chairs in India. When you think about it, Randolph, they are quite uncomfortable."

"Chairs? They are not."

"Lately, I have been sitting on the floor in my bedroom to study the Scriptures. I find it far superior to a chair and desk."

"You had better get yourself back to India, brother, or I shall fear to take you to church next Sunday."

Edmund laughed. "I should preach the sermon in Bengali. That would give everyone quite a turn."

"You would not save any souls at that rate."

"No, yet I very nearly did the same thing in India. I kept myself such a proper Englishman that I led not a single soul to Christ."

"Well, you shall have your first soon. No

doubt, Miss Rosse's soul will shine as a bright star upon your heavenly crown."

Edmund dismounted at the stable and handed the reins to a cyce. "Do you believe this is why I seek to lead Miss Rosse to Christ, Randolph? Can you think that I am after heavenly reward?"

"Are you not? That is certainly a valorous aim. Christ taught us to store up treasures in heaven."

"Yes, but that is hardly my goal. I seek to reap a harvest of souls for the glory of God and for the benefit of the abundant life He brings to His followers."

"Have you had an abundant life, Edmund?" his brother asked as they strolled toward the house. "All those mosquitoes and tigers. All that heat. And no converts. How can you call such an existence abundant?"

"Christ promised His followers persecution and strife upon this earth. It is a lie to believe anything different. But my life is abundant, Randolph. In all things I have the certainty of God with me and in me. He is my strength. He is my rock, my fortress. He holds me in the palm of His hand, and without Him I am nothing."

Randolph paused at the door and suddenly caught his brother in a warm embrace. "Edmund, I am grateful for you," he murmured in a husky voice. "I thank God that He made us brothers, and I commit to pray for you daily. If we do not meet again in this life, know this: I love you."

Edmund clapped his hands on Randolph's broad shoulders. "No man knows what God holds in store for him. It may be that my time on earth is short. But as long as I live, I shall remember your words. And you must hear them from me as well. I love you, my dear brother."

Side by side, the two men stepped into the hall and then parted toward their rooms. But as Edmund started up the stairs to his quarters, he spotted a valet hurrying toward him.

"Mr. Sherbourne, sir!" the man called out. "A letter came for you. A messenger arrived shortly after you and Lord Thorne left the stables on horseback this afternoon. I sent out several footmen, sir, but none could find you."

He presented a silver tray, and Edmund took the letter. "From which direction did the messenger come?"

"From York, sir. He said the letter was most urgent."

As Edmund broke the seal, he recognized the signature at the bottom of the letter. Malcolm Rosse.

★ ★ ★

Violet stepped into the drawing room and greeted Edmund and his brother with an elegant curtsy. It was perfect, in fact. She had practiced it a thousand times in the past three weeks, and she felt certain that not even the rajah of Krishnangar could upset her balance now.

Arrayed from head to toe in finery, Violet knew a surge of victory at the look of astonishment on Edmund's face. *Yes,* she thought as she strolled across the carpeted floor toward a settee, *you have my permission to stand in awe of my glorious beauty.*

Beautiful she was. Her two mentors, Lady Thorne and Mrs. Richmond — or Olivia and Ivy, as she now called them — had at last convinced Violet of her loveliness. Her golden locks, they insisted, would be the envy of all their society. Violet bore the most stunning head of shimmering gold tresses they had ever seen. On this night, they had piled them upon her head in a mountain of rolls, curls, braids, and ringlets. Jeweled butterflies perched here and there among the coils, but such paltry baubles could do but little to embellish the stunning magnificence of Violet's coiffure.

As she seated herself on the settee, Violet straightened her back into the perfect posture of elegant repose. Her gown — a flowing confection of pale lavender satin — molded over her feminine shape in a sweep of genteel neckline, silk ribbon tied at the empire waist, and folds of fabric that fell to her ankles. Pretty slippers, a shawl of ivory cashmere, white gloves, and a necklace of garnets accented the splendid array. Assured by her devoted teachers that she must surely dazzle the assembled guests with her beauty and culture, Violet began to recite her accumulated knowledge of the feminine arts.

"How well you are looking this evening, Lord Thorne," she said, laying her fingertips beguilingly at her throat. "I believe the winter air suits you, sir."

He tipped his head. "Thank you, Miss Rosse. I believe it does. My brother and I spent the afternoon on horseback. I have always said there is nothing like a good ride to get one's blood flowing."

"Very true, indeed," she replied. She had never been on horseback, but Violet thought such an activity would certainly make her blood flow. She turned her head and awarded her host's brother with a demure smile and a flutter of eyelash. "Mr. Sherbourne, did you enjoy your afternoon out of doors?"

"Yes, very much." He cleared his throat. "Miss Rosse, I wonder if I might have a word with you . . . in private."

Violet glanced in alarm at Lady Thorne. This was not done! Young men were not to seek out private conversations with unattached young ladies. Why was Edmund violating the rules? Had he forgotten them? What was she to say to him?

"I believe Miss Rosse must take a moment to refresh herself after the journey from Longley," Lord Thorne spoke up. "Surely your mission can wait, brother."

"But I —"

"Tell me, Miss Rosse, how does your health fare these days?" Lord Thorne asked. "Do you find the conservatory to have a healing effect?"

"Very much, sir." Violet let out a breath of relief. Her tutors had told her that a true gentleman could redeem any conversation that went astray. "My lady's maid and I go to the conservatory each day to stroll among the flora."

"Miss Rosse has taken charge of my tropicals," Mrs. Richmond enlightened them. "She has a magnificent touch with all the philodendrons, many of the ivies, and certainly the ferns. I believe even the roses respond to her careful hand."

As the conversation progressed, Violet discreetly studied Edmund, who sat across from her. He appeared dreadfully uncomfortable, his fingers gripping the arms of his chair and his jaw tight. He must be in shock over her transformation, Violet decided. Pleasantly shocked, she hoped. She had not seen the man for three weeks, and the whole time, she had missed him terribly. Though Ivy and Olivia had occupied her with lessons and drills, not even the conservatory had been able to take her thoughts from Edmund for long.

What was he doing? she had wondered as she tended her plants. Had he gone back to India without saying good-bye to her? Did he know that she had done exactly as he suggested and turned her whole life over to Jesus Christ? Could he possibly imagine how very different she felt because of it? And did he know how desperately she had grown to love him?

"I cannot think that winter will win Miss Rosse's heart immediately," Ivy Richmond was saying as Violet tried to concentrate again. "But as the years pass, she may learn to take some joy from the change in seasons."

"I found it difficult to accept winter myself," her husband observed. "A life in the tropics attunes one to a different rhythm. In India, the seasons change only from wet to dry."

"Or from hot to cool," Lord Thorne added. "Is that not what you told me, Edmund? The monsoons effect a cooling, but the dry season typically brings stifling heat?"

Everyone turned to Edmund, who had risen and walked across the room to a long window overlooking the front drive. He seemed to be paying no attention whatsoever, and Violet knew a rush of discomfort on his behalf. Surely he recalled the rules of society. He had employed them all too often himself. Talking of weather and the time of day had been his regular occupation aboard the *Scaleby Castle*, but now he seemed to have forgotten his manners altogether.

"Your brother is correct, Mr. Sherbourne," she called to him across the room. "After the monsoon rains, Calcutta becomes much cooler . . . does it not?"

He turned to her. "Truly, Miss Rosse, I must speak to you at once. Will you walk with me in the gallery?"

"Edmund!" Voicing a tone of displeasure, Lord Thorne stood. "Miss Rosse is displaying her accomplishments for us. Leave off your proselytizing for once and join us in conversation. Perhaps she means to play the pianoforte for us or recite a poem."

"Proselytizing?" Violet asked.

"My brother longs to convert you to Christianity — a worthy aim, of course. But it is all he thinks about. He began the task upon your last conversation, and now — etiquette to the contrary — he means to finish it."

"The task? Is that what it was, Edmund?" Violet rose and walked toward him. "You saw me as one of your heathens? Some poor lost soul you must save?"

"Violet, come to the gallery with me at once." Edmund took her arm. "I insist upon it."

"No, I shall not!" She drew away from him. "Your words had their effect, Edmund, and I am already a Christian. There, you may rest from your labors. Lady Thorne and Mrs. Richmond have endeavored to enrich my understanding of Christ and His place in my life. So, you have succeeded. Moreover, you have made a missionary of me, for I was so taken by my newfound hope and peace that I told Moumita all about it, and she has become a Christian too. Your task is done, then, if that is all it was."

Edmund stared at her, his green eyes

ablaze. "Miss Rosse," he said in a low voice, "if you do not come to the gallery with me at once, I shall be forced to turn you over my shoulder and carry you there."

"I beg your pardon! You shall do nothing of the sort. I am a lady now, and —"

He reached for her, and Violet let out a shriek. Grabbing up her skirts, she leapt onto the nearest chair. "Whatever is the matter with you, Edmund Sherbourne? This is not how a gentleman should act!"

"Hang politeness; I must talk to you! It is your father — I have had a message from him."

A chill spilled down Violet's spine. "What has happened?"

"Speak plainly, brother," Lord Thorne declared, approaching Edmund. "What have you learned from Mr. Rosse?"

Edmund studied Violet, who realized she was still gripping her skirt — showing her legs all the way from ankle halfway to the knees. But how could she care about manners now?

She jumped down from the chair. "Is my father well, Edmund?" she demanded. "You must tell me at once!"

"He is well enough. But I fear he may not be so for long." He regarded the group. "Randolph, I prefer to discuss this matter in private, as the ladies may be highly offended to hear of this development."

"But I am a lady," Violet said, "and you intended to tell me. Why not Ivy and Olivia, too?"

"Very well. But I assure you, this subject is of a most delicate nature." He squared his shoulders. "Mr. Rosse wrote to tell me that he has entered into a violent conflict with Mr. Cunliffe. The topic of their disagreement is the death of Mrs. Cunliffe — an event which Mr. Rosse privately investigated himself in London and by means of his barrister in York. Yet uncertain of Cunliffe's character, Rosse undertook to question the man in person. Their discussion led to an argument that included many vulgar accusations and insults which I shall refrain from repeating in this company."

"Absolutely," Lord Thorne affirmed.

"At some point in the heated argument between the two men, Cunliffe took it upon himself to refer to Mr. Rosse as an impertinent scoundrel."

Everyone in the party gasped at the heinous insult, and even Violet knew that such degradation could not go unchallenged. To cast general aspersions upon a man was one thing. But to call him impertinent was to imply that he was wholly insolent and rude.

"What did my father do?" Violet ask, fearing the answer.

"He struck Mr. Cunliffe a blow to the chin."

"Oh, no!" Ivy Richmond cried out, and both she and Olivia quickly moved to take Violet in their arms lest she swoon from the shock of this revelation.

"I must go on," Edmund said, "for the worst cannot be kept secret now. Upon recovering from the blow, Alfred Cunliffe immediately challenged Mr. Rosse to a duel."

"Upon my word, this is preposterous!" Lord Thorne sputtered. "It cannot be permitted!"

"It can, and it will," Edmund said. "Although dueling is outlawed in England, Mr. Rosse states in his letter that King George is unusually tolerant of such means to the settlement of a dispute. Rosse writes to me that the king provides would-be duelists with a pardon which they carry in their pockets to the dueling ground."

"Then my father must apologize to Mr. Cunliffe at once," Violet cried. "He cannot be permitted to duel!"

"No apology can be received after a blow," Edmund told her. "Such an offense is too great."

"My brother is correct," Lord Thorne

confirmed, taking his wife's hand as if somehow to protect her and their unborn child from the calamity. "The rules of the duel state that a blow is strictly prohibited under any circumstances among gentlemen, and no apology can be accepted for such an insult. The selection of the weapons rests with the offended party, and Cunliffe is certain to choose the sword over the pistol."

"He has already done so. Rapiers will be used."

"But my father is no swordsman!" Violet protested. "He is a merchant, and a very fat one at that! He cannot fight Mr. Cunliffe. He will be killed!"

"Calm yourself, Miss Rosse," Lord Thorne said. "We must make further inquiries. Perhaps a written apology may suffice — or a monetary inducement."

"Randolph, there can be no delay whatsoever," Edmund stressed. "The forty-eight-hour period in which a challenge to duel may be resolved will end at ten o'clock tomorrow morning." He fell silent for a moment. Then he let out a breath. "Mr. Rosse has asked me to be one of his seconds."

"But you hardly know the man!" his brother protested. "Certainly you have no strong relationship or connection. As you are in line to hold title to Thorne Lodge, Edmund, you must deny this request. I insist upon it!"

"You will have a child and an heir soon, Randolph, and my conscience will not allow me to refuse Mr. Rosse. It is the duty of the second to decide upon the necessity of the duel and to state his opinion to the principal. I shall consult with Mr. Rosse and urge him to pursue all means of avoiding a duel. Likewise, I shall meet with Mr. Cunliffe's seconds and endeavor to settle the business amicably. In this way, I may prevent violence altogether."

"My father will never agree to settle amicably," Violet said, dropping onto a settee. "I know him too well. His temper is quick to rise and slow to subside. You remember how insolently he treated you in Calcutta, Mr. Sherbourne. You heard the insults and the names he called you, yet you bore them as a gentleman. But my father is no gentleman. He will fight Mr. Cunliffe, and he will be killed."

"I fear it may be so," Lord Thorne said. "Cunliffe's reputation is not a good one, Miss Rosse. We kept this information from you out of concern that we not discourage you further. But we do believe he may have been responsible for the death of his first wife. Your father's efforts to investigate that claim put him in his present predicament."

"Oh, dear God, please help us!" Violet moaned, lowering her head to her hands. "Where are You now? Where are You?"

"He is here with us, Violet," Edmund said, going to one knee beside her. He took her hand in his. "We must trust Him."

"Trust Him for what?" She lifted her head and looked at him through her tears. "Can God tie this up in a pretty packet, Edmund? Can He transform my father suddenly into a man who thinks before he acts? Will God make Mr. Cunliffe choose not to fight? Is that what you are telling me?"

"God can do anything He desires, and we must pray for peace. But it is likely that in this case, earthly sin may prevail. Yet, we shall hold to the promise of our heavenly Father that He is with us always."

Violet clenched her fists, fighting the urge to run to Moumita and insist that they set up an altar with their old gods. They could pray and light incense and beg for help. At least those little clay and brass figurines could be touched and kissed. This new God was nowhere to be seen! How was it possible to cling to a God who was nothing more substantial than a Spirit? How could she really trust in something she could never prove to herself was real?

"It is *kharma* that my father will die," she sobbed. "Unpleasant as he can be, my father is all the family I have. He is my protection and my sustenance, and in my way, I do love him. But he has been a bad man, and now Mr. Cunliffe will kill him, and he will be reborn a pig — or worse."

Edmund folded her into his embrace. "Violet, we do often reap the consequences of our sin. The Scriptures agree with *kharma* on that, and your father may pay a heavy price for his rash behavior. But I shall do all in my power to prevent the duel, and you must pray."

"I cannot pray! I cannot find God. Oh, Edmund, where is He?"

"Here. Inside you. Inside me. Among us. He is watching over you even now as you weep."

"I cannot feel Him!"

"He says to us: 'Be still, and know that I am God. Take My yoke upon you, . . . for My burden is light. Put thy trust in Me.' "

Violet brushed the tears from her cheeks. She had only belonged to Jesus for three weeks, and until now, she had been filled with such joy. Even though the winter winds blew outside, she knew a wondrous warmth in her heart. All her many errors were for-given. All her blunders and sins had been washed away by the sacrifice of His blood. The Holy Spirit had seemed so present in every moment of the day — when she rose to a tray of tea and scones, when she chatted with Ivy and Olivia, when she and Moumita walked in the conservatory . . . God had been with her, and she had known His pres-ence with certainty.

But now she was afraid and full of doubt. She wanted to go back to Calcutta and the people and sounds and smells she knew. She wanted Moumita and the barefoot ser-vants and the *mali* in the garden. She wanted the idols in the closet and the muez-zins calling from the mosques.

Yet, Edmund was here, and he told her that God was with her still. Was He? She gulped down a ragged breath. *God, are You here?* she prayed silently. *It is I, Violet. My father will be killed tomorrow, and I shall be left all alone.*

"You are not alone, Violet," Edmund spoke up, almost as though he had heard her prayer. "God is with you. He holds you in the palm of His hand."

"And we are here, too," Lord Thorne added. "Miss Rosse, we are your friends. No matter what the outcome tomorrow, you can be certain of our constancy."

"Of course, dearest," Ivy told her. "We have grown to love you as one of our own. You must not be afraid."

"You will always have our protection and assistance," Olivia promised. She laid her hand on Violet's arm. "Dear friend, do you know how a Christian can see God?"

"No, for I cannot even feel Him now."

"Look around you. We are His ambassadors. God's love shines in our eyes. His warmth surrounds you in our embrace. We Christians are to represent Christ on this earth, and by our tender mercies, you will know Him."

The gentle smiles that encircled her drew a new round of tears from Violet. She hugged each of them, and when at last she came to Edmund, she held him the longest of all.

"Save my father's life," she whispered. "I beg you."

"I shall do my best." He pressed her tightly against him and then stepped away. "Randolph, call for a horse. I must away to York at once."

"We shall follow you by carriage," Olivia said. "No, Randolph, do not protest. The baby will not be nudged out into this world by a mere carriage ride. I must go with

Violet to York. I insist."

Standing near the window, Violet watched as Edmund sprinted across the room and vanished into the corridor. The two ladies hurried to alter the dinner plans. And Lord Thorne spoke to his valet, who went to gather the footmen.

Violet gazed out the window for a moment, and in the pane of glass she saw her reflection. The mountain of golden curls had somehow fallen askew and the confident poise had gone. But her friends were right. God did dwell within her now, and in their faces she saw His love.

Picking up her skirts, she stepped to the door. She must call Moumita at once.

# Sixteen

Violet stood at the edge of an exercise ground in the private garden of a man she did not know, a Mr. Wolmer of York. Along with Edmund Sherbourne, her father had chosen a colleague in the cloth trade, an elderly merchant, to act as his second. Though the party from Thorne had traveled most of the night to reach their destination in time, their haste was in vain. Edmund, who now stood beside Malcolm Rosse, had been unable to prevent the duel.

Across an expanse of dry winter grass, a formidable foe strutted about, chatting with acquaintances who had gathered for the occasion and whipping his rapier back and forth as if practicing to lop off Mr. Rosse's head. His two seconds appeared equally fit and as hostile as their friend. Near the gathering, an eminent surgeon awaited the outcome of the violence.

Sick with fear, hunger, and exhaustion, Violet held tightly to Moumita's hands as the two women watched the proceedings unfold before them. Lady Thorne and Mrs.

Richmond stood close by, offering what words of comfort and hope they could muster.

The only relief Violet could find in this day was that she most certainly would not have to marry Alfred Cunliffe. She had disliked the scoundrel from the moment she laid eyes upon him. A boastful, self-important man, he laughed and teased with the crowd — as if killing portly, middle-aged merchants from India was as common to him as eating breakfast. With thick black hair and an imposing jaw, Cunliffe was handsome enough to tempt many women. But Violet found no appeal in him whatsoever.

She much preferred a gentleman like Edmund Sherbourne — tall, broad-shouldered, and confident in his white shirt, tan breeches, and knee-high black boots. He was speaking to Mr. Rosse even now, reminding him of the intricacies of swordsmanship. But Violet knew Edmund's instruction would be lost on a man whose whole adult life had been spent poring over ledgers, meeting with other merchants, swilling rum, and dallying with Betsys.

And now Mr. Wolmer, to whose house the garden was attached, called for the duel to begin. Edmund and the other three seconds marked out the spot where each combatant would stand, leaving a distance of two feet between the points of their weapons. Mr. Wolmer measured the swords to ascertain that they were of equal length.

Satisfied, he gave further instruction. "Throw off your coats and lay bare your chests, gentlemen." Both men complied, stripping away coats, shirts, collars, and cravats — and the sight was a sad spectacle indeed. While Mr. Cunliffe sported a fine display of manly muscle and sinew, the doughy white mound of his stomach was Mr. Rosse's prominent attribute.

When Mr. Wolmer had assured himself and the other seconds that neither combatant wore any armor or other defense against the sword, they were permitted to put their shirts back on. Now Violet knew for certain that her father must lose his life on this day, and she held her breath as Mr. Wolmer stepped forward again.

*"Allez!"* he shouted, signaling the duel to commence.

Edmund and the other seconds moved into position close to the combatants. Each second also held a sword, point downward, in readiness to stop the fight the moment any rules were transgressed.

As Violet watched in dismay, the two

combatants went at each other with their rapiers. In the first pass, her father rushed wildly at Alfred Cunliffe, and somehow he managed to cut his foe slightly below the left knee. Cunliffe expertly blocked all subsequent thrusts, then struck with lightning speed, puncturing Mr. Rosse's shoulder with the tip of his rapier. As the cries of the watching throng died down, the seconds assessed the wounds and declared that the duel might continue.

At the next pass, Malcolm Rosse again threw himself into the contest with a frenzy, his rapier flying as he cut Cunliffe in the left hand and grazed him on the right side. Cunliffe seemed to stand perfectly still, his own sword only moving forward in a single thrust. But as her father fell back from the fray again, Violet saw at once that Cunliffe's weapon had found its mark. Mr. Rosse dropped to his knees, and blood began to ooze from an ugly injury to his neck.

"I am wounded!" he cried to signal that the duel must come to a halt.

"Stop!" The elderly merchant called out as Edmund raised his sword.

Cunliffe moved a step back, his rapier remaining on guard. At this moment, the surgeon hurried to tend the victim. Violet started for her father as well, but Lord

Thorne held her back.

"The duel is not ended," he said. "The seconds must assess the situation. If they determine that your father is unable to continue, then it will be over. But if your father elects to rise and attempt to fight again, he must be allowed."

"But this is preposterous! He lies bleeding there on the grass."

"The sahib is very foolish," Moumita murmured. In the past weeks, the tiny woman had packed away her colorful saris and worked her long black hair into stylish ringlets and a bun. On this day, she wore a soft gray gown, a wool bonnet, and a warm cloak. She shook her head glumly. "*Meye,* your father will die very soon. Why do those other men not defend him?"

"It is not permitted for the seconds to take his place unless asked," Lord Thorne said.

"This English way of fighting is not good. Sahib Rosse is too fat. He cannot win."

Knowing her *ayah* spoke the truth, Violet clung to Moumita in the long minutes as the surgeon tried to stanch the wound and wrap a bandage about Mr. Rosse's neck. At last, Dr. Dunbar stood and lifted his hand to those watching.

"Alfred Cunliffe's sword has pierced the right side of Malcolm Rosse's neck to a depth exceeding two inches," he announced. "The point of the sword passed between the jugular vein and the carotid artery. Mr. Rosse will survive. This duel is at an end."

Violet let out her breath as her two friends hugged her warmly. "There, you see!" Ivy exclaimed. "It has all come out well. Your father will live, and you are free of Mr. Cunliffe. God is always —"

"I declare myself unsatisfied," Alfred Cunliffe spoke loudly over the hubbub of the crowd. "The duel has not atoned for the insult."

"Impossible," Edmund retorted. "You have nearly killed the man. How dare you call the result unfair?"

"Mr. Rosse struck me as the result of an allegation made to him by one Randolph Sherbourne, Lord Thorne. I have been defamed by this spurious allegation, and I demand satisfaction. Lord Thorne is here today, is he not? Let him stand in for Mr. Rosse."

At his challenge, Lady Thorne cried out and clutched her stomach. Violet hurried to her aid, assisting as Ivy and the others escorted the heavily laden woman to a chair at the edge of the lawn. Immediately, Lord Thorne and Edmund approached Cunliffe, as did the other seconds. The group upon the green began a heated discussion of the situation. At the same time, the surgeon assisted Mr. Rosse in tottering off toward the house. His shirt covered in blood, Violet's father moaned as though he were facing his final hour.

Violet herself hardly knew which way to turn. If Lady Thorne began to have her baby at this moment, what could they do but carry her into Mr. Wolmer's house and summon a midwife? At least the surgeon would be nearby to lend a hand. But surely Violet ought to go to her father instead, for soon Dr. Dunbar would be cleaning and stitching his wound. Yet, how could she leave the garden when Alfred Cunliffe had called out Lord Thorne? Surely this could not all end so badly!

But it was worse than she could have imagined, for at that moment, Edmund stepped free of the others and made a pronouncement. "According to the rules of the duel, a second is to be of equal rank in society with the principal he attends, inasmuch as a second may either choose or chance to become a principal. At this time, I elect to take the place of my brother, Lord Thorne, as the principal in a duel with his accuser, Alfred Cunliffe."

"But the forty-eight hours!" Lady Thorne called from the chair upon which she reclined in obvious pain. "Oh, Violet, remind my husband of this! His brother must be allowed time to prepare. Edmund must practice!"

Violet took up her skirts and raced out onto the green. "Edmund," she said, catching his arm, "you have time. Forty-eight hours are permitted from the moment of the challenge."

"Cunliffe declares the allegation by your father to have begun the clock. Mr. Wolmer agrees. Violet, I have no choice in this. Your father is too weak to continue the duel, and I cannot permit Randolph to risk his life."

"But you may lose yours! Look at that man. Cunliffe is a monster!"

"God is with me, Violet. If I lose my life, I have my brother's love and my faithful service in India to comfort me in my last breath."

"You have my love as well," she gasped. "Oh, my dearest Edmund, I do love you so! I cannot think of life without you!"

He smiled. "You hold my heart, dear lady. I shall love you always."

"Do not fight him, then. Please, Edmund —"

"If I die, Violet, know that I go to a better

place. I shall be with God, the one I love most dearly of all."

So saying, he pulled away from her and returned to the field of battle. As Moumita drew Violet back to the gathered throng, Edmund stripped off his shirt to show that he wore no armor. As he pulled it on again, Randolph stepped to his side to take a place as his second. Colin Richmond assumed the same role. While the men conferred, the three women huddled together to watch the nightmarish proceedings.

And then it was too late to stop anything. Edmund took up his rapier. Mr. Wolmer measured it against that of Alfred Cunliffe. The seconds assumed their places, and the cry rang out: *"Allez!"*

Quite unlike the one that preceded it, this battle stunned Violet in its immediate intensity. The combatants advanced step by step, each extending his blade. Cunliffe made a forward leap, followed by a lunge. Edmund countered by driving his opponent's blade into a bind — a diagonally opposite line. Cunliffe feinted and forced a change of engagement. The hiss of steel cut the winter air as the swords kept up their deadly conversation. The clang of steel on steel rang out across the green. The men circled, slashing, parrying, dancing away from one thrust and feeling the sting of another. Suddenly Edmund flicked his blade, and the point found Cunliffe's right arm, causing bright specks of blood to fly through the air. The seconds immediately called a halt, and the wound was examined.

But Cunliffe would have none of the cautions offered. He returned to the fight at once, as if the sight of his own blood had made him all the more eager to defend his name. Edmund stood on guard, and when his opponent was ready, Mr. Wolmer gave the call.

Cunliffe attacked. Edmund feinted, and his blade slid along his opponent's. Hilt to hilt, both men shoved and fell back. Cunliffe advanced and attacked again. Edmund counter-parried, forcing Cunliffe's rapier high into the air, then following with a deception and a cut. But Cunliffe dodged the sword and engaged again, sweeping Edmund's blade through a full circle.

Violet gasped, certain Edmund must fall victim to the clever move. But he expertly pressed away his rival's blade and retreated. Now he poised to lunge, drawing Cunliffe into a defensive position — but instead he feinted and made a whirling cut that caught his opponent on the left thigh. The gash was deep and wicked, and Cunliffe dropped to one knee, crying out, "I am wounded!"

Again, the seconds halted the duel.

Violet let out a shaky breath. "Surely Mr. Cunliffe cannot continue!" she said. "He is nearly cut through."

But Ivy shook her head. "Look how he rises again. The man is driven with some sort of bloodlust."

"I believe by this duel he means to convince his society of his innocence," Olivia said. Her discomfort appeared forgotten as she watched the dangerous dance.

Edmund's skill with the sword was obvious to Violet. Yet she knew Alfred Cunliffe was no barely trained guard at the palace of Krishnangar. Worse, he fought with a rage that seemed unquenchable. Perhaps Olivia was correct in her assessment. No doubt rumors that Cunliffe had murdered his wife still echoed in the city. His business must have suffered, and perhaps even his friends shied away from him now. A duel with a soft merchant could have little effect. But this battle against Edmund Sherbourne must be seen as a message to any who might dare mention the possibility of Cunliffe's guilt. Let the accusers come forth, he seemed to say, and they will face the wrath of my blade.

His shirtsleeve and leg now soaked in

blood, Cunliffe rose again and stood on guard against Edmund. This time the man's swordplay held nothing of the disciplined conversation he had displayed before. He went at Edmund like a madman, his rapier whipping through the air as he attacked again and again. Forced into defensive moves, Edmund parried, disengaged, and dodged at each engagement. And then Edmund stumbled momentarily on a patch of uneven ground, and Cunliffe's sword found its mark, piercing Edmund deeply through the side.

He cried out, "I am wounded," but Cunliffe refused to back away. At this flagrant infraction of the rules, the seconds rushed to halt the combat. Olivia screamed as her husband took a quick cut to the shoulder, and the green erupted in violence. All four seconds now engaged, while Cunliffe continued his attack on Edmund. Mr. Wolmer's voice calling for a cessation of the violence could hardly be heard over the ring of steel and the shouts from the watching crowd. Violet tried to see what was happening, but the observers had pushed forward, and the swordsmen now battled in the midst of a melee.

"We must help them!" Violet cried. "They will be killed!"

"No, Violet!" Ivy grabbed her arm. "We are women. We have no training. And look at Olivia. See how her condition worsens. We should take her into the orangery just there at the far side of the garden. Someone must run to the house for the surgeon, for I fear her agitation has brought on labor pains."

"But your husband, Ivy! Mr. Richmond is just there. And Lord Thorne! And — oh, Edmund, look behind you!"

"You come now, *meye,*" Moumita commanded. "This is the play of men, and it will end badly. We must help Lady Thorne."

Torn, Violet gathered her skirts and assisted Moumita and Ivy as they lifted Olivia and forced their way through the throng toward the small glass house. But as the women reached the orangery, Edmund and Cunliffe broke free from the circle, left the flat expanse of lawn, and began to battle their way across the rose garden. Leafless, thorny canes caught at their breeches while mounds of mulch threatened to trip them. They reached a dry stone fountain with marble fauns and fairies playing at its edge. Edmund leapt onto the fountain's wall and slashed at Cunliffe, but the other man's sword found an opening and grazed Edmund's calf. Tumbling down into the fountain pool, Edmund rolled away from his foe while Cunliffe's sword cut and cut and cut at him again.

Crying out, Violet abandoned the others and raced for him. But as she reached the fountain, she saw Edmund spring to his feet. His sword streaked through the chill air, and its point came to rest directly above Alfred Cunliffe's heart. The man's eyes grew wide with shock as he stood awaiting his death.

Cautiously Violet approached the scene, realizing now that the skirmish in the distance had broken apart and the others were running to see what had happened. There was Lord Thorne, limping but well. A scratch on Colin Richmond's cheek was all that marred him. And now Edmund.

As Edmund held his position, Mr. Wolmer ran gasping to his side. "The rules of the duel were broken by Mr. Cunliffe," he declared. "Mr. Sherbourne has given the charges full satisfaction, and the duel has ended! All parties must disperse."

Edmund drew back his sword, and several men rushed forward to restrain Cunliffe, lest he attempt to start the fighting anew. Before he could protest, they hurried him away.

As the crowd began to leave the grounds,

Violet touched Lord Thorne's shoulder. "Your wife, sir. We have taken her to the orangery. You must see to her. I believe the distress of the day may have brought on her labor."

Thorne briefly gripped his brother's shoulder and hurried away. Colin Richmond joined him. Violet hurried to Edmund and took his hand.

"The Lord will hold you blameless in this conflict," she said softly. "I have been reading the Bible, and does it not speak of an eye for an eye and a tooth for a tooth? Your brother is correct when he states that Mr. Cunliffe meant to kill you."

"Perhaps he did," Edmund said. "But the Bible also instructs us to love our brothers as ourselves."

"Mr. Cunliffe was hardly your brother. He would have killed my father had the duel not been ended, and he wished to strike you dead. He practiced nothing of Christian virtue or charity, and you were not wrong —"

"Excuse me, Miss Rosse," a man's voice interrupted. She looked up to find the elderly merchant who had served as her father's second. Though spattered with blood, he made her a polite bow. "I am sorry to intrude, but Mr. Rosse has sent me to fetch you. His wound has been stitched, and his strength is returning. He means to quit York at once for London."

"London!" Violet exclaimed. "Why?"

"He has made arrangements there . . . for you and for himself."

"What arrangements?" Violet asked. "You must tell me, sir. I cannot think of leaving my friends at such a time as this."

"I believe your father has worked out a sort of engagement for you. You are to stay with his brother in London until I am able to settle my affairs here in York and join you. And then, when all is well . . . when the matter is concluded . . . Mr. Rosse will return to India."

Edmund stood at Violet's side. "Which matter is this, sir? Speak plainly."

"Why, the matter of Miss Rosse's marriage. Clearly Mr. Rosse knew she could not be wedded to Cunliffe, so he undertook a different arrangement. A different man."

"Which man?" Violet demanded.

The merchant gave a little cough. "Uh . . . me."

"You? But you are . . . you are . . ."

"I am James Oxmartin, at your service." He made another bow. "Your father and I have engaged in trade for some sixteen years. I own a large market square here in

420

York — several fine buildings, actually — and I provide many of the merchants with fabric. Mr. Rosse has been a steady supplier of Indian cottons as well as Chinese silks."

Violet stared at him in astonishment, her heart nearly frozen with the shock of this news.

"Do not dismay, dear lady," Mr. Oxmartin said. "It is true that I am older than you, but I shall make you a very good husband. My wife and I were married nearly twenty-eight years before she passed away. I have missed her sorely, and for some time I believed I could never consider remarriage. But your father spoke convincingly, and now that I meet you, I feel we shall make a good match. My character cannot be questioned, I am a Christian, and my house and business will supply all your needs. My children are grown and now work in my trade, but they have homes and families of their own. They will not trouble us except to make us all the merrier by their presence."

He smiled, his pleasant face folding into gentle lines that fanned out toward his thatch of thick white hair. "Please, Miss Rosse, do not fret. You will have time to adjust to this news in London. And when I am able to join you there, I am confident that we shall discover much happiness."

Unable to speak, Violet merely continued to stare at him.

Edmund shifted from one foot to the other. "Is this not rather sudden, Mr. Oxmartin?" he asked. "After all, yesterday the young lady believed she must marry Alfred Cunliffe. And today she learns she is to marry you instead."

"It is not sudden to me or to her father, for we have been discussing the matter at length. But Miss Rosse will have plenty of time to accustom herself to the situation. Come then, dear lady; you must be anxious to see to your father's health."

"Yes, but I . . ." She shook her head, trying to comprehend that she must now leave Edmund. Leave Olivia in the throes of her labor. Leave Ivy and her sweet friendship. "I must find my lady's maid!"

Without another word, Violet fled to the orangery. Inside, she found a calmer scene than anticipated. Olivia's pangs had abated, the men had washed their wounds, and all were seated on benches in the midst of a grove of potted orange trees. Quickly Violet told them the shocking news of her intended marriage to Mr. Oxmartin, but none could conceive of any way to help her delay her father's departure for London.

At last she had no choice but to bid her

friends farewell, take Moumita's hand, and hurry back out into the chill. At the fountain, she found Mr. Oxmartin awaiting her, his gentle smile still in place. Edmund was gone.

"Where is Mr. Sherbourne?" she asked.

"He departed for the city. He asked me to wish you well in your future life."

Violet glanced down at the bloodstained spot where Cunliffe had fallen, and then she searched the edges of the garden for Edmund. He was not to be found. Before she could think what else to do, Mr. Oxmartin slipped his arm through hers and began to lead her toward the house.

"It is a long journey to London," he said in a kindly voice. "You and your father will wish to be on your way at once."

Violet allowed him to take her into the house, for she could see nothing through the tears that streamed from her eyes.

The outline of Calcutta against the horizon beckoned Edmund as he stood at the ship's rail. A mosque, its minarets gleaming pink in the setting sun. A jagged hill of makeshift houses, one rising upon another. The gentle whisper of palm trees, banana trees, and flame trees. And nearer, thin masts of the small canoes that plied up and down the Hooghly River, pierced the golden clouds.

Along the shore, familiar sights sent an ache of welcome through Edmund's chest. Coolies raced from one street to another as they carried a wooden door or a load of sun-baked clay bricks or a tray of sweetmeats. Rickshaw wallahs ran by, barely avoiding naked children playing in the roadway or black-veiled Muslim women gliding along toward unknown destinations.

And the smells . . . Edmund could hardly bear to recall how Violet Rosse had chastised him for disparaging the city's distinctive aroma. Now his senses drank in everything that once had displeased him — drying fish, sacks mounded with spices, ripe fruit, and a river teeming with humanity and life.

But he could not permit himself to think of Violet as he returned to her beloved city. Five long months on board a ship had taught him that. He had not seen Violet since the day she hurried away from him toward the orangery at Mr. Wolmer's house in York. She had gone to London later that day, he knew. That was all the information he had of her until a letter arrived from Mr. Rosse some three weeks after the duel.

He had recovered his health entirely,

Rosse wrote to Edmund. His business in England was settled happily, and he was married to Mrs. Congleton, who — to everyone's surprise — had suddenly divorced her husband. They would be returning to India in the following year.

Thanking Edmund for his services in the unfortunate conflict with Mr. Cunliffe, he had enclosed a deed to the former Hindu temple in Calcutta that once had been intended as a warehouse. It belonged to Edmund now and could be used in whatever manner the young man chose. Mr. Rosse also wrote to say that he had sent a petition to the British authorities in Calcutta and that a permit to preach should await him upon his arrival there.

And finally, he mentioned almost as an afterthought that his daughter was to wed Mr. Oxmartin on the following Saturday. The pair were content in their match, and they would return to Oxmartin's estate in York after the wedding. Violet, he reported, was very happy.

Edmund had not been able to purchase a ship's passage soon enough after that. And now his future awaited him. He had left behind him his two brothers: William, who could talk of nothing but the mill; and Randolph, who could talk of nothing but his new son. Lord and Lady Thorne considered themselves blessed indeed by the birth of Robert John Sherbourne, heir to the title of baron and to the entire estate at Thorne. Sharing in their happiness, Edmund had said farewell to new friends and old at Otley. The Richmonds had become close companions of the Thornes, and they had enjoyed talking with Edmund of their own plans for travel to India. Colin Richmond's father lived in Bombay, and they were eager to visit him.

Finally, Edmund had sailed away, leaving family, friends, and the only woman he would ever love. He must accept that God had put Violet Rosse into his life only for the purpose of showing her the truth of Jesus Christ.

Violet would be married five months to Mr. Oxmartin by now, Edmund realized as the ship burst into activity at its approach to the harbor. She would have a lovely house in York. Mrs. Choudhary would be at her side to remind her *meye* of India whenever the young lady grew homesick. And soon, if God willed, she would bear children to give her even greater joy.

Swallowing his pain, Edmund stepped away from the railing as the ship dropped anchor. He must make certain his trunks accompanied him ashore and did not wander off with some overeager coolie by mistake. The oppressive heat bore down even in the evening, but thanks to Violet and her *ayah,* Edmund had not made his former mistakes. This evening, he wore a soft white shirt and brown cotton breeches. In Ceylon, he had purchased a pair of sturdy boots made of water buffalo hide and a wide-brimmed planter's hat to keep the sun from scorching his face.

"Those trunks are mine," Edmund said to a coolie in Bengali. The man's jaw dropped for an instant in surprise. Then he burst into laughter and shook Edmund's hand.

"You are an Indian!" the fellow cried. "Welcome home!"

Edmund chuckled in return. "*Dhanyabad,* sahib," he replied. "I am happy to be home in Calcutta again."

And he was. Despite the empty place in his heart, Edmund knew he was where God meant him to be. The long journey had been delayed when the ship was becalmed off the coast of western Africa. During those windless, silent days, Edmund had spent many hours on his knees in prayer. And at last he knew — knew beyond any shadow of doubt — that God wanted him in India.

Handing the coolie a couple of coins, Edmund pointed out the remainder of his baggage. Though it was nearly dark, he intended to hire a small boat and make the eighteen-mile trip upriver to Dr. William Carey's house. There the two men could discuss future plans, and Edmund could set the course for his work in Calcutta.

Slapping at a mosquito, he set off down the gangway toward the wharf. The cries of the wallahs made sense to him now that he better understood Bengali, and he smiled in satisfaction. He would increase his vocabulary in the months to come, and his work among the heathen must profit from —

Edmund paused on the length of damp wood, uncertain at the vision that greeted him. In the distance, shadowed by the setting sun, stood a slender young woman in a glowing turquoise sari. A blonde woman. A woman who spotted him, gave a jump of joy, and ran forward waving her hand in glee.

"Edmund! Edmund, you are here at last!"

He could not move. She was a vision. A dream. A glimpse of heaven itself. His heart soared, yet his feet remained planted on the gangway as disbelief assailed him.

And then she stood before him. "Oh, Edmund, I have come down to the docks to meet every ship that arrived from England for the last month." Violet threw her arms around him and danced him off the gangway onto the wharf. "Where have you *been?*"

Still unable to believe his eyes, Edmund stared at her. He looked back at the ship. And then he found her again. The same blue eyes he had loved. The same sweet pink lips. And the same long golden braid.

"Violet?" he asked.

"Yes!" she cried, jumping up and down three times and laughing out loud. "You are shocked! I have surprised you!"

"Violet, what on earth are you doing here?"

"I ran away!" She giggled. "Oh, stop looking askance, Edmund. I left my father a very nice letter, and he wrote me back and is not the least bit angry. For he understood it all. You see, I was staying with my uncle in London and trying to prepare myself to marry Mr. Oxmartin — whom I should tell you is a very fine man and would have made me a good husband, even though he is older than my father but very much better in moral character and virtue. So one day as I was praying, I realized that I had been unable to stop telling everyone about Jesus — from Moumita to my father to the carriage drivers to the gardeners to the fine ladies who came to call on my aunt. I could not stop, Edmund. I simply could not."

"Violet . . ." he began. But instead of following it with something sensible, Edmund merely mumbled her name again and went on staring at her.

How his heart had ached at the loss of this vibrant, beautiful woman! At times aboard ship he had thought he must go mad for want of her. The sound of her voice had haunted him. The sweet beauty of her smile had played through his dreams. And now she was here. In Calcutta. *Violet.*

"And that is when I knew!" she exclaimed as if blissfully unaware of his consternation. "I was meant to be a missionary. Can you not see the great plan? God has been preparing me all my life. He allowed me to be brought up among Hindus and to speak their language and to understand their beliefs — all for the purpose of teaching them that they do not have to go on making sacrifices and trying to earn good *kharma* and fearing being reborn as an ant. So, what could I do but take a carriage from my uncle's house to the missionary society, which was very difficult to find, mind you, but I did find it. The society are all men, I discovered, and they did not take well to the idea of a young lady going out on her own as a missionary. This I learned immediately upon making application to them. I had thought I ought to go to India at first, but then I realized you would be here, and you did not really wish me to be near you."

"Upon my word!" he blurted out. "What could have given you that idea?"

"You told me again and again that God had meant for you to be an unmarried man. And you tried very hard not to love me, and when you kissed me, you apologized immediately and never did it again. And then in York you hurried off and never wrote to me or came to sweep me away from dear old Mr. Oxmartin. So that is how I knew you did not want me."

At this obvious misunderstanding, Edmund shook his head. "But, Violet —"

"I am not finished, Edmund. Before talking with the missionary society, I had decided I would go to Africa, you see. I thought about Cape Coast and all those poor slaves. And then I thought about Mombasa and the old church. I am certain God wants missionaries there. But in the end, the missionary society — with a push from your dear friend Andrew Fuller — decided I ought to go to India after all."

Edmund took off his hat. Amazement

thundered in his chest. "Violet, do you mean to tell me that you have been commissioned as a missionary?"

"Well, in a manner of speaking . . . as I said, they did not like me going off on my own. They wanted to marry me to someone, but I said I was already nearly married to someone, and I did not fancy it to be the best idea. I told them that if a man like you could go off on his own, why could a woman not do the same? That is when they realized that they knew you, and that we knew each other. And after that . . . well, I left for India."

"Then you are not commissioned?"

"No, not completely. They know where I am, and they have committed to pray for me. But I came back to Calcutta on my own. I sold my jewelry to pay passage, and I am living in my father's house."

"And Mrs. Choudhary is with you?"

"Oh, you will not believe this! Moumita fell in love with Michael Hedgley, the gardener at the conservatory in Longley Park. They have married!"

"Upon my word, this is too much."

"It is indeed." She smiled. "Dear Edmund, I am very happy to see you again."

"I am utterly astonished and pleased to

see you, of course." He stood helpless with shock and pleasure and uncertainty. "But Violet, what does the missionary society say about your work here in Calcutta? Surely if they committed to pray for you, they must have some opinion as to which direction your efforts must take."

She shrugged and looked away. "They wished me to teach Bible studies to ladies, which I am doing. They wished me to teach children, which I am also doing. They were happy to let me continue my work with Dr. Wallich at the Botanic Garden, for they believe it important that missionaries engage in other work that may lead to opportunities to share the gospel. That is why they were happy for Dr. Carey to translate the books on flora."

"This is wonderful then," Edmund concluded, feeling the first surge of real joy since his astonishment began to abate. "You are here! You are in Calcutta!"

"Yes, I am! And you are too! And . . . well, the missionary society did suggest one other thing to me. They would be very happy to hear that I . . . that you . . . that we . . ."

Unwilling to wait a moment longer, Edmund threw down his hat and dropped to one knee on the wharf. "Violet," he said, "Violet Rosse, will you marry me?"

"Yes!" she burst out, the word a laugh of joy. "Oh, Edmund, I began to wonder how long it would take you to come to this! I began to think you must never see how perfectly God has fitted us for each other."

"Of course I see it," he said warmly. "I was blinded to you once before, unable to see that you did not truly know Christ. And after that, I allowed myself to be deceived again. Such a fool I am. I thought you could not want me. I believed I must remain unmarried. But God was preparing you to be my wife all along. Everything I lack — a full understanding of these people and this land — you provide."

"And what I lack in understanding of Scripture and doctrine, you may teach me! The society suggested we marry, and of course, I wanted such a union, but —"

"Violet, my darling love!" He caught her up in his arms and kissed her lips. "I thought you were in York . . . Mrs. Oxmartin . . . and here you are! I have spent the last five months in agony trying to forget you ever existed."

"But I have been here waiting for you. And you took so long to arrive!"

"The ship was becalmed off the coast of Africa."

"I have been here nearly a month, dying

of anxiety, so worried that you would not have me!"

"Silly girl! I love you. Oh, Violet, I love you with all my heart."

She laid her head on his shoulder, and Edmund drank in the stillness of this moment. Violet. Here in his arms. By his side. Working with him. A labor of love.

"Darling Edmund," she sighed. But just as quickly, she sprang away. "Come, dearest! We must find a *nouka* to take us to Serampore!"

Edmund watched in utter joy as she hurried ahead of him, the bells on her ankles jingling beneath the folds of her sari. "You are going to Serampore tonight too, Violet?" he asked, catching up to her.

"Of course! Dr. Carey is waiting for us."

"Dr. Carey?"

"He has promised to perform our wedding upon the very hour of our arrival."

Edmund laughed aloud. A wedding! A wife! Such a blessed life awaited them!

# A Note from the Author

Dear Friend,

There's an old song that says, "This world is not my home; I'm just a-passin' through." So often, I feel like I just don't *fit*. I know part of this comes from growing up in a missionary home in Bangladesh and Kenya. My heart will always belong to Africa. Many of my responses and emotions stem from the languages, cultures, and varied experiences with which I was raised. Like Violet, I can't seem to get truly comfortable anywhere. And like Edmund, I make a lot of mistakes in trying to relate to people who were brought up so differently.

Our younger son, Andrei, came to us from a Romanian orphanage. At almost seven, he'd had lots of experiences in a very unusual culture. He, too, has a hard time figuring out how to mesh with the world around him. When Andrei arrived with his immigration green card, our older son, Geoffrey, liked to tell people, "My little brother is an alien!"

Though it's no fun feeling like a stranger in a strange land, this is actually the condition of *all* Christians. This world truly isn't our home. We're just passing through on our way to God's heavenly throne where we belong. To the world, what Christians say sometimes sounds foolish (1 Corinthians 1:18–29). Our choices and behaviors may look strange. Dear Christian sister or brother, when you feel out of sorts and uncomfortable with the world, remember what the apostle John taught: "The Spirit who lives in you is greater than the spirit who lives in the world. These people belong to this world, so they speak from the world's viewpoint, and the world listens to them. But we belong to God" (1 John 4:4–6).

If you're not a Christian, my precious friend, I assure you that the discomfort of living in this world is only temporary. It keeps us believers on our toes. We can't quite relax, so we're always in need of divine reorientation. God has provided prayer, the Bible, and His church to give us a deep breath of fresh air from the "homeland." This puts us back on our feet and sets us on our way through the world once again. We look forward to the day we'll finally get to go and live with God. We'll see Him face-to-face, and we'll know we're *truly* home. I can't wait!

Blessings,
*Catherine Palmer*

# About the Author

Catherine Palmer's first book was published in 1988, and since then she has published more than thirty books. Total sales of her books are more than one million copies.

Catherine's novels *The Happy Room* and *A Dangerous Silence* are CBA best-sellers, and her HeartQuest book *A Touch of Betrayal* won the 2001 Christy Award for Romance. Her novella "Under His Wings," which appears in the anthology *A Victorian Christmas Cottage*, was named Northern Lights Best Novella of 1999, historical category, by Midwest Fiction Writers. Her numerous other awards include Best Historical Romance, Best Contemporary Romance, and Best of Romance from the Southwest Writers Workshop; Most Exotic Historical Romance Novel from *Romantic Times* magazine; and Best Historical Romance Novel from Romance Writers of the Panhandle.

Catherine lives in Missouri with her husband, Tim, and sons, Geoffrey and Andrei. She has degrees from Baylor University and Southwest Baptist University.

The employees of Thorndike Press hope you have enjoyed this Large Print book. All our Thorndike and Wheeler Large Print titles are designed for easy reading, and all our books are made to last. Other Thorndike Press Large Print books are available at your library, through selected bookstores, or directly from us.

For information about titles, please call:

(800) 223-1244

or visit our Web site at:

www.gale.com/thorndike
www.gale.com/wheeler

To share your comments, please write:

Publisher
Thorndike Press
295 Kennedy Memorial Drive
Waterville, ME    04901